CONTENTS

READING ORDER

Some confusion has been shown in what order the books should be read in this series, so I am providing this now to solve the issue.

While this novel IS intended to be a new starting point, with character introductions and all the information a new reader needs to go on, you can spend more time in the universe if you want by following the chronologically ordered novels listed below.

Optional Prequel
Holy Ground - https://amzn.to/3uOjOv2

Main Series

Oddyssey One : https://amzn.to/3j3erFC
Heart of Matter : https://amzn.to/3FZC1fP
Homeworld : https://amzn.to/3FRBblc
Out of the Black : https://amzn.to/3FsZKU4

Optional Side Story
King of Thieves - https://amzn.to/3YoqU7h

Warrior King - https://amzn.to/3W8r40I

Odysseus Awakening - https://amzn.to/3uPceAq
Odysseus Ascendent - https://amzn.to/3PwPMWo

Archangel One - https://amzn.to/3j2A1Kl
Archangel Rising - https://amzn.to/3Bvszy4
Imperial Gambit - https://amzn.to/3FQsYO7

Odyssey One : King's Fall - https://amzn.to/3We5zeB

THE SEEDS THAT WERE SOWN

After the Apocalypse...
the real work begins

CHAPTER 1

Gaia's Revenge, **Approaching Orbit of** *Rogue's Nest*

"Inbound contact, declare identity. You are within our defensive envelope and have one minute to identify. Say again, declare identity."

"Roger that, Nest. Transmitting ID."

There was a brief pause as the signal was sent out, lightspeed lag being what it was. Within a few seconds, however, the channel crackled back to life.

"Roger transmission, ID received. Welcome back, sir."

"Pleasure to be back," Stephanos answered as he leaned into the controls and sent his old beast of a ship gliding in toward the rogue planetoid that was barely visible across his sensor suite.

The Rogue's Nest was one of the forward posts, located deep inside what was once the territory of the Starsbane Empire, though the locals might have sworn differently back in the day. It had come a long way from when he and the Archangels had first discovered it, the sunless world had barely served as a navigation point for them at the time.

Now, however, there were several million full time inhabitants, all living right in the middle of formerly Imperial claimed space, while none of the locals had *any* clue they were even there.

No one paid any attention to rogue worlds unless they were actually threatening to mess with an inhabited system or had drifted into a major transit lane. Almost all of them were lifeless iceballs, without enough raw materials to bother with when you had much richer and more energy dense star systems to pick from, after all.

The Nest, however, had something that even most worlds inside a star system lacked... a single large moon, slightly larger in ratio than Luna was to... Earth. That provided for a great deal of tectonic activity, actually warming the world from the inside and providing an irresistible temptation to many Terran fleeters who wanted both a place to call their own... and a place from which they could watch the people of the former Empire.

Thirty years. Thirty damned long years... and we're still doing this. When does it end?

He was officially an old timer now, not that he looked it thanks to various bits of life extension technology they'd begged, borrowed, *stole*, and even came up with for themselves over the years. Not that it prevented Steph from feeling his years all the same, he just didn't look them.

The Nest lit up the navigation lights as he came in on approach, guiding his *Revenge* in by the book.

There had been a time when he wouldn't have been able to resist hot dogging in, just to give the controllers a panic attack, but those days were behind him. He'd been on the other side too many times now to see the humor in it.

"All hands, standby for atmospheric insertion." He intoned over the ship's intercom.

The *Revenge* was running light on crew, he was just back from a paid escort mission that hadn't required a complement of Marines. Leaving them at the Nest had made more room for cargo in the small gunship, and supplies were... while not desperately needed, still in tight supply and high demand.

After the war, humanity... the Terran variety at least... had been scattered to the stars. Most never heard from again, by design. Steph wouldn't reveal the location of the Nest with a gun to his head, after all, and any fledgling colony that did so had a fool for a leader. The Empire had been shattered by Earth's counter attack, but not destroyed.

Once burned, Steph thought dryly as the ship shuddered a little through the thickening atmosphere of the ice world.

Researchers said that the Nest had once been a living world... well, technically he supposed it still was, and not just from the human inhabitants. Frozen bacteria had been found in the deeper cores they'd sourced, and in some deep lakes there was still single and simple multicellular life aplenty.

That meant that there was actually a lot of oxygen in the atmosphere, relatively speaking, though it was mostly locked into carbon dioxide molecules. It made for a good thick atmosphere for control surfaces to bite into, but with surface temperatures reaching minus two hundred Celsius it wasn't much of a garden spot.

"*Revenge*, we have you on final approach. You're clear to the wall, Bay Five is all yours. Call the ball."

"Roger that, Nest. *Revenge* making final approach." Steph said clearly, "I have the ball."

"Roger Ball."

Can you tell we're all carrier brats? He thought, amused as the lights became more clear, showing him that he was lined up properly.

Putting his ship down inside a stationary bay wasn't much of a challenge compared to much of what he had become familiar with over the years, and in a few more minutes the old gunboat shuddered under reverse thrust as he slowed to a hover and then settled down onto the marked pad.

"*Revenge* is down."

"Roger that. Securing docking bay. Welcome home."

*****

Steph grabbed his duffel on the way down the corridor to the rear ramp, slinging it over his shoulder without pausing in step. He nodded and returned the greetings of the Nest's maintenance crews as he joined his own crew, all eager to breath air that hadn't been recirculated through their own lungs a million times over.

They were all tired. Worn down, really. There were never enough crews to go around, but the Nest needed supplies, outside currency, and *intelligence* badly.

So they went out.

As many times as they had to, they went out.

And he knew that they'd do it again.

*****

"*Revenge* is secured, Ma'am, and being unloaded as we speak. The Manifest is in your system now."

"Good," The slim woman nodded, waving off the messenger as she wiped her eyes and pushed off the desk to lever herself to her feet.

A simple gesture sent the newly received file to her heads up display, where she quickly perused the list to see what had been brought in.

Mostly foods, seeds, and the like... cheap to buy elsewhere, expensive to grow on the Nest where basics got the focus, just to ensure no one went without. Luxuries were valuable, of course, but it was the smaller section of the list that she focused on.

He found the medical supplies. Thanks to whatever Gods still give a damn, I suppose.

Keeping what was, essentially, a fully formed colony in good form on a world like *Nest* was no small feat, but they'd managed. It wasn't something she'd believed possible when they started, the entire idea seemed preposterous even.

Steph had pushed, however, as he always did... and, as was common, he turned out to be right, even when he didn't have much evidence to back his *gut* up.

Life on the Nest wasn't easy, but it was manageable... and the benefits were worth the cost.

Milla Chans wiped the manifest from her HUD a moment later as she checked and straightened her uniform briefly in the cameras monitoring her office, then took her leave.

"I'll be out for the rest of the day," She told her aide as she walked past.

"Yes Ma'am," The young woman smiled at her as she left.

*****

"Boss!"

Steph half turned, smiling as he saw Tyke approaching, and shifted the weight of his duffel to quickly wrap a free arm around the other man, clapping him on the back.

"Good to see you," Steph said, "How did your run go?"

"Well enough," Tyke confirmed. "Mostly anti-pirate patrols, a little escort stuff. You know how it is."

Steph nodded. The galaxy was a much less peaceful place in the aftermath of the Earth/Imperial war, that much was certain.

The current most prominent power in this section of the galaxy, at least, were the Priminae by default more than any intent on their part. The peaceful people were good allies, but relatively poor at projecting power beyond their borders. Inside Priminae controlled space things were mostly nice and law abiding.

Outside?

Not so much.

The shattering of the Empire had opened the door to all manner of scofflaw types, and few of the governments that survived or emerged seemed inclined to change that.

"Good for business, I suppose," Steph shrugged as he stepped back from Tyke and re-adjusted his duffel.

"There is that," Tyke admitted, a frown on his face, "but some of them are really pushing my tolerance, let me tell you. The Empire was bad, but at least they'd just kill you and be done with it, you know?"

Steph nodded, "Yeah."

There was a reason why Terran Marines were rather popular among the peoples of the former Empire and its vassal worlds.... Not that any of them *knew* that the Marines were anything other than Mercenaries for hire, particular not that they were from Terra...

Marines were hell on Pirates, however, and that made them *very* popular among the peoples who'd been ravaged by the depredations of the lawless.

"You get a chance to visit Prometheus?" Tyke asked, seemingly out of left wing, but Steph knew what he was really asking.

"Yeah," Steph confirmed, slapping the side of his duffel. "Have the latest pull as of a few days ago."

Tyke hesitated, like he didn't really want to know the answer, but asked anyway.

"What's it like?"

"Jupiter's finally gone," Steph sighed, shaking his head. "That's the last of the inner worlds. The Network has expanded out into the Oort cloud, starting to pull apart the Plutoids."

Tyke winced, but nodded.

"And...?"

"Earth and Luna are still untouched," Steph said firmly. "No sign of life that I could see, but it's a big world, even for Prometheus."

"Yeah... still, the network isn't tearing it down, so that's something... I guess?"

"Yeah."

It was a weak hope, Steph thought, but hope was all many of the old guard had at this point. The Imperial Fleets had only controlled Earth's orbitals for a few days before Admiral Gracen's parting gift tore them to *shreds*, but it had been a few days too long.

The orbital bombardment endured was the least of things, in many ways. Liberty Station, or the remains of it, had crashed uncontrollably into Europe as best they could tell, and that was just the start of the debris field coming down.

Global warming had stopped being a problem in the aftermath of the Imperial invasion, with a new ice age sweeping across the planet, burying easily ninety five percent of the world's key industrial and food production sectors under hundreds of feet of contaminated snow.

In the aftermath of the battle several had tried to go back, look for survivors to evacuate or run supplies to... but Gracen's Middle Finger, the Kardeshev Network she'd unleashed on the enemy when defeat became certain, kept everyone out.

A massive self replicating network of satellites that essentially weaponized the power output of the *sun* itself had turned the Sol system into a memorial to a civilization that dared stand up to the aggression of a Galactic power and, though it lost, had *broken* the Empire in the process.

No one had been able to work out why the network refused to accept Confederate IFF codes, but at this point there wasn't much anyone could do about it. Assaulting that fortress just to get to a dirty snowball floating alone in the void... well, even if they *had* the resources, Steph suspected that it would be a hard sell.

And the longer anyone waited... well, the more of those self replicating satellites there would be, having scavenged material from every last object in their range to build more of themselves.

If Sol isn't impregnable by now, it will be soon, Steph thought.

It had a sobering irony, he supposed.

Earth was now so well defended that he doubted anyone *could* get through to do it harm...

All the dead are locked in, while we're locked out. I'd be tempted to think it was too little too late, but that's bullshit. Too late? Yeah, but goddamn if the Admiral didn't go out in style... they all did.

"I'll get you the files when I get unpacked," Steph promised. "Not much to see, but..."

"I know, thanks. Lot of people are interested."

"Old farts like us, no doubt," Steph chuckled wryly.

"You'd be surprised. Lot of young brats have some romantic ideas about going home," Tyke sighed, rolling his eyes. "Won't happen, of course."

"Probably not," Steph shrugged. He'd laid those hopes to rest some time ago, home was where his ship was parked, and...

"Steph!"

Tyke's hand snapped out automatically, snagging the duffel before it could hit the deck as Steph dropped it without a thought, turning to the speaker. The pair met a bit down the hall, Steph wrapping arms around the smaller woman and easily sweeping her into a swing before setting Milla down and catching her face between his hands.

"Missed you, love," Steph told his wife before he kissed her deeply.

*****

CHAPTER 2

World Kraike, Former Center of the Empire

The being once known as Emperor, or Empress, as it suited them stood silently amid the shattered remains of what was once the seat of power for *dozens* of systems.

It didn't know how things could have gone quite so wrong, in quite so spectacular a fashion, and it was… irritated by it. A thousand years or so of work had been wiped away in an instant, by a species that… to the very best of its knowledge only held one singular world.

A world!

Not even a fully developed system according to all reports.

Just one miserable world.

A single, simple, misstep and everything is back to the beginning… or near enough.

Kraike was slowly being reformed, both through the efforts of the inhabitants, but also through the entity's machinations. Factions were being created, and destroyed, at his nudging… each moving the world toward consolidation of power once more.

Controlling a single seat of power was far easier than dealing with dozens of conflicting sides, though there were occasional advantages to that of course.

Re-establishing the Empire would take time, of course, but time was something that was in great abundance. For the moment, the entity was more focused on controlling the factions that either did have, or would soon have, significant forces in orbit. The rest were of little import in the long run, and would most likely be absorbed into one of the larger groups or wiped out.

*At least **that world** was ended too, but the fleeing ones will have to be hunted down.*

It had dealt with other evolutions of the species in the past, and it was a frightful mess. Humans were frustrating, petty little beasts. Useful, of course, but fractious and... difficult to control if left to their own devices for too long.

Every other species in his experience slowly adapted to the world.

Humans? They adapted the world to them.

It was a powerful trait to be certain, but an incredibly dangerous one in the hands of foolish little creatures like humans.

It might be different if the little cretins were able to adapt their thinking as well, but no... they stayed stuck in the mire and morass of their primitive little worlds, largely unchanging in more than a *hundred thousand years*!

Primitives in mind, wielding the power of the tools the few actually intelligent members of the species could concoct.

Utterly disgusting, depraved, and destructive.

So he had set out to tame them, and succeeded. Giving them a constantly moving frontier, while ensuring that the core of the Empire was ruled with an iron fist, it kept the balance humans seemed to need in order to flourish in a useful manner.

That had worked for a not insignificant period of time, his people grew strong under his tending care... powerful, but peaceful.

That had been his first mistake.

When the *others* were encountered, his people had not been ready.

That war had been... eye-opening.

The fighting had been short by his way of marking time, but brutal by any measure. When the fighting cleared, the enemy had offered surrender.

Surrender!

After they'd *slaughtered* so many.

No, he would not allow his people to be tricked so foolishly. With whispered suggestions, occasional intervention in more direct ways, and other bits of subterfuge, it had ensured that no such surrender would be accepted. The Xeno would be purged.

Only *HIS* people deserved to live.

Not all of his agreed, however. The civil war that followed was, if anything, even more destructive than the invasion. Millions died, a billion were left destitute after losing everything... and when it was over, the dissenting group mustered their last strength and...

They left.

A thousand years he looked for them, using those who stayed as his eyes and hands.

A thousand years.

Even he hadn't realized just how deeply the pain of their betrayal had cut him, but now as he looked back on it... likely they had gone too far when they found them.

The Drasin.

Those ancient war machines, those Xeno creations. They should have been destroyed when the ancient cache had been discovered, but it seemed so obvious that they should be controlled and put to good use.

The entity sighed in his pained remembrance.

If only.

No sadder concept was known to him than those two words.

If. Only.

*****

Imperial Cruiser, *From the Flames*

Ship's Commander Kaela Eurydice glared at her screens, a hint of smouldering satisfaction only just visible in her eyes as the ship centered there burned as its atmosphere escaped into the void.

Good riddance to bad filth, She thought grimly as the pirate ship died the death it deserved.

Since the shattering of the Empire the internal conflicts, world to world and even within individual planets, had torn the remnants down faster than anything could be rebuilt.

She'd only been a child when the fires came down from the skies, burning down anything connected to the Imperial Military it seemed, but she remembered the day like it had happened just moments earlier.

The terror of the attack had filled the air, she'd been able to *smell* it... taste it, practically.

It was a day that had changed everything. Changed *her.*

Worst day of her life was when she'd been accepted into the military and they had told her that the enemy that had done that to the Empire... was already dead. She'd known it might be the case, the message that accompanied the fires had certainly indicated that it was, but she had hoped they were lying.

Kaela had *dearly* wanted to kill them all herself.

In the end, though, she had to content herself with

killing pirates and bringing a rule of law back to the Imperial Worlds.

A poor substitute for revenge, she supposed, but it would have to suffice.

"Enemy ship is cooling, Ship's Commander," Her Sub-Commander informed her. "No sign of life remaining."

"Good. Drop a spread of proximity mines," She ordered. "Then we'll be on our way."

"Yes Commander."

The Mines would ensure that any of the Pirate's fellows that tried to reclaim the ship or anything on it had a bad day.

Perhaps she'd get lucky and kill another ship or two.

"Mines deployed."

"Then take us out of the system," Kaela ordered. "Make course for the next waypoint and engage the drives as soon as we're clear of the gravity well."

"Yes, Commander."

The *From the Flames* shifted slowly in space until it's warp drives came up to full power, and then it sped up quickly as it climbed away from the system primary, heading for deep space.

Her patrol orders were to show the flag across all of the Empire's holdings, and remind the more unruly neighbors… such as those in the so called Free Stars… that while the Empire may be hurt, it was still the supreme force in the Galaxy.

*****

Prometheus Facility Colony

"Governor, welcome."

"Thank you Admiral," Ian Kale nodded as he was directed to a seat at the table in preparation for the day's meeting.

Admiral Aiden Pierce took his seat at the head of the table as the highly ranked analysts, researchers, and administrators finished filtering into the room and took their place. The Prometheus gravity lens made them possibly the most informed group in the known Galaxy, but they were badly hampered from making anything happen with that knowledge due to a severe lack of real *reach*.

They could watch… they could *burn*… but they couldn't really do much in between.

So they learned what they could, tried to figure out what it meant, and then passed the intelligence on to the Rogue's Nest, and from there it would be sent on to the Priminae or whoever else might be able to accomplish something with it.

"First point of order, the ongoing search for human colonies," Aiden said, looking around and pausing at the Analysts. "Are there any new breakthroughs there?"

"Not particularly, I'm afraid," Doctor Brenda Flores said with a shake of her head. "We've located some potential worlds for colonies, but keep in mind that we are strictly limited by lightspeed limits. Most of the worlds we're examining are well over thirty lightyears away. Realistically, it will be another century or more before we can confirm whether the colony ships made it to any of those targets."

Aiden nodded. It wasn't new information, but it got repeated a lot. People seemed to forget that the Gravity lens wasn't some magical way to beat physics. Light took the time it took to get to them, even if they had a far better way of collecting it than most.

"Understood, Doctor. Compile the possible sites and we'll pass the intel along to the Nest. It's possible that they may be able to shake a ship or two loose to go looking."

Unlikely, of course, and they all knew it but it wasn't impossible.

"We have been monitoring likely FTL Comms," Flores said, looking concerned, "however I'm fairly certain that those are of Imperial origin. They're pushing out more, and more aggressively."

"Yes, we've been getting reports from the Free Stars contacts that indicate as much," Aiden nodded. "It had to come. I'll make sure that the Nest knows to pass that along to the Priminae. Governor, how are things going with the colony?"

Originally the Facility had been little more than a research base reinforced by enough firepower to flatten a small fleet, but after... well, after, it had become more.

The facility, much like the Rogue's Nest, was built upon a rogue world. That was to say, a planet without a star.

They had yet to determine just why this was the case, but the common belief was that originally it was deemed vital that the observatory not have a nearby star to create light pollution. Over the centuries, likely millennia or more, or drifting through space it had slipped into the system it was still currently in range of, but with enough speed to guarantee escape velocity that would prevent it from being trapped by the primary for long.

Soon enough, in planetary terms, Prometheus would slip out of the system and back into deep interstellar space.

That would largely disable the offensive capacity that the gravity lens gave them, of course, but the world below had clearly been modified to use the lens to gather light and heat from great distances.

An entire world existed in the dark depths below, one that the human colonists had been cautiously pushing into. Clashes with the local fauna had been inevitable, and as such required constant monitoring.

"Our population continues to increase, which is

bringing both good and bad effects," Kale told them. "More of the population is chafing at the restrictions. They want us to open up frontiers in the world below."

"That's insane," Flores scoffed. "The place is teeming with hostile life, pitch black, and has no resources worth the effort."

"None we've found," a voice spoke up from across the table.

"Do you have something to add to the discussion, Mr Jones?"

Raymond Jones sighed, "Just that we don't *know* what's down there. Marines locked the area off from the public, and no one has done any significant exploration since the first discovery. We found the lens and the records... and we called that everything."

"Several deep forays were conducted, Mr Jones," Aiden said wearily. "Nothing of import was located."

"it's a *planet*," Jones said, exasperated. "It will take centuries to explore."

"The lives lost if we opened up access would be..."

"Let them decide if they want to risk it," Jones cut off the governor. "Otherwise we will be dealing with more and more dissent. People want to be free, or the want the illusion of it at least. Some of them want it so much they'll kill for it. I'd much rather they were killing the dragons than their fellows."

That set Aiden back slightly, and he frowned in thought.

"Is it that serious?" He asked after a moment.

Jones sighed unhappily, "Not yet, I don't believe, but it is trending that way. We have space still in the secured areas, places for people to expand into... but they're all heavily regulated, by necessity I know, but that chafes on people. A certain percent of people are just different. They need the frontier, the lack of rules and the pretense of freedom that offers. All I'm saying is that we need an outlet for them."

"It would be safer to simply offer them transfer to the Nest," the Governor snorted.

"Another location just as regulated, again by necessity... but that won't change the way they think," Jones said. "We need to address this now, before it becomes a problem we need guns to deal with."

Aiden shook his head, but couldn't refute the other man's words.

"Very well," He said finally. "We'll put it on the docket and see if we can't figure out a reasonable way to open up exploration options. Is there any other new business?"

"Just one, Admiral."

Aiden turned, eyes falling on the old man who'd spoken, "What would that be, Doctor Palin?"

Edward Palin looked around the table at the people, all of them young fools to his way or thinking, but far from the worst group he'd ever worked with. Unlike most, he had not partaken in the anti-aging technologies that had been made available, other than health improvements at least.

So he was a very healthy man in his seventies now, and reasonably happy with it. Living forever... might have sounded good when he was younger, but he had killed far too many people to want to cling to this life any longer than nature intended for him. His time would come, and he would face whatever judgement there was for what he had done.

But that was not today.

"I've been analyzing background signals," He said, "ones that generally get filtered out because they largely fit in with what we expect to see in nature."

"Why?"

Edward shrugged, "Because I don't think they're natural after all, and I've seen similar encoding in the past. If it is what I'm worried about, ignoring them would be a potentially fatal error."

*****

CHAPTER 3

Rogue's Nest

"How was it this time?" Milla asked as she walked along side Steph as he took the chance to stretch his legs for the first time in weeks.

"Not much different," He said, "We've been doing the same thing for years, not even trying to fix things. It… it's frustrating, and sometimes I forget that we're working for the enemy… we don't want them to fix things."

Milla sighed, understanding his frustration.

It wasn't quite the same thing for her, her world hadn't been lost among many other differences, but she had experienced the same battles by and large, and seen the same acts committed over and over again.

For Milla, she'd been brought up in a wildly different culture than either Steph or the enemy they shared. The Priminae were concerned with building rather than destruction. Defense was certainly something they strove to be capable of, though it had become clear that they had failed in that for quite some time, but her people simply did not glory in the destructive arts.

The Terrans and the Empire were far more alike than the Terrans were in comparison to the Priminae.

Too alike, she thought on darker days. Far too alike to tolerate one another, perhaps, but those were her darker days. When she had more light to view the problem, she saw the differences between them in far more stark clarity.

The Terrans might glory in the battle, but they didn't in the war... somehow. The glory was not in the destruction, but in the intent that rested behind it. The Empire had wrought destruction for little other reasons than they were told to do so. They didn't question the orders, they simply... destroyed.

That was what the Priminae warned of, the deep cultural fear that had chased her people across the centuries. A warning of what would happen if they pursued weapons and destructive capabilities. A warning of what they would become if they began down that path.

Steph and... Eric, they had taught her and her people a very different way.

You didn't meet destruction with kindness. You met it with more powerful destruction.

Kindness was reserved for afterwards... and before.

Once the decision was made to bring hostility to another, though, the Terrans seemed to change wildly from one moment to another. From nearly Priminae in their enthusiasm for building things, to a force that didn't merely match the Empire... but *broke* them, even if it was at a horrifying cost.

Honestly, Milla often wondered if Terrans were entirely sane.

Her relationship with Steph had not, in any way, disabused her of those dark concerns.

"I believe I understand," She said as those thoughts passed through her mind. "I too would rather fix the galaxy than continue to fight."

Steph nodded thoughtfully, gesturing to a passing person in a friendly manner as they arrived at one of the domes that peaked out over the world they'd claimed from the black.

They stopped and looked out over the icy surface beyond the glass. Thick carbon dioxide fog was flowing down the glacier flows, almost a river in how thick it was and how you could see the flow move. The sky, such as it was, was dark. The light was reflected from the stars almost exclusively, leaving the scene looking like something from a dream more than anything related to reality.

"It would be a herculean task to fix the galaxy," Steph said wryly, "but I have to admit... it has a romantic draw."

"Where would we even begin?" Milla asked, laughing as she leaned into his shoulder and looked at the planet beyond the glass. "There's too much."

Steph nodded, humming thoughtfully.

She wasn't wrong, he knew that. There was *far* too much out there to fix.

His logical mind told him that there was no way they could significantly change that. Then he thought about Eric, and Gracen. They had, in their own way, faced impossible odds. The outcomes they'd achieved were far from ideal, but when the impossible faced them down... both of them refused to flinch.

They might not have been able to *fix* the galaxy but they had each, in their own ways, tackled some of the worst problems... and *removed* them.

"I don't know," He admitted. "But there has to be *something* we can do."

"If you figure it out, love, please let me know."

*****

The Free Stars had been all but official Imperial Protectorates for their entire existence, the constant looming threat of an Imperial Battle squadron had, more often than not, been the only real thing that kept them from waging unlimited war upon one another.

The fall of the Empire had, oddly enough, been a traumatic event for the peoples of the Free Stars as they at first struggled to comprehend what had happened.

That period took… years. Not because anyone was actually able to come around to understanding the situation, but more because none of the worlds had been prepared to take proper advantage of the situation.

For almost the entire decade that followed the fall of the Empire, life for the citizens of the Free Stars had been steadily growing better.

Work was easily available, and with workers in high demand the quality of life had increased even as they heard of the depredations that the former Imperial worlds had suffered.

Most took a vindictive satisfaction in hearing the plight of the Imperials, but few understood what was really happening.

The first military strikes happened just over nine years after the collapse of the Imperial worlds, one free star world striking out at another over some old grudge no one really remembered.

It was the first, but far from the last, as the peace that had briefly come to the Free Stars was shattered again.

From that point forward, it became clear that the new normal was not going to be the exceptional experience they'd gone through over the previous decade. It would be brutal raids, back and forth, unchecked by even the depredations of the Empire.

In the years following, more than a few of those in the Free Stars had found themselves thinking about the Empire and the good old days as their worlds spiraled more and more into a cycle of war and rebuilding. Each time, falling a little more behind as resources were used up and they were forced to look to ever more difficult sources to maintain their war machine.

The entire region became rife with piracy of the worst kind, a place where fortunes could be made or lost in an instant, and no true laws ruled.

For the surviving Terrans, it was a gold rush.

*****

Rogue's Nest, Citadel

The Citadel, a name that was more than a little tongue in cheek, was a combination of the small colony's administration offices as well as the primary command and control that handled the comings and goings of visiting vessels.

Raymond Jagger's footsteps echoed as he walked the corridors, heading for the Administration's office. With the return of Gaia's Revenge and her small crew, the colony had a few more much needed supplies as well as news from the outside galaxy.

The first was much needed, but in many ways it was always the second that drew the most attention.

"Ah, Mr Councillor, welcome. The Admiral is expecting you."

"thank you, Jan," He smiled to the secretary and walked on past.

Inside the office, he found Admiral Passer looking out at the brutal landscape beyond the tower. Carbon dioxide snow, methane rivers, and other such nightmares were a fact of life when it came to living at the Nest. It had a stark sort of beauty, but he had gotten over it a long time earlier.

The children born here just considered it home, but Jagger remembered Earth still... it was a fairy tale to the new generation, and perhaps it was one for his generation as well.

The difference being who was telling the tale, I suppose, he thought ruefully.

The children learned of Earth in the style of Disney, perhaps. For the older generation, though, it was a tale with a far more horrifying turn than anything the house of mouse had ever delivered.

"Ah," Passer looked up at him with a weary smile. "Ray, welcome. Have a drink?"

"thank you," Raymond said as he took a seat across from the other man, accepting the tall glass of purified water that appeared from inside the desk a moment later.

"Here for the reports, I take it?" Passer said, not really asking.

"As always," Ray shrugged, "Any news is in demand."

"Well, can't say we have much change," Passer said, "The Kardeshev Network has continued with its work back home, but so far seems to be leaving Earth and Luna intact. No one has attempted to approach it since the last time..."

Ray nodded, wincing as he recalled the last attempt to secure access to the network. The Rogue class destroyer had been intercepted in the Oort Cloud, warning shots driving them back with significant damage to the ship. No one doubted that if they'd pressed on, the system would have diced the ship into easily digestible pieces and turned it into more platforms.

"I don't know what they were thinking, creating that thing in the first place," He sighed.

"Gracen had an impossible task," Passer shrugged. "She made it possible. Somehow."

Ray didn't have anything more he could add to that, but that wasn't abnormal as much as he hated to admit it. The stresses that Earth had been facing up to the end there, well he couldn't even conceive of how it must have felt.

"What about the others?"

"No contact," Passer shrugged. "If they survived, they're keeping their heads down."

"Well, Can't say I blame them there," Ray nodded.

"Yup."

Any of the human colony ships, whether they be sponsored by governments or by corporations, had every incentive to keep their heads down. None of them would have any real idea of what happened to the Empire, after all, when the last of them fled Earth no one outside the upper command had any idea about the contingency plans Gracen, Weston, and the others put into place in the event of the Empire making their ultimate play.

If he were in charge of any of them, he'd be keeping low too.

*Probably for a century or two, at least, until I had a **fleet** or five at the minimum.*

"The Priminae have put together another shipment, should arrive in a few weeks," He said aloud. "And we have a list of new contracts for our ships."

"Anything interesting?"

"Mostly anti-piracy, escort missions, nothing that stands out," Passer said. "We'll give priority to existing clients, probably flat out turn down a few from what I'm reading. Looks like a couple Free Star worlds have decided to get a little too cute."

"Oh?"

"These look more like raiding contracts than anti-piracy," Passer shrugged. "Not surprising, there aren't many good guys out there right now. Most of our contracts are with worlds that hire us to keep pirates out of their systems, and pay others to go pirate on their neighbors."

Ray grimaced, but knew that was part and parcel of how the Nest and Prometheus were getting by.

Neither group really wanted to throw in with the Priminae, despite them being solid allies and good people in general. It just didn't feel right, so they were cutting their own path through the universe.

It was far from an easy task, but despite the constant complaints, Ray didn't know of anyone on the Nest who seriously wanted to change direction now. Of course, in large part that was because any one from the Nest or Prometheus were welcome to visit, or even flat out emigrate to, the Priminae worlds.

It wasn't an easy life, though, and most of the young men and women from the Nest and Prometheus both, tended to wind up on ships performing dangerous duties in order to provide for the colonies.

It was… irritating that a great deal of their efforts to prevent piracy ultimately went to supporting it, just from another source.

"There is at least one interesting contract in the batch," Passer said, tapping on a screen in front of him. "Not so much the contract, though, but the *contractor* now? Very interesting."

*****

Steph and Milla's apartment was buried deep below the ice of the Nest, cut into the planet itself. A few kilometers of ice had to be traveled through before you got down to the surface, but once there the temperature rapidly went from minus two hundred or so to as warm as minus twenty in the first hundred meters below the surface. It warmed up rapidly from there, and the colony used deep drilled wells to cycle meltwater down to the tectonically active warmth beneath their feet and provide warmth for the inhabitants.

They didn't have a ton of room, but after coming from the *Revenge* it felt palatial to Steph as he tossed his duffel into the laundry room and let himself collapse on a simple couch.

"Argent, cycle through views from Earth please," Milla asked the computer as she slid a pillow over for Steph to prop himself up with.

The walls, floor, and even ceiling shifted in an instant, showing a wild view of what Steph believed was a plateau in South America... possibly Africa, he wasn't certain. A lot of green and blue, colors he didn't get to see much of anymore.

"You look tired," She said, shaking her head. "You push yourself too hard, Stephan. Every time you come home, you seem... less."

"I'll be ok," He said, shaking his head. "It was nothing new, just the same old missions."

"Exactly," She said with a shake of her head as she sat down beside him. "but I know you will not stop."

"Someone has to go out."

"It does not have to be you."

"Yeah... it does."

Milla shook her head, both with deep fondness and a rising frustration. It was a combined emotion that she was quite familiar with.

"Next time," She told him firmly as she rubbed his shoulder, "I am going with you."

Steph twisted, looking alarmed, "Milla, there's no reason..."

"For me to stay here now, I agree." She smiled. "So, if you wish me to stay here, all you need do is turn down the next mission. Otherwise, it will be... like old times, I believe you say, no?"

Steph groaned.

He wasn't going to win this, he knew it, but he still felt like he had to fight.

Damn it.

*****

CHAPTER 4

Rogue's Nest

Amanda Michaels groaned as she slumped onto her bunk, feeling like she'd just been worked over by one of the interrogation specialists. Every muscle in her body ached, along with her bones, teeth, fingernails, and *somehow* her hair.

*Why does my **hair** hurt? **How** does my hair hurt?*

"Hey Mike, you good?"

Amanda sighed, not wanting to move as she responded, "Yeah I'm good. Just need to get some energy back before I take a hot shower."

Her bunkmate nodded, "How did it go?"

"I did it," She said, smiling slightly.

"Well congrats, not that anyone is going to be surprised. So, do I salute you yet?"

"I get my bar in the morning, so nope. Not yet."

Sarah Liv tossed her a sloppy salute anyway, "Well you deserve it. Top in the class, I'm assuming. You put in for your assignment yet?"

"Yeah, I want an Angel slot."

Sarah whistled, "Damn. Not a lot of those to go around. You know what ship they'll give you?"

"Not the Revenge, that much is certain, but I may get the Ranger."

Sarah whistled, "Good luck. How'd your brother do?"

"He graduated too, don't know how well he did but I'm sure it was solid at least," Amanda said, still staring at the ceiling over her bunk. "He's looking for a berth on a Rogue."

"Well no shock there," Sarah laughed, "If Mik and Mike didn't graduated, what chance would the rest of us have had?"

"Oh bugger off," Amanda grunted as she sat up and began stripping down as she lurched off the bunk and headed for the small shower.

Sarah laughed at her as she stumbled in and punched the activator for the shower, groaning as the heat washed over her.

*****

Rogue's Nest, The Citadel

"Graduate records for this session, Sir."

Passer nodded wearily, taking the slate.

"Anything noteworthy?"

"Nothing unexpected," His secretary told him. "We're still going to be undermanned, but this graduating class will fill in a lot of the empty spaces in the Rogues and Angels."

That was good news, he knew, but it wasn't quite enough. The Angels were their only real connection to the worlds of the former Empire and its array of worlds. The Rogues were a known Terran design, which meant that those ships absolutely could *not* be seen by the Empire... at least not in conjunction with any of their normal operations.

The few cruisers they had left were functionally identical to Priminae vessels, which meant that they could come and go readily with little issue even if they were seen it didn't matter overly.

Unfortunately, trained crews were the limiting factor.

Thank god we have so many volunteers.

He'd had to leave his ship a few years after the last

battle, putting the Auto in the hands of Daiyu Li, who still commanded her to this day. Passer longed for the days when he was a Ship's Captain, but duty's call couldn't be ignored and he was needed where he was. Few of the Captains left after the war had been properly experienced with the logistical rigors of command, which made him the man on the hill he supposed.

"I see a couple names I recognize here," He said after a moment's perusal. "Right at the top. I trust there's been no favoritism at play?"

"No sir, that order came down from both parents in no uncertain terms after they'd applied," his secretary snorted, amused at the idea. "I believe they both made it clear that if the kids couldn't cut it, they didn't want them anywhere near a ship."

Passer nodded, satisfied. He hadn't really expected there to be any, and was quite certain that there was, in fact, *some* degree at play... but with an order like that, he expected that for as much favoritism the pair might have enjoyed, they likely caught a lot of harsher treatment as well.

"Good enough," He said. "Assignments?"

"Eric put in a request for Rogue duties, I'm guessing he's looking for Command eventually," She said. "Amanda applied for a slot with the Angel's Marines."

Morgan nodded thoughtfully, "What slots are open?"

"The Auto could always use a young officer with some promise, but we have a few alternatives. Marines, well, there's no shortage of those places."

"True, but I think young Eric may be misestimating the chances of promotion with the Rogues," Passer said mildly.

They didn't have enough ships, and their best officers tended to stay right where they were until they were ready to move on of their own accord. Morgan didn't want to cripple a promising young officer's career, such as such things were these days, because they made a bad assumption before they were even commissioned.

"There's truth there."

The Rogue's were rarely involved in action in these days, generally only striking from the shadows when there was almost no chance of being found out. Keeping them as even less than a rumor was a strategic advantage that he wasn't about to give up.

"Cardsharp has a spot open."

Passer looked up, surprised briefly but then he nodded slowly.

"Yes, that'll do. Send him over there, if she'll take him."

"Jenn will take him, Sir."

Passer didn't doubt that for a second, but it was polite to leave the option open.

"Find a Marine squad that needs new meat for Amanda," He went on, "*Not* on Cardsharp's crew, nor the *Revenge* either, of course."

"Of course, Sir."

With the top two candidates out of the way, Passer and his secretary moved on to the rest of the list as they worked to get the graduating class all spread out to where they were needed.

"And tell Blackbeard to get his ass up here," Passer grumbled, "As soon as he and his wife finish getting reacquainted at least."

"Yes sir."

*****

Steph checked out the changes as he made his way to the Honcho's office, glad that he'd managed to get out from behind the desk for a rotation back to space duty a few years back.

They were always short of trained personnel, but that held just as true for good logistics and command officers at base as it did for experienced ship's commanders.

Passer had left his ship to his first when he took over the job here, and by all accounts Captain Li was providing a good accounting for the Thief as anyone could, though she was shackled by the need of the Rogue Class Destroyers to remain hidden from the enemy.

Of the three main ship classes available to the Terran survivors, the Rogues were the most problematic. They were known Terran designs that no other faction used, whenever they showed up or were spotted, the Imperial remnants tended to converge quickly. That had led to the loss of many of their fellows in the early years, and now the Rogues tended to live and die by the adage of run deep, run silent.

"Ah, Captain Michaels, welcome, the Admiral is waiting."

"thank you, Idra," Stephen said as he walked past and into the office that rested at the top of the spire.

Not the best location in some ways, he knew, but while deeper down would be more defensible they were far enough out in deep space that any approaching enemy would be spotted with plenty of time for the Base Commander to withdraw to a safer location... and the view from the spire was, well... better than looking at rock walls at least.

That was a bit of an exaggeration, honestly, it was a spectacular view when you could see it, but this far out from any star meant that the nights were constant and redefined dark in many ways.

"Ah, Captain," Passer said as he got up and walked around the desk. "How have you been?"

"Can't complain, Sir."

"None of that," Passer rolled his eyes, "otherwise I'll have to call you sir next time you take the job."

"Let's just hope that's a ways off," Steph laughed, shaking the offered hand. "What makes you summon me, oh great one?"

"Smart ass," Passer grumbled, but without any heat to it. "Mostly just wanted to talk about a couple new recruits."

Steph nodded slowly, "Ah. I have been informed that they graduated and did well. I trust there was no coddling?"

Passer snorted, "I gave them to the Marines, Steph. Even if they were coddled, I doubt they'd agree."

Steph smiled, "There's truth there. So what's the issue?"

"Just a friendly heads up, really, I'm sending them both to the Angel teams."

"Not the Revenge, I assume," Steph blinked, not quite surprised, but not really having expected it either.

"No, Eric is going to the Casino," Passer said. "Not sure about Amanda yet, but some other ship. I won't berth them together either. We're tight up for manpower, but not that tight."

Steph nodded, thinking it through. "Jen has a spot for a young officer?"

"She does," Passer confirmed. "And well, there are always places for a young Marine."

"That's a sad truth," Steph replied. "I didn't need a squad on my last run, but most times... yeah."

Passer nodded somberly.

The highest casualties were always among the Marines, with good reason he supposed. Marines were the ones who met the enemy face to face, and that was hardly a safe position to be in. Even when a ship was in combat, well, the Marines were just as much at risk as anyone else.

"I'll probably assign her to..." Passer paused, considering

the thought before he spoke.

"I could send her to the Bell or the Bo," He offered after a moment.

Steph held up his hands, "Don't make decisions based on me, Sir. If that's where she'll fit in, send her there, but if you need a Marine elsewhere, she's chosen her path."

Passer nodded, "Understood. I just wanted to let you know, anyway. How is Milla?"

Steph smiled, "Same as always. Just informed me that she's coming with me on the next run."

"May as well just clear out your berth then, that woman may seem meek but..." Passer shuddered.

Steph laughed, "Don't I know it. I'll fight anyway, just for the sake of it, but yeah I expect she'll be on board when the Revenge next tastes deep space."

"Won't be long, I expect," Passer told him. "Unless you want to take some more down time, I already have several missions lined up."

"I'll talk with Milla, let you know."

"You do that," Passer said. "Meanwhile, how are things out there? I mean, really."

Steph sighed, gesturing to the seats as he started thinking about his impressions of the state of affairs beyond the Nest.

"That's a hard story to tell, I think," He admitted.

"I have time, Captain."

*****

Steph made his way back to the lower levels were the habitation sections of the base were located. He still remembered locating this planet, at the time it had just been a convenient stop off point to coordinate navigation for their missions into the Free Stars and Imperial space.

Back then, he'd never had considered that it might become one of the hidden bastions of Terran civilization in the region. Before Earth fell the colony ships had been departing the system as fast as they could be built and crewed. So fast that he personally expected that the loss rate for those ships would turn out to be atrocious, assuming anyone was ever able to find out what happened to them all.

Those ships that survived, well they were all headed out as far from the Empire as they could possible, and even if they survived it was more than merely possible that he wouldn't live long enough to hear from them again, life extension technology be damned.

Assuming they follow the protocols we put out last going off, they'll start putting out their own colony ships as quickly as they can manage as well.

The Empire had tried to crush Terran humanity in one stroke... but all it had succeeded in doing was scattering the seeds to the wind.

Those thoughts in mind, he had some hopes for the future even if things were rather like being grain in the mill at the moment. Steph crossed the public spaces and headed for his apartment. He had a long discussion in his near future, whether he wanted it or not.

As the door slid open he heard voices inside, "Hello the room."

Steph grinned as his call stilled the sounds and rushed movement could be heard. A moment later he saw Eric and Amanda rush out of the inner room, followed slightly more sedately by Milla.

"Dad!"

"Hey guys," Steph said as he grabbed both up in a single hug. "I hear you passed the academy and are due for your first assignments. Congrats, both of you."

*****

CHAPTER 5

World Kraike

For ages practically immemorial for humans, albeit merely a long time for him, the entity who had nearly as long been known as either Emperor or Empress as it suited, had sat at the very center of Imperial intelligence. All the data of every world under their banner had, in one way or another, passed through his web.

At its height, it made him very nearly omniscient across multiple worlds in something that closely approximated real time. It hadn't been quite as potent as his abilities on his own world had been, but it had been an impressive multiplication of his capacity nonetheless.

Nearly a hundred worlds feeding his growing understanding of the universe.

Now, while not entirely gone, his capability was far from what it had once been. Merely maintaining order within Imperial space was now the focus of his abilities to a disturbing degree. More and more incidents of piracy and incursions from the frontier worlds that had once been an outlet for the Empire were taking away resources from more important goals.

Oddly, perhaps, the group that had caused all this... were not causing issues.

The Emperor knew that they had survived, in one manner or another. Reports back from the front had made it clear that some ships had escaped the system before the Hammer of the Empire could be brought down on them, and not every enemy ship had fallen in the final battle.

In the aftermath, however, there had been no sign of them.

The fires that had been the enemy's retaliation, utterly burning military facilities across the Empire to ashes in a single blazing moment of time, had been the final stroke.

After that?

Silence.

The silence worried him more than nearly anything else.

This group of Xeno did not act as the first. They were certainly capable of violence, and a brutality that had stunned even him, but they held back… even in the face of annihilation, they *held back*. Their retribution had been swift and brutal, but then they didn't press their advantage.

*They held **back**.*

And he did not know *why*.

More than anything else, that gnawed at him. Humans were many things, but being capable of delaying the gratification of their base instincts… whether it be pleasure or revenge… well, that was not one of their core strengths.

Which left him worried for what was sure to come. The Empire had struck against a foe and failed to end them with the blow. That could only bring trouble.

The Emperor was shaken from his musings by a report entering his sphere of influence, the information becoming part of his consciousness as soon as one of his humans read it. The human in question didn't see much to be concerned of with it, but he saw a signature that brought his entire focus to the communique.

A few nudges later, and a missive was sent, assigning ships to investigate the report to determine whether it was as he believed or something else entirely.

With his 'daughter', the former Empress dead, and the current political climate still in uproar as Nobles jockeyed for position to replace her, his direct influence had waned and would take at least a full generation of *stable* rule to properly replace… but he was still the *Center of the Empire* and all lines of communication led to him.

He controlled the information, he controlled the *Empire*.

*****

IC *From The Flames*

"Ship's Commander, Pulse Band direct from Kraike!"

Kaela shifted, eyes falling on the Comms officer who was approaching hurriedly. "Understood. Transit."

"Yes, Commander. Transiting." He said, immediately sending the data ahead to her terminal.

Kaela waved him off casually then as she opened up the file and looked over the intelligence and orders sent along from the seat of Imperial Hegemony.

She had never set foot on the First World before joining the military, and since then only briefly as her orders required. Still, like any loyal member of the Empire she had pledged her works to the benefit of the seat of the Empire and intended fully to see that through.

Still, her orders often left her confused.

The files sent along were curious, she supposed, but she saw nothing that explained the urgency applied to the attached orders.

Not that her lack of understanding made much difference, she supposed.

"Navigation," She called, standing.

"yes, Commander."

"New course to your station," She said, flicking the nav

points over with a gesture. "Set it and have the crew readied for motion."

"As you will it."

As I will it indeed, She thought, mind still focused on the data.

Why would such signals be so concerning?

She didn't know the answer to that, but ultimately it wasn't something she needed to know.

Kaela and her crew merely needed to do their duty.

*****

Bellerophon

Thirty years. Longer really.

Captain Jason Roberts... technically an Admiral now, he supposed, given his responsibilities, was a tired man. Not physically. He had rarely felt better, physically. The help the Priminae offered included amazing health benefits, and compared to his pre-war peak almost fifty years earlier... he was actually in the best shape of his life, by far.

Mentally?

That was a different story.

It's not the years, it's the mileage, he thought with grim amusement. *And by any measure, I've put a **lot** of miles behind me.*

Since the War... yes, he capitalized it in his head, everyone he knew did the same... since then, it had felt like he was running a race with no finish line.

No goals, no endgame, *no point* to any of it.

He knew that wasn't true, if anything what he and the others had been doing were possibly the most important things anyone in *history* had done... but that wasn't what it felt like.

Roberts and many of those who'd served during the War couldn't help but feel like everything had ended with the loss of Earth. They'd defined themselves for so long as the last line of defense for the planet, and when they'd *failed*...

What was left?

My people.

Roberts steeled himself as he had done often before, refusing to allow any *hint* despondency to enter his thinking. That way lay ultimate, unintentional or not, dereliction of his duties... and that was one thing he would **not** allow.

"Sir."

Roberts glanced aside as a young officer approached, "Yes Nichelle?"

"Flash Traffic from Prometheus," Nichelle Swayel said, passing him a chip. "Encrypted, Captain's Eyes, Sir."

"Thank you, Ensign. That'll be all," He said, accepting the chip.

Encrypted flash traffic from Prometheus.

No way that's good news.

Roberts sighed deeply but didn't delay dropping the chip onto the induction reader and reading the file that was immediately projected above it on his station.

Hmmm... not good news, but hard to say if it's bad. I can see why they wanted someone to take a look, though.

Roberts nodded to himself and closed the file after pulling out some key bits of data for the ship's systems.

"Bell," He said, "make sure that navigation gets the coordinates I just put into the system."

"Aye sir," The entity known as Bellerophon, the soul of his ship and crew, said with perfect military diction. "Coordinates received. Orders?"

"I'll give them myself when I get to the Deck," Roberts said, "but you can let them know that we're on mission the moment my boot lands."

"Aye sir."

The entity vanished with that, leaving Roberts alone as he checked his uniform before leaving his office.

The Entities had taken time for him to get used to, since the Odysseus had somehow... given *birth* to the first? Honestly, no one... least of all him... had any idea about what exactly had triggered the first to appear, but they had since worked out how to repeat the event.

Only ships powered by the massive singularity reactors or Priminae and Imperial vessels could create, or hold, an entity. They were beings that existed in the gravity well and electromagnetic influence of the reactors... much as certain others appeared to exist within the wells of inhabited planets.

Each of them were a Gestalt creature, a sum of all the parts in their system. A system that included the *crew* of the ship they embodied.

Those that existed on planets... Roberts still shuddered at the *thought* of them. The combined experience of *thousands of generations* of people, all crammed into one being with unknown motivations.

Before the War, his experience with the entities had been... essentially nonexistent, and that had been the way he liked things if he were being honest. Other than a few short encounters with Odysseus, the soul of the entity's namesake ship, he'd been happy not to have dealt with any of them.

It had mostly been Eric who handled those situations, by design or otherwise, Jason didn't know which.

Since then, however, every Terran Cruiser had an entity born within. The Bo had come first, during the last days of the War, providing the Boudicca with the added support of what was essentially a super intelligence compiled from her own crew's experiences. Jason hadn't been eager to duplicate that accident, but the Odysseus...

Oh Lord, the Odysseus...

One man, one ship, and one entity... in that final battle, Eric and Odysseus had *lain waste* to their enemy until they were dragged down by sheer force of numbers.

Whether he liked it or not, Roberts was a military man and that made him practical above all of his personal inclinations. He may not like someone, but if the mission called for it, by damn he'd not only work with them but he'd call them *brother.*

In the years since, though, he found himself rather liking Bell.

The Soul of the ship was a firm and practical minded personality, adhered to military discipline as though born to it... likely because it *was...* and had little of the free spirit playfulness that had irritated Roberts in the few dealings he'd had with Odysseus.

No incidents with Bell wearing makeup, thank God.

The Ship Souls were essentially a Terran secret at this point, one of the few military secrets they had left. The only ships that he knew of that held one were the surviving cruisers of Weston's squadron... and for the foreseeable future, that was all there would be.

The Priminae were good allies, but they were not Terrans, and their intelligence and more importantly *counter-intel* capabilities weren't up to spec as far as he was concerned. One day this secret too would leak out, he knew for certain, but until then...

Any advantage is a good advantage.

Jason laughed grimly to himself as he made his way to

the Deck.

*****

"Captain on Deck!"

"As you were," Roberts said firmly as he emerged from the lift. "Ops, are we ready to move?"

"Aye Captain," Jessie Kale, the Lieutenant at Operations, answered without hesitation. "All departments report green to go."

"Excellent, let the locals know we're leaving orbit," He said, "Then make to warp space."

"Warp Space, Aye skipper."

It would only be a few minutes more before the Bellerophon left the orbit of the Priminae agri-world, stocks resupplied and a mission in hand.

*****

Prometheus Facility

Edward Palin scowled as he looked over the scanner data that he'd requisitioned from the facilities antennae.

He couldn't determine for certain what the source was, but it was the location that concerned him above all else.

There wasn't anything out that way according to any of the available data he had. No Imperial worlds, certainly no Priminae colonies, and none of the known Earth ships had gone that way… though, admittedly, not all of those had properly filed their destinations.

Partly for security reasons, but mostly because the early ships in particular were guessing at likely destinations more than setting out with a solid plan.

*If it's an Earth colony, we need to get to them fast and **shut them up.** The Empire will notice this before long,* Palin knew for certain.

And, if it were anything *else*, they needed to know what the hell was out there now.

The Galaxy had proven dangerous enough in their ignorance, Palin wasn't willing to settle for anything less than accurate knowledge going forward.

*****

CHAPTER 6

Rogue's Nest

Steph smiled easily as he relaxed in the living area of the small apartment. The kids had headed off to their own places, base housing for both as he understood it, leaving he and Milla alone for the night.

"You have that look on your face again," Milla said with a smile as she dropped into the seat beside him, leaning in to his side.

"What look?"

"The content one," She answered, "you don't wear it nearly enough."

Steph laughed lightly at that, dropping an arm easily around her and pulling her closer.

"I suppose I don't at that," He admitted. "It's hard to be content when you have so many worries and responsibilities."

Milla nodded, "I remember after the children were born. You got very serious, for far too long."

Steph nodded, his smile dropping a little as he thought back to those early days.

"I think... they reminded me of what I'd lost, things I'd tried to forget... stupidly," He said somberly. "Eric, Gracen... everyone else. I spent *years* after the War just trying to forget their faces. The kids reminded me of my failures, I was determined not to fail again... and damned it if I didn't drive myself right down that same road. Almost missed their childhood, trying to keep that promise."

Steph shook his head, "would have been worth it, if there had been anything I could really do to ensure their safety... but the universe isn't a safe place. Took me too long to accept that, I guess."

"You came around," She said, teasingly, "even if there were times I was tempted to hit you very hard with something, just to see if 'percussive maintenance' was what you needed."

"That might have worked," Steph said amused before he sighed. "They're going to get their first assignments soon."

"I know, it worries me too."

"Eric will get an Ensign's slot, probably on an Angel, the Casino was mentioned specifically." Steph said, "though Morgan suggested maybe one of the Heroics for Amanda."

Milla shifted, looking up at him, "Seriously?"

Steph nodded, understanding her tone.

The Heroics were prime assignments, and generally not something that went to young officers without experience... not even Marines.

"I said no special treatment," Steph went on, keeping his tone level. "If she fits there, fine, otherwise... well, wherever she does fit."

Milla nodded reluctantly. They'd had this conversation many times in the past, occasionally even getting heated. The pair of them held a lot of influence with the fleet as it currently sat, both from their current authority and from their legends. There were few ships that the children *could* be sent to that wouldn't result in them receiving *some* sort of special treatment.

She was proud of the pair, but worried for them as well. The times that she and Steph had gone through over the last half century, near enough by Terran reckoning, were such that she'd much rather her children *not* experience anything equitable.

As her husband was fond of stating, however, the universe was not a safe place.

*****

The Casino

Jennifer *Cardsharp* Samuels leaned into the controls that floated around her, bringing the Angel up to full power and throwing her ship through space at high acceleration. The forward screens were visible through the HUD, lighting up with the impacts of dust, debris, and cosmic radiation but the system tied into her central nervous system allowed her to look through it with long range scanners adjusting for the doppler effect of their acceleration.

"Target located," She said firmly. "Stand by weapons. Marines, get ready."

"Weapons Standby, Aye."

"Oorah, Ma'am."

The enemy vessel was an old one, not of Imperial make nor anything from the major players in the War, but rather a destroyer from one of the Free Star States. They'd been tracking this one for a while, jumping system to system trying to get ahead of it.

The contract was Imperial, ironically enough, but their money spent as well as anyone else's... and it kept the Angels close to the enemy, a knife at their back.

Not that she had a problem with this contract.

The destroyer didn't have a name as best she had been able to determine, whatever markings it once might have had were long since blasted off... either intentionally to hide its identity or from damage due to fighting. Cardsharp didn't much care which, if she were honest.

The ship was a piece of crap, but the crew were worse.

Pirates in the worst sense of the word. They'd looted several worlds, including an Imperial protectorate which was what brought her down on their heads. If they'd limited their deprecations somewhat and focused on Imperial combatants, well they might be getting a *very* different sort of visit.

Wouldn't be the first outlaws we've recruited over the years, She thought amused by the return to the Age of Sail rules they'd undergone, *but we don't recruit slime.*

"All points, Cardsharp," She spoke. "We're starting our run. Stand ready."

She ignored the acknowledgements, focusing on the drives as she brought her fighter gunboat up to it's highest in-system velocity... well, highest without requiring a rebuild next time they made port at least. The relatively small ship was a fraction the size of the destroyer they were about to tangle with, and still completely hidden in the vastness of space but that wouldn't last much longer.

"Weapons hot. Clear the safes."

"Aye Skipper. Weapons charged and ready. We've got rounds in the chamber, Ma'am, ready to roll."

Cardsharp keyed a single beep response to acknowledge that, her mind hyperfocused on the target not. Gun emplacements were identified and Haloed in her mind as they were on the HUD.

"Target designations received... locked. Finger on the trigger ma'am."

"Send it."

The weapons of the Archangel Class gunboat didn't *roar* exactly, lasers generally made a quiet clicking sound as their capacitors were discharged... maybe a whine if something needed tuning, but for the enemy on the receiving end of it Cardsharp suspected that the difference was rather moot.

At ten light seconds out, less than a minute to the destroyer, the lasers hit their targets with the practiced accuracy of professionals who knew their job inside and out. Armor grade metal just vaporised under the tuned energy weapons, gun ports being blown apart from the heat expansion even if the armor was enough to slow the beam's destruction.

The destroyer didn't seem to react immediately, but by the time they'd crossed half the distance to the target it was beginning to maneuver… either to escape or to try and bring its undamaged weapons around, she didn't know which… and didn't care.

Too little, too late.

"Marines, Cardsharp," She intoned, "Deploy at your discretion."

"Oora Skipper. Boarding teams away."

*****

Iska Niver slammed a hand onto the side of the console in front of him, trying desperately to get his weapons system tracking again.

"Where did those strikes come from?" Jasin Corr, the Ship's Commander, demanded in a tone that sounded a lot shakier than Iska believed he intended.

"Calculations being made, Commander," The much calmer ops officer responded, "however we're having issues…"

"What issues?"

"Source must be moving, *fast*, closing on our position," The Ops officer said, "We're trying to predict where it is *now*, not where it was when it fired, and it's taking time."

"We don't *have* time!"

As though that was a portent, the conversation on the ship's Command Deck went silent a moment later as a series of loud *thuds* could be heard reverberating through the ship.

Everyone just stopped for a moment, looking up and around in silence.

Iska broke the silence first.

"W... what was that?"

****

Colonel Keenan slapped the Marine beside her on the shoulder as he grabbed the ragged edge of the hole they'd just blown through the armored hull and swung himself through it and into the ship beyond.

"Next, move it," She called. "Secure the breach!"

"Oorah Ma'am."

She pushed her squad through as quickly as possible before shouldering her own rifle and jumping through feet first.

Inside the ship the squad had set up a perimeter, securing the breach as ordered.

"Good work, Martinez, Chin, move up and get that junction covered. Parker and Saul, you cover them while they set up."

The Marines moved quick, the two heavy weapon grunts lugged their kit forward while the Gunmen followed as security.

"Well boys," Keenan said casually as she checked the surroundings and compared what she was seeing with the sets of blueprints she had on file for Free Star ships on her HUD. "Looks like we've got ourselves a heavily modified Woodpecker Type Destroyer, directions coming to your systems now. Stay tight, don't trust the directions if you can help it, these boys may have done some extensive mods since this baby was new."

The Marines nodded, grabbing more gear as it was

passed through the breach by the support squad.

"We have five squads on this tin can, and I do not want to be the last one to the prize, so let's pick up the pace boys."

*****

"Sir… we've lost contact with the forward decks, I can't get any communications through to the repair teams that were dispatched."

Corr scowled, tapping in commands at his console only to come up similarly blank.

"We must have taken more damage than we thought," He grumbled. "Do we have a lock on the enemy yet?"

"Yes, Commander. They blew past our perimeter too fast for anything to lock on and are now moving away at high speed," The Ops officer replied. "They are beyond the range of our close in weapons, and are staying in the firing arc of the emplacements their attack destroyed."

"Bring us around," Corr ordered. "I want live weapons on that target *immediately*!"

"Coming around, yes Commander."

The deck rumbled a bit, which caused them all to pause again.

"Was that… the drives?" Corr asked, incredulously.

The drive mechanism shouldn't have done *that*.

*****

"Careful with those, Chin, we want the ship intact," Keenan said dryly as she walked up past the heavy gunner, who somehow managed to look chagrined in his environmental armor.

"Sorry Ma'am, I overestimated the enemy's emplacement," The Marine admitted. "Didn't think they'd break so easily."

"They're pirates, son," Keenan chuckled low in her throat. "Break and bleed is all they're good for. If they were tough, they'd have picked a real job."

"Oorah, Ma'am."

Keenan mentally cataloged the damage as they passed, noting that the new heavy weapons designs were possibly a little good for shipboard use.

Oh well, if it gets broken, we'll sell it for scrap.

Her team was moving steadily through the ship, moving to the protected inner decks where the command deck would be. Shutting down communications was easy enough, Free Star ships almost exclusively used hardline systems that were incredibly durable, reliable, and impossible to block... unless you were on board.

If one could reach the optical cables, on the other hand, that same perceived security had made it such that few of the Free Star *state* actors bothered with significant encryptions... Pirates like this group? Probably didn't even know the meaning of the word in the first place.

Only the fact that the Command Deck had hardline access to key stations that originated there prevented them from taking over the ship entirely from where they stood.

"Secure that door," She called, pointing to a security door up ahead, with people working feverishly around it. "Don't let them seal it!"

Her Marines surged forward, the Gunmen taking the lead as they fired on the run. The lack of appropriate cover made the charge dangerous, but the enemy were more focused on the door and only a couple were firing back with the sorts of weapons they'd come to expect on board a Free Star built ship.

Flechette type rounds pattered on the Marines armor, like a hard rain more than a battlefield weapon, while the much heavier rounds from the Marines' rifles blew great big holes in their targets as the squad *bodily* slammed into the few that remained standing to push them away from the door controls.

"Door secure, Ma'am." Parker said as she approached.

"Good work." Keenan said, looking to the left. "Plans say that the Command deck should be right over there. Secure the survivors and leave em where they lay, we have bigger fish to fry. I want a word with the Pirate Captain."

"Yes Ma'am."

Keenan waited a moment while the team got everything squared away and then they were moving again. The breaching team were setting up at the sealed door to the Command Deck when the second squadron arrived.

"You're late," She said dryly, nodding to the Lieutenant in charge.

"Apologies, Ma'am. Took the scenic route."

"Ah well, as long as you have a good reason," She laughed. "Alright, ready to breach?"

"Oorah!"

"Then knock knock, motherfuckers." She said, taking a step back.

"Fire in the hole!" The Marine EOD man called, hitting the manual striker on his detonator.

The door blew in, with the Marines charging through the smoke and fire before it even began to disperse.

*****

CHAPTER 7

Rogue's Nest

"Ship inbound, Sir."

Passer nodded, rising from his desk. "ID?"

"Tentative, we're waiting for challenge response still, but it looks like the Casino, Sir."

"Took them longer than expected," Passer said mildly as he left his office and made his way to Ops. "Must have had trouble hunting the target down."

The hubbub in the operations center was about on par with the norm he found as he stepped in, people actively scanning the void beyond their little world for anything that looked out of the ordinary. The large screens showed the view from orbit through the observation birds they had dotted around the area, as well as anything interesting being reported back from farther out.

"Challenge response cleared, it's the Casino!"

"Stand down from defense alert," The deck commander said calmly, taking a sip from her coffee. "Issue approach instructions, clear a bay for them."

"Aye Ma'am. Bay thirty is clear and the crews there have been alerted."

"Good work, retask our birds out there to watch the Casino's wake, make sure there's no uninvited guests following her home."

"Yes Ma'am."

Passer nodded silently to himself, pleased with the responses he was seeing. The odds that Jen Samuels had slipped up enough to allow someone to follow her back were beyond slim, but it was bad discipline to assume that. The safety of the *Nest* had been secured with secrecy and, while they might not be at nearly as much risk now as when they got started, there were still plenty of threats out there that could gut them.

"Casino has transmitted mission report."

"I'll take that, to my system please," Passer spoke up.

"Yes Sir, file dispatching. It'll take a few, we're still pulling the data down from the satellites."

"No worries, I'm a patient man when I have to be," Passer smiled. "Good work people, as you were."

*****

Morgan made his way back to his office and found that the data was already loading into his system. He ignored most of it for the moment and went straight for the text report that had been front loaded with the files.

Job complete, of course. Pay has been accepted, good.

Morgan didn't much *like* operating as a Mercenary, but needs must. They were still rebuilding their industrial capacity, but such things just took inordinate amounts of time. He, and many others, couldn't decide if they were regretful or thankful that the Kardashev technology had essentially been lost when Earth was.

While self replicating manufacturing would be an incredible asset, no one who looked to the Sol system at the moment was entirely comfortable with the idea of replicating Gracen's Middle Finger anywhere else at the moment.

At some point, he supposed they would have to rebuild even that, but that point was a distance off. Which meant that they had to do things the old-fashioned way. That meant building infrastructure and manning it.

The first wasn't that hard to do, but population wise... well, the second was proving difficult.

Human population trends on Earth had been slowing since before the end of the twentieth century, at least in developed nations. As health services improved, those numbers dropped even more as more nations reached a point where they didn't need to be afraid that their children would die in the crib. The numbers weren't helped by the presence of so called "forever chemicals" in over *ninety seven percent* of the human population by the 1970s, of course, as those chemicals in combination with lead, cadmium, and other pollutants had devastated human fertility, but ultimately cleaning things up had begun to reduce those issue at least marginally by the time the Block War happened.

The minor population boom after that had been a boon to Earth's activities as it pressed out into space, and found itself fighting the War against the Empire... but now they had found themselves with even more issues.

Their base population had been composed of a few tens of thousands of people, mostly military and research scientists, after the fall of Earth. The colony ships, with all the resources to actually build that infrastructure... well they'd vanished into the Black, as they should.

It was what Morgan and his fellows had fought for, after all. Getting as many people *out* as possible, while they held the door.

When it was over, though, it was just them left.

Less than a hundred thousand Fleeters, Marines, and research scientists, basically no construction workers or any of the rest of the jobs that made society actually function. Sure, they had their logistics people... thank *god*, because without them Morgan had no doubt that they'd have had no chance at all.

Most likely would have been forced to sign on with the Priminae if it had come to that, he expected.

With the logistics people, however, they had a chance.

The last three decades had been an exercise in banging everyone's head against the wall until the wall gave way, or that was how it felt much of the time. The initial focus had been entirely on military logistics, they'd desperately needed to be able to fix their own ships so as not to be overly reliant on their Priminae allies.

Self same Allies had been invaluable, however, with several thousand of them actually joining up with the displaced Terrans despite the grueling nature of life on places like Prometheus and The Nest. Some out of gratitude for what the Terrans had done for them before and during the War, but a good many because even the Priminae had those who thirsted for challenge and adventure, even if it came at the cost of a loss of freedom and comfort.

In recent years, though, they'd *finally* begun establishing the pieces of infrastructure they desperately needed to bootstrap themselves past their current limitations.

The day was coming when the Terrans wouldn't need to be mercenaries any longer, but until them he was just glad that teams like the Angels were willing to go out and put it on the line for the rest.

*****

The Casino, on final approach

The turbulence shook the gunboat as it got in deeper into the cold and thick atmosphere, making Jennifer focus more as she concentrated on getting them down in one piece.

"*Casino,* we have you on final approach. You're clear to

the wall, Bay Thirty is all yours. Call the ball."

"Roger that, Nest. *Casino* making final approach." Jenn said clearly, "I have the ball."

"Roger Ball."

Green lights led the way through her HUD as she took them in, heading into an ice wall with an opening she could barely see from the current distance. It got larger as they closed, though, and Jennifer kept the light green as killed the forward power, letting the gunboat drop along the glide path naturally before she hit the reverse power and eased her down into the bay on thrusters.

A clunk reverberated through the ship as the weight was returned to realspace when she cut the countermass system, the landing pads taking up the strain as Jennifer toggled the ship-wide.

"All Hands, Cardsharp. Welcome home. Get some rest, get plastered, enjoy yourselves. You've earned it. I'll see you all when we go out again. Cardsharp out."

She dropped out of the null-gravity field that allowed her to interface with the system that let her treat the ship as an extension of her own self, feet landing on the deck as a pain shot up through her knee.

Wincing, Jennifer leaned over and rubbed it out for a moment before she limped out of the command deck.

Need to see a doc, spent too much time floating.

Bone density loss, weakening of ligaments, and the like were an ongoing problem for those who spent time in space. It was worse on the Rogue's by a large margin, as those beasts didn't have artificial gravity at all, but anyone who spent time in space on anything less than a Heroic class cruiser could expect similar issues.

"Hey Jenn, welcome back."

Jennifer looked up at the voice as she limped down the deck and was surprised to see Steph grinning at her from a little ways off.

"Crown! I didn't know you were in," She called out, waving to him.

"Got in a couple days before you," He said, nodding to her leg as she limped off the ramp, "You good?"

"You know how it is, Doc'll fix me up," She brushed off the concern.

Steph just nodded without commenting, something she appreciated since she had too many people bugging her about it as it stood.

"Well good to see you," He said, "I headed over when I heard that Casino was inbound. How'd the mission go?"

"Green as grass," She answered. "Even took the Destroyer mostly intact. It's in our dock in Free Star space, local teams will check it out and determine whether it's worth adding to our fleet or scrapping for materials. I give it fifty-fifty. Damn pirates couldn't be bothered with proper maintenance."

"If only that was the worst of their sins," He told her dryly, earning a laugh in response.

"Ain't that the truth. What's the board look like," Jennifer asked as they walked along.

"A few missions up," Steph said, "Nothing crazy, just standard stuff."

"You heading out?"

"Soon." He nodded, almost reluctantly.

"What's wrong?" She asked, reading him easily enough after all the time they'd worked together.

Steph sighed, but smiled slightly through it, "Milla says she's coming with this time."

Jennifer snorted, "Is that all? You're lucky she was willing to stay out of the mess this long. Those kids of yours are the only reason she wasn't glued to your side, and you know it."

"I know, and she wouldn't be Milla otherwise, but…"

"But you're a chauvinist, and sometimes a pig," Jennifer laughed, "though rarely a Chauvinistic Pig, much to your credit I suppose. Buck up, boss, you'll deal."

Steph chuckled, "True enough I suppose."

"How are those kids of yours?"

He shot her a side eye that caused Jennifer to feel something run through her she didn't recognize entirely, but knew meant something she wasn't sure she was going to like.

"Graduated, and signed up." He sighed.

"Well, you knew that was coming," She shrugged. "Mandy made it through Indoc ok?"

"Seems like. Morgan said that he's considering a post with the Casino's Marines for her."

Jennifer just managed not to wince, now knowing what that look was about.

"Ooof. You asking for anything, Boss man?" She was honestly curious.

"No, it's her life, and that's the service," He said, before shrugging, "well, other than that you don't cut her any slack you wouldn't give to anyone else. Better she bleed in training than in the field."

"You've got it," Jennifer said, understanding.

Some men would have asked for their daughters to be treated carefully, but Steph had come up first through a World War and then an Interstellar one. He knew the value of training, and the consequences of special treatment. Most military people did, of course, so that sort of pressure for special treatment wasn't something that showed up much as of late.

"What about your little secret?" She asked, grinning.

Steph snorted in laughter, shaking his head.

"That poor kid is never going to live that down, is he?"

"You named him after the Big Boss, did you really think he ever would?" She laughed.

"I guess not," Steph admitted, shaking his head with a smile, "anyway, I don't know where Eric is going. Might end up with the Angels, might get on elsewhere. Rogue or even Heroic is being considered."

"Seriously? A Heroic slot?" She asked, surprised.

Those were few and far between, since Heroic cruisers tended to stay closer to Priminae territory where they would generally be mistaken for being aligned with the Prims. Being identified as a Terran Heroic by the Empire would be bad for, well, everyone probably.

"There's talk of bringing them more into the fold soon," He said. "We're not quite ready to come out of the closet and all, but we've got what we need to crack the door."

"Ah..." She breathed out. "Well now, that's going to set the fox amongst the chickens."

"You know it. Listen, I wanted to check in and say high, give you some heads up and all, but I have to get back." Steph grinned a bit, before the smile dissolved into a frown. "hey, get that leg checked out ok? I see you limping up that ramp when you head out... well, don't let that happen. Clear?"

"As crystal, boss. Heading there as soon as I drop my kit off anyway."

"Good... welcome back, Sharp. Damn good to see you."

*****

CHAPTER 8

Bellerophon, in Transit, Deep Space

Times have changed.

Roberts casually glanced over the reports as the Bell barreled through empty space en route to its destination. Back in the day they'd have simply transitioned closer to the target, only using the warp drives for tactical maneuvers.

There was intelligence that the enemy had figured that trick out, to one degree or another, however, so the Transition Drive... effectively a Tachyon based teleporter... had been decreed for strategic and emergency use only.

It wasn't something that most of the crews familiar with the technology were sad to see happen. Transition sickness was like the worst hangover of your life, and you most often *had* to work through it because whatever was waiting for you at the transition point wasn't likely to be patient in their experience.

Warp drives were slow by comparison, of course, but easily made several thousand times light speed without undue strain on the ships' infrastructure. For almost all real uses, that was more than enough for the ranges they generally were tasked within.

He still had the Bell do occasional Transition jumps just to keep people acquainted with the sensation, as did the rest of the Heroic cruisers that remained, but by and large even the Priminae who had been gifted the technology in return for their help during the Drasin invasion had agreed that it wasn't a good idea to poke the Empire with that particular stick for the moment.

Terran forces were, especially right after the War, critically vulnerable while the Empire was a badly wounded tiger. Poking that angry beast could have brought it to a killing rage while it was in shock and licking its wounds.

Not something we would have survived.

So for the moment they were cruising along at the lethargic rate of merely thirty-two hundred times light.

How Pedestrian, Roberts thought with an amused smile.

*****

Rogue's Nest

Amanda checked her breath as she saw the note on her console, alerting her to a new priority message. The return address told her all she needed to know about what the message contained.

It's the official assignment. Oh God...

She'd been training for this for so long, and now she was almost scared to open the damn thing and find out what the results of her training would be.

Moving quickly, before she could second think herself into some sort of stupid inaction, she tapped the message to open it up and read through the posting as fast as she could manage. When she was done, she slumped back into her office chair, letting out a breath she hadn't even known she was holding.

The Casino.

She was going to be one of the *Dealers.*

A smile slowly grew on her face.

"Yes!"

Her bellow was accompanied by jumping up with one fist pumping in exultation. The *Casino's Dealers* were the tip of the spear when it came to operations these days. They went out and engaged with pirates, enemy state actors, and occasionally even *Imperial* forces. Granted the third option was rare and required that no one identify them, which generally meant that getting cleared for it was... unlikely.

Still, you didn't get a better assignment than one of the Marine units assigned to the Angels. She'd known that her scores were good, but there were no public postings of ranking for various reasons, so she hadn't been certain if she'd scored high enough to get her first choice of assignments.

Oh shit, I have to check with Eric. See if they got his posting listed yet.

She knew that her brother wouldn't be assigned to the *Casino*, of course, that would be beyond the pale. Still, she wanted to know, and grabbed a light jacket on her way out of the dorm.

"Amanda? Where are..." One of her roommates started to ask as she bolt past.

"No time! I got the Casino! Talk later!" She blurted on her way out the door.

Eric was bunked with the Naval Officer trainees, in a separate section of the base tunnels, so she made her way over as quickly as she could, only stopping at the guard post.

"Marine Tra..." She paused, shaking her head and smiling, "Apologies, Second Lieutenant Michaels to speak with my Brother, please?"

The guard looked her over briefly before nodding, "Congratulations, Lieutenant. Go on through, I believe your brother just got in a short while ago."

"Thank you, Corporal," She said as she passed through.

*****

Eric Michaels stared at the screen, not blinking as he

tried to determine exactly what it meant.

He'd been doing that for the last several minutes without pause, and his eyes were frankly starting to itch. Before he had to force himself to look away and blink a few times, a banging on his room door broke his focus and made the call for him.

Getting up in a stupor, rubbing and blinking away the grit in his eyes, he stumbled over to the door and hit the activator. It slid aside on its air bearings, revealing his twin standing there practically vibrating though to phase through the door in a macro example of quantum tunneling.

"Got your assignment, I assume?" He asked dryly.

"yes! You?"

"I... I'm not sure," He admitted, shaking his head as he stepped aside and let her in.

That caused her to calm quickly, confusion overriding her excitement he supposed.

"What do you mean you're not sure?" Amanda demanded, "How can you not be sure?"

"In a minute," He waved casually, "What did you get?"

"The *Casino!*" She answered, the vibration making its return. "I got in with the *Dealers!*"

Eric whistled, "Nice. Congratulations, Sis. You worked damn hard for it."

"Yeah, yeah, yeah, now what do you mean you aren't sure?" She demanded.

Eric gestured to the terminal, "Check for yourself."

She frowned, but turned to the computer and read through the screen quickly.

"Graduated, top honors... congrats, by the way..." She mumbled, "Ensign rank, awesome... here go, assignment... to be determined. What the fuck does that mean?"

"That they'll determine it later, I presume?" He shrugged.

"That's bullshit!"

Eric laughed at her, "Welcome to the service, Sis. New here?"

Amanda shot him a sour look, "Not new enough for that joke to be funny. Seriously, though, you don't have any idea?"

"Not a one," He shook his head, "I'll take it up with Commandant tomorrow, I guess. Still, that's for then. You're going to be *Dealer*? Damn sis, I hope you're ready for it. Archangel Marines are no joke, not one of them."

Amanda nodded happily, her grin a little feral, "I'll show them a thing or two."

Eric snorted, that response was so very much like his sister. Of the two of them, she was the reckless one, boisterous with the sort of confidence that stood out like a beacon to everyone around her. It served her well, but it got her into trouble too.

"I have no doubts," He told her.

"Bah, you're annoying as always," She rolled her eyes. "Doesn't anything every get you revved up?"

Eric shrugged, "Well, Kelly down on…"

"Gross! Not like that, and you know it! I do *not* want to hear about your sex life," She cut him off instantly and just glared while he laughed at her.

"You asked."

"Not what I meant," Amanda sighed. "Seriously do you have to be so damn calm? It's aggravating."

Eric just shrugged.

That was how things always were between them.

Amanda led the way, generally with a war cry on her lips, while he followed along and… more often than not… pulled her butt out of whatever mess she got herself into.

Opposite personalities in many ways, with her taking after their father while he favored their mother's approach to life.

Others often compared them to their namesakes, but those comparisons tended to break down quickly to his thinking. Eric Weston, often jokingly called 'granpa' by his father when telling stories about the man, was a calculating man… who wasn't above rolling the dice or charging in as the case warranted it.

Eric didn't see that in himself, nor did he see the Admiral (their father *never* referred to Amanda Gracen as anything else) as a particular match to either of their personalities.

Still, that was neither here nor there. One thing that both their parents had stressed near constantly was that they were not their namesakes, nor were they their parents. He and his sister would find their own way.

And right now, he had a good idea where that way would be taking both of them.

"Come on," He said, grabbing his jacket.

"What? Where?"

"Let's grab who can and go out and celebrate," He told her with a grin. "Not everyday you get a slot with the *Dealers*."

Amanda paused, thinking about that, then grinned.

"Damn straight."

*****

Morgan scowled as he looked over the reports, fighting an urge to pull out his hair. Crew assignments were not usually this aggravating as a rule but something had just thrown a bunch of their assets into motion without much warning.

"Where's the Bell going?" He shook his head, backtracking through their records, looking for the orders.

It didn't take too long to find the message that had gone out from Prometheus, which put him in a bit of a quandary.

He *had* wanted to send young Second Lieutenant Michaels to the Bell for her first assignment. There was room in their roster at the moment, which was a lot better than he had in most of the ships based out of the *Nest* at the moment. Unfortunately, they were in motion and currently out of contact, which really only left the *Casino* with a free slot at the moment. They'd lost a man to injury on the last mission. He'd make it and recover back to active duty in time, but they needed warm bodies and she'd *requested* a slot with the Angels.

Without any free slots at the time of the request, he'd easily just put her down for the Bell. Now, however, with the Bell out of contact and the *Casino* with a slot open...

Morgan sighed.

I'm a dead man.

Ensign Michaels, on the other hand... well, there were some wrinkles there too.

It was a different problem than usual, which he supposed he should appreciate. Not long ago they were *starving* for personnel, so having to hunt a little to find a slot for a promising young officer should be a relief by comparison.

If only the silver lining didn't have a dark cloud with it.

The cloud in question was that they now had a distinct lack of *ships*.

Progress it might be, but trading one bottleneck for another was just a pain in the ass that was completely throwing off his earlier plans.

Steph is going kill me.

He had an idea for the Ensign, though he wasn't going to

post it as an assignment. Better to give the kid a chance to turn it down, he felt, without a black mark on his official record.

He doubted that the kid would, but it was just barely possible that the Academy program had turned out a new young officer who was smarter than he was eager, but Morgan doubted it as he made the note and sent off a summons for the kid to come to his office the next afternoon.

Yup. Steph is going to murder me. Shit. I better give him a heads up before he finds out through the grapevine.

Morgan idly wondered if he could find some local Marines to protect him who weren't inclined to look the other way in favor of *Stephanos*, The Archangel's Crown.

Yeah, I'll have better luck dealing with him myself. The Marines might choose to help him.

*****

CHAPTER 9

Rogue's Nest

Eric Michaels had a pounding headache when he rolled out of his bunk in the morning, blearily blinking the sleep from his eyes as he stumbled across the room to the small integrated bathroom to wash up. The previous night had rapidly degraded into a party that he doubted he either would, or would want to, remember when Amanda's Marine graduated class… all of them, as close as he could tell, joined them in small groups.

*I am **never** partying with Marines again. Jesus, how much did I drink last night?*

A quick wash, followed by downing as much water as he could manage in combination with painkillers, and he made his way back toward the bed to collapse back into it for the rest of the morning. Only he stopped before he got there, a flickering light catching his attention out of the corner of his eye.

Ah crap. That's a priority message. Better check it.

Priority flagged messages basically only came from a few sources, most of which he didn't want to ignore. Slumping into the desk seat he waved his hand over the interface to bring it to life, wincing as the screen's glare struck his eyes like a pair of daggers to the back of his brain.

Blearily he squinted, trying to make the letters stop swimming, but that stopped in a hurry as a cold ice water rush flushed right down his spine.

The Admiral's Office? What the f...

No way in hell he should have anything from Admiral Passer's office, no matter what he'd done. At most, Eric might expect something from the Commandant's office about his assignment, but not the Admiral.

*Shit. What the hell did I **do**?*

Any thoughts of crashing for the rest of the morning was gone now as he got up and stripped off his skivvies and headed for the shower this time. Even with the meeting scheduled for the afternoon, he wasn't taking any chances.

*****

Steph was stewing a little, having gotten up early after not getting much rest the night before.

He wasn't really angry with Passer, he understood the exigencies of the service and how things could change in the blink of an eye. That said, he was less than happy with how things were rolling out for the twins first assignments.

Amanda's assignment was bad enough. Marines on the Angels tended to see a *lot* of action compared to pretty much any other assignment. In general, this meant that they were the best and most experienced gunmen in the service, but it wasn't a requirement for assignment to the platforms. He knew that the men and women on the *Casino* would take care of her as best they could, just as they would any new meat coming on, and while he wouldn't expect or want Jenn to offer any special treatment, he also knew that she'd keep an eye out too.

Eric, though, that was a whole different story.

God damn, what the hell is Morgan thinking?

*****

Eric turned up at the Admiral's office a good fifteen minutes early and waited around outside the outer office for another five before stepping in.

"Ensign Michaels here for a meeting with the Admiral," He told the Assistant at the desk.

"Ah yes, Ensign. You're a little early, take a seat," She told him. "The Admiral with be will you as soon as possible."

He just nodded curtly and did as he was bade, sitting stiffly in place as he tried to keep his head from building up various horrific scenarios that might have brought him to the attention of the Admiral. Newly graduated Ensigns *didn't* get called up to the Base Commander for good reasons as best he could tell… but at the same time, they didn't get called up for anything short of *epic* screwups, and he didn't *think* he'd done anything like that.

Though there are some patches in my memory from last night… fucking Marines.

Without being able to remember, though, Eric just did as he had been trained.

He sat there at attention and waited.

*****

"Sir, young Ensign Michaels is here."

Morgan got up and casually leaned a bit so he could look out through the door without being spotted. The kid looked like he had a board shoved in the back of his uniform, but his eyes told the story even from the side. Morgan winced.

"Damn," He said, "Must have been a hell of a celebratory last night."

"MPs were called a couple times according to the reports," His assistant told him, laughter bubbling in her tone even if it wasn't in her words. "It seems his sister's entire class invited themselves along."

Morgan shook his head, chuckling, "Good to know. Leave him there for another ten, then send him in."

"Yes sir."

Morgan was grinning as he sat back down behind his desk and continued to go over reports, mostly logistical needs and such, remembering similar nights when he'd been a young officer. Working with a hangover was a long tradition in the military, and practically a requirement for promotion it often seemed.

He'd known officers who didn't drink, but rarely liked any of them.

Morgan made a note to read through some of the reports of the celebrations, just for amusements sake if nothing else.

Ten minutes later as he was signing off on a transport order his assistant knocked on the door again.

"Ensign Michaels, Admiral."

"Send him in."

Morgan didn't look up as the Ensign walked in stiffly, coming to attention in front of the desk.

"Ensign Michaels, reporting as commanded, Admiral Sir."

Morgan just grunted and kept working for a moment, letting the young man stand there, stiff as a board for a few moments longer. Finally he closed the files he'd been working on and looked up, taking in the boy in detail for the first time that morning.

Yeah, definitely a party.

The kid looked like he was suffering, but was determined not to show it. Morgan didn't smile at that, though he dearly wanted too. Kid didn't have a clue how to hide his suffering, but he'd learn.

"At ease, Ensign," He drawled out. "In fact, you might as well take a seat."

Eric had started to shift to the at rest position, only freeze partway through as Morgan's second statement filtered through. He hesitated visibly before uncomfortably shifted and took the offered seat, where he sat much like he had out in the outer office.

"Relax, Ensign, before you strain something," Morgan told him as he started loaded up files from a different folder to his desk system. "I'm sure you're plenty confused as to why you're here."

The boy looked like he wanted to say something, but ultimately remained silent.

"That's not rhetorical, Ensign."

"Sorry Sir, yes sir, very confused Sir."

Ah, have to love fresh graduates.

Outwardly, Morgan just nodded, "I'm also sure that you noticed some… discrepancies with your assignment board."

"Ah… Yes Sir."

"We ran into a bit of a snag with your assignment," Morgan told him honestly. "I had intended to send you over to the *Bellerophon*, they have a slot open and it seemed a good fit. Unfortunately, they're on the move now and out of communication. We don't have a lot of open spots, most of your class were already assigned and that pretty much filled the berths out there for the moment."

*****

Eric felt his guts drop at that statement.

He'd busted his ass to get a good berth, and to hear that he'd actually been positioned to take a spot on the *Bell* of all ships only to lose it to happenstance felt like a knife through his chest.

"I… I understand, Sir."

What else could he say? It was *lie*, but the truth wasn't going to set him free here.

The Admiral seemed to suppress a smile, maybe, at that. Eric wasn't sure, but he didn't want to think too hard on it just then.

"Well, that's good of you son," Passer said in a friendly manner, "but it now means that you have a choice to make, and a few options open to you. We could wait for the Bell to come back up, but I'll warn you… I have no idea when that will be. They're on a deep run, checking out some signals quite a ways out."

Eric forced himself to nod and not to grimace at the idea of just sitting around, waiting like that.

"Alternatively, there are permanent spots open here on the Nest, and at Prometheus," The Admiral offered.

He wasn't quite able to hide the wince that time. It wasn't that those duties weren't important, but he'd spent a lot of time planning to get into the deep black, like his parents. Eric didn't want to spend the next couple years ground side, even in an important slot, if he could avoid it.

"Now, there is another option, but I'll warn you it's not exactly the Bell, son," Passer said, eyes coming up from the desk and piercing Eric's own.

Silence stretched out between them for a moment, forcing Eric to listen to his own heart as it pounded in his chest. Finally he couldn't take it anymore and he broke the quiet.

"And that is, Sir?"

Passer smiled slightly, tapping his desk and bringing up a projection.

"The *Casino* is heading out again shortly," He said, "They'll be making a stop at one of our rented shipyard facilities within the Free Stars. At that facility there is a Tin Can just captured from pirates that's been declared worth restoring to service. A prize crew is with her now, and they need bodies."

Eric froze even more in place as he considered that.

A Destroyer berth wasn't exactly the Bell, or really up to the standards of *any* of the Terran built ship assignments, but it was a deep space mission.

"Imperial build?" He asked curiously.

"Free Star, not sure which polity," Passer shrugged.

Eric hid a wince at that. At least Imperial builds were likely to be solid, even after being in the hands of pirates. A Free Star ship might have been a death trap when it was new, though if the ship was being considered fit to bring back to the service it was probably one of the better ones.

"You'd be assigned to Ops," Passer said. "Seconded to the helm. It's not a fancy assignment, and I know that you earned consideration with your position at the Academy, so I do apologize for that."

"I understand that situations change, Admiral," Eric said dully, as he considered his options.

Passer just nodded to that, "Well you can have the day to think it over."

"No need, Sir. I'll take the Tin Can," Eric said firmly.

Passer stared for a moment before he nodded again.

"I expected you would. Very well, The *Casino* heads out in forty eight. Best get your kit together, say your goodbyes, and be ready by then."

"Sir."

"Dismissed, Ensign."

*****

Morgan watched the kid leave, feelings mixed on the

assignment he'd just handed out.

Serving on a Destroyer would be a mixed blessing, at best, for the kid. Possibly a mixed curse might be a better description.

Captured Destroyers made up a fair chunk of their security fleets, mostly ships that they would hire out as escorts and the like. It wasn't glamorous, and it sure as hell wasn't comfortable. On the other hand, if you wanted a fast track to promotion, a distinguished tour or two on a Tin Can would get you as close as it got in the current service. The reason being that captured ships were about the only way new vessels came into their fleet at the moment, though that would hopefully change soon. New berths opened up regularly, and new ships meant that experienced crews were needed in the command slots.

Of course, it was also dangerous and dirty work.

He wished the kid well, and a shitload of luck.

He's gonna need it.

*****

CHAPTER 10

IC *From The Flames*

Kaela Eurydice glanced up as the footsteps approached her position, acknowledging the messenger.

"Speak."

"Ship's Commander, We're nearing the border to Free Star Space."

Kaela sighed, "Of course. Thank you, I'll be out shortly."

"Yes, Ship's Commander."

The Free Stars.

What a joke.

However, joke or not, since the aftermath of the war the inhabitants of the Free Stars had been causing more and more problems. Prior to the losses from the day of flames they would never have dared, but the Empire's reach wasn't what it once was, and now it was actually possible that they would assault a lone Imperial Cruiser if they had the chance.

So she cleared up the logistics work she had been keeping up on and made her way out to the Command Deck to check the current situation so that she could officially sign off on breaching the border.

"Report," She ordered as she stepped into her position on the deck.

"Yes, Ship's Commander. No signs of any activity along this sector of the border space," Her scanner chief, Merrick Sunnam, said instantly.

"Communication Intercepts?" She asked, glancing aside.

"All quiet there as well," Sirra Mnemone said with a shake of her head.

"Very well, I am officially clearing the ship to exit Imperial Space and proceed through Free Stars jurisdiction," She ordered formally. "Proceed."

"Yes, Ship's Commander," Yseb Corran, the helmsman confirmed as he returned power to the drives and pushed the ship forward, out of Imperial space.

*****

Hele Protectorate Destroyer, *Perdition*

Ship's Commander Dural stretched as he made his way forward as the soft chime summoned him with a persistent urgency that had quickly become irritating.

"What is it?" He asked, swinging onto the Command Deck with a casual motion born of long familiarity with his command.

"Contact, Commander." His second offered with barely a glance back. "Imperial cruiser by the looks of things."

"Cruiser? As in solo?" He asked, leaning in.

"So it would appear. We're running reception scans only, however, to avoid detection. There could be more we've missed so far."

Dural grunted, thinking about it.

His second was certainly right about that. Reception only scans were quiet, of course, by virtue of simply *not transmitting* anything out to be heard. That said, the void was *large* and that made missing things a veritable certainty.

"Continue tracking," He said, shifting to check out the deck crew for a moment. "Get ready to move. We'll track them for a time. Determine whether they're alone or not."

His second looked over, "And if they are?"

Dural grinned, "That'll be up to Central Command, but I imagine we'll get to see a few of the Empire's dogs get a much needed lesson."

"Yes Commander."

*****

The small destroyer, nearly invisible in the depths of space, lit off it's drives and began to warp space as it shifted onto a new course. Leaving its picket, the *Perdition* moved into place in the wake of the much larger Imperial cruiser and began to tag alone quietly as the larger vessel breached the territory of the Free Stars.

*****

The Casino, Departing the Nest

"That's your bunk, kid," Keenan, nodded as Amanda followed her through the narrow corridors, duffel slung over one shoulder. "Get settled in, we're on stand down on the outward trip so find something to entertain yourself without getting in anyone's way."

"Yes Ma'am." Amanda said, trying not to reflexively salute the Colonel every time the other woman spoke.

"Relax before you hurt yourself," Keenan advised her with a shake of her head. "Your with the Dealers now, not in boot. We do things a little different out here, but don't go thinking you can forget your discipline either. We may not be as worried about saluting, but if you fuck up out here, people die. You get my people killed, you better have joined them."

Amanda flushed, but nodded quickly, "I'll get it right, Ma'am."

"I know you will, because I won't accept less," The hard faced woman said simply. "Now go on, get settled. I'll be back around later to give a walkthrough of how we do things on the

Casino."

"Yes Ma'am!"

Keenan shook her head, but didn't say anything as she turned and left, leaving Amanda too take a deep breath as she found the locker to toss her bag in and took a seat on the narrow bunk.

The rooms on the Casino were cramped, even by the standards of the Academy's dorms… and they weren't exactly luxurious.

Still, she was *there*.

The ship was humming slightly, she could feel it through her feet more than in her ears, but it was there. Power was surging, and they were in motion she knew, heading out for whatever missions the Captain had either been assigned or opted to take on.

She. Was. There.

Amanda leaned back against the bulkhead the bunk was butted up against, closed her eyes, and just grinned.

*****

Sylvana Keenan wasn't in the greatest of moods as she headed forward to the cafeteria for a cuppa. Losing an experienced Marine never put her in anything that *resembled* a good mood, but getting a fresh recruit to replace him wasn't helping.

The kid's record looked good, for what little there was of it. Top of the class, brains, guts, and determination aplenty. It all sounded great, aside from the fact that none of it had been proven in blood.

She sighed.

Well, no one is proven in blood until they are, I suppose.

Chen would recover from the injuries he'd taken when

they assaulted the command deck of the pirate vessel, and she'd have him back one way or the other. Until then, though, she would deal with the new meat and make sure that they didn't turn themselves or anyone else into hamburger.

She was surprised to find the Captain in the Cafeteria, sitting at the small table the crew had to hotswap, with a body she didn't recognize.

"Ah, Colonel, welcome. Did you get your new member settled away?" Captain Samuels asked, looking over as she entered.

"Yes Ma'am." Keenan said, eyes settling on the young man sitting across from the Captain, taking in the Ensign's insignia briefly before returning to the Captain.

"This is Ensign Michaels," Samuels told her.

"Michaels?" Keenan asked suspiciously.

Samuels smiled and nodded, "Yes, on both counts. Your new member is his sister, and they're Archangel Legacies, the pair."

Keenan nodded through a jaw that was clenching up slightly. Another inexperienced recruit was bad enough, but brother and sister on the same ship, assigned to a Captain that had served with their parents? That smacked of nepotism of the bad sort.

"Relax, Colonel," Samuels chuckled softly, apparently reading her easily enough. "The ensign is payload on the outward journey only. We're transporting him to his new assignment."

Keenan nodded and relaxed a bit, turning to grab a cup before walking to the coffee maker. "What assignment would that be?"

"He'll be joining up with the prize crew for our recent acquisition."

"Oof," Keenan winced, pouring the beverage. "Rough first assignment, Ensign."

The Ensign just shrugged, "I will manage, Colonel, but thank you for the warning."

Keenan nodded absently as she took a drink and leaned back against the bulkhead. "We have anything official on the docket yet, Captain? I didn't see anything in the pre-launch brief."

Samuels waggled her hand, "Several requests for the standard. I'll review them and pick out the likely ones, then pass the list along. You know how it goes."

She nodded as she drank the coffee.

She did indeed know how it went. Mercenary jobs were prone to revision, often on the fly, and they'd have little to no warning if things went tits up on them. The employers, assuming they weren't lying, often didn't have all the intelligence needed for the job. Since they were paying for disposable assets… from their points of view… they didn't put much care into working out the details.

It had some upsides, of course, since it really freed up the TOE and made things easier in that regard. But whatever they gained from looser Terms of Engagement, they tended to lose out on when it came to intel and other basic preparation.

And, again, that assumed they weren't *lying*.

Hiring mercs and just flat out lying to them about the mission was far more common than she would like, especially considering that she was playing the part of the Merc, like it or not.

"I'll be waiting for that then," She said, pushing off the bulkhead, turning to leave though not before sending a pair of nods to the table. "Captain. Ensign."

"See you Colonel."

*****

Jennifer Samuels watched the Colonel leave for a moment before looking back to her young guest.

"So, first time off world?" She asked.

"Aside from training runs, yeah," Eric admitted. "What did you mean, about how things go? If it's ok to ask, I mean?"

Jennifer just shrugged, "it's fine to ask, even if you were under my Command, kiddo. It's just that the sort of missions we handle tend to be... looser than a proper military would ever allow as a matter of course. Can't trust the clients, they lie... even when they think they're being honest. Keep that in mind when you're in the hotseat, Merc work is dirty at the best of times. We try to be professional soldiers, but most of them just want hired guns."

Eric nodded quietly, though he wasn't sure he fully got the gist of that. He knew what she was saying, of course, but still...

Jenn just grinned at him, "Don't drive yourself around the warp trying to work it out. You don't need too yet, just keep it in mind."

"Hmmmm," He nodded again. "What are the Free Star people like, I mean really?"

"They're people. Good people, bad people, politicians. Watch out for the politicians, they're the ones that cause the most trouble," She said with a smirk.

"Not the bad people?"

"We can *shoot* the bad people if they give us too much trouble. Shooting politicians tends to be more trouble than it's worth."

Eric snorted, amused by that, but then drew back a little as he caught the look in her eye that told him that Jennifer... while being humorous, wasn't actually *joking*.

"Seriously?"

"Seriously." She sighed, "Look, most of the time, politicians are same as anyone else. Some good, some bad... more bad than you'd expect from the general makeup of the population... but when you have a job that provides power, people who *want* power are the ones who are most likely to want the job. Most good people just want to be left alone to live their lives, and there are *always* people who are more than happy to step up and *take care of things* for the good sorts."

Eric nodded, "Makes sense I guess. Explains a lot of the history books anyway."

"Doesn't it though?" Jennifer said wistfully. "You've heard the expression, those who don't learn from history...?"

"Are doomed to repeat it," Eric said dryly. "My dad was fond of that one."

"Yeah... no one learns from history, kiddo. Least of all historians." Jennifer said. "Not the right things anyway. People focus on the obvious signs, the really nasty stuff. Thing is, by the time *that* shit happens, it's too late. Every dictator in history got into power the exact same way, by telling good people that he would take care of things for them. Forget the pretend ideology they talk about, forget everything except *that*. If you're going to learn from history, learn this... take care of your own shit, kid. If you need help, trust a friend or hire a professional, don't elect someone to do it."

Eric shook his head, "I'll keep it in mind."

"No you won't," Jennifer told him soberly. "No one ever does, and I include myself in that."

"Didn't get a lot of classes about political theory in the academy," Eric admitted. "Never realized you were so much against politicians."

Jennifer laughed, "I'm not against politicians, kiddo. I'm against people giving them jobs that they shouldn't have to deal with in the first place. If we handle our own shit, they won't have to. If we leave it to fester until it becomes *someone else's* problem... well, then someone else has to deal with it and we have no one to blame but ourselves. Don't leave problems for others to deal with, or *someone will*, and you probably won't like how they do it. That's what you need to learn from history."

*****

CHAPTER 11

Private Shipyard Facility, Star Kingdom

Eric found himself turned around as he made his way across the orbital facility, looking for the bay he'd been directed to. The crew of the *Casino* had barely had time to drop him off with directions, tossing much of their cargo off as quickly as they could before turning back out to deep space.

He was the only person being dropped off on this run it seemed, which left him making his way through the station alone and feeling more than a little overwhelmed but it all. There was more of a variety of people just in passing than he'd ever seen in his life, as relatively isolated as that life had been.

His training had actually covered just that situation, so he wasn't coming at it completely from the black, but knowledge and experience were far from the same things as he was now learning for himself.

Having to stop multiple times to check the Facility's directory, he finally found himself at the entrance to Bay Four and the location of his new assignment.

He hoped.

There was a guard at the entryway, no weapon obvious but the uniform and posture were clear giveaways.

"Excuse me," He said, walking up. "I'm Ensign Michaels. I think I'm supposed to be here?"

The guard looked mildly amused and annoyed, checking him over.

"Yes sir," he said, "A moment."

Eric just nodded as the guard stepped back and activated a comm, speaking sub-vocally for a moment before waiting for a response, then going back and forth a few more times. Finally he nodded and stepped back up as Eric felt a buzz through his implanted computer system.

He checked the request, recognizing it as a challenge code, and sent the reply with his documents.

The guard was distracted briefly as he checked them, then nodded.

"Yes sir, you're clear into the bay," He said as he stepped aside and pointed. "Follow the red line down a hundred meters, then take the green line left. Stay on that to the end and you'll be at the plank. Someone will meet you."

"Thank you," Eric said, hefting his bag over his shoulder as he started forward.

Behind him he could feel the guard shift back into place without a word.

*****

First Lieutenant Beverly Quinn consciously forced herself not to tap her foot as she waited at the plank to the ship.

Not that it was really a plank, of course. The captured Destroyer had been secured into an enclosed bay for safety reasons, with a single flexible air-locked tunnel that linked back to the station.

She had been checking on the repairs when the call came down from the Command Deck for her to go meet a newly assigned Ensign just in from the Nest, and she was anxious to get back to work because the sooner they got done the sooner they could get the ship out into space where it belonged.

Must be him now.

She eyed the baby faced kid as he approached, evaluating him at a glance. He was so green it hurt, which almost made her laugh since she wasn't an old timer herself, but working out in the Free Stars tended to age you fast, in career terms at least.

"Ensign Michaels," She asked as he approached.

"Yes Ma'am," He said, dropping the bag and throwing her an academy textbook salute.

She flipped a more casual one in return, "As you were. Come on, we're busy here so let's get you squared away so I can get back to it."

"Yes Ma'am, lead the way. Apologies if I'm holding you up."

"Don't worry about it," Beverly said, turning and leading him back to the lock and starting the cycling procedure as soon as he was in. "Name's Quinn, by the way. I run guns and related systems."

"Ops and Helm," He answered. "Guns? That make you my direct supervisor?"

She shot him a look and laughed sharply, "Technically you're mine, if you want to run it by the books."

He choked slightly, "Excuse me? I don't think I heard that right."

"Relax," She advised him. "We run things a lot more casually out here. These beasts are basically irregular by definition, and we rarely get a proper and traditional chain of command in place, especially not for a new capture like this. It's catch as catch can when initially crewing prize ships."

The cycle completed and opened up to the slightly swaying tunnel to the ship. She caught his shoulder as he started forward.

"Zero gee, be ready for it." She said.

He nodded and she kicked off the station's gravity, using the rails to guide herself across while checking that he was keeping up.

"Anyway, Ops is technically over Guns," She answered, "and we've been waiting for someone to take that station for a bit now."

His look of mild panic amused her, though she hoped it was over what she said and not from the feel of micro-gravity.

"Shouldn't someone with more experience be in this slot then?"

Good. If he was space sick vulnerable, this would suck for him.

"Ideally, sure, but experienced people already have their slots, and few of them want to downgrade to a Tin Can," She told him. "Relax, this is a shakedown cruise. You're mostly ballast, not that you should take that as an excuse to slack off."

He nodded, a little jerkily as they pulled themselves along toward the ship.

"You fly, I believe you said?" She asked, mildly curious.

"Yes Ma'am. NICS certified, Triple A rated," He told her with a snort. "My dad wouldn't accept anything less."

"Your dad?" She asked, quizzically.

"Not important," He waved it off. "I've been flying since I was barely old enough to walk."

"Well, the Chief is our Helmsman so I don't know how much stick time you'll get, and we don't have a NICS system on board anyway." She said. "You'll need to get the Chief to sign off on your certifications before the Commander will let you handle this beast anyway. Free Star constructions can be a little... odd."

"Looking forward to it," Eric said honestly. "Love to get my hands on a new bird, always."

"Well, we're here," She said as she punched in the code to

cycle the lock on the ship side. "Commander is expecting you. He'll be on the Deck."

"Yes Ma'am."

*****

Lieutenant Commander Marcus Reid examined the latest round of reports from the crews working on getting his ship back into shape.

Pirates, He thought with disgusted.

There was no excuse for the sheer level of incompetence that had become evident as they overhauled the Destroyer. Even *neglect* wasn't enough to explain the state of affairs he'd found when he arrived with his crew to begin the project. The previous owners had to practically have gone out of their way to make some of the crap they'd found on board happen.

Still, the Tin Can was in better shape than many they'd taken over the years. Recoverable, at least, which was saying something. Any ship they could still manage traveling through space was worth more than then most realized, given the current lack of yard facilities among the Terran survivors.

Reid was just happy to have a Command, but the work thus far had been a nightmare and a half.

"Sir."

Reid glanced up, "What it is, Mac?"

Chief David McKenzie nodded his head to a spot over Reid's shoulder. "New meat."

Reid glanced around and, indeed, there was a fresh looking kid there with a duffle over his shoulder, looking around with wide eyes.

Well, at least his jaw isn't wagging open.

"Ensign Michaels, I assume?" He called across the Deck.

"Uh, Yes sir," the kid dropped the duffel instantly,

saluting.

"At ease, kid," Reid said, waving him in. "You just graduated, right?"

"Yes sir."

"Well, shouldn't matter much," Reid said. "You've got Ops, that station over there."

Michaels looked over, nodding as he spotted the position.

"You certified on Free Stars tech?"

"Much as anyone can be from a book, Sir."

Reid almost chuckled at that, knowing how true a statement it was, more so than he suspected the kid did.

"You'll figure it out," He said. It wasn't a question.

"Yes sir."

"Mac here is the Chief," Reid gestured. "He's our Helmsman. I understand you fly?"

The kid nodded, "Born to it, you might say. Triple A certified at the Academy, but I was flying everything in stock before I was out of primary schooling."

"Impressive," Reid drawled, not letting himself sound impressed. "Chief will spec you out. He says you can fly, we'll put you in the schedule. He doesn't sign off, you don't touch those systems. Understood?"

"Understood, Sir."

"Good." Reid looked around, then waved to an Able Shipman, "Little, take the Ensign to his quarters. Ensign, go get settled in, I want you back up by the start of the next shift. I'll be here, walk you through the systems."

And make sure you won't fuck anything up, Reid added mentally. Academy certified didn't mean much when it came to actual Free Star gear.

Oh, it might if the ship were still stock off the line, he supposed, but a prize ship taken from pirates generally didn't have a stock bolt left in the hull to his experience.

"Yes sir."

"Aye skipper."

Reid waved the pair out before returning to his reports.

*****

The Casino

"Cargos off, Skipper. We're clear to move."

Cardsharp nodded absently, eyes skimming the intelligence download she'd taken when they docked.

"Good work, secure the rigging then, we'll be moving in five."

"Aye ma'am."

There were a number of jobs on the board, most of which she wouldn't touch with someone else's ship.

The Free Star Polities were barely different from Pirates themselves, and the jobs they tried to hire people for reflected that by times. Raids, piracy, all manner of nastiness that she wasn't about to sully her ship and crew with were on the board.

It really hit her in the gut, sometimes, just how far it felt like they'd fallen. How much they'd all lost.

She was a Navy pilot, not a pirate or a merc, but here she was trying to pick from the least objectionable jobs that offered the best pay.

Jennifer did her best not to think about that, but it snuck in every now and then.

This time, though, there was an interesting request on the board.

A lone Imperial Cruiser crossing Free Star space? That's

bold, these days.

They didn't take jobs openly harassing Imperial assets as a rule, or at all honestly. This was ostensibly because they didn't want to piss off their best client, at least as far as the Free Stars were concerned. The real reason was that they didn't want to alienate an enemy they wanted to keep *close*.

She normally wouldn't take a job involving the Empire as a potential OPFOR, but this one specified no combat, just observation.

Frankly, she was curious about what they were up to as well, and knew damn well that the Nest would want to know too.

"Alright, I've got our next job," Jennifer decided, looking up to the small cadre of officers. "Should be a cake walk, but let's not get too relaxed, clear?"

"Yes Ma'am. What's the gig?" Roy Parker, her XO asked curiously.

"Shadow gig, Imperial Cruiser. Locals are worried, if I'm reading this right, might be setting up an ambush, don't know about that," She said. "Either way, it's a non-combat job. Pay isn't much, but I think Higher would love to know what the Imps are up to, sending a lone cruiser into the Free Stars like this."

"Huh," Parker nodded slowly. "Yeah, raises some flags doesn't it?"

"Does indeed." She said, getting up. "Let's get everyone squared away. Time to suck vacuum again."

*****

CHAPTER 12

IC *From the Flames*, Transiting Free Stars Space

Kaela didn't like taking the *Flames* into potentially hostile territories like the Free Stars without considerably more force than she'd been afforded for this passage, but times had become tighter for the Imperial forces, and unless missions called for considerable force... they generally just didn't assign it any longer.

An Imperial cruiser could deal with almost everything they were likely to run into, short of a concerted assault, but it was that second possibility that was keeping her on edge as they moved through the Hele Protectorate and began pushing into the next Polity's space.

"Wide scans clear, Ship's Commander."

"Good work, continue with scheduled scans," She ordered.

"Yes, Ship's Commander."

Kaela forced herself to relax, at least marginally, and returned to the review of the mission parameters.

With only the *Flames* currently being assigned, it was obvious that little more than scouting could be reasonably expected of them. If they found anything that required significant attention, well it would have to be up to the Imperial Forces Command to dispatch more ships because as potent as an Imperial Cruiser was... just one ship could only manage so much.

The issue was that no one in Command seemed to know

just what in the abyss it was that they were supposed to be scouting, and that left her with a distinctly bad taste in her mouth as she considered the possibilities.

Most likely, of course, was that it was nothing of much import.

The truth was, strange signals were very nearly commonplace if you knew what to look for and were looking anywhere *near* inhabited systems. Polities sent ships out, pirates made bases in the far reaches, and any of innumerable other possibilities that didn't necessarily comprise a direct threat.

However, when it was a threat, it was better to know about it as quickly as was possible, and that was why you sent scouts.

For herself, Kaela could *almost* hope that it was flame bringers... somehow. The official word, of course, was that they'd been wiped out, but rumors said otherwise.

Normally she wasn't one to bother much with rumor, they generally weren't worth trying to thresh out the kernels of fact from the overwhelming balls of fiction that were wrapped around them. In this case, well, she had wanted to face off with the flame bringers for most of her life and so she had some deep hope that those particular rumors might be true.

It wasn't a hope she allowed her rational thoughts to entertain, however, and logically she very much did *not* want there to be any truth to those stories. The flame bringers were a threat to the Empire, or had been, and her duty was to protect the Empire rather than serve her own ego.

Still, though... deep down.

Rational thoughts often conflicted with emotional desires.

Not that she really wanted to face the flame bringers

with only her Cruiser and no support, to be certain.

She wasn't always rational, Kaela knew, but she rather didn't consider herself either insane... or stupid.

*****

Perdition

Dural was well passed feeling stressed as they continued to shadow the Imperial ship as it left Hele space. His orders were to maintain contact until relieved, until it fully left Free Star claimed space, or until he had new orders. Frankly, he was beginning to wish that they'd simply never spotted the damn ship in the first place.

"Any sign they spotted us?" He asked tersely.

"No, Ship's Commander. The Imperial vessel appears focused on forward scans, and we're holding position far enough back that I do not believe even a direct scan would surpass their detection threshold."

Dural nodded, "Very well, continue."

"Yes Ship's Commander."

Where are our support and reinforcements? He wondered. The Imperial ship had transited Hele space without incident, which he was relieved for to be sure, but long experience told those within the Protectorate that one didn't trust that the Imperials wouldn't cause trouble just because they appeared to be uninterested.

For *generations*, Imperial forces were considered to be forces of nature or close enough that the Free Stars Navies treated them as such.

You didn't fight a Nova, and you didn't stand against the Empire. They were all too willing to bring regular and overwhelming force to a conflict, and would often initiate a conflict with little to no reasons that anyone could determine, other than just because they could he supposed.

"Burst Comm traffic, Ship's Commander. To your station."

It's about time, Dural thought as he leaned in and opened up the communication, waiting with impatience as it was decoded.

Let's see what they want from us... well, that's interesting.

The Protectorate had employed the services of the Gaian Mercenaries, a name applied to them after the ship that led their mercenary fleet, Gaia's Revenge. Revenge against what, well no one seemed to know and the mercenaries weren't telling so all that was left was speculation and rumor, none of which was likely to be the truth.

Bringing them in was an unusual play, he had to admit. Historically, the Protectorate and that particular Mercenary group had a someone... rocky relationship. The Hele Protectorate had lost their Neutronium Mine due to the interference of the Gaian forces, and even now to this day they remained as close to allied with the former slaves that worked that mine than they were with almost anyone else.

They were an effective force, though, and well known for both being picky about what contracts they took... but also holding the contract as very nearly inviolable once they'd made an agreement. They didn't tend to like facing off against the Empire, however, which made this bit of news doubly curious.

Not that he blamed them on that part of things. No one sane actively *wanted* to fight the Empire, not in his opinion. The Empire generally chose to fight *you*, not the other way around. Not that there was any lack of insanity in the universe, mind.

The Gaians, however, were not a group that seemed to show that as a rule.

For the moment the task they'd been employed for

was merely to provide another ship running shadow on the Imperial cruiser.

Makes sense, Dural thought. *Their small attack crafts are notoriously difficult to spot at the best of times.*

Over the years since their first appearance as an organized group in the Free Stars space, the Gaian forces had actually triggered something of an arms race in the opposite of the usual direction. Prior to them, the general direction of new military constructions had always trended to bigger and more powerful ships, following the Imperial model.

That was still a legitimate direction that took up a lot of spending, of course, but the small vessels the Mercenaries could field had proven shockingly effective within their niche and had become a hot area of interest for development over the past years.

New classes of fast attack craft had been produced by nearly every member of the Free Stars, though even to this day, there remained elements of capability that the mercenaries had that no one could quite seem to duplicate. Which of course begged the question that had been going around the military research circles he knew of... where did those ships come from in the first place?

The best guess anyone seemed to have was that they were prototypes built by a polity that had lost a major war. Too little, too late, and the plans had been destroyed to prevent capture while a few were smuggled out by fleeing crews under the Command of Captain Teach.

It was a nice and neat theory, Dural supposed, but there was an element of it that bothered him.

Teach and his men weren't the sort to flee a fight... at least not without causing a hell of a lot of *noticeable* chaos on their way out the proverbial door.

Yet *no one* had any record of that sort of action, either

involving them directly or even *seemingly*.

Operating for years within and without the Free Stars, and the Gaians remained somewhat of a mystery... however, they were a known element as well, and trusted not to betray their employers the way many of the less savory ships for hire might.

He would actually feel a great deal better once they were in the area, all things considered.

*****

The *Casino*

Flying an Archangel Class gunboat was a lot like flying in space, exposed to the elements as if you were *born* to it.

Jennifer was pushing the ship hard, wanting to get on station as quickly as possible, as much from her own curiosity as any desire to do the mission she'd agreed to take on. The Empire had been quiet for a good many years after the War, licking their wounds and rebuilding infrastructure and ships lost when Prometheus called down the fires from on high.

Post-war estimates had the Empire losing damn near *half* their military infrastructure, including almost all of their space borne repair and construct capability.

Most of their fleets had been in motion, which spared the actual ships... Prometheus could *hit* a moving target, but realistically getting them the targeting data needed to do so was generally contraindicated.

Still, that had left them with a fleet of ships many of which were badly damaged after the invasion of Sol Space, with no way to institute repairs.

To this day, Jennifer was aware that the Empire maintained what were effectively massive star system wide ship graveyards that were filled with vessels that normally would have been put right back into service after repairs were done, but now just floated in the Black, silent tombs and reminders of the former Empires greatness... and hubris.

Something was changing, however, because she had noted an increase in Imperial incursions into the Free Stars and surrounding polities of late.

So far they're not pushing into Prim space, but that's so much farther away that I doubt they have the logistical capability to pull it off yet. It'll come, no question.

She loved the Priminae, she really did, but Jennifer wished that they would throw off their old tendency toward complacency and *change*. Just a little was all it would take, but the entire culture was remarkably conservative and set in their ways. It had worked for them for so long, of course, that even when many of their number had seen the light... well, it was like pushing a boulder uphill to get any change implemented, while everyone *else* seemed intent on pushing it right back *down*.

Adapt or die, she thought grimly as she pushed on through the void.

Eventually, she knew that they would figure it out. Jennifer just hoped that it wasn't too late.

It was for us, after all.

*****

Second Lieutenant Michaels wiped off the contact patch for the induction trigger of her rifle before slipping it back into the receiver and locking everything into place. The Marine issued M-96A was a chunky beast of a weapon, but it weighed considerably less than it appeared and she was easily able to flip it around to confirm that she'd done the job right.

The daily grind on the *Casino* was perhaps less exciting than she'd envisioned, at least in her heart. Her head had known that it would be the proverbial long durations of boredom, punctuated by short bursts of terror, but the reality was still something of a revelation to her.

This morning she was checking her weapons and kit, along with everyone else in her squad. The other three squads on board were split up, with one resting, another doing PE, and the last running sim drills. There was only so much space on board a ship as small as the Casino, so they had to split their time accordingly.

With her rifle cleaned and checked, Amanda set it carefully back into her locker and snapped the catches tight around it before she took the time to check her magazines for readiness as well.

Unlike older weapons, these were not spring loaded devices and thus were quite a bit more durable and less prone to misfiring... as long as the gun was running at least. The weapon itself used Priminae technology, which gave it the capacity to tune in the needed power that could be brought to bear on a situation as needed, the gravity accelerator within the gun would simply pluck each round up from the magazine as needed before sending it on its way.

At the moment she had it set to the lowest lethal setting, which was intended for fighting on starships... when you might want to shoot through body armor, but would rather not put holes in the hull.

At the higher ratings, well she'd only gotten to fire it that high the one time and it had been... impressive.

*****

Colonel Keenan watched over the squad, especially the new meat, with a baleful eye. She'd taken the young officer onto her own team, both because Chen had been one of hers before he was injured and because she wasn't going to ask the other teams to deal with a newbie until she'd properly checked the girl out for herself.

Thus far, though, she wasn't disappointed.

The girl was methodical, meticulous, and quick in her motions. She knew her gear and wasn't sloppy... which was better than she got with a lot of new recruits.

Whether that would hold over in a fight, well that was something Keenan didn't know yet. A lot of otherwise excellent recruits fell apart when the rounds began ablating all about their ears. Not everyone was cut out for this sort of thing, that was just a fact.

Well, we likely won't find out on this run anyway. A little shadow spying generally doesn't require Marines, and it's not like we have the forces to take on an Imperial Cruiser's crew if it did.

There were worse things than a quiet run, though, and after the last one she wasn't going to be complaining anyway.

*****

CHAPTER 13

The Casino

Jennifer dropped from the control field, boots clicking on the steel deck as she turned.

"Roy, police our transmissions, we're coming into range of the target."

"Aye, Ma'am," Parker said. "We're running quiet."

"Good. Any sign of the Hele ship that we were told would be shadowing them?"

Parker shook his head, "No but they'd be running silent too, if they were smart."

"If they weren't, then they're beyond our help anyway," Jennifer said simply. "Alright. I have the system running on auto, so we'll maintain our distance from the target, but it doesn't look like they're doing much that I'd call objectionable. Where are they going?"

"We're running the trajectory numbers now, but there's nothing inside Free Star space of interest along it, I can tell you that for free," Parker told her from where he was leaning over the navigation console. "Given their speed and course, I'd say that they're just transiting Free Star space."

"Alright, extrapolate out, look for anything along their course beyond that," Jennifer said. "The Nest will want to know what the Empire is taking an interest in."

Parker nodded, "If they keep on that course it won't be far, relatively speaking, before they leave the Galactic Arm, so unless they're planning on crossing over to the Perseus Arm, there's not much out there."

Jennifer thought that it was probably safe to assume that the Imperial ship wasn't planning on *that*, at the very least.

"Cross reference our database with anything of interest along that course," She said, "Tell the system to run everything, cast a wide net."

"Aye Ma'am…" Roy entered the commands and then waited as the computer began to respond. "Well… shit."

"What is it?"

"There's a hit, but we don't know what it is. New upload, just before we left the Nest," He said, "it's not entered in the main database yet, the computer had to pull it from the update files. Unknown transmissions in that region, no match… just a note from an Edward Palin that we should take care with any attempt at approach."

"Palin?" Jennifer's head snapped around, "Doctor Edward Palin?"

"You know him?"

"We've breathed the same air," She said slowly. "Does he say *why* he suggests caution?"

"Not in this update," Parker shrugged.

"Cagey bastard."

"According to this, however, the *Bell* is already moving to investigate."

Jennifer nodded, "Alright. That makes sense. The Empire detected the same signals our systems did, and they dispatched a cruiser to check on it. Again, same as we did."

"What do we do then?"

"Fulfill our contract," She said simply. "If it turns out that we happen to be in a position to help the Bell while on someone else's dime… well that's just happy coincidence, right?"

"Right you are, Skipper."

*****

EC *From The Flames*

"Edge of Free Star Space in twenty lightyears, Ma'am. No contact from the locals."

Kaela nodded, pleased that the mission through the Free Star territory had gone as quietly as it had. They could have handled some moderate resistance from the local powers, of course, but it would have slowed them down and negated the value in cutting across their claimed space in the first place.

Not a problem that would have afflicted her a few decades earlier, but it was an unfortunate reality of the Empire as it stood now.

"Standby all hands for a full sweep once we leave Free Stars territory," She ordered.

"Yes Ship's Commander."

There was no point in doing such while they were within the territory of potential enemies, all it would have done would be to call attention to them. The Free Stars people weren't the sort to bother chasing down anyone outside their space, however, so the risks were minimal and a scan would turn up anyone attempting to be sneaky about things.

*****

Perdition

"Imperial ship is slowing, Ship's Commander."

Dural hesitated a moment, cocking his head to one side, "There's nothing along their course to stop at, is there?"

"No, Ship's Commander. They're aiming for a zero speed relative stop in deep space."

Dural shook his head, confused.

None of that made any sense as best he could tell.

Meeting a contact this far out, perhaps? He considered briefly before casting the thought aside. *No. We're barely in the space of any Free Star polities, and there's nothing anywhere close to be worth that sort of clandestine meeting. Not with so many more equally quiet areas much closer to practically every world or place of interest.*

"Should we slow to match?" The officer at the Helm asked nervously.

Dural considered it, before leaning in. "Slow, yes, but not to match. Ease us in closer, I want to get a look at them. Optics up, best magnification, full enhance protocols."

"Yes, Ship's Commander. Optics on screens, raw imagery on peripheral screens, augments to full on the center screens."

The image on the screen flickered, the side screens showing little more than a blob of light as the enemy warp fields effectively scrambled the visual imagery beyond recognition. In the center, however, the computer had adjusted for the interference and added a number of other enhancements to show the Imperial cruiser in it's full.

Dural put a fist on his knee as he leaned forward, eyes on the screen. The imagery was still a few minutes old, of course, they were far enough out that light would take that long to reach their sensors from the Cruiser. A glance over to the raw imagery clearly showed the red shift as the cruiser slowed.

"Target to thirty micro-lights and closing..."

The tension built, among them all as the imagery got better with slow certainty.

"Easy," Dural ordered. "reduce speed, don't push too close."

"Yes Ship's Commander..."

Dural was looking for any sign of another contact approaching the Empire ship, or any hint of them picking something up, perhaps, or jettisoning something as an alternative. It wasn't common practice, certainly not for the Empire, but some were known to use deep space drop points to transship less than… well, legal or ethical cargo.

He had done it himself more than once.

But never this far out. It would be a miracle to actually find anything that didn't have a powerful transmitter attached.

"Wideband scan, is anything out there transmitting?" He asked curiously.

"Scanning, Ship's Commander, but… no, nothing we can detect."

"They're maneuvering, Ship's Commander…" Sunnam started, before he paused and bolted upright. "They're coming about!"

Abyssal Sow! Dural swore under his breath, "All stop all systems! Don't *breathe!*"

"All Stop, Ship's Commander! We're drifting."

*****

The *Casino*

"Imperial Ship is coming about, Skipper," Roy Parker said as Jennifer quickly crossed back to the Command Deck and activated the suspension field.

As she lifted off the deck, her body braced by the field, Cardsharp glanced back, "Status of our stealth systems?"

"All green. We're a black hole to any active transmissions, Ma'am."

"Good. HUD Up," She commanded, letting the computer fill her vision with an augmented view of deep space.

Numbers and vector lines filled her view, masking the

stars for a moment before Cardsharp dialed them back in priority. The Imperial ship was haloed in her system, so she focused in and watched the imagery zoom in until she could see the ship.

It was far enough away that she knew the view was several seconds old by this point, but it was already beginning its maneuver.

"She's clearing her baffles," Roy said firmly. "Crazy Ivan."

"Roger that," Cardsharp replied. "Check that we're secure, and watch our six. Are there any stellar objects in the danger zone?"

"Negative, already checked. Nothing at the right distance for us to eclipse noticeably," Roy assured her. "All transmission locked down, nothing leaking. We're secure."

"Alright, then we just sit tight and let them scan away," Cardsharp said firmly, her iron control keeping any hint of the nerves she felt from entering her voice.

"You've got it, Skipper."

*****

Perdition

Dural's fingers were clenched around the arm of his seat, knuckles white as he prayed internally.

"Active scans, Captain," Sunnam called out. "Below detection threshold for now, but climbing."

He nodded curtly, feeling the tension through down to his bones.

What do I do? If they spot us...

"Reverse thrust," He ordered. "Back us off."

"Ship's Commander, they *will* detect that," Sunnam warned.

"They'll detect us anyway," Dural snapped. "Back us

away! Full warp!"

*****

IC *From the Flames*

"Contact. Drive just powered up."

Kaela stood up and walked casually across the deck, "Identity?"

"Destroyer Class, no telemetry transmission obviously... no specific profile match, but it matches the general class for a Free Space vessel."

Kaela snorted, mentally giving them credit for shadowing her ship as far as they had, but also took it away and then some for getting as close as they had only to lose their nerve at the last second. A small target like that, she could have missed it.

Probably not, but better odds of that than they had now.

"Lock in the target, full power to beams."

"Yes, Ship's Commander! Beams powering."

*****

The *Casino*

"Free Stars Destroyer, Ma'am. Lit off their drives, backing away at full power," Roy reported.

Cardsharp shook her head, mumbling under her breath, "Turn and run you idiots. Damn it."

"Should we intervene?" Roy asked uncertainly.

She grimaced, but shook her head a little, "Negative. Job is to track and watch only. Poor bastard."

The only way the *Casino* could take on an Imperial Cruiser would be by lifting the current weapons restrictions they were operating under and hitting them with a full array of HVMs and Pulse Torpedoes. Doing that, however, would definitively identify them as Terran in the eyes of the Empire.

She'd have to ensure that the enemy didn't survive if she opted for that, and she honestly wasn't sure she could guarantee it.

They watched as the Cruiser opened fire from range, beams visible in the augmented display as they cleaved space and quickly bracketed the destroyer, fencing it in from all sides. The little ship had nowhere to go as the beams began to tighten up.

As the Imperial beams cut into the Destroyer's warp field, wild twisting divergences were shown on the HUD, the beams being turned aside by the warp at first, but Cardsharp knew that couldn't last.

Sure enough, the Imperials found the sweet spot in the Destroyer's warp field, the point were the beams came out of the warp at close enough to the angle they'd gone in, and flash explosions lit up space as the small ship's armor was vaporized and the inner decks exposed to space.

"They're toast, shit," Roy swore. "We couldn't have saved them if we'd tried."

"No, we could not," Cardsharp agreed as the Destroyer's warp field vanished, and the Imperial lasers went to work, no more space time warping interfering with their task.

It only took minutes for the Imperial Cruiser to leave the smaller Destroyer in smoking pieces, fires burning from the escaping atmosphere as the ship was gutted and left in pieces.

*****

CHAPTER 14

Captured Destroyer

Marcus Reid shifted in the seat, trying not to visibly squirm as he found the command post distinctly uncomfortable. Most of that was probably his imagination, as he had actually been the one to clean the damn thing off and he was still remembering the filth he'd had to scrape out of the crevices with a fair degree of disgust.

It wasn't like he'd ever had much in the way of romantic notions of the age of piracy, but if he had... well, they were dead now.

The ship had been *filthy*, right down to the air filters, to the point that more than one person on his team had expressed honest shock that the crew hadn't managed to asphyxiated themselves before the Marines had taken the ship from them.

Speaks volumes of just how tough Free Star constructions are, I suppose, he thought as he looked over the crew currently manning the stations as the ship flew through deep space on its shakedown run.

Most of them had been with him for a while, and this wasn't their first rodeo as the phrase went. There were a number of 'professional prize crews' among the Terran forces, and his was one of those. These were men and women who specialized in refitting, sometimes retrofitting, ships that were in... less than spectacular shape.

They'd likely run a few missions in her before another one came up that needed their touch, then they'd cycle off with a new crew that would take over for the duration while they went off to refit another one.

It wasn't the most glamorous job in the fleet, he knew, but it was good work. High levels of satisfaction, generally low levels of risk by and large. If the ship didn't meet their specs, they didn't take it out, and if they took it out it was good to go. There wasn't really anyone riding herd on them, making them cut corners. Reid was the final authority on his ships, as his mentor had been before, and that was how he intended to keep things.

If the Nest needed something, well they'd do what they could to make it happen, but Reid wasn't going to get his crew killed for it unless it was *damned* important.

This time around they had a new face though, which was odd... and not.

New faces weren't uncommon, often enough some members of his crew had to stay with a ship when they left for varying reasons. Sometimes they requested it, sometimes their skills were needed, whatever the cause it did happen. Then they'd get fresh faces who rotated in from other crews normally.

A baby face out of the *Academy*, however? That was... unusual.

He's handling the post well enough so far, though, Reid thought as he looked over to where the Ensign was standing at Ops.

While there had been some expected hiccups, the boy hadn't made the same error twice, and once he got it into his head that the system wasn't going to match the specs he'd learned in classes, he made a lot fewer of them too. That was about as good as Reid could have hoped for, and a lot better than he'd honestly expected.

Mac had checked the kid out on flight systems too, and had actually written a report that was positively glowing... if you read between the lines and knew the Chief well enough to know what he meant rather than what he wrote.

Reid had been forced to make a couple addendum notes to the report, just to ensure that the poor kid didn't have a black mark following him around because of Mac's backhanded compliments in a couple places.

It had been enough for him to look closer at the files the kid had presented when he came on board, including his records and associated documents.

The Academy records were impressive and all, but it was the personnel jacket that was eye opening.

Stephen Michaels wasn't the sort that anyone in the fleet didn't at least know *of*, but Reid had completely missed that name on his first read through. It was only mentioned once, as the boy's father, and then never showed up again in *any* of the documentation. The only reference the kid himself had made was that he'd been born to fly, and that he'd told Lieutenant Quinn that his father wouldn't have settled for anything less from him.

Reid suppressed the urge to snort at that, unsurprised by the sentiment in the slightest.

Still, the kid hadn't invoked his father's name at any point, so Reid didn't mention it to anyone else either.

"All systems green, skipper," The Chief said from his position at helm. "We're good."

"Excellent, Chief," Reid said, bringing himself out from his thoughts. "We have a list of minor jobs that need seeing to, set a course to the first spot on the list I sent to your console."

"Aye sir, course already laid in. Execute?"

"Very well, Chief, if you want to be eager about things, make it happen."

The Chief didn't look around, just tapped a single

command that sent a shudder through the ship as the warp bubble formed. There was a brief sensation of falling as they began doing exactly that, sliding down the incline of space time as the generated wave rose up behind them and fell ahead of them. Then the gravity systems on board adjusted and they felt their weight solidly return.

"Warp bubble holding," Ensign Michaels said softly from Ops. "All green."

"Confirmed green," The Chief said, satisfied. "We're solid."

"My compliments to the crew," Reid said, pleased. "Another lady brought back from durance vile."

The Chief smiled, very slightly, as he half turned, "She'll need a name, Sir."

"She will indeed."

One of the advantages, or perks perhaps, of being a refit crew was that they got to name the ship they brought back from the service of the less than honorable sorts they took them from. No doubt the Pirates named the ships, something, he supposed. But rarely were those names recorded anywhere except in the minds of the pirates, and Marines didn't care what pirates thought beyond whether they knew were to find more pirates, as a general rule.

"We'll setup a crew poll," He said, "but Chief?"

"Sir?"

"Give the crew a choice, but don't let them make suggestions… or, at least, police those suggestions. I am *not* sending a name with profanity, puerile humor, or the such back to the Nest, clear?"

"Takes some of the fun out of it, Sir, but crystal." The Chief answered, sounding amused.

Reid was as well, but not amused enough to actually let

the crew come up with a name for the ship unsupervised. He'd made *that* mistake.

Once.

Only once. That was enough, and an excellent object lesson of just how one had to approach managing the sorts of misfits who were smart enough to do this job, yet dumb enough to volunteer for it.

Reid sighed, running a ship wasn't that far removed from managing a day care center to his mind, aside from the fact that four year olds were less childish most of the time.

*****

There wasn't much to do at the Ops console, Eric found with some levels of relief and chagrin combined.

Most of his job at the moment was really just to take a little of the load off the Engineering teams, and that just because they were too busy to be handling the minutia that normally would be running through the Engineering console.

If they got into a fight, well that would be a different matter, but he'd checked the mission brief and that was fairly unlikely. The first mission up was just a simple stop and check job, paying a quick visit to a new colony that didn't have a star-comm link installed yet.

The expansion of several of the Free Star polities since the Empire had began to degrade had resulted in quite a few small, and unfortunately vulnerable, colonies to pop up in previously marginal worlds.

The Empire had previously been fairly harsh on unlisted colonies, for whatever reason they had. Eric assumed it was some sort of means of controlling the size of the Free Star polities, though he wasn't sure by any means. Whatever their reasons, the degradation of Imperial influence had directly translated into a burst of colonization among the Free Stars, and that brought about a new era of pirates in the region as well.

It made for a lot of work for a mercenary force, with jobs all across the spectrum from the simplest to some of the most dangerous imaginable.

Eric couldn't help but feel a thrill nonetheless, however. He was finally on his first mission.

Into the black we go.

*****

Gaia's Revenge

Steph dropped from the suspension field, both pleased and a little apprehensive to be back in space.

Pleased because, after all the years he'd been doing it, the Black was his home more than any planet was. Especially since Sol fell. Apprehensive because his wife was on board on this run, and he worried too much.

He knew it was too much.

Lord knew, behind the mild and meek exterior, Milla was a survivor and a lady he would not want to cross swords with in anger. Not the least reason of which was that he'd likely be bringing a sword to a terawatt laser battle if he tried.

But even he fell for the image she presented, bringing out the chauvinist in him and making him puff up his chest like some white knight wannabe.

Steph grinned at the thought, because when he stepped back from things and looked at it from a distance, he could tell he was being an idiot… but it didn't make any difference, because he couldn't help himself.

Speaking of…

"Hey love," He said, wrapping an arm around her, after checking around to make sure they were alone, sliding up behind Milla's station. "How are we looking?

Milla leaned back into him briefly, craning her neck to look up at him with her brilliant smile. "All systems are as I demand they be. We are ready as we can be. What mission are we assuming?"

"Nothing too crazy, most likely," Steph said, "Just a patrol around the perimeter of the Free Star polities, we have a few deliveries of key materials scheduled, including a shipment from the Neutron Star and we don't want any of them to be disrupted."

Milla nodded, understanding that.

Neutronium, in the stable form that was harvested from the ancient hulk of a broken star, was incredibly valuable in the construction of new ships that used a singularity power core. The material was so incredibly dense that it would actually *suck in* any other matter that contacted it, creating more Neutronium mass in a near runaway reaction.

It was a cheap way to kickstart a singularity, assuming you had access to the initial seed material... which was incredibly rare of course.

The Priminae, by contrast, had developed a method that Terrans called a Kugelblitz Reaction to do the same thing. By focusing multiple lasers, two orders of *magnitude* above combat grade, to a single point it was possible to create a warp in spacetime such that the beam energy became trapped within by its own event horizon.

The Kugelblitz method neatly sidestepped the need for exotic materials that could only be harvested from easily assaulted locations, such as a known Neutron Star... but the level of energy required was daunting even by Priminae standards.

Only the Forge, a facility *literally* built inside the corona of their *star* had enough power to birth new starship cores.

With Neutronium, you could fire up a new core literally

anywhere you had sufficient matter to feed to the fuel seed.

"I understand, it will be like old times, yes?" She said, smiling as she exaggerated her accent slightly, amused by the reaction it always got her.

"Minx," Steph told her, "We don't have time to play Gomez and Morticia right now. Later."

"Later then, I will hold you to it," She told him firmly.

He shot her a look that sent a thrill through her, but refocused on the conversation they'd been having.

"Hopefully not too much like old times," Steph said reluctantly. "I doubt my old heart could take that again."

"Your heart is as healthy as it every was," She told him archly. "I've seen your medical records."

Steph smiled softly, "The heart is more than just a muscle, love. Come on, let's get some grub and check in with the others. We have some work to finish before we reach our first waypoint."

"Of course."

*****

Prometheus Facility

Edward didn't like what he was seeing when he looked at the signal patterns, but he couldn't tell if it was due to a real concern or more because he couldn't... yet... decode what he was looking at.

The patterns were familiar, but nothing he could quite decode, which was *incredibly* frustrating.

It made him, literally, want to throw up his arms and scream the frustration out.

Instead he just turned the volume up on the audio conversion he was listening to as he leaned back and closed his eyes.

For someone who can literally decode alien signals from just hearing them, this is proving to be unreasonably difficult. If it weren't so potentially important, I rather think I'd be enjoying the challenge.

In his younger days, he had no doubt that he'd be doing exactly that.

Over the years, though, Edward had learned the hard way that the puzzles he was tasked with solving had a deadline.

Dead often being the operative word.

It took a little shine off the challenge when he thought about it that way.

*****

CHAPTER 15

IC *From the Flames*

Kaela Eurydice eyed the results of their recent cleansing operation with satisfaction, glancing over to the scanner station.

"Any sign of other followers?" She asked archly.

"Scan is nearing completion. No signs of any other ships."

"Very good," She said, "We'll complete the scan before proceeding."

"Yes, Ship's Commander."

Kaela didn't really consider the elimination of a random Destroyer to be much more than a some easy exercise for a ship of the magnitude of her *Flames*, but it was good to see that the crew had performed as expected nonetheless. It was a clean kill, bracketing the enemy with beams so that they had nowhere to go before ultimately closing the trap with very neat efficiency.

The rest was just a matter of cleanup, and frankly she didn't care much for the mess they were leaving behind.

"Scans complete, no sign of pursuers Ship's Commander."

"Very good. Bring us about," She ordered. "Full warp is authorized."

"Full Warp, Yes Ship's Commander. Coming about as ordered."

The ship listed slightly, or felt like it did, until the gravity systems caught up with the maneuver and she felt the usual lightness in the pit of her belly as they began to accelerate clear away from the debris in their wake and the Free Stars entirely.

*****

The *Casino*

"Any chance of survivors," Cardsharp asked as she plugged in the pursuit course, eyes on the receding image of the Cruiser as it blue shifted away from them.

"Highly unlikely, Ma'am," Roy answered with a shake of his head. "They were thorough."

"Not impossible, though…" Jennifer hummed to herself, making an adjustment. "We'll do a flyby. Standby active scans."

"Yes Ma'am. Active scans up."

She leaned into the suspensor field, banking the ship over as Cardsharp guided the Casino in a long arc that brought them into range of the remains of the Free Star Destroyer.

"Scanning… Multiple heat sources, all too hot for life. Penetrating Spectroscopy looking for air pockets… Negative match," Roy said as the systems ran. "All fields show negative, Skipper. Can't promise there isn't some poor bastard floating around in a suit, but we'll never find him if there is."

"Understood, clearing the AO," She said, putting power to the warp field as she spoke.

The small fighter/gunboat flickered and stretched slightly as seen from the outside of the warp field, vanishing in a blue flash of Cherenkov radiation.

Inside the bubble, other than a brief sensation of almost freefall, nothing changed as the crew's reference frame remained consistent.

"They're moving fast," Cardsharp said, clucking her tongue while she kept her eyes on the HUD. "Moving loud and noisy through the Black. Not bothering to even try masking their presence."

"Typical Imperial," Roy shook his head.

She nodded, knowing he wasn't wrong. The Empire were anything but subtle, long used to being the biggest gun in the Galaxy as far as anyone knew, she supposed that they didn't have much need to learn the art of subtleties.

One would think they'd learn some value in it after what happened with us, but I suppose it's a lesson they need beat into them more than once. Hard-headed bastards, I'll give them that.

"Can you stay hidden while keeping up?" Roy asked, sounding a little concerned.

She didn't blame him. Unsubtle or not, that cruiser out there had more than enough firepower to turn the *Casino* to expanding plasma if they fucked up like the Free Star Destroyer did.

"As long as I stay in their baffles, yeah," Cardsharp answered. "But that means we need someone in the float the entire run. If they opt to pull another Crazy Ivan, they'll spot us in a second."

"Damn." Roy swore softly.

"It's worse than you think," Jennifer grinned a feral smile. "We'll have to be *close* if we want to stay hidden. Under a light minute, minimum, under ten lightseconds ideally. Otherwise, when they move to clear their baffles, not only will we be unable to react in time, but even if we manage that they'll still be able to see us due to the lightspeed time lag."

Roy's next words were definitely unfit for mixed company, Cardsharp was pretty sure her Marines would blush at a couple of them in fact.

"Ma'am... Jenn, I don't think I'm good enough to ensure we stay undetected at those ranges," He admitted.

She sighed, knowing he was right. Roy was a damn good pilot, but while he was NICS certified, he didn't have the instinctual reflexes she had come to cultivate and take nearly for granted. At those ranges, she wasn't even confident of her own ability to stay clear of the detection threshold of Imperial scanners.

The safest option was to hang back, far enough to run if they were spotted, but doing that would almost guarantee that they *would* be spotted. Getting close was risky, because if the enemy got wise to them, they'd be range of those lasers… but it had the benefit of having better odds of not being spotted in the first place.

Well fuck it. Didn't get where I am by playing it safe.

"Don't worry about it, Roy," She said as she leaned into the power of the ship, pushing it faster. "I have this one."

*****

The Marines looked up and around them as the sensation changed, and they could tell that the ship had gone to high warp.

"Back on the trail, I'd guess," Corporal Parker said, a little nervously even as he breathed a sigh of relief.

The others all nodded in agreement, a lot of the tension in the hold bleeding out.

They were Marines, one and all, and had no fear of any fight you might care to name, but there was something about just sitting there and praying that you didn't catch a beam amidships that wore on a person's nerves like little else could ever hope to compare to.

Amanda tried to hide her own relief, at least until she saw the others weren't even bothering with the attempt. So ultimately she just closed her eyes and slumped back against the bulkhead behind her, taking deep breaths to slow her heart.

"You ok, meat?"

She opened her eyes, glancing to the side to look at the speaker.

"I'll be fine, thank you Sergeant," She said dryly, idly tapping the name badge she wore. "Call me Michaels, if you must."

"Willco, Meat," The Sergeant just grinned at her, "Just as soon as you earn it."

That statement put her in an irritating position, and one she had to consider carefully. Technically, and really, she outranked the man who was clearly taking the piss out of her at the moment. On board the *Casino*, however, and especially to the *Dealers*, she was just fresh meat. Pissing off an NCO was a sure way to fuck her position in the squad before she even got established, but at the same time she couldn't just let it pass for that very same reason.

"Oh really, Sergeant," She drawled out slowly as she turned her head to pin him with a fairly mild glare. "And what would I have to do to *earn my own name*?"

He smiled slowly in response, "You'll work it out, Ma'am."

"No doubt." She said, closing her eyes again and rest her head back. "Ma'am works fine until I do then."

"As you say, Ma'am."

*****

IC *From The Flames*

Kaela rarely felt quite the way she did when she was able to take the *Flames* to full power without worry of censure. Out in the deepest regions of space, with no authorities for a hundred stars or more in any direction, the *Flames* could really stretch out and show what it was capable of.

She'd catch some heat for it upon return, of course. The

stress on the ship's infrastructure would need to be checked, measured, and possibly compensated for... but that was a problem for later.

At the moment she was just pleased to be where she was.

A glance down at the screens by her position told her that they were now mere hours out from the edge of the target region. Locking things down more than that would take a few drops out of warp to scan for signals and begin triangulation procedures, but it wouldn't take too much to accomplish.

Her mission was listed primarily as a reconnaissance pass, no combat, but there was a lot of leeway for the Ship's Commander to use their own initiative in the best interests of the Empire.

While in warp they were, while not entirely blind by any means, certainly more limited in what they could see of the outside universe. Photons, like every other particle out there, tended to get trapped in the forward warp trough, which made pretty much all of their primary scanners effectively useless.

Only the few hardened spires with attached scanning instruments that were pushed out right up to the edge of the warp could properly see, and they had limited resolution.

So dropping out of warp would be non-negotiable in order to see much of anything that wasn't a blur.

She did wonder though...

What is out this far, that has attracted the attention of the Empire?

*****

World Kraike, Imperial Capitol

Why do I return here?

It was a question that the Emperor, past, present, and future, often asked him/her/itself as the entity sat on the ruined thrown in the charred black tower that had yet to be cleaned up.

The place had been the seat of power for ages, generations nearly uncountable in fact, but for him... if really should have been just the same as any other place on the entire planet. Limited omniscience was not something that generally led to a fondness for any given place over any other, as a point of fact.

Despite that, this room had a deeper meaning that escaped his mental grip.

So when it was time to think, to plan, the Emperor found itself settling here in the throne almost without thought as he examined the new information and worked to formulate plans going forward.

Imperial Fleet Command has reported unknown signals out beyond Free Stars Space, near the edge of the Galactic Arm. One ship dispatched. Insufficient, but understandable.

Resources were not what they once were, and demands were higher than they had been in centuries. A single ship was unlikely to be able to deal with any situation of concern, but it could report back quickly enough and that would trigger a more significant mobilization.

Not how things were done in recent years, but it would suffice.

The Emperor briefly looked over the signals, noting that they certainly were not of any natural occurring phenom. That did not do much to reduce possibilities, however, so it determined that waiting for more information would be the only reasonable course for the moment.

There were too many situations to deal with at the moment and far too few assets.

Worst, despite what the Imperial Military Authority was telling everyone, the Emperor was well aware that the *Xeno* had not been eradicated.

Reports had shown them launching colonial class ships even during the last battle itself, and that meant that he had to assume that they had done so far earlier as well.

The enemy has gone to seed, and the window to eradicate the infestation has likely closed completely by this point.

That would mean nothing but destruction in the future, the Emperor knew with certainty. The Xeno would have to be eradicated wherever it was found, which would cost resources and lives every single time. It would take *thousands* of cycles to eliminate them all, even assuming that was possible, but there was no other option.

For now, I rebuild.

If only he wasn't absolutely *certain* that they were doing the exact same thing.

*****

The *Casino*

"She's hauling serious ass," Cardsharp said as she pushed the Casino in closer, coming into a little under five light seconds from the Imperial Ship.

"Think the Imps know something we don't about what's out here?" Roy asked from where he was standing the relief station, just in case she needed to swap out despite what she'd said earlier.

"Maybe, hard to say though," Cardsharp said with a shrug that caused the ship to bump a little in space, not that they felt it from the inside, "they weren't moving like this through Free Star space, so maybe they're just stretching their legs for the exercise."

"Not sure that's how that works, boss," Roy chuckled.

"Says you. A ship needs to run from time to time, Roy, trust me."

Roy laughed, shaking his head, but didn't argue. They'd

been following now for a few hours, and he was watching his Captain to make sure she was holding up. The suspension field made it so that you didn't get cramped or sore while flying an Archangel, but the mental stress still wore you down.

He figured he'd give her a few minutes relief in a bit, if only so she could use the head and grab some black caffeine sludge before taking over again.

"Hold up! Blue shift! Blue shift! Blue shift! All hands, secure stations! Crash Crash Crash!" Cardsharp called sharply as she abruptly *killed the warp field* and dropped them out into the black in a rough transition that set the whole ship flipping end for end as it tumbled along their previous course.

*****

CHAPTER 16

Captured Destroyer

"System challenge, Sir."

"Flash our creds," Marcus ordered casually, reaching over to check something on his own system.

"Aye sir. Challenge response sent. Locals… no immediate response," Eric said from where he was standing at Ops. "I know they received our response."

"I doubt they have much reason to hurry out here, Ensign," Marcus told him easily. "Don't expect people in the Free Stars to be as on the ball as the control teams at the Nest. We have reason to be paranoid, and it's fresh."

"Yes sir, sorry."

"Don't be," Marcus said with a shake of his head. "The Free Stars takes some getting used to. Imperial Space is run a lot closer to how we'd do things, believe it or not. Those bastards run a tight ship, even today."

Marcus saw the Ensign nod and thought he'd heard him mumble something, but didn't catch it. "What was that, Ensign?"

"Apologies, sir, just remembering something my Dad told me," Michaels answered. "He used to say that the Empire and us, we had too much in common to ignore, that we'd either be at each other's throats or call one another brother, there was no inbetween."

Marcus snorted, amused by that, the more so because he'd looked up the kid's file and knew who he was referring to.

"Might have a point at that," He said after a moment. "We have more in common with them than we do the Priminae, I'll say that for sure."

He was considering say more when a chime from the Ops console got the kids full attention.

"Challenge response cleared, Sir. We have an approach corridor."

"Send it to the Chief."

"Aye Captain."

*****

The still unnamed Destroyer followed the spiral corridor through the Free Stars defense system, such as it was, heading down for the fourth planet in the system that was their destination.

Ships were moving steadily in and out of the system, but most were smaller than the destroyer by a good measure, clearly local tugs and the like moving out to the outer system and pulling material from the Comet Shield that surrounded the star.

The colony was a young one, barely two decades old and still in the process of a Colonial Terraforming Project that could be detected from *lightminutes* out.

Tall stacks were puffing greenhouse gasses into the atmosphere by the gigaton, bulking out a thin atmosphere with the vaporized contents of countless comets that had been already deposited on planet.

*****

"People *live* on that rock?" Michaels blurted, shocked as he read the numbers being fed back through their scanners.

"Just at the poles," Marcus answered casually as they settled into orbit. "The comet strikes are all directed for equatorial impacts. Give it a another century or two and they'll have themselves the beginnings of lovely garden world."

"Until the stellar wind strips it all away again," The Chief snorted.

"I imagine they have a plan for that," Marcus said lightly. "Likely a EM umbrella out around Lagrange One. It'll be a power hog, but it'll do the job unless they want to move a good size moon in to wake that dead rock up."

"Would that work?" Ensign Michaels asked skeptically.

"Maybe, but probably not. You'd have to get the core spinning again even if you got the mantle heated up," Marcus admitted. "No idea how you'd go about that. The Umbrella is the best bet, I think. Course, I'm a prize captain, not a exogeologist, so who knows? Not our concern anyway, we're just dropping off a shipment to them and moving on."

"Yes sir."

"Comms, tell the locals we have their product," Marcus said. "Get a delivery point and get the shuttles sucking vacuum. I want to be moving on as soon as we're clear."

"Yes sir. Opening comms."

*****

Everyone tended to think that Mercenary jobs were all about fighting, but truthfully a lot of the work available in the Free Stars boiled down to deliveries as much as anything else. High value cargos tended to be attractive targets for the pirates, and the legal polities, of the region so for larger shipments escort jobs were common.

Smaller deliveries, however, were more economical to just load onto the warships in the first place and forgo the big, slow, interstellar transports.

Far more expensive per ton, of course, but also less risk of losing everything in one shot.

Hiring even a single destroyer wasn't cheap by any

means, but it was far less expensive than losing a convoy was.

So there was no shortage of work, all to the benefit of the Terran forces that remained active.

*****

Delivery went on without a hitch, and in a few hours the shuttle was back on board, a hundred tons lighter than it had left, and they were clear to leave.

There was no safe flight corridor required for leaving a system in general. Most planets didn't worry about things that were fighting gravity to move *away* from them, all things considered.

So by the time third shift was in full swing, the Destroyer was nearly out of the system's gravity well and already calculating navigation vectors for their next stop.

Marcus was policing his personal kit for the evening and preparing to turn in for the evening when his comm chimed.

Sighing, he pushed away from the little sink in his quarters and leaned over to grab the comm.

"Reid."

"Captain, emergency call from the planet, they want to negotiate a contract."

What the...

"Was there a problem with delivery?" Marcus asked as he grabbed his jacket and boots.

"No, Sir. Mayday call from outsystem, looks like pirates."

Fuck.

"I'll be right up."

*****

Marcus strode onto the command deck, eyes immediately centering on the ass in the hot seat.

"Details, Lieutenant. If you please."

"Light on those, Sir," Quinn told him as she got up, "Locals had a big convoy inbound, just sent up a Mayday before comms were cut off. Pirates. No idea how many."

"Shit." Marcus said with a shake as he dropped into the seat. "Locals on the line?"

"Yes sir. They actually launched a negotiator in a fast ship to catch up, so the delay will be minimal."

That would make things easier, Marcus knew, but he wasn't sure just what he could do for them anyway.

"Alright, put them on," He ordered.

"Aye sir. Comms up!"

Marcus settled in as the screen flickered to show a distraught looking man in a ruffled uniform, cramped into the back of a fast ship with crap piled around him.

"C... Captain Reid?" He stammered.

"That would be me, yes." Reid responded, looking down as he read the transcript between Quinn and the planet to familiarize himself and see if there was anything she hadn't had the time to convey. "I understand you have a pirate issue."

"Yes Ship's Comm... I mean, Captain..."

"Either is fine," Reid said, smiling as he looked up, "I won't take offense to you using your terms. I have to inform you, we are not currently at full capacity. This is a prize crew on a shakedown run, we're a long way from being ready for a fight."

"I... yes, we understand. Your Lieutenant said as much," The man slumped. "We had hoped..."

"Hope is a dangerous thing," Reid said, expression serious. "Here is what I am willing to do. We will contract with you to investigate the mayday call, you will cover fuel and operating costs plus our normal non-combat fees for the duration of that investigation. Should I feel that we can accomplish the mission, there will be a combat clause in the contract that I will invoke. In that case, you will be responsible for any costs incurred during the fight. If I feel we cannot, you only are on the hook for the basic fees I mentioned before. Acceptable?"

The man looked almost pathetically relieved, nodding furiously.

"Good. I'll transmit the contract, you countersign and send it back," He ordered, flicking his fingers to the Communications console, where the officer quickly got to work. "Do you have a last known location for the convoy?"

"Yes, I… uh, transmitting now."

Marcus glanced over to Comms again, and got a quick nod.

"Helm, recalculate our course," He ordered, "Comms, send Helm the data."

"Aye skipper!"

"Yes Captain."

Marcus turned back, "We'll be moving to military power shortly. Please send the contract terms back, signed, as quickly as possible otherwise I will not be able to take on the job."

"I will, Captain, and thank you!"

"You're paying the bills, Sir," Reid smiled. "thanks are not needed, but much appreciated. Now, I need to get to work."

"Of course… I… yes, I understand."

"Good. Reid out."

The Comms cut, leaving the command deck in silence for a moment.

"Are you sure about this, Captain?" Quinn asked,

sounding concerned.

He didn't blame her, really. The Destroyer wasn't ready for a fight, at least not officially. Off the record, they had a full charge to the onboard systems, the power core was running well in the green, and everything was *probably* good to go. On the record, however, until all of that was confirmed and signed off on *after* the shakedown cruise, the ship was still technically a wreck.

Beyond that, however, one Tin Can wasn't much of a pirate breaker as a rule.

It really depended heavily on what they were dealing with, and that meant gathering intelligence before he could decide.

"I'm sure we're going to investigate," He said aloud. "We'd probably be best doing that, paid or not. Intel on pirates is always in flux, so getting some fresh is just good news for us top to bottom. Past that?"

He just shrugged, "Past that I have no idea what we're going to do, so let's plan on going in *cautious*, alright everyone?"

"Aye Skipper."

*****

Eric was awakened in the middle of his downtime by the alert sirens on board, jolting him from a fitful sleep due to the less than stellar bunk he was trying to get used to straight to full awareness that left him halfway to the door in his underwear before he remembered where he was.

"Shit," He mumbled, back tracking and grabbing his uniform and boots, quickly jamming himself into them.

A minute or two wouldn't change a damn thing in space combat, not likely anyway, and running around the ship in his underwear was hardly conducive to either good discipline or, ultimately crew morale either… even if, right at this moment, they'd likely all get a kick out of the new kid running around in his skivvies.

The instructors at the Academy had hammered that in, confirming what his dad was known to say.

In space combat, if seconds counted… you were screwed. Take your time, do the job right. Better than ninety nine point nine times out of a hundred, you probably had hours to think your way through an emergency. If you didn't, then whoever was standing your post was going to be better informed than you would be if you rushed up there *anyway*, so let them do their job while you focused on yours.

Still, he didn't take his time so much as jammed his body into his uniform and boots as quickly as possible, ignoring the discomfort when some things didn't quite slip on the way they should, and only then charged out of the room and started heading for the Command Deck.

Halfway there the alarms went quiet as the corridors filled up with people, everyone running to their duty station or alternate, without any care as to which shift it currently was.

*****

CHAPTER 17

The *Casino*

"Shit! Someone grab my clean kit!"

"Damn it, Carl, get a grip on your rifle!"

"Everyone shut the fuck up!"

The room went dead quiet as people who were fighting to keep from being thrown around the room by the sudden shift in acceleration vectors all turned to look at the red faced Sergeant who was bracing himself in the doorway.

"Not a damn word," He hissed, holding a finger up to his lips as his eyes swept the bulkhead and deck.

The Marines froze, looking back and forth in some disbelief.

"Um... Sarge," One braved the stretched out quiet to whisper back, "You do know that sound doesn't travel in space, right?"

He quailed back as he was fixed with a glare that could have scoured the hull.

"That's the kind of shit someone always says right before they give away their buddies positions to the bad guys in a movie, Corporal."

Everyone just stared for another long moment, uncertain if the Sarge was serious or not, until a quiet but clear voice spoke up.

"The Sergeant's um... concerns aside," Second Lieutenant Michaels cut in, shooting her own confused look in the Sergeant's direction, "let's keep the roar down. Corporal, get your kit squared away, everyone make sure that nothing was lost or knocked loose. If that happens again, I'd rather not catch an LMG across my skull."

"Yes Ma'am."

Amanda watched over the squad as they got to work putting their gear back into shape for a bit before moving carefully over to the Sergeant.

"Any idea what that was?" She asked softly, back to the squad.

"Based on the Skipper's warning, I'd guess that the Imperial ship cut warp unexpectedly," The Sergeant answered just as softly. "Since skipper cut the drive power, we must be running silent, hoping they miss us."

Amanda nodded grimly, "Alright. Get everyone ready to move."

He eyed her for a moment, "You think we're going to deploy onto an Imperial Cruiser?"

"No, but it'll keep them from worrying about shit they can't do anything about, besides" She said with an easy shrug, "never a bad time to ready to move, Sarge."

"Right you are, Lieutenant," He nodded, "I'll see to it."

Amanda stepped away, leaving him to it, and made her way to the door. She did a pressure check instinctively, then popped the heavy door open before stepping over the knee knockers, then closing and dogging it tightly behind her as she checked up and down the empty corridor briefly before heading for Officer Country, such as it was on a small boat like an Archangel.

*****

Command Deck

Cardsharp hung there in the suspension field, holding

herself motionless as she flipped slowly one end for the other, mirroring her ship as her eyes alone moved to track the Imperial warship as it came slowly about.

The cruiser had taken her by surprise, dropping from warp without warning as they had, but they didn't seem to be in a rush to clear their baffles. Indeed, it seemed that the cruiser was almost languidly coming about, no hint that there was even the slightest reason to rush in any of its motions.

"They're scanning, Skipper," Roy said quickly from where he'd clawed his way back to the secondary controls.

"I can see it," Cardsharp whispered. "can feel it."

She could too, the faint shivering along her skin was a sign of high frequency scans bouncing off the hull. She was familiar with the Archangel's detection threshold for Imperial Scans, however, and knew that they were comfortably under the line.

For now.

The cruiser was visible in her HUD, and for the moment they'd escaped a direct hit from the big ship's scanners. Getting accurate and detailed scans of anything in space was a function of power and distance, often modified by the scanning arc of the technology in question. That generally put the advantage in this sort of a game of Cat and Mouse firmly into the paws of the mouse.

That knowledge did nothing to keep the cold sweat she could feel gathering at irritating sections of skin from coming, however.

"Weapons free, Ma'am?" Roy asked nervously.

"Negative, don't touch *anything.*" Cardsharp ordered firmly. "No stray bleed from our own systems, nothing…"

"Yes Ma'am."

She took a deep breath, considering, "That said… get

down to the powder monkeys and tell them to get reading for a *summoning.*"

He froze up, looking at her blankly.

"Just in case," She assured him. "Make sure they *don't* start, just... be ready to."

Roy nodded slowly, "You've got it, Skipper."

Cardsharp watched him go for a second before she returned her unblinking gaze back to the holographic HUD and the circling predator out there in the Black.

*****

IC *From the Flames*

Kaela silently observed every motion as her crew got ready to tackle the mission they'd been sent out for.

Most of them at least.

"What is going on?" She asked, approaching the scanner station.

"Not certain, Ship's Commander, likely a false hit." The watch officer said as he guided the younger woman at the station through the system's check feature. "Looked almost like a warp wave, but we probably caught a reflection of our own bubble as we turned."

Kaela nodded in understanding, "Very well. Make certain, then log the error. We have a mission to conduct."

"Yes, Ship's Commander, It will be done."

"I know it will," She said, moving away without a glance back at the officers.

Minor scanner glitch aside, she was pleased with the performance shown on this mission thus far. They'd made good time, cutting through Free Space territory to ensure that the response to the Empire's demands met the required level of alacrity and, aside from a minor incident when leaving, the transit had gone entirely without issue.

She was eager to move on to the next stage of the mission, but that would first require establishing a solid scan of the surrounding stars before they made their approach to gain more detailed intelligence as needed.

The unknown signals had been shown as intermittent from the start, which would certainly serve to make her task more difficult, but they had what should be more than sufficient to build a fairly precise triangulation map in reasonably short order.

Once that was accomplished, it would be time to begin a detailed search and examination.

Her orders were to return with intelligence above all else, which limited her freedom to operate slightly, but it was rare enough to get direct orders to preserve her ship and crew above all other considerations that it was a fresh approach in her mind.

Just how necessary such orders might be, well she would have to determine that for herself, Kaela supposed.

*****

The *Casino*

"Get every Marine into kit," Keenan said, "I don't care if they're off duty... Ah, Lieutenant, come in."

Amanda nodded sharply and stepped over the knee knocker into the small conference room that the Colonel had taken over for the time being.

"What's the status of your squad, Lieutenant?" Keenan asked, looking her way.

"Kitting up as we speak," Amanda replied. "They'll be ready to deploy upon my return."

The Colonel nodded curtly to her, "Good work. Now, I doubt we will be moving, of course. That's an Imperial cruiser out there, and unless I very badly misread the situation, I expect that the skipper will cut and run rather than throw anything pointlessly at a cruiser, but let's be ready just the same."

"Oorah, Colonel!"

"Dismissed," Keenan said, "Lieutenant Michaels, please stay a moment."

Amanda waited as the rest filed out, it only took as long as it did because they were cramped enough to have to file out nearly single file, getting a little more nervous as the seconds ticked past. Finally she was alone with the colonel, and let the door swing shut at a nod from Keenan.

"At easy, Lieutenant, I just wanted to see how you're handling things," Keenan said simply.

"Nothing out of the ordinary to report, Ma'am," Amanda said simply. "My squad seems on the ball, and the Sergeant definitely knows what he's doing."

"He does at that, good of you to notice," Keenan told her, an amused glint flashing in her eyes. "I hope it goes without saying that you should listen to him."

"Of course, Ma'am," Amanda nodded. *Aside from when he's being a turd.*

Keenan just looked at her knowingly for a moment, making Amanda wonder if the Colonel could read her mind, but ultimately didn't opt to say any more on the subject.

"Go on then," The Colonel said instead. "Make sure the squad is ready to move."

"Oorah, Colonel."

*****

Command Deck

Roy Parker slipped back onto the deck quietly, not for

fear of the enemy detecting him of course but just so as not to disturb the Skipper as she worked.

"Everything ready, Roy?" Cardsharp asked from where she was drifting in the suspension field.

"Ready to be made ready, at least," He confirmed. "What's the cruiser up to?"

"Running a standard survey, best I can tell," Cardsharp said without looking away from the Imperial ship. "So far they've missed us, but they're barely a couple lightseconds out. If those scanners sweep directly at us... we're blown."

Roy nodded as he slipped into the secondary control station, grabbing the loop straps to wrap around his shoulders.

If they were that close, he knew she was right. Even with the black hole armor settings probably wouldn't be enough to hide them from a direct scan at that range.

Thankfully a direct scan was fairly unlikely, at a couple lightseconds, the arc the cruiser had to cover was fundamentally *massive*, which made it easy to hide in the vastness of empty space.

"Think they're establishing a baseline," He asked, calling up the positions on the secondary systems so he could keep up on the situation.

"Seems so. They should be ready to start their actual mission shortly, if so," Cardsharp said.

"Hmmm," Roy mumbled as he checked their database. "The unknown signals were tracked to this region, but there's a fairly wide area just the same. Hang on a moment..."

"What is it?"

"We have the detection vector from Promethus," He said as he pulled up the data and plugged the vector into the overlay map. "Prometheus narrowed it down to a few hundred stars in this region of space, but look at this..."

He called up the Imperial cruiser's vector and laid it over the data from Prometheus, then tapped the screens where they overlapped.

"If we assume that the Imperial ship departed from where they detected the signals, we have triangulation data."

Cardsharp nodded slowly, "They probably dispatched the closest available ship, not one from wherever their deep space scanners are, however."

"True, but it still should have narrow things down a little."

"That it does. Ok, run the numbers, compare it to the star charts we have of the area, see if anything interesting pops," She ordered. "I'll see what I can do to keep us out of their gunsights in the meantime."

"You always get the fun jobs, Ma'am."

Cardsharp just rolled her eyes.

*****

IC *From the Flames*

"Survey complete, we're ready Ship's Commander."

"Excellent work. And the scanner glitch?" Kaela asked mildly.

"Unable to replicate, logged for maintenance teams to worry about."

"Very well. Initiate search vectors," Kaela ordered. "Time to be about our mission."

"Yes, Ship's Commander."

*****

CHAPTER 18

Captured Destroyer

Eric was fighting his nerves as they decelerated from warp in the region that had been reported as the source of the mayday call. The rest of the command crew seemed tense, but far from his near onto shaking in his uniform at least.

"Scans," Reid ordered calmly from the hotseat.

"We're passing through a radio wave, Sir, looks like standard ship to ship comms," Lieutenant Quinn responded. "Nothing unusual. Still looking for the convoy."

"Understood," Reid said, glancing aside, "Anything on active comms?"

"Negative, Skipper. No active comms in range."

Reid sighed, settling back as he considered that. "Chief, we are where we're supposed to be, I'm assuming?"

"Yes sir," The Chief said from the Helm, not looking up from his instrumentation.

Reid grimaced, but didn't respond for a moment as he considered the situation.

"Alright, sound General Quarters," He ordered. "A convoy doesn't just disappear, so we'll assume the worst."

The alarm began to sound through the ship as the tension continued to ratchet up.

"They can't be far," Eric said, thoughtful but confused by the situation, "I mean… it's a merchant convoy, right?"

Reid looked at him in silence for a long moment before

nodding, "Kid's not wrong. Ok, Ensign, what do you think is going on?"

Eric masked his instinctual grimace, recognizing that he'd just given the Captain a chance to impart a lesson using him as the 'lessonee', something he'd have thought he'd would have stopped doing by now, given how often he goaded instructors at the Academy in the same way. Luckily it *was* familiar territory, however.

"Two options jump to mind," He said, "Either the Pirates raided the convoy in a hit and run, destroyed what they couldn't take, and are long gone…"

"Possible," Reid tipped his head. "And the second option?"

"The pirates have control of the convoy," Eric suggested. "Either they had inside help, or they managed to get boarders on all the ships. Either way, the pirates and the convoy are both out here somewhere, playing hide and seek."

"And we're 'it'," Reid said with a thin smile. "Though it's also remotely possible that the Pirates *and* the convoy are playing hide and seek with each other. Unlikely, but possible."

Eric considered that and shrugged, "Requires too many variables. Not impossible, but if the convoy is a normal sort of merchant group, I wouldn't expect the discipline to hold. Someone would have made a run for it."

"And maybe they did," Reid suggested. "Lone runners are easy pickings."

"Fair point," Eric said, before wincing. "Apologies, Sir."

"For what? Answering a question I asked?" Reid chuckled, "I'm not that much of a martinet. I think your second point is more likely, we have some snakes in the grass to flush out. Since you're at ops, suggestions?"

With one Destroyer as our only asset? Eric grimaced at the thought.

"We don't have enough intelligence to make a good plan," He said immediately.

"In the field you often don't get that luxury, Lieutenant," Reid chided gently. "We make plans anyway, and deal with the unknowns when we can, as we can."

"Yes sir," Eric agreed reluctantly as he considered his options. Really he didn't see many. They could just poke around, scanning quietly, looking for the convoy and pirates... but they could be a *lightyear* away by this point.

Alright, that was pretty unlikely, but even lightseconds would make for a stupidly large search area and the low powered ships like Merchants and Pirates were likely to use wouldn't show up on gravitational scanners with the same brilliant spotlight as a larger singularity based vessel.

"Go active," He sighed. "We're here, chances are they know it. We go loud then, convince them that we're scouting for a larger force if we're lucky."

"And if we're not?" Reid asked.

"Then at least we'll have a good chance of knowing where the bad guys are."

Reid nodded slowly, a hint of a smile on his face, "Finesse the situation by *not* finessing the situation. Interesting approach... Alright, do it."

"Sir?"

"You're at ops, Ensign. Get loud," Reid ordered simply.

"Uh... Yes sir," Eric said as he tapped in a few commands, putting everything in order and then, with one last glance to the Captain, he took a breath and sent the final order through the system.

*****

Lancing through interstellar space, the Destroyer lit off it's primary scanners at full power, sweeping the area with abandon, FTL scans reaching out to every object in the vicinity that they could interact with.

The number of such objects was, however, both limited and specific. Tahyon particles, as a class of sub-atomic elements, didn't interact with many things in the sidereal universe as a rule. They had a zero to negative mass, which meant that for the most part there was very little in the relativistic universe that they *could* interact with.

One of the very few things, other than intense warping of spacetime, were the various mechanisms that could *create* such warping. Extremely deep gravity inclines would twist the particles, either toward the disturbance or away from it depending on the specific type of particle, giving away some degree of information about what was out there.

Natural sources were not exactly common, though they did exist, which left the most likely of objects that might be spotted using such scanners being constructs of some type or another... almost all of which would be ships.

Unfortunately, of course, any ship with sufficiently advanced propulsion technology to be easily spotted with such a method was also extremely likely to be able to *detect* the pulse that detected them.

*****

Captured Destroyer

"Contact," Quinn snapped, "Multiple contacts... Drives lighting off, Skipper!"

"Wake up call seems to have worked," Reid mused. "Vectors to my station and the main screen."

"Aye skipper," Quinn said, flicking her fingers across the board in front of her, sending the data as requested.

On the big screen the augmented details showed as the view skewed to port, focusing in on a small group of rocks a few lightseconds away.

"Wait for it…" Quinn said softly just before lights began to appear from among the rocks. "There we are."

"Bring us about, interception course, best military power," Reid ordered. "Full scans, target beams up. Power all weapon systems."

"Coming about, interception course plotting!"

"Reactor is winding up, you want power, it's on tap."

"Weapons charged, safeties cleared," Eric said from Ops. "All stations report ready."

"Sir," Quinn half turned, "Request permission to transfer to my Guns."

"Denied," Reid said, "I need you on scans for now, and if this comes down to a fight, we're probably screwed anyway. Ident on the pirates, ASAP, assume the merchants are *under control* but not actively hostile."

"Aye Sir," Quinn said, wincing slightly at the language in use.

A Person Under Control was just another term for what used to be called a Prisoner of War, for the most part, with the main exception being that a POW could expect certain rights to be granted them by whatever agreement existed between the warring polities.

A Person Under Control or, in this case, a Ship Under Control… well, you might get treated according to some code of honor or treaty, but you very easily may not, all depending on who had their hand on the leash.

If that hand belonged to a *pirate*, well you were almost certainly PUCed… and that meant your life just SUCed.

For them, however, it was worse in a way.

They knew that the Merchant ships had civilians on board, people they'd been asked to rescue if it were possible. At the same time, they had to treat the ships as potential combatants, because if they were armed it was sure as shit the pirates with their finger on the trigger… and if they weren't, those ships were still gigaton massed projectiles in potentia.

Either way, there were no good answers.

"Start transmitting, use Imperial encryption…" Reid said, "The one we know was broken a while back. Fill it with coordinates, scan details, everything we've got. Request immediate backup to our location, transmit on repeat."

That caused a brief pause as most of the command deck half turned to look at the Captain, expressions warring between disbelief and impressed.

"What?" He drawled, "I'm just going with our dear Ensign's plan."

"Oh don't give me credit for this one, *please*," Eric said, shaking his head, which immediately started the rest laughing as the young woman at Comms leaned over her console.

"On it, Skipper," She said while laughing. "It'll take me a few seconds to compile."

"Understood."

*****

Pirate Destroyer, *Gia Corvo*

"Scans! Wide area, find the task group that Destroyer is attached to," The man pacing the command deck snapped angrily.

He knew that they shouldn't have hit the convoy this close to the destination, but they'd not been able to get together their force as quickly as he'd wanted, and time had played against him.

"Searching, Commander. Nothing yet."

Nothing.

"Keep looking," He ordered. "No way a destroyer is charging us like this without backup. I need to know how far they are away!"

"We're scanning!"

Could they mop up this destroyer quickly and then get clear with their prizes before the rest of the task group arrived?

He didn't know, and didn't love the odds, but there was a *lot* of wealth on the table. Too much to easily give up.

"Power weapons," He grunted. "We'll meet them, but keep *scanning*!"

*****

Captured Destroyer

"They don't seem to be falling for it, skipper," Quinn said, shaking her head. "Enemy weapon systems are charging. Be ready for beams."

"Roger that. Hold course," Marcus ordered. "Ops, can you pick out the lead ship?"

Eric paused, considering the query for a moment before he quickly brought up all the scan data and started throwing elimination prompts at the computer to narrow down the possibilities.

"Maybe," He said after a moment. "Honestly, I give it fifty fifty with the available information, though."

"I'll take those odds," Marcus said cheerfully. "Lock your best guess in, full weapons cleared."

"Uh... Yes sir," Eric said quickly. "Target locked in, all weapons with an arc are linked."

"Send it."

*****

The beams of Imperial and Imperial derived weaponry were generally well into the Terrawatt range as a matter of necessity. Vaporizing armored hulls required an immense application of power, and if you had power to spare as Imperial designs tended, there was little need to look into more efficient ways to make things work.

The Captured Destroyer didn't have the Terran's latest generation adaptive technology, it was true, but the prized crew had made adjustments to the system as best they could while prepping the vessel for their use.

Among those changes were setting the most common frequencies needed for best absorption against the likely targets they were going to see in the course of their duties. A minor thing in terms of work, but the payoff potential was far too great to ignore.

A cage of beams erupted from the Destroyer, lancing out ahead of them as fast as anything could manage in the sidereal universe, each spoke of which could easily slag a large asteroid with a single pulse.

*****

CHAPTER 19

The *Casino*

"They're moving on," Cardsharp said after a moment, finally letting out a deep sigh of relief.

The Imperial Cruiser had ceased it's scanning of the local area and was now again warping space, though far less enthusiastically then previously, beginning what she thought was the start of a search pattern.

"That was too close," Roy said wearily as he slumped a little.

Jennifer just nodded as she dropped out of the suspension field, feet connecting with the deck and sending an audible clicking sound echoing around the room.

"Monitor the situation," She ordered. "I need to hit the head. Stay on passives for a while, but run our own baseline. We might be racing the Empire here, so let's see if we can stop playing follow the leader and get out ahead of them."

Roy nodded as she walked past, "Got it."

He didn't know what was out in this sector, but whatever it was did seem to have the Empire hot under the collar and that was good enough reason to be looking into things. So he spun back to the console operations and made certain that the passives were running on full, dumping the data directly into the ship's interrogative AI system to let that filter out the majority of the chaff that was no doubt being recorded.

Little, if any, would be deleted of course. There was no

such thing as bad data when you relied on space travel as much as the Terran survivors did. Every spectroscopic analysis of a star, every minor black hole, every pulsar recorded was valuable data... but for the moment they were looking for things of a more direct and pressing value.

So with the computer happily chugging through the flood of data he'd firehosed into it, Roy kept a more physical eye on the departing profile of the Imperial Cruiser. They were moving away at sublight, but accelerating as they warped space with the power and casualness only a singularity driven vessel could match.

They weren't looking back however, so he split his focus more than he might otherwise and ran their scan vectors against the data he already had from Prometheus and the approach vector the Empire ship had used.

Jennifer was right that they'd likely dispatched from whatever patrol zone was closest to the unknown signals, so he called up data from the Rogues' to see if they knew where the Empire had deployed their best deep space scanning systems.

The Rogue class destroyers were among the stealthiest ships in known space, and also well associated with Earth's forces since Earth was the only polity that had ever deployed anything similar. That had deeply affected their roles in the post-war scattering that had occurred when Earth fell.

Unlike the Heroic Class cruisers, the Rogues couldn't blend in with any other force, so they did what they did best. They went deep, and they went silent.

A Rogue's detection profile was even smaller than an Archangel could manage, despite massing well over ten times the size. That made them valuable for intel gathering, but also as strategic weapons of last resort if it came that.

Since the war, the remaining Rogues had been pulling

everything they could about surviving Imperial infrastructure as well as new construction, and all if it went into Prometheus' database. That mountain of data was too large to be copied to every ship, but the Archangels routinely downloaded applicable data before dispatching on a new mission.

Given the range, the Imperial facility just inside the border with the Free Stars is the most likely to have detected the signals, He noted with interest, allowing the computer to draw a new line through the stars.

It crossed with the Prometheus scans in three dimensions, highlighting a section of space right on the edge of the galactic arm. It was a relatively sparse sector for the size of the overlap, only about fifty stars or so across the entire sector, few of which were likely to be a home port to any sort of inhabited world.

"Anything of interest?"

Roy glanced back as Jennifer leaned over his shoulder, looking at the screens.

"Maybe," He pointed to the overlap. "If we calculate the Imperial vector using their closest listening post, those stars are the most likely sources."

Jenn nodded slowly, "How strong a detection did Prometheus get? And across which bands?"

"Fairly weak, mostly in the hyperlight bands," Roy responded. "We can probably assuming radio and other signals as well, but it'll be years before Prometheus picks those up."

"Right," Jenn nodded thoughtfully. "What range do you suppose before we pick anything up?"

Roy grimaced, considering that for a moment.

"Not sure, but we'll have to be close." He said after a moment. "our gear isn't wideband like Promethus is capable of. We're tuned for specific frequencies, the ones our comms run to be precise. Most of the stuff Promethus detected out this way would only show up as interference bleeding into our own channels, and our systems are designed to filter that out."

"Fair enough," She said. "Disable those filters and keep our own passives moving, scan each of those stars while we're on the move ourselves. Full spectrum, even lightspeed limited. We're getting close enough that we might spot Radio, depending on how long ago the started broadcasting... if they're broadcasting, I suppose."

"Agreed. And the Imperials?" Roy asked.

Jenn reached over his shoulder, tapping a couple commands into the system. The ship's drive activated and in moments the Archangel was moving again, automatically trailing the Imperial Cruiser as it delved deeper into the sector.

"We follow."

*****

Amanda watched quietly as the squad put their kit away, cleaning and securing everything in the wake of the standdown from immediate alert.

She was glad that everything had, thus far, turned out reasonably but she'd be lying to herself if she hadn't in some small part been hoping for some kind of action.

Her teachers had all told her the same thing, her parents as well for that matter, and all of the veterans she'd known growing up. They all said that boring was good, and once you've seen action you'll probably stop looking for it.

That was likely true, her brain told her, but Amanda couldn't help what her heart was demanding all the same.

For the moment, however, the possibility had passed.

"Ma'am," The Sergeant got her attention. "Squad's kit is put to rights and to bed."

"Very good. Have the squad stand down, we're off alert

for the moment," She confirmed. "Get some rest, read, spend some time in Virtual, whatever."

The Sergeant nodded, "Yes Ma'am. I'll pass that along."

"Second squad will need the room shortly," She said, a quirk of a grin. "So they don't have to go to bed, but they can't stay here. Make sure to pass that along."

"Yes Ma'am."

*****

IC *From the Flames*

"Scans running, Ship's Commander. No confirmed identification as of yet."

Kaela frowned, but said nothing as she waved off the report.

The unknown signals they were looking for had opted to be recalcitrant it appeared, but that was unsurprising of course. The sheer size of the void made finding the source of anything over any reasonable distance an exercise in near futility. Even with the very best of equipment, it could take months to quarter out the sector here and perform a rigorous search.

Thankfully that outcome was not the likeliest outcome either.

Armed with the originating data, the *Flames* should be able to eliminate the majority of potential stars based entirely on their suitability for housing people likely to have created the signals they were hunting.

The most likely of stars would get their attention first, with some flexibility based on proximity. Unless they got unlucky in the extreme, Kaela expected that they would have the origin locate within a few days at most.

That knowledge did little to alleviate her nervous energy, however, or the bubbling desire she had to have her ship do what it had been *built* for.

Soon, She thought with fondness.

Kaela could feel that in her bones.

Soon.

*****

Bellerophon

"Sir, we're entering the designated area."

Jason Roberts looked up and nodded, "Thank you, Lieutenant. I'll be right out."

The young officer nodded and vanished without a further word, leaving Jason to finish up the desk work he'd been using to pass the time.

For someone used to the instant transport of the Transition Drive, moving across the stars at a measly thousand times light or so was rather pedestrian. The thought never failed to get a smile from him when it occurred, however.

A thousand times lightspeed… pedestrian.

It was a laughable concept, but one that he felt deeply from time to time.

They still used Transition from time to time, just to keep a toe in so to speak, but the decision had been made to allow any knowledge of the technology outside the Terran survivors and the Priminae to fade into history if possible.

They knew that the Empire had begun to piece together the existence of the tech just before Earth fell, but in the chaos that had erupted in the wake of that, it seemed that most of the Empire had forgotten it… if they ever really *knew* in the first place.

So over the last decades, Transition tech had been considered a strategic technology and thus had been employed judiciously so as not to attract any untoward attention from the, now distracted, but still quite dangerous remnants of the Empire.

So, Jason found himself with inordinate amounts of time to do his desk work and fill out all the forms needed to keep his ship in space.

Thoughts pushed aside, he finished up quickly and closed the applications, rising to his feet and walking around the desk to head for the Command Deck.

*****

"Welcome, skipper."

Jason Roberts nodded to his XO as he joined the man on the center deck, looking over the array of posts and displays that tied the ship's Command and Control Deck together.

"We've begun our survey," Commander Dereck Kay said, "but at this point we're mostly just establishing a baseline for the region. It's a little outside the norm for this section of the Galactic Arm..."

Roberts glanced over the feeds briefly, "How so?"

"Higher degree of interference across the spectrum, even into hyperlight," Kay answered. "We can filter it easily enough, but it's going to require a baseline to do of course."

"Of course," Roberts nodded. You couldn't filter interference without a baseline, at least not with the degree of precision needed to keep from fouling any high detail scans you wanted to make.

"We're also registering several anomalies that aren't making a lot of sense," Kay grumbled. "Frankly, I'm a half step from pulling our systems offline piecemeal for calibration tests."

That brought a concerned look from Roberts.

That sort of recalibration would take time, and was a mess to do while under power anyway.

"You think it's needed?"

"I don't know," Kay admitted before going on, "No, probably not. Not necessary at least, even if it were needed to some degree. No, it's just the interference, I think, that's causing cascading issues in our data models."

Roberts grimaced, but nodded in understanding.

Anything that disrupted your raw data was a problem, because everything else was *derived* from that. Small mistakes, or holes in the data, would propagate up through the systems, utterly devastating any hope of gaining accurate interpretations of the scans you'd taken so much care to acquire.

"Get the baseline done," Roberts said firmly. "We'll determine what, if anything, we have to do once we have that."

"Yes, Sir."

"In the meantime, what sort of anomalies are you recording?" Roberts asked curiously.

Kay laughed derisively, "Better to ask what we're not recording. There are small issues with the data across practically every metric, that's why I expect it's a cascading fault. EM interference, HL instability, even some gravimetric anomalies among other, even more obscure faults."

The Commander shook his head and lowered his voice slightly before going on.

"I had to look up what some of the faults *meant*, sir. Never even heard of a couple of them before."

Roberts snorted, amused, "Anything interesting?"

"Only if you're really into quantum mechanics, I expect."

"Not really my thing, but I'll take a look anyway."

"Good luck with it, Boss," Kay said with honest feeling. "Probably going to need it."

*****

CHAPTER 20

Pirate Destroyer, *Gia Corvo*

"Beams, Commander! Locked onto the *Mikala*!"

The Ship's Commander snarled, half turning as he checked the screens monitoring the rest of the small squadron. The *Mikala's* telemetry was screaming as the ship came under fire from the full power of the enemy destroyer.

That's not right. A Destroyer shouldn't have that much power?

"Confirm those readings," He snapped.

"Confirmed, Ship's Commander. Checked twice, they're accurate."

The Commander flinched as he watched the *Mikala's* hull buckle in multiple points, the outer armor ablating away, but sufficient heat transfer making it through to the inner hull walls to *melt* them in situ, leaving bubbling globs of molten material to float away from the hull as the breaches blew out across the ship.

He swore, "Tell them to withdraw! I don't want to spend the next months trying to find a new Destroyer to replace them."

"Orders sending, Commander. Mikala's Commander acknowledges but is uncertain if he can comply. Damage is severe."

The Commander snarled, turning back to the primary screen, "All ships, full beams. Slag that piece of filth from my space."

"Yes, Ship's Commander. Full beams confirmed. Engaging."

The whine of the ship's slightly off tuned beams discharging filled the command deck with an ear splitting sound that was somehow barely audible and extremely painful all at once.

*****

Captured Destroyer

"Increase warp, adjust course positive fourteen degrees relative altitude," Reid ordered. "Watch for incoming beams, Helm. Ops, coordinate evasive maneuvers with Helm."

"Aye skipper."

"Yes sir."

Eric felt a tension flooding through him, but at the same time just couldn't take the time to pay it any mind. He linked quickly to Helm, so he could send data directly, getting a quick handshake back from the Chief who didn't even look up in the process.

A quick check showed that they were still several lightseconds apart, but that range was closing *fast*. In a few moments they were going to be at point blank range against multiple ships capable of delivering multi-terrawatt per second beams against a hull that had *no* chance of taking it.

Part of him was honestly wondering if the Captain had lost his goddamn mind, but even if he had there was nothing Eric could hope to do about it. At this point they were committed, and the only thing worse than the Captain being completely off his rocker would be any confusion or hesitation, of which there would be plenty if anyone started questioning their orders now.

He snuck a glance over to the Captain and was honestly surprised by how calm and… *cheerful*… the man seemed to be.

Eric honestly wasn't sure if that was a good sign, or a sign that his concerns were in fact warranted. He supposed it didn't really matter, at least not at the moment. He put his attention fully back to his duties, eyes on the scans as he looked for any sign of incoming fire.

Lasers were all but impossible to detect before they struck, just due to the nature of the weapon system. Travelling at lightspeed, of course, the beam would strike before any relativistic scanners could see it. It *was* occasionally possible to pick up the nearly imperceptible interference pattern of the enemy weapon discharging if you were close enough, but at that range the warning was generally well under a second, and warp drives or not, moving thousands of tons of warship took longer than that.

What he was relying on instead was using the forward warp well to divert the beam long enough, while using the extended sensor masts to detect and triangulate it, hopefully before the energy of the enemy got the angle right to breach the well close enough to score a hit.

In a flash, though, Eric realized part of the Captain's madness.

Unlike the Pirates, Reid's Destroyer *was* under full warp. It's primary defense was the very thing that was pulling them headlong into the enemy formation.

It was an incredibly reckless maneuver, though, and that sent a chill down Eric's spine as he finished setting up several automatic responses to various potential conditions he was expecting could happen.

The man is out of his mind, no question.

Eric's board chirped, causing him to looked down to the live feed and blink.

"Captain, target ship is moving away."

"Speed?"

"Low," Eric said. "They're damaged."

"Good. Burn them from my sky." Reid ordered coldly.

Eric swallowed, but nodded, "Aye, Sir. Tracking, continuous fire."

*****

Pirate Destroyer, *Gia Corvo*

"Enemy continuing to charge, they'll be among us in seconds, Ship's Commander!"

The man in the center of the command deck had ceased his pacing, now staring at the screens in open shock that had seemingly left him frozen with indecision as he tried to find where the task force he *knew* had to be out there would be coming from.

"Commander, they're tracking the *Mikala*... fire intensifying," His scanner officer sounded pained. "The *Mikala* is losing life support on all decks... reactors dead. She's drifting... enemy fire is *not* diminishing."

The Commander snapped his head around, not quite believing that he'd heard that right.

What insanity causes a lone destroyer to burn a ship out while it's attempting to leave when they're outmanned, outgunned, and certainly outmatched?

The only thing that made sense, other than the enemy being completely *insane*, was that the task force was closer than he knew.

"All ships, withdraw." He ordered.

"Ship's Commander, we have boarders..."

"I said withdraw!"

"Yes Ship's Commander. Orders dispatched."

"Go to maximum warp, get us out of here."

*****

Captured Destroyer

Eric gaped as he saw the vectors on the enemy ships change, massive ballooning gravity fields appearing across his board.

"I... Sir, I think the enemy is bugging out," He managed to stammer out.

Reid just smiled, "So it would appear, press the attack as they leave. Helm, reverse our warp power and bring us to a stop, relative to the convoy."

"Sir, firing into their rear warp field... we, we won't penetrate to the ship." Eric said, confused.

"I'm aware of that, give them a proper send off anyway."

"Yes sir," Eric furiously entered the command set and quickly engaged it as the enemy ships accelerated away.

Firing into the Warp Well, the 'forward' angle of a ship's warp, was challenging but possible. It mostly came down to getting the angle right, like playing a deadly game of snooker as you attempted to angle your beams such that they came out of the well at the right angle to hit your target rather than becoming trapped by the well or throwing off randomly into the universe.

The Warp Wave, which was the trailing aspect of a ship's warp, however, was quite different. Spacetime was bent in such a way there as to repel all matter, whether of the positive or negatively charged variety. This was primarily used to repel, or push, the ship itself... but it also provided an effective defense that was all but impossible to reliably breach.

Nevertheless, Eric did as commanded and put the full power of the beams to the Warp Wave of the closest pirate, and wasted *petawatts* of power over the next few minutes as the enemy fled out of range.

"Enemy cleared from range, Sir." Eric said, voice not *quite* shaking as he spoke.

"Excellent work. Quinn?"

"Sir?"

"See if our Marines would be interested in taking a walk, if you would?"

"Aye skipper. I think they'll be willing to be convinced," She said with satisfaction as she rose from her station. "With your leave?"

"Be about it," He nodded as she left.

Reid rose from his own station, stretching out a bit, "Well that was a bracing bit of fun. Chief, put us where the Marines need us, alright?"

"Aye skipper."

Eric could feel the shakes coming on, but couldn't seem to hold them back as he just did his best to focus on the board in front of him. He almost jumped out of his skin when Reid dropped a hand on his shoulder.

"Call for relief," The Commander ordered. "I'd like to see you in my office in five. Alright?"

"Yes sir," Eric nodded, hand already moving to summon someone to take his station.

"Good. Relax, kid, you did well." Reid said, turning away as he gestured to his XO without words, telling the other man to take Command.

Similarly without words, the First Lieutenant casually stepped around the command station and took a seat.

*****

It was a little over four minutes later when Eric knocked on the door to the Captain's office and ready room.

"Come."

He hit the release and let the door slide open, stepping in nervously.

Reid was sitting at his desk, working on something, but he pushed it aside as Eric arrived and just nodded to the seat.

"Take a load off, before you collapse kid," Reid said with twist of his head. "You look like hell."

"Sorry, sir, can't seem to..." Eric clenched his fists together, stiffening up as much as he could, but the involuntary shaking wouldn't cease. "Can't seem to stop the shakes."

"First combat, I assume?" Reid asked.

Eric just nodded wordlessly.

Reid grunted, shaking his head, "You shouldn't have been at Ops for that. I'm sorry."

"What?"

"First time in a fight is bad enough, being in the *hot seat* with lives on the line for that time? Shouldn't have happened," Reid said, sighing, "but life doesn't care about should. You did well, this isn't a reprimand, I just wanted you off the Command Deck in case you broke down or lost your lunch."

"I..." Eric shook his head. "I don't understand."

"Understand what?" Reid seemed genuinely confused.

"Well... any of it," Eric blurted before shaking his head. "No, sorry... I... No, Sir, permission to speak freely?"

"Granted."

"Are you *insane*?" Eric blurted before realizing what he'd said, his eyes opening in panic.

Reid just laughed.

"not what I was expecting you to ask, I'll admit," The Commander said, still chuckling. "I could probably guess, but why don't you tell me why you're asking."

"We just charged a squadron that massively outgunned us, outnumbered us..." Eric said hesitantly. "You didn't even blink, and... Sir, you were smiling. What if the enemy hadn't fled?"

Reid nodded, leaning back.

"You know, I've often wanted to ask my commanding officer if they'd lost their goddamn mind," Reid said musingly. "Never had the balls. I rather think I like you, Ensign. Alright, before I answer your question, can you tell me the tracking speed of Free Stars Destroyers."

Eric blinked at the non-sequiter.

"Average is around a hundred and twenty degrees per tenth of a second, mostly limited to that because of mechanical restrictions."

Reid nodded, "Very good. At the range we were making our approach, and our closing rate, how fast would we have crossed their guns before our Warp Wall was between us?"

For that Eric needed to think a bit.

"Not exactly sure without the raw data in front of me," He admitted, "but we'd likely have crossed their arc in a little under a hundredth of a... second."

Eric's eyes widened as he looked at Reid, "You... planned it?"

"Kid, to answer your original question," Reid said with a wide grin as he completely ignored the last one, "Yes, but that doesn't mean I'm stupid too. Consider that something to keep under your hat... if you have to pick between stupid and crazy, pick crazy, but don't *ever* pick both."

He winked at the confused Ensign before nodding to the door.

"Dismissed. Go get something to eat and take a bit of time to unwind before you step foot back on the Deck."

Eric nodded numbly, later barely remembering getting to his feet and shambling out of the office as Reid returned to his desk work without another glance.

*****

CHAPTER 21

IC *From the Flames*

Ship's Commander Eurydice stood in the center of the command deck, arms crossed behind her back as they continued to scan through the sector, looking for the source of the transmissions that had so bothered the Imperial Central Command.

Thus far they'd come up empty, but she knew it was just a matter of patience. Searching through *star systems* was not a matter that one could call either fast or easy, but it was not a complex issue either. Merely one of methodical patience, though Kaela would be one of the first to admit… privately, if not aloud, that patience was not her strongest point.

"Stellar object X37-4G9T has been cleared, Ship's Commander. Negative contact." Chief Sunnam said, "Moving on to object X37-4G9U."

Kaela suppressed the urge to sigh, or do anything else that would show her internal impatience.

The system was proceeding on automatic for the most part, with Sunnam merely checking the work of the automated systems and providing his confirmation between targets, and as such she could see that he was similarly hiding his irritation with the job.

"Any progress on the local anomalous scans?" She asked once the systems were fully onto the next level of scanning.

Their systems had been reporting something off about the region, relative to their records at least. It wasn't unusual, considering that the last time a survey ship had even been *close* to this region was far enough back that the scans had been filed in the historical section of the archives.

"Not as such, Ship's Commander," Sunnam said with a shake of his head. "We have luminosity anomalies across the sector, but haven't yet determined the sources. Most likely a large dust cloud has moved across the region in the last century or so."

Kaela nodded curtly, "Keep at it. I would prefer to know than to guess, but I agree with your assessment."

"As you will it, Ship's Commander."

*****

Heroic Class Cruiser *Bellerophon*

Jason Roberts was on edge, but couldn't place the reason why, which was frankly putting him even more on edge.

The Bell was proceeding into the investigation sector, their armor running in neutral mode as they relied primarily on passive scans for the moment while they were getting their feet under them so to speak.

The sector was largely quiet, and he knew that was part of what was bothering him.

A tap of his fingers brought up the scans of the local area, and he ran comparisons with another gesture, looking at how they compared to other known parts of the Galactic Arm he had on file.

If anything, the signal noise is too low. A good, what? Twenty percent under the galactic average?

Roberts had run the numbers in every way he could, but nothing he did seemed capable of squaring that circle. The stellar age was the same as the rest of the region, so that wasn't an explanation. There weren't any big anomalies he could point to that would explain any of it either, at least not that he'd found thus far.

He leaned forward in the command station, fist to his jaw as he considered the matter.

"Lieutenant Smith," He said finally.

A young officer standing watch at the sensor station turned immediately, "Yes sir?"

"Have a job for you, in between your current duty," He said.

Smith nodded, "Yes sir. What do you need?"

"Bring up *Prometheus* scans of the local region and start running one to one checks."

The young officer's eyes popped, her jaw dropping slightly.

"Ah... Of course, sir... Sir..."

"I am aware that it will take time, Lieutenant, don't worry I'm not asking for miracles," Roberts assured her. "Pull in anyone who has time, though."

Sandra Smith nodded, "Aye skipper... what are we looking for?"

"I don't know," He admitted, eyes sweeping the displays around the deck, as though willing them to tell him their secrets. "If you find it, I'll know it."

"Yes... sir."

Roberts didn't blame the young officer for being confused, but trusted her and the rest of his people to do their tasks regardless. Honestly, he wasn't able to claim a lack of confusion himself at the moment.

Something was nagging at him, but he couldn't put his finger on it.

Experience told him to figure out what the hell it was, before it put a finger on *them*.

*****

The *Casino*

Jenn checked the scans she was keeping aimed at the Imperial Cruiser, noting that they were remaining on their predictable survey schedule. That made things a great deal easier for her, if nothing else. She was able to dart off and run her own surveys at a rate that exceeded the Imperial clearance rate by a factor of *three*, but thus far she'd been disappointed in the results.

"Cleared another target, skipper," Roy said with a shake of his head. "I know Prometheus reported something out here, but I'm honestly starting to think this is a wild goose chase, Ma'am."

"Can't say that I blame you," Jenn admitted, "but let's not go making assumptions yet. There's a lot of space out here for someone to hide in."

"Aye, there is that," Roy said wearily. "Well, at least our friends out there aren't having any better luck."

Jenn chuckled, "One way to the look for the silver lining, Roy. I'm going to cross their wake again, bring us to the next scan."

"Aye, Ma'am," Roy responded and he checked the ship's systems. "Stealth is good, but we'll need time soon to vent heat or it'll get a smidge uncomfortable here."

"Got it," Jennifer answered, glancing at the current heat cap for herself.

Roy wasn't wrong, she saw instantly. They were still good a while, but ultimately heat was a delicate balance for a starship to walk. Space, while technically cold by certain definitions, was also the ultimate insulator. Dumping waste heat from the *Casino* was no small technical challenge, as there were limits to how much of it could be converted into other, more useful, forms of energy.

Run too long without venting, such as when you were operating with all your stealth systems maxed out, and just the *body heat* of the crew would be enough to eventually turn the small ship into a rather large oven.

The *Casino* had a lot more than just the crew putting out heat.

"We'll run parallel to the Imperial ship after the next system scan," She decided, "Pump heat out through the radiators opposite their position. It won't be the most efficient, but risk of being spotted will be negligible."

"Aye, Ma'am."

"Meantime, tell the crew it's about to get warm in here." Cardsharp said firmly. "Heat protocols are in effect."

"Aye Ma'am."

*****

"Alright everyone, you know the drill," The Sergeant snapped. "If it's using power and doesn't have to be on, time to kill it."

The Marines grumbled, but there was nothing really to be done or said about it, so other than those sounds of discontent everyone shut down whatever they had running."

"It's going to get warm in here," The Sergeant said, "so uniform regs are suspended for the duration, but I swear if I catch anyone running around bare assed, we *will* be having words and you *won't* be enjoying them. Clear?"

"Hooah, Sergeant!"

Amanda silently watched the interaction, not having any reason to intervene. For the moment she kept her uniform to regs, however, even as many of the others took the opportunity to loosen up on theirs for comfort despite the fact that the heat hadn't yet become uncomfortable inside the ship.

She knew enough about ship operations to know that it

could get *very* hot very quickly, depending on the situation.

From what she knew they were currently running high stealth, which meant that their external armor was actually running in maximum absorption mode. That made the *Casino* all but invisible to scans, only a very lucky and good scanner tech or AI would be able to spot them as they eclipsed stars, but it also meant that they didn't radiate *anything...* including heat.

Worse, they were actively absorbing thermal energy from the surrounding environment. Granted, in a vacuum that didn't amount to a lot, at least not this far out from any Stellar object, but when you weren't radiating anything away it didn't take much either.

"Freezers are going to be shutting down," the Sergeant said softly as he slipped over. "If you want to requisition some Ice Cream or the like, now would be the time."

She glanced at him in surprise.

"Just letting you know, Ma'am."

"thank you, Sergeant. I believe I will. In fact, let's see what we can get for the squad," She said. "And a couple decks of cards, perhaps?"

"No need to worry about that," The Sergeant snorted. "If they're not sitting on half a dozen decks of different types, they're not worth their BDUs, Ma'am."

A quick glance told her that the Sergeant was right, as she could see the marines already settling in at the tables with various decks appearing from nowhere.

"Very good then, let's see what we can get from the freezers before they're cleaned out then."

"Right you are, Ma'am."

*****

IC *From the Flames*

"Object X37-4G9U cleared," The chief mumbled out, "Moving on to object X37-4G9V to begin..."

He cut off, which brought Kaela's attention from what she'd been distracting herself with.

"Sunnam?"

"A moment, Ship's Commander," Sunnam said slowly, checking his system again and cocking his head from side to side as he stared at the terminal in front of him.

"What is it, Sunnam?" Kaela articulated firmly.

"I can't seem to find Object X37-4G9V, Ma'am." The Scanner Chief admitted reluctantly.

Kaela stared at the back of his head for a moment.

"I... beg your pardon?" She said slowly, wondering if she'd misheard.

"The stellar object is on the Imperial records, but it's not *here*, Ship's Commander. I don't know how to explain it."

"Put the location on screens," Kaela ordered.

"Yes Ship's Commander. On screen now."

Well... I suppose he did warn me, She thought dryly as the screen just showed *nothing*.

"Overlay the records."

"Yes, Ship's Commander. Record overall up."

A ghostly star appeared on the screen, along with the recorded details from the previous... albeit long obsolete apparently... survey data.

*White dwarf star, potentially valuable resource system, negative for colonization however. Well, unless the survey team fabricated their data, something **very** odd is going on here.*

"Cross spectrum scans the same?" She asked.

"Visible through higher frequency all match."

"What about lower frequency?"

Sunnam glanced down, "It's not in the standard scan, data is more efficiently derived from higher frequencies."

Kaela nodded, she'd known that though only in a vague sort of way.

"Run lower frequency scans anyway," She ordered. "Let's be thorough."

"Yes, Ship's Commander. Shifting down past the red wavelengths into thermal..." Sunnam responded before trailing off as the scan abruptly changed.

"Well..." Kaela said softly. "It seems that the previous survey wasn't making things up."

"I'm not certain about that, Ship's Commander, because whatever *that* is, it's not a white dwarf star." Sunnam said as he stared at the screen that was showing a *massive* bloom all across the thermal spectrum.

"No, it most certainly is not," Kaela said slowly. "Rig for Combat, just in case."

"Yes Ship's Commander, Rigging for combat operations!"

Alarms began to wail as the lights on the big cruiser shifted subtly, but for those on the command deck it was all ignored as they just stared at the screen and the bizarre object that shouldn't *be* there.

*****

CHAPTER 22

The *Casino*

"Skipper, something's up."

Jenn shifted from where she was taking a brief break, grabbing some food and a cuppa before getting back into the suspension field that allowed her to become one with her ship.

"What is it, Roy?" She asked as she ambled back over.

His voice was more curious than concerned, so she figured she had time to be casual about things.

"Imperial ship just went a little wacko," Roy told her, shaking his head. "Pretty sure they just went to full alert, but they're just… sitting there."

Jennifer straightened up, her casual manner vanishing.

"Full Alert?" Cardsharp asked intently.

"Combat grade warp field just went active, we could see it from here if we were half blind," Roy answered, "they're holding position, however."

"No sign of anyone else?" She asked as she stepped into the center of the Command Deck and activated the field, lifting easily into the air and twisting as she matched the position of the fighter/gunboat in space.

"Negative contacts, no sign of any other ships."

Cardsharp hummed grimly, eyes blinking open the HUD that fed the full sensory apparatus of the *Casino* into her field of view. Slowly she turned in space to get a good look at the Imperial cruiser.

"Got them," She said, frowning. "Now what just got up your ass, I wonder?"

Roy shook his head, knowing that she wasn't really asking him, but opted to answer anyway.

"Doesn't look like they're gearing up for a fight, the warp fields aside," He said. "More like they're... looking at something?"

Cardsharp nodded, "I think you have the right of it. System, extrapolate Imperial Cruiser's angle of attack. Match any and all stellar objects along their most powerful scan vector."

The system paused briefly as the computer processed her command and began analyzing the scanner data, running comparisons and looking for matches that fit her criteria. It only took a few seconds, really, but it felt longer.

Error. Data Mismatch.

Cardsharp blinked, "What the fuck? What mismatch?"

Roy shook his head, checking his own system.

"Huh," He said. "That's weird."

"Roy, if you *wanted* to freak me the fuck out, you couldn't have done it any better than that. What's weird?"

"We have a match in the database, but no match in the observational data," Roy answered. "There's supposed to be a star out there, but it's not on our scans."

That sent a chill down Cardsharp's spine.

"What do you mean it's not on our scans?" She asked, "Did it go Nova? Black hole?"

"Neither match, hold on... vector to your HUD," He answered.

Cardsharp blinked and shifted position, looking now where the Cruiser had apparently been focused. There didn't seem to be anything out there, as far as she could tell just more black space.

Wait.

"System," She said again, "Compare our charts to the live view. How many stars are missing?"

Roy stiffened, looking up in shock.

The computer again took a moment, running star chart comparisons was intensive work.

Data Mismatch Error. Four local stars are missing, unknown number in the next Galactic arm are missing, Eighteen Galaxies are missing.

"What the fuck…" Roy blurted.

"System scan, thermal overlay," Cardsharp said, her voice sounding dead.

Instantly the view changed from black to a deep reddish glow that took up a terrifyingly large chunk of the sky.

"Holy shit… what the fuck are we looking at?" Roy stammered out.

"A Dyson construct." Cardsharp muttered. "God help us, it's another one."

*****

IC *From the Flames*

Kaela just stared at the screen, unable to quite comprehend what she was seeing.

"What is it?" Someone else asked, and she was glad of it because at least it meant that she didn't have to voice her ignorance so cleanly.

"Unknown," Sunnam answered. "However it's *massive*."

Kaela heard someone snort at that, but didn't bother looking to see who.

"Any of us could have told you that, Merric."

"No," Sunnam shook his head, "I mean it's *massive*. As in, I'm scanning the gravimetric interference we would expect from an entire star system. Whatever that is, it's not just a dark star, it's... beautiful."

"It's an anomaly," Kaela said coldly. "And likely our cause for being here. Do not romanticize it, Chief Sunnam."

"Apologies, Ship's Commander," Sunnam said quickly. "I... just have never seen anything like it, and there is beauty in the unknown, but also threat I am aware."

Kaela nodded, "Now that we have a direct target, are there any signs of the signals we were dispatched to investigate?"

"A moment," Sunnam said, running a check through the systems. After a moment he straightened up, "Possibly. Faint signals that could match the ones we detected are present... however..."

"However what, Chief?"

"They're far too faint to be detected by the Imperial long range systems, Ship's Commander," Sunnam said apologetically. "If they're this well shielded now, why were we able to detect them before?"

"I don't know," Kaela said grimly, "however we are going to find out. Helm, take us closer. Cautiously, now, Yseb."

"Yes ship's Commander," Yseb said nervously as he set to work, putting the big ship into motion.

*****

The *Casino*

"Skipper," Roy growled warningly, "Movement on the Cruiser."

"What? Right," Cardsharp took a breath, "We'll back off

too."

"Skipper, they're closing on the contact."

Cardsharp twisted in the suspension field, putting her eyes directly on the Imperial cruiser.

"What? No, No! What are you fools doing?" She snarled, yelling into the ether, "Get back from that *thing*!"

"Skipper, doubt they can hear you."

Cardsharp pulled herself together, seething but getting a handle on it.

"Fucking Imps, they of *all* people should know better," She snarled, shaking her head.

"What the hell is it, skipper? I mean, besides the obvious," Roy asked, confused. "You clearly know more than I do."

"Before your time, Roy," Cardsharp sighed, thinking back. "You know about how we were introduced to the Priminae?"

"Sure, the alien spider monsters," Roy said, grinning for a moment before he suddenly got it and lost the smile. "Oh no."

"Yeah. That out there is what they can do when they have a star system all to their own for a little while." Cardsharp said. "Gracen's middle finger was reverse engineered from captured Drones, ones we took when they tried to *eat* Earth."

"Drasin," Roy breathed out, "but why the hell would the cruiser be *approaching* it? Weren't they the ones who set the Drasin on us?"

"Not us, they set those nightmare monsters on the Priminae," Cardsharp growled. "We were collateral... *that time*. It was the start of the war, and the point when the Empire realized that they needed to take us *seriously*."

"but then why approach that thing?" Roy asked again.

"I don't know," She said with a shake of her head. "Might be they have the command codes they used originally, but our intel says that the Drasin managed to toss off that leash, so I'm not sure I'd want to trust my ship to them."

She considered it for a moment, "Maybe they don't know what they're looking at."

"How?"

"The Empire wasn't exactly open about the evil shit they got up to, Roy," Cardsharp said. "Bossman actually spent some time on their homeworld, even got an Audience with *her Majesty* before Prometheus turned the bitch into a matchstick. They're like any other group of people, telling themselves over and over again that they're the good guys... even more strongly when they know that they're not."

"Still, you think the Empire would send a cruiser out here to die like this? I mean, what do they get out of it?" Roy asked. "Wasteful unless there's a payoff."

"Don't know," Cardsharp answered as she leaned in slowly and brought the drives up.

"Whoa!? What are you doing?"

"Tailing them," She said firmly. "We *need* to know, Roy."

"Oh boy."

*****

IC *From the Flames*

"Gravimetric interference is increasing, space warp is becoming less stable," Yseb announced as a shudder passed through the big ship.

"Is it a threat to the *Flames?*" Kaela demanded simply.

"No, Ship's Commander. All systems holding, no stress beyond the normal range."

"Continue."

"Yes, Ship's Commander."

The *Flames* was closing on the anomaly, the massive thermal specter growing in their screens with every passing moment.

Kaela was staring at the data pouring in from every scanner they had, not that any of it made much sense to her.

This construct is insanity defined.

It was farther across than the diameter of her *home planet's* **orbit**.

Nothing natural she knew of even came close, at least not as a single construction. There were, of course, massively larger structures in the universe, but those were connected by *gravity*, not by a physical linkage!

This thing, whatever it was, did indeed appear to be a physical construct however. The scans they were running could not penetrate it, though she had yet to bring their full active scans to bear on it… not that Kaela expected them to be significantly different.

Their best view was actually from passive thermal scans, through which she could see the geometric construct in areas of hotter and cooler sections where the thermal radiation grew stronger or weaker.

All that heat, it's almost unfathomable… Kaela considered that, and really there was only one logical explanation.

The star must still be there, inside that thing.

It made sense to her. Kaela was a Ship's Commander. One of the many things that anyone in her position had to be well aware of was the thermal nature of operating in a vacuum. Energy could not be removed easily, or destroyed at all. The heat of the core at the center of a cruiser was a significant issue that they had *multiple* systems to deal with.

Radiating that energy out into the void was a last resort,

of course. Among other things it was wasteful, energy was energy after all and in the correct form it could be utilized for more productive or practical affairs.

However, it was also extremely easy to spot a ship that radiated heat, assuming you were looking for it.

The reason that the *Flames'* scans hadn't been looking in such frequencies from the start was because no combat ship in the Empire or their enemies, simply *radiated* heat into the void if they could avoid it.

But… heat from a star? It might be too much, even for whoever built **that***, to handle in the more useful of ways. Radiating some may be unavoidable.*

She did, almost, want to laugh at the idea that the sheer level of thermal radiation she was looking at could be considered 'some' of the heat involved, but logically she knew that it must be. A star's entire energy, trapped in a bubble?

What could be done with such power…

*****

CHAPTER 23

Heroic Class Cruiser *Bellerophon*

"Skipper… got something here."

Roberts shifted, eyes moving over to Comms in some surprise. If anywhere, he'd have expected something from Sensors.

"What is it, Max?"

Maxine Curran tilted her head, "Degraded signal, but it looks like an IFF. One of ours."

That got his attention, "Excuse me? Are you certain?"

"Can't say that I am, but it's hitting about thirty percent of the markers," She told him. "Not enough for me to clear the contact, but enough for me to say it looked familiar, boss."

"Can we triangulate?" He asked intently.

"Not with one hit, sir. This far out, there's no telling how long that signal has been traveling either."

Roberts grunted, eyes setting as he looked over to ops.

"Get the ready squadron and a couple SWACS into the black," He ordered. "I want that signal localized."

"Aye, Skipper. Vorpals are scrambling, it'll take a bit longer to get the SWAC Shuttles into space, however."

"Just get it done."

"Aye Sir."

*****

"Move, move, move!"

Lt Command Jenson Mayfield called loudly as his crew ran across the deck for the waiting shuttle.

The old bird was a member of a dying breed, one of the first… and last… countermass shuttles every built on Earth, but it had never failed him and Jenson had no doubts that she'd see him through this mission too.

The Venture Class shuttle was a lifting body design that traced its lineage back to Lockheed's work on a replacement for the Space Shuttle at the turn of the last century. Big, beefy, with a now well worn white heat reflective paint that hadn't been touched up in years, engines with enough power for the damn thing to operate as a tug, and enough cargo room to make it a very useful piece of kit indeed.

His bird was loaded with a Spaceborne Warning And Control System, a compact scanner system with damn near the same power and resolution as the *Bell* herself, capable of tracking a thousand hostile targets at once all the while keeping an eye on a hundred times that number of natural threats ranging from big rocks to *dust clouds*.

"All aboard, Sir," His left seat confirmed. "Vorpals are clear, and we're next up."

"Alright, boys," He called over his shoulder. "Launch in three. Brace. Brace. Brace."

At the end of the third brace, Jenson hit the thruster, which triggered the ship's cat into action, and the big shuttle hit the better part of Seven Hundred Knots before they even left the deck.

"Clear. TigerEye One, in the Black," Jenson said as they continued off away from the Cruiser that was quickly shrinking away behind them.

"TigerEye Two, in the black," the second shuttle announced moments later.

"Roger that. Proceeding to point Alpha."

"Roger One. Two proceeding to point Bravo."

"Ok, Paul, get that beast fired up. Time to go to work," Jenson called over his shoulder.

"You got it, Sir," Paul Bradley responded from the back seat. "Deploying the SWAC."

Jenson could feel the rumble through the seat he had strapped on, the big actuators in the rear hold powering up as the bay doors slid smoothly open to let the system lift the shielded scanner disc out above the shuttle's dorsal section.

"Spinning up. We'll have full resolution in thirty seconds."

*****

Captain Roberts watched the varying feeds as the shuttles, with their fighter cover, got into position.

"Do we still have the signal, Max?"

"Faint, but yes Sir."

"Good. Do your thing."

"Yes sir. We're running the triangulation now, but resolution will improve when the shuttles get to the assigned positions. I'm running interpolation software on the signal now, let's see if we can clear it up." She said, entering commands into the system. "Feeds are up. Let's see if we can't fill in some of these holes."

Roberts waited as patiently as he could project, but inside his mind was running a mile a minute.

We never had anything out this far, not even close. How the hell would one of our IFFs get this far out?

It didn't take long to get a partial answer to that, at least.

"It's not one ours," Max announced a moment later.

"You sure?"

"Yes sir. It's Priminae, *post* tech share."

Jason leaned back, considering that bit.

It made more sense than one of Earth's at least, he supposed.

"Identity?" He asked.

"Reads as the *Corusc Ment*, Sir."

Roberts froze.

"Please confirm." He said evenly.

The young Lieutenant looked back at him for a second before running the signal again.

"Confirmed, Sir. *Corusc Ment*."

"That's impossible." He said firmly. "The *Corusc* went down almost three hundred *lightyears* from here. I was there when it was lost to the Empire during one of our skirmishes after the first invasion."

Max just looked helplessly back at him.

"I... I don't know what to say, Sir."

"I do. Locate the source of the signal," He ordered. "As soon as we have it, recall the shuttles and their cover. We're going to track down that transmitter."

"Aye skipper. Working on it."

Roberts walked back to the center seat and dropped into it, silently watching the crew work as thoughts swirled in his head.

Something very wrong is going on out here.

*****

Prometheus Facility

There was something wrong in the data.

Doctor Palin didn't know what it was, and he couldn't

point to anything specific to support his conclusion, but that didn't change his determination that he was right to believe it.

Since scanning the unknown signals he'd been scouring that section of the Galactic arm with every available resource, using every bit of his pull to get more computer time and, when that didn't work, he just took the time anyway.

The problem was that it wasn't getting him anywhere, and that was driving him completely mad.

"I have to be missing something," He muttered to himself as the loud screeching sounds of the recordings he'd made played through his lab on high volume.

Some of the patterns were known to him, he could hear Confederate encoding, Priminae, and even Imperial patterns in the mix. Something that made no sense to him at all.

The evidence kept coming back to an Earth colony... with both Priminae and Imperial technology?

Palin shook his head.

No, that didn't make sense.

A confederate colony with enough access to have *both* of those technical assets would know better than to broadcast sloppily out into the galaxy for anyone to hear.

It had to be something else.

Palin angrily stomped back to his seat and dropped heavily down into it, glaring at the screen in front of him as it showed the audio levels across the entire spectrum.

And what are these? They're clearly in the non-audible spectrum, is it encoding? Doppler shifting of the signal? No, we've adjusted for that. Why would they be broadcasting audio that isn't audible?

It was almost like the source didn't really understand what it was broadcasting in the first place.

Like they baited a...

Palin froze, his blood chilling in his veins.

"Baited a trap." He mumbled. "System, isolate the non-audible frequencies."

"Frequencies isolated."

"Drop audio encoding, compare signals to known data transmissions from Imperial, Priminae, and Terran ships."

The computer went to work, his brain racing along in other directions as he waited.

*The Empire wouldn't do this, **we** didn't do it,* he thought grimly, *and the Priminae certainly have no reason.*

"Data match. Signals are encoded data from multiple ships of Terran, Priminae, and Imperial origin."

"List the ships." Palin leaned in, eyes on the names that rolled by, as he grew paler with each name.

The last one set him swearing.

NACS Odyssey.

They're all ships that contacted the Drasin.

"Show me the contents of the data files."

The information was broken and chopped up, but he didn't need the whole files to know what he was seeing.

This is just copies of combat communications from the Drasin conflict.

Palin stared for a moment before his hand moved of it's own accord as he reached out and slammed his palm down on the emergency alert.

He barely heard the alarms screaming around him as he sat there, listening to the past... a past that had been chopped up and recombined into a Frankenstein's monster and blasted out into the universe to get attention.

And it worked. God help us. It worked.

*****

Heroic Class Cruiser *Bellerophon*

"Skipper, we've got a contact."

"Kill the warp," Roberts ordered. "Full active scans, pin it down. I want to know the sub-atomic composition of the damn thing and everything around it."

"Aye skipper. Going full active."

Roberts leaned back, taking a breath, "Bell?"

Bellerophon shifted into place beside him, the entity standing at ease. "Yes, Captain."

"I have a bad feeling about this," Roberts said quietly.

"I am aware, Sir."

Of course he was, Roberts thought. Just as the entity was aware of what he was thinking even then. That was why he didn't worry about sharing his concerns with the Soul of the Ship, the entity already knew them.

Possibly better than he did.

"Be ready for a fight," He said.

"Always, Captain," Bell said with a faint smile that would have been unsettlingly feral had Roberts not spent a good amount of time with a similar look on his own face before a fight.

"Analysis complete, skipper. Looks like debris, definitely scans as Heroic class materials."

"Find the mission recorder," Roberts ordered, getting back to his feet. "That'll most likely be the source of the signals we scanned."

"Zeroing in on it now, Sir. I think we have it."

"Good. Send a shuttle to retrieve it," Roberts said firmly.

"Tell them to grab some debris too, if they can. I want to see what we have here with my own eyes."

"Aye, Skipper."

*****

CHAPTER 24

The *Casino*

"Jesus, it's getting hot in here."

"Put a sock in it, Corporal," The Sergeant snapped. "We're all sweating, you don't need to bring it to everyone's attention every two minutes."

Amanda leaned back, eyes closed as she tried to think of cooler times though, honestly the heat wasn't too crazy yet. They were all just far too used to living on the Nest, or working in ships with precise climate control. It honestly wasn't a common issue for ships to run for long periods without radiator cooling active.

Not for an Archangel or a Heroic Class, at least, She mused. She, like everyone else, had heard nightmare stories about the things that crews of the Rogue class ships had to deal with.

She quietly mourned the vanishing of the ice cream she'd polished off, her share from what had been dumped from the freezers when they were shut down to limit the heating caused by those systems.

Of course, the cold treat had really only been a brief respite that was followed by an increase in how much heat she felt. The Colonel's offer of a hot coffee had made her give her superior a look that elicited a sharp bark of laughter from the older woman, but surprisingly the hot drink seemed to have more cooling effect on her than the ice cream managed.

Go figure.

For the moment Amanda was focused on the current

situation, though she didn't know all that much about things, she was trying to learn as much as she could manage on the fly.

The discovery of a Dyson Construct had shaken everyone up a bit, and there hadn't been any chance of keeping it quiet. Not on a ship as small as The *Casino*, at least. She supposed it might be different on a Heroic, though Amanda rather doubted it.

Scuttlebutt travels faster than a Transition Drive.

And bad news moved faster again, she supposed.

The Drasin. Unreal. I really kind of considered them to be nothing more than ghost stories, She realized as she thought it through.

Not in the way that she believed her parents were making things up. Logically she knew that their stories were true, or at least based in the events as they saw them... but she hadn't really connected that with the monsters being *real* all the same. Part of her had just called them legends and stories, and that had been the end of it.

Until now.

The news of what they'd found out there, and that the Skipper was moving *toward* it had put everyone on edge. She could see it in the Marines of her squad, their games and humor had taken a brittle edge, a nervous energy that was swirling beneath the bravado.

Amanda wasn't sure if she had even now quite processed the threat, though, because she didn't feel nervous.

And that scared her.

*****

"These fucking idiots..."

Jennifer was seething as she followed the Imperial cruiser in toward the Dyson construct, hating every passing AU as she did.

"Data on the object is getting more detailed, if nothing else, boss." Roy told her from where he was running the Ops system.

"I'm sure someone will find that fascinating, assuming we don't get *eaten* before we have a chance to pass it on," Cardsharp growled. "Why are they getting closer? You're close enough, you idiots!"

"Still don't think they can hear you, boss."

"Oh shut up, Roy," She groused, rolling her eyes.

"Sensors are starting to get detail differentiation on the composition of the sphere," Roy said, not paying her words any mind. "This thing is *amazing*."

"I already know all the details I need to know about that thing," Cardsharp responded. "I know what made it. That's enough."

"That may be, but check this out." Roy told her, entering a new set of parameters and sending them over to her HUD.

The view changed as the overlay affected the frequencies she was observing the sphere in, and Cardsharp sucked in a breath of air.

"What the hell?" She whispered.

"It's a thermal overlay with better detail, combined with motion tracking data of the independent elements of the sphere," Roy answered. "We're tracking movement, heat, and energy conduits."

The new image of the Dyson construct only vaguely looked like the last, the spherical shape still evident but much of the previous structure now invisible as the image focused on motion and energy tracking.

"Looks like a tree growing in space," She muttered.

"Fractal growth pattern," Roy answered. "It's a common design in nature, if I invert the image it looks more like a lightning strike. Same thing really, but that's not what caught my attention."

Cardsharp hummed, eyes falling on what undoubtedly *had* caught her XO's eye.

"What is that?" She wondered. "Enhance that object."

In an odd orbit within the construct, they were able to discern a second large sphere. Certainly smaller than the Dyson construct, but still big by any measure, and radiating even more thermal energy than the shell itself.

"Still analyzing, but there are only a few theoretical constructions that fit the data," Roy said. "Had to look them up. One in particular, though, well it stands out."

"And it is? Come on, Roy, we don't have time for guessing games."

Roy sighed, "I think it's a Jupiter Brain."

*****

IC *From the Flames*

Kaela Eurydice stared in ill disguised awe as the ship's scanners were able to differentiate between the components that made up the massive construct they were approaching.

Each individual component was larger than *any* inhabited world she knew of, and all of them were operating in a stable orbit that frankly defied everything she knew about the physics of orbital motion.

Each of those must be under some type of positive guidance, She supposed, but the power and sheer data crunching needed to maintain anything that large and complex was beyond anything she'd ever even heard of.

"Ship's Commander, there are… gaps in the construct," Sunnam told her.

"I can see them," Kaela confirmed. "Can you estimate the

size? Will the *Flames* fit through?"

The Chief choked a little.

"Ship's Commander…" He said hesitantly, licking his lips, "The *homeworld* would fit through. The scale of what we're seeing it beyond imagining."

Kaela frowned, "Not beyond someone's, clearly."

She considered the options for a brief moment, but finally nodded, "Take us in."

A long quiet pause filled the command deck before anyone spoke.

Finally, Yseb nodded and began setting new commands.

"Yes, Ship's Commander."

*****

The *Casino*

"Oh you mother…" Cardsharp began spewing a long, seemingly neverending, diatribe of slurs and vile oaths that Roy just tactfully ignored as they watched the Imperial ship start moving again, heading for the gaps in the shell ahead of them.

"Are we following them?" Roy asked when she paused for a breath.

Cardsharp hesitated, shaking her head.

"I… I don't know," She admitted, hating the thought of doing just that.

The construct was, among other things, one of the singularly *largest* imaginable gravity scanning networks you could conceive. The *Casino* was small, and heavily stealthed, to be certain but inside that beast… there was literally nowhere to hide.

She suspected that the thing could track *individual* dust motes by their gravimetric footprint within the sphere.

Going inside the sphere was like inviting a Vampire into your home. Whatever power you might have had, well you just surrendered it.

However, if she didn't follow the Imperial ship, she'd never find out what the ever living *fuck* they were up to.

"Set a buoy," She determined. "Flash traffic, any recipient, re-trans to *Prometheus.* Put in the location, situation, and a request for backup."

Roy grimaced, but nodded as he called up the software needed and put in the parameters.

"Buoy set," he confirmed a few moments later.

"Launch away from the sphere, set it to broadcast once it loses contact with our telemetry laser," She ordered. "That should put us far enough away, just in case those fuckers intercept it."

"Aye, skipper."

Decision made, I guess.

Cardsharp was *not* in a good mood, but she supposed that no one ever gave a damn anyway.

"I'm going to get closer," She said, leaning into the field. "Hide our mass in the Imperial's warp field."

"You're going to *what?*" Roy blurted, albeit too late as they were already moving.

*****

IC *From the Flames*

"Construct perimeter approaching, Ship's Commander."

"I see it. Penetrate as planned."

"Yes, Ship's Commander."

The gaps in the construction were objectively massive, but subjective appeared like gossamer threads until they approached and the threads began to expand, seemingly without end.

Who or what builds such a thing?

There was no answer, of course, but she supposed that was why she was here.

"Penetrating Perimeter…"

The tension ratcheted up, seemingly endlessly, as the massive slabs of material slid smoothly past the cruiser as they broached the perimeter and could finally see the dim glow of the white dwarf deep within.

A shudder went through the ship, startling each of them, and driving Kaela straight up in her seat.

"Report," She snapped.

"Anomaly in the warp field," Yseb answered, cocking his head slightly as he took in the data. "It's stabilized now. Likely interference from the construct, Ship's Commander. We have no data on making an approach this close to something of this nature with warp fields."

Kaela grumbled, but nodded, "Understood. Monitor it going forward, but continue."

"Yes, Ship's Commander."

"Anomaly detected, Ship's Commander," Sunnam announced.

"*Another* one?" Kaela demanded archly. "Unless you've somehow forgotten, this entire situation is anomalous."

"Another one, Ship's Commander," The Chief confirmed. "heat source in orbit of the star. It's the only significant source of gravity we can detect beside the sphere and the star."

"Show it."

"Main viewer."

The image on the large display wavered briefly, then

focused in on a thermal image of *another* ball floating out in the depths.

"What is this now?" She demanded, frustrated.

"Unknown, however it is several times the mass of the gas giants in the home system… *combined*."

That shouldn't have come as a shock to her, given the nature of the construct they were currently flying *through*, but the numbers staggered Kaela nonetheless. Nothing she was learning made any sense, but somehow it all just kept coming in defiance of sanity all the same.

"Are we still scanning those signals?" She asked.

"Yes, Ship's Commander. Source is now localized," Sunnam confirmed, nodding to the screen. "They're coming from *that*."

Kaela grimaced, lips pulled back over her teeth.

*Because of **course they are**.*

"Very well, adjust vectors for a stable insertion orbit around… whatever that is."

"Yes Ship's Commander," Yseb responded. "Vectors calculated and entered."

"Take us in."

*****

CHAPTER 25

Captured Destroyer

Eric was surprised by how little they ultimately had to do after the Pirates had fled, leaving behind their own boarding forces.

The Captain had called in the local patrol group from the colony and then basically told the remaining pirates that either they gave up… or he'd send in the Marines.

That was all it took for the smarter examples.

I guess they've been making a reputation for themselves over the years, Eric thought dryly.

Of course, they were pirates, so there were more than enough of the less than intelligent type as well. That meant that over the next day or so they'd run boarding operations with the Marines on board, which was really a minimal team who wound up worked to the bone while being surprisingly happy about things.

Marines were known to be crazy, but despite his Sister being nuts enough to want to join their ranks, Eric hadn't really internalized just how much they deserved their reputation.

Still, though, they got the job pretty much done by the time the local patrol made it to their location and the Convoy was freed up to finish its journey and deliver the cargo to where it was needed. Eric was standing watch, technically in charge on the Destroyer while the more experienced officers grabbed some sleep, with orders to bug out in a hurry if anything happened while screaming for everyone to wake the hell up the whole way until he was relieved.

It was odd, He would have thought that he'd object to orders like that as if they were an attack on his pride or something, but when the Skipper laid out his instructions he was just happy to *not* have to make any decisions.

Listen to the Noncoms, Reid had told him. They've forgotten more than you've learned, and if anything happens. Anything at all... you get the hell out first, then call for someone who knows better.

He could do that.

Thankfully it didn't look like he would have to. The last of the freighters had been cleared by the locals, which meant that he just had to watch them head out on their way and wait for new orders.

It made for a peaceful way to pass the watch, though a bit boring he supposed. He might complain, but at this point he was too happy that his nerves were calmed down and that he *could* be bored. For a little bit there, Eric had honestly been worried that something physical was wrong.

Logically he knew that there hadn't been, but it still felt like it.

"Lieutenant..."

Eric looked up from the hotseat, a thrill running through him that he didn't understand.

"Yes?" He asked the Petty Officer who was standing Comm Watch.

"Pulse Traffic reception, Sir. Looks like it's from the *Casino*." The Petty Officer said, scowling at his board. "Encrypted deep, highest priority though."

"Copy me on it."

"Yes Sir."

Eric felt the thrill settle into a chill, moving in deep in his bones as the Pulse Traffic message appeared on his station and he looked over it quickly before immediately reaching over and tapping out a command.

It took a minute, but in short order a bleary sounding voice filtered out over his system.

"What is it, Lieutenant?" Reid asked, clearly still asleep but struggling through that anyway.

"Flash Traffic, skipper, from the Casino. They want to retrans to *Prometheus*, and a general call for reinforcements. Details are encrypted."

"Shit. Right, ok, retrans as requested," Reid ordered. "I'll be right up."

"Aye Sir."

*****

Marcus hadn't bothered with his uniform jacket as he made his way onto the Command Deck of the destroyer. He wasn't technically on duty, and wasn't much of a stickler for rules at the best of times, which was why he'd volunteered for Prize Crew duties in the first place.

The Deck was quiet as he stepped on, third watch lighting was lower than the day watch settings, at least while things were nice and boring. The minimal crew were all doing their jobs quietly, but it was relaxed quiet rather than an oppressive one.

Good sign for the new Looie, at least he'd not a Martinet, Marcus supposed, not that he'd expected the kid to be. *Speaking of...*

The kid was sitting in the hot seat, looking as uncomfortable to be there as he should be, which was also good to Marcus' mind. Kid was a good long time from being experienced enough to be comfortable in that seat. Shouldn't even *be* in it yet, but the rules were different on Prize crews, and Marcus figured he had a pretty shrewd idea of the kid's competence already.

Good enough to follow orders, smart enough to know better than think he could handle most problems himself yet, but somehow still with enough knowledge to do the job.

Most people with a *little* knowledge were a threat to themselves and the people around them, specifically because they had the knowledge to know what to do but not the experience to know whether they should do it.

The kid didn't seem to have that logical fallacy floating around his brain... yet. Marcus would make damn sure it never had a chance to develop if he had anything to say about it too.

"Hey kid," He said softly as he walked up. "Show me what you got, no stay seated. This won't take long, I hope, then I'm going back to bed."

Eric paused, halfway out of the seat, before nodding and relaxing back into it.

"Yes sir. Flash traffic from the Casino," He told Marcus, tilting the screen over so the Commander could see it. "Request for retrans, completed by the way, and a request for any available reinforcements. Everything else is encrypted, including their coordinates. Not sure what the point of putting the reinforcement request out in the clear was if they were going to encrypt the coordinates, though."

Marcus grunted, "Just making it clear to anyone who caught this that the message was serious, I expect. Ok, let me see this encryption..."

He took control of the display, twisting it fully to face himself as he put in his authorization into the system and was surprised when it didn't decrypt immediately.

"Ok, this is no joke it seems," Marcus hummed to himself, reading the query/response code that was being presented to him. "Cardsharp must be seriously spooked. I've read about this code, but never seen it in action. Alright, let's see here..."

He navigated through the challenge/response code, mostly from memory but having to stop and check his own records twice to be sure of the answers. The process took several minutes, during which the silence on the command deck *did* become more than a little oppressive as everyone paid far too much *obvious* attention to their duties, while simultaneously trying not to lean in his direction too obviously.

Marcus ignored them as he got the code cleared and finally unlocked the data.

Less than a minute into reading he paled and stepped back, twisting his head.

"Up," He ordered the kid.

The young Lieutenant jumped out of the seat like he had a CM field boosting him, and Marcus immediately dropped right in, pulling the screen in close.

"Lieutenant," He ordered. "Take the Helm please."

"Aye sir," Eric Michaels responded, immediately crossing to the station currently being stood by an inexperienced Petty Officer. "I have the Helm."

"Aye Sir, you have the Helm," The young woman confirmed, moving aside.

"Lieutenant, prepare for high warp," Marcus ordered. "We will be underway in short order."

"Yes sir."

"Coordinates incoming. Plot best course, full military power, engage when ready."

Eric swallowed, but nodded firmly.

"Aye sir. Plotting course, full military power. Estimate to departure... three minutes."

"Good work."

*****

Gaia's Revenge

"Skipper, Flashtraffic with Prometheus tag, looks like a retrans from one of our Destroyers. All Ships Attention." Tyke announced, half turning from his station to where Steph was flight checking the systems.

For the past few days they'd been running patrol patterns, hired on as an anti-piracy gig they'd primarily been showing the flag for the local colony. It was about as safe a mission as his teams ever got, and Steph generally tried to ensure that they grabbed on similar to it every now and again if only because constant combat missions had a way to wearing a man down to the bone... and then keep on wearing on him.

Most Pirates in the Free Stars and beyond were unlikely to want to tangle with even a single Archangel, primarily because they'd built their reputation by taking on *combat* vessels from major polities in the region and had similarly developed a near *legendary*... distaste... for pirates of the conventional sort.

Given his *nom de plume* in the region, that is Captain Teach, and many of his earlier operations, that legend always amused him greatly. Of course, historically, there were Pirates and then there were *Pirates*. Often both groups got mixed up a lot, both being pirates and all, but the key difference was that some crews had a *code*, while others at best pretended to.

Steph had initially used the infamous Pirate's true name more as a joke he was playing entirely for his own amusement more than anything else, but as such things were wont to do on occasion, the joke had quickly taken on a life of it's own.

And so, Captain Teach was once again one of the most feared ship Captains in the regions he prowled, and his *Revenge* might be deadlier than the original, but Steph honestly liked the link back to home... especially after the invasion and its aftermath.

He grunted as he made a final adjustment to one of the alignment sensors, ensuring that it passed checks and was tuned in to a sub-millimeter accuracy, then closed the panel and slid out from under the console.

"What's it say?" He asked as he rolled to his feet and clapped his hands clean.

"Coded, skipper. Captain's eyes."

Steph raised an eyebrow, surprised by that.

All transmissions from Prometheus were hard encrypted, of course. You needed a physical decryption key to decode *anything* from that facility, in additions to the officer's codes as well as a host of other protections all intended to secure the location and even *existence* of Prometheus... however, that was usually enough.

It was rare that they'd toss an Eyes Only lock on top of it all, given that Archangel crews were among the most trusted people they had by definition.

"Got it," Steph said as he slipped into a cramped side console and slid his hand into a scanner.

The system lit up the scan instantly, heating his hand as the energy penetrated through his flesh, blood, and bone and was analyzed on the other side. Everything from blood oxygen levels all the way up to a rough DNA analysis was conducted in that few seconds, ensuring that he was who he claimed to be, and the system beeped once as it unlocked the file.

Removing his hand, Steph tapped the screen to open the file and immediately stiffened.

"Boss?"

"Code Delta," He said, slightly numb. "Shit."

Tyke frowned and had to think about what that meant. He'd heard it before, but only in a briefing he thought, but he did remember that it was high profile.

"Sorry, don't recognize it. I know it's big but..."

"Drasin," Steph said. "They've been spotted again."

"Oh fuck me."

The Drasin were a threat Tyke had only seen once, and most of that encounter had been him bunkering down and hoping to survive the event because he couldn't leave his daughter alone, she'd been so young at the time. He remembered the terror when they hammered through Earth's defenses, listening to the reports of combat coming in from around the world.

After they'd been beaten off, however, the alien beasts had just... vanished. Logically he'd know that they still existed, everyone kind of did, but most were too happy to forget them if they could.

Tyke was startled from his thoughts by Steph suddenly bolting upright, face drawn white and pale.

"Boss? Boss, what is it?"

Steph didn't answer as he grabbed a comm unit and slapped it onto his jaw.

"Colony Riva, Teach." Steph growled out. "I am invoking the exterior threat clause of our contract and will be leaving the system momentarily. Your payment for our services will be refunded in full, and an option for a discounted operation will be made available on your account at a later date assuming I survive to offer it. Teach out."

He sent the message and got up, standing shakily.

"Boss... the fuck."

"It's the *Casino*, Tyke... Amanda's on board." Steph said dully.

"Oh... oh shit. Right," Tyke nodded. "Ok, let's go."

"Coordinates are in the file," Steph said. "Get us moving. We'll Transition once we're in Interstellar."

"Where are you... oh... yeah, alright, got it covered." Tyke nodded.

"Thanks," Steph said, patting the man on the shoulder as he moved on past and headed for the aft compartments.

*****

Bellerophon

Jason stood watch over the cargo bays that held the material they'd recovered from the debris field they'd located. It included a mission recorder from the *Corusc*, of course, but quite a lot of other material as well. The mission recorder had little of interest, at least for his current purposes.

The ship had been destroyed during action with the Empire, and the mission recorded never recovered due to the nature of the fight and its location. Having it back now would fill in a few holes in the records, make some historians happy, and certainly answer some questions the Priminae had held for a while… but that was really all.

The debris, though, there was something off about that.

He had full analysis running, of course, but he could already tell that whatever happened to it wasn't the normal damage from beam fire or even a reactor collapse. He just hoped that analysis had some answers, especially as to what the *hell* happened to bring all of it out this far.

Sure as hell didn't drift out here, not in a mere thirty odd years.

"Sir."

Jason turned, hot drink steaming in his hand as the entity appeared at his side, "Yes Bell?"

"Emergency Flash Traffic from the *Casino*," The entity told him. "Heavily encrypted."

Roberts snorted, "What does it say?"

He knew that there wasn't any encryption that would stop the entity from decoding the information, basically on instinct. Anything in the electromagnetic spectrum was basically an entities bitch, trying to keep them out was only marginally harder than permanently reversing entropy.

"It is not good news, Sir. The *Casino* has been tracking an Imperial cruiser, likely also investigating the signals we are…"

Roberts bit back a curse, *If some idiot colony just brought the Empire down on their own heads with their foolishness...*

"It does not appear to be a Terran Colony, Captain," Bell stepped on his thoughts with alacrity.

Roberts grimaced, "You know I hate it when you respond to my thoughts. Wait until I say something."

"Time appears to be of the essence. The Casino has requested immediate reinforcements."

Roberts straightened up, head snapping fully around.

The Archangels didn't generally ask for reinforcements. There wasn't much out there that they couldn't fight, hide, or run from. Given time, one of those little gunboats could likely take on a Heroic cruiser... maybe even a Task group... and make them *pay* for tangling with the smaller ship.

"Are there any other Archangels or Destroyers available?" Jason asked, almost dreading the answer.

"You misunderstand, Captain, Samuels has requested any and *all* reinforcements. No limiting criteria," Bell said.

"That's impossible."

"The Imperial ship located another Dyson Construct."

Jason felt himself physically stagger and reached out for the bulkhead to steady himself.

"I need to hear the full report," He croaked out. "but first, let's get this beast moving."

"Aye, Sir."

*****

CHAPTER 26

IC *From the Flames*

"Target object entering range, Ship's Commander."

Kaela nodded, "Continue as ordered, reduce approach velocity. I want to give the scanning stations all the time they need."

"Yes, Ship's Commander."

The interior of the massive stellar construct was… oddly quiet, Kaela noted with some *disquiet*. She wasn't certain what she'd been expecting, but the utter silence that had greeted their scanners as they penetrated the construct wasn't it.

It is as if there isn't even **dust** *remaining within this sphere,* She thought with a slight shudder.

It made some sense, of course. Where would you get the material to build such a thing if not by cannibalizing everything else within the system, afterall?

However much since that might make in theory, however, the reality of it was hard to accept for someone used to the natural state of affairs within a star system. On a low warp, such as they were using now, the forward well of spacetime that tugged the ship forward wasn't sufficient to trap and prevent dust and such from reaching the hull.

Normally that would result in the occasional impact warning along with a minor ablation of the outer surface of the armor, which would have to be reapplied after a time in order to maintain the integrity of the inner hull and pressurised sections of the ship.

Here, though?

Hours they'd spent within the construct now and there was nothing. No minor impacts, no hits on any of their scanners, and even the *interstellar gasses* were measurably lower within the construct.

The precision of it is... terrifying.

It was not something that Kaela would admit aloud, of course, nor would she show such a reaction to any of her subordinates.. nor, frankly, to any of her peers or superiors, or anyone else for that matter... but it was there anyway.

"Scans to my station," She ordered, reaching for her display.

"To your station, Ship's Commander."

The object they were guiding toward was truly massive. Under almost any other situation, in fact, she would be marveling at how something so impossibly large could even *be built*. That, however, felt like a silly notion to be entertaining while she was guiding her Command *through* a structure that was nearly incalculably larger.

The size of a particularly large gas giant, the artificial construct radiated nothing other than thermal energy, making her wonder if the builders had somehow trapped another dwarf star within the system and built a second, smaller, shell around it.

To what end, though, she honestly had no real idea.

"Reduce to station keeping relative to the target," She ordered as they got close enough to maximize their scanning capability. "Hold until further orders, begin analysis."

"Yes, Ship's Commander. Adjusting to maintain position relative to Target Alpha," Yseb responded.

"Scanning and analysis beginning," Sunnam spoke up a moment later, "Request from analysis team to go active, Ship's

Commander."

Kaela grimaced as she considered that.

On the one hand, of course, going active meant revealing their presence and position, but she honestly wasn't sure it was truly possible for them to have been *missed* given the completely empty nature of the environment they were currently within.

"Granted," She sighed, knowing that the active scanners would be *far* more effective. "Proceed with full analysis."

"Yes, Ship's Commander."

*****

The *Casino*

"Whoa. Heads up, Skipper. We've got active scanners."

Cardsharp grunted, opening her eyes.

"Threshold?" She asked immediately.

"Well below detection levels," Roy answered, wiping sweat from his eyes. "Primarily directed away from us, we just caught some of the reflected energy."

Cardsharp nodded, wearily making her way across the command deck so she could get the full HUD feed for the best idea of what was going on.

The suspension field lifted her off the deck as the holographic HUD came to life again, feeding information to her through all of her available senses once more. She took in the view of the full spectrum analysis of all radiation the ship could detect, could *hear* the thrum of both the drives of her own ship and the Imperial cruiser so close ahead through their warping of spacetime, feel the sensation of heat radiating from the Jupiter Brain on her skin... the feed of data from the NICS interface never ceased to take her breath away, but she was long used to controlling that reaction and kept her focus on the matter at hand.

"They're scanning the object," She said, "Make sure that we're recording *everything*."

"Roger that," Roy said, "Nothing like using your enemies scanners against them."

Cardsharp smiled slightly, though it was tinged with a bitter expression. "Truth, but I'd rather we were a *lot* farther away from them than we currently are. If they attract... unwanted attention, we're going to be right at ground zero anyway."

Roy grimaced, "There is that... whoa. Check out the composition on that thing."

Cardsharp glanced over the spectral analysis and whistled, "Damn thing is a girl's best friend... well, aside from an Archangel gunboat... a loaded rifle... clear lines of fire..."

"I get it already," Roy rolled his eyes, "but that is a *lot* of diamond material. The outer shell has to be several earth masses of diamond *alone*."

"Good heat dispersion through that," She noted. "Explains why it's so hot, they're using Diamond as a radiator. Also durable as hell, won't ablate away easily if there's any micro impacts."

"There are more efficient options for heat dispersion," Roy noted.

"But probably not more accessible," Cardsharp said. "You said it yourself, there are multiple Earth masses of it there. Graphene would be better, but that shit is hard to make in quantity."

Roy grunted, "Scanning large quantities of graphene too, though nothing like the Diamond. Where do you even *get* that much diamond anyway?"

"At a guess? Forged in the gas giants these bastards ate to build all this crap."

"Point," Roy tilted his head.

They fell silent as they continued to examine the data they were getting from the reflections of the Imperial scanners then. The object they assumed to be a Jupiter Brain had some of the most insane compositional data either had ever seen, which actually meant something in Jennifer's case as she'd personally been inside a similar construct, and been present during the initial phase of construction for Earth's own Kardashev Network.

"Skipper, look at this data... it's on a sub-band, passive scans, not coming from the Imperial cruiser I don't think," Roy said, flipping a feed to her.

Jenn checked it quickly, then stopped and went back to the beginning to look it over in depth.

"What the hell are we looking at?" She whispered, confused by the sheer complexity the scans were showing.

"I think that's the EM radiation residue from the processing being done," Roy noted. "It's *massive*. That thing could conceivably run simulations on a *universal* scale..."

"I doubt the Drasin give two shits about simulating a universe," She shook her head. "What do they need *that* kind of processing power for? It's insane."

"No idea, skipper."

Cardsharp curled up her lip, head shaking very slightly side to side, "Whatever it is, I guarantee you it isn't good for us."

*****

Enemy proximity. Plan success.

Indecision. Query?

Suggestion.

Amendment. Caution.

Acceptance. Adjust Plan, factors favorable.

Agreement. Proceed.

Proceeding.

*****

IC *From the Flames*

"Scanning proceeding as planned, Ship's Commander," Sunnam said. "Data analysis thus far is… interesting."

Kaela snorted, suspecting that was a vastly underwhelming choice of words.

"Anything of note?"

"Extreme use of crystallized carbon in various forms, in amounts that I've never even heard proposed before," He admitted. "Beams would have a very difficult time cracking that shell, Ma'am."

"I don't believe I'm quite to the point of firing on it, Chief, but thank you for the information," She said dryly, amused but still rather tense about the whole situation.

"Ah, yes Ship's Commander. I was just pointing it out."

"Understood. Anything of immediate use?"

"Not as such, though we are scanning odd background interference," Sunnam admitted. "That has been prioritized for analysis but nothing as yet has been determined."

"Very well," She said. "Continue scanning."

"Yes, Ship's Commander. I…"

Sunnam paused, as did everyone else, as a dull thump could be heard and felt through the deck of the ship. Distant, but significant.

"Chief, I thought there wasn't anything in system to strike."

"We haven't detected anything, Ship's Commander. A

moment," Sunnam said quickly, "Adjusting primary scanners, looking at local space… uh…"

Kaela didn't much like that pause.

"What is it, Chief."

"Something… Ship's Commander, there's something out there."

Kaela bowed her head, wanting to swear, but instead just looked up again.

"Sound combat alert, retask all scanners to close in support," She ordered sharply. "Bring all point defense beams online, tracking up to may station."

"Yes, Ship's Commander. Combat Alert! All hands, Combat alert!"

Kaela pulled her display closer as the tracking data began it's feed directly to her, spotting the multiple contacts that were registering on it now.

What the hell is going on?

She picked one of the closer contacts and focused the scans on it as it approached, her features growing taught and pale as it came into view just seconds before landing down on the hell of her ship with another audible thud.

"Beams up," She ordered sharply. "Fire at all targets!"

*****

The *Casino*

"Whoa, they just went full combat mode, skipper…"

"I noticed," Cardsharp said through gritted teeth. "Their warp field is trying to squeeze us out like a peach pit between its fingers. I'm not sure I can hold position much longer."

Roy shook his head, "I'm not sure we *want* to. Scan up, skipper."

Cardsharp's eyes glanced aside to the video file he'd sent her, the box popping up in her peripheral vision on command.

As she focused on it, a shape emerged from the black background of local space, spindly looking at first, then firming up to show a solid core and an evil visage of sorts. Cardsharp paled as she recognized the image and stopped fighting the enemy warp, letting it spit them out and away from the Imperial cruiser.

"Drasin." She spat the word like it was a vile epithet. "General quarters, Roy. I want every soul on board ready for a fight."

*****

Amanda bolted upright from where she'd been napping fitfully against the bulkhead, trying to ignore the heat as the sweat caused her tanktop to cling to her skin like it was glued there.

It took her a moment to recognize the sound, and another to fully get her brain in gear and start moving. The Sergeant was *way* ahead of her as he moved through the room, slapping Marines awake and shoving them toward their lockers while they were still half asleep.

"Wakey wakey, boys and girls," He said with a wide grin. "It's time to earn those oh so magnificent paychecks!"

Amanda left him to it, focusing instead on getting her own kit from the locker she rushed to.

She didn't know what was going on yet, but it looked like the mind numbing boredom part of the operation was over.

Time for the bowel clenching terror portion to begin.

*****

CHAPTER 27

Prometheus Facility

The retransmitted message from the *Casino* had set the fox amid the hens, Palin noted with dry amusement that was tinged with bitter hints of personal recrimination for failing to see it before.

Only the Drasin had access to all the signals he'd been detecting, they were the commonality that he'd not been able to find. Likely because, over the years, Edward had tried very hard to forget the nightmarish little beasts.

The Drasin were not truly what one might consider sapient creatures, not in the human meaning of the term at least. Self awareness only came to them in the Gestalt, the group, and even then it was far from anything a human might comprehend or even recognize.

Individually they were more like components of a single being, but even that failed to fully describe the nature of the beasts.

Guided first by instinct, and only second by anything resembling rational thought, the Drasin were a swarm of annihilation for anything that crossed their paths.

Every bit of research that the Confederacy had managed to put into discovering what the aliens really were had been largely for nothing, because they were not like anything humans had ever really encountered.

They could be compared to arachnids and insects in some ways, but were more like Fungi in others, and were clearly none of the above in almost all ways that mattered. Silicon based, with molten metals and other elements forming their 'blood', the Drasin were not even alive by some definitions and had very neatly shown just how bad many common definitions for such things were.

The Admiral had, of course, brought Prometheus to it's full military capacity... which was no small threat, Palin was aware. However, if they were forced to deploy Prometheus in such a way that the *Empire* was able to witness its use... well, that would be... suboptimal.

For his part, Palin was focusing less now on attempting to decode the signals they'd received and instead look for the *reason* behind them

The Drasin might not be rational, in the human sense of things, but that did not mean they were stupid or incapable of planning.

They were up to something, and he had to figure out what that was.

*****

The *Casino*

"Fuck!"

"You ok, Skipper?" Roy asked without looking up from the secondary controls he was running.

"Just got spit out of the warp field, hold on... going to get a little rough," Cardsharp spat out as the ship twisted under them, sending his guts into freefall for a moment before up and down reasserted themselves.

"Ok, we're clear. Don't know if anyone spotted us," Cardsharp said a moment later. "I'm trying to stay out of the line of fire, but those little fuckers are hard to spot on passives."

Roy nodded grimly, knowing that was the god's honest truth.

The Drasin drones he was tracking were largely only due to the Imperial Cruiser going full active and just *plastering* local space with enough energy to ignite a small sun. It was bad enough, in fact, that their camplate armor in its black hole setting was absorbing enough to become dangerously radioactive.

"Not sure we can stay stealthed much longer boss," He said, "We're absorbing a *lot* of rads being this close to that monster. Shielding is holding, but it's just a matter of time before our *shielding* starts picking up enough rads to glow in the dark too... once that happens..."

Cardsharp nodded grimly.

Once that happened, The *Casino* was a write off.

Camplates could be cleaned or, worse case, replaced. The internal radiation shielding would have to be completely gutted to remove the radiation, however, and even if the ship's superstructure was clean, the cost of doing that and then putting it all back...

No, that was better to be avoided.

"Pulling back, thrusters only." She said through gritted teeth.

That was a risk as well, since to withdraw directly she would need to fire thrusters that were aimed directly *at* the enemy ship. In their current state, there wasn't a chance this side of hell that they would miss that.

The Empire were bastards. Evil bastards in many cases... but they were *not*, unfortunately, *stupid* evil bastards.

Instead she fired thrusters that were aimed just off from the Imperial Cruiser, adjusting them on the fly, which resulted in a slowly increasing orbit away from the bigger ship.

*Which is great and all, but that means I might just be flying us **through** the Drasin swarm. **Fuck.***

"Passive imagery of the ship, Skipper. Check this out."

An image appeared in her peripheral view, out of the line of her sight directly so it would distract her while she was focused on the task at hand. When Cardsharp had a moment she flicked her eyes over, then back, and then over again to star for a moment.

"What the hell?"

*****

IC *From The Flames*

"Pressure loss, Dorsal decks, Ship's Commander!"

Kaela gripped the arm of her command station in frustration. They'd been throwing everything they had into the void, and wiping out the targets by the *hundreds* but they kept coming.

*They can't be what they look like. They **can't**.*

She desperately wanted that to be true, but everything she was seeing matched the classified briefing she had received upon promotion to Ship's Commander on certain dangers that exist beyond the void.

The Drasin were one of those dangers, albeit a very nearly mythical one. She'd wondered why bother with a briefing on such an unlikely threat, but had sat through it all despite that, and now wondered just what she *hadn't* been told.

Regardless, however, it didn't matter for the moment.

"Issue weapons to security, dispatch people to the access points to the affected decks," She ordered. "Orders are to *kill* all boarders. Confirm."

"Confirmed orders, Kill all boarders, Ship's Commander."

"Good. Enact."

"Enacting."

"Yseb," She snapped, coming to her feet.

"Yes, Ship's Commander!"

"Pivot us into the swarm," She ordered grimly. "Full power to the warp field. Reverse the rear warp to match forward intensity."

He twisted, staring at her in stark incredulity.

"Sh… ship's Commander, that will…"

"Put an incredible strain on the hull, I am aware. Do it."

"Yseb swallowed, but nodded, "Yes Ship's Commander."

He set to work and in short seconds the *Flames* was sweeping around to face the swarm of monsters drifting toward them. Kaela could first *feel* and then hear the creaking of the hull as the warp field was brough to full power with wells forming *both* fore and aft of the ship.

This resulted in a gravitational shearing force that attempted to tear the ship apart right down the middle, but it *also* put a near *singularity* between them and the Drasin.

Kaela sneered in satisfaction as the scanners showed the *beasts* being sucked into the forward well where they were crushed together by the warp field.

Good riddance.

"Pressure loss! Doral level two!"

She snapped around, "I gave orders to hold the entry points!"

"Ship's Commander, they didn't come through any of the entry points. They're coming *through* the decks!"

*****

The *Casino*

"Well… that's a thing."

Cardsharp nodded slowly, "It honestly never occurred to me to use a warp field like that."

"Doubt the *Casino* could do it, not without being torn in two, boss."

She nodded absently, "That's a point."

She didn't have any doubts for herself, there was *no chance* her ship would survive if she tried even a hint of that. They'd not built the Archangel class for that type of durability. The ship actually leveraged the fact that, under normal operations, the warpfield actually operated effectively to *nullify* stress on the hull and superstructure.

"Some got on board, though, venting from the dorsal hull is visible."

"Show me."

The imagery moved over and as Cardsharp watched, a hole melted through the tough armor of the Imperial cruiser came into sight. Sure enough, there was plenty of venting there, however what really caught her eye was the fact that more Drasin had landed on the ship and were beelining straight for the hole.

That caught her attention and kept it focused as she watched several more scramble through the hull and into the ship through the hole just because it was so atypical for the Drasin as she knew them.

"Why aren't they making more holes? Eating the hull, and ship, from the outside in like they have before?" She murmured.

Jenn did *not* like it when the enemy changed tactics.

"No clue, boss. They seem to be trying to take the ship intact?" Ray offered with a shrug.

That idea sent a chill down her spine, though Cardsharp couldn't quite figure out why. They certainly would be any more dangerous if they somehow took over an Imperial Cruiser, that was the god's honest truth.

The only reason she could think for the chill was that it *was* such a bit departure from their previous actions.

*I do not like new things from eldritch monsters that **eat planets**, goddamnit.*

"Monitor that closer," She ordered, working to keep the ship clear now from both the Drasin and the Imperial warp fields that were trying to pull everything in close to be crushed by the gravitational flux.

"Aye Ma'am."

"Whatever the fuck they're doing, I don't like it."

*****

IC *From the Flames*

"Security reports contact, Dorsal Deck Three!"

Kaela twisted, "Why wasn't I informed of a breach on deck three!"

"We didn't detect one, Ma'am. No pressure loss."

Kaela paled, considering that.

If the beasts were now sealing their entry points to prevent pressure loss, there was no way to know how far into her ship they had penetrated.

"All crew members are to arm themselves," She ordered, opening a lock box installed in her station and pulling out a sidearm. "Report all contacts with boarders as quickly as practicable, preferably after they're *dead*."

"Yes, Ship's Commander. Crew wide order dispatched."

She nodded grimly, considering the situation more as her head spun with the details.

This is not how the brief suggested the Drasin would act. What has changed?

*****

Within the Imperial Cruiser, the Drones continued to penetrate through the decks, now taking time to preserve the environment as they moved toward their target.

Likely, it wasn't necessary, however the fewer variables that were entered into the operation the better. The loss of the target would be an unacceptable outcome according to *the mind*.

The life filth onboard were unneeded to the *plan*, however, and were dealt with appropriately when contacted despite significant resistance. The beam weapons brought to bear were of little import to the drones, only massed fire could overwhelm their very nature sufficiently to bring any inconvenience, let alone cessation of activity.

The same could not be said of the life filth, however, who fell neatly to the drones in return as beams of photon and other particles cut them apart and left them scattered across the environment with ease, the drones quickly cleaning up the mess to continue to fuel the operation as it moved forward.

The target would be near the center of the ship, though not quite, according to *The Mind*.

That left a certain area to search, which would take time.

That was acceptable. The Drasin were close now. They could wait… a little longer.

*****

CHAPTER 28

The *Casino*

"There's more of them, still slipping in through the same access point," Roy said, "It really looks like they're boarding the ship to take it intact."

"Drasin don't *do* that," Cardsharp insisted, rubbing her face briefly before resuming her careful piloting, trying to keep the ship away from the drifting monsters *and* the scanners of the much larger Imperial vessel. "What is their endgame here? I don't like this."

"What's to like?" Roy asked, shrugging. "Aside from the Empire getting a little of their own medicine, I suppose?"

"Karma is a fine thing, but I have a bad feeling that the Empire is just getting a taste ahead of the game," Jenn said, "and if we don't figure this out… we'll be eating the same damn dish soon enough."

Roy sighed, "I can't disagree, boss, but what's the play? If we do *anything* we let the Empire *and* the Drasin know that we're here."

Jenn laughed bitterly, "No. If we do anything, we let the *Empire* know we're here. The Drasin? They already know. We're in the middle of a gravity detection system the size of a *Solar System*, there's no chance that they aren't tracking us already."

"What are you talking a… oh. Shit."

Cardsharp chuckled freely at the shift in his tone.

"You sound a lot like Weston did, or so I'm told by those few who were present when he realized that exact same thing," She said after a moment. "It came as a nasty surprise, apparently."

"You knew? And you came in here anyway? Are you out of your goddamn *mind* Boss?" Roy exclaimed, staring at her.

"Probably," She nodded. "Whether I am or not doesn't change the facts, though. We *need* to know."

"Oh I don't like the look on your face…"

Cardsharp raised an eyebrow, "Lock and load, Roy. Tell the boys that we're going to war."

"Fuck me." He whispered before turning back to the console. "Alright, we're ready to fight. Beams charged, secondary Beam Capacitors… charged. Tertiary Capacitors charged. What about special weapons?"

"Arm them," She ordered, "But secure the systems. Fire only on my order."

"Aye Ma'am."

"Tell the powder monkeys to be ready for potential damage," She ordered. "I do *not* want to have to kick their asses in the afterlife because we lost containment. Clear?"

"Crystal."

"Alright… going hot in three… two…" She said, her voice dropping. "One."

*****

IC *From the Flames*

"Ship's Commander, we've lost contact with Dorsal Five. Dorsal Six is reporting beam flash from multiple sources."

Kaela gritted her teeth.

*Five decks lost, and I can't even be certain that we're inflicting any damage on the… attackers at all. This is **impossible!** The Empire doesn't fall like this! It doesn't **happen!***

"New swarm detected, they're closing along our most efficient exfiltration path, Ship's Commander!"

"Beam! Retarget to the new contacts," She ordered, swinging to observe the screens that showed the swarm. "Fire on my..."

She was shocked into silence a moment later when a blazing net of beam fire from blow the *Flames* aft quarter tore through the targets, slagging them into molten puddles that conglomerated into wobbling spheroids from the surface tension of the material in seconds.

"New contact! Profile match, it's one of the Free Stars' Mercenary groups, Ship's Commander," Sunnam said, sounding shocked.

She didn't blame him.

"Which one?"

"The Gaians, Ship's Commander. It's one of the pocket Destroyers."

Gaians... Kaela had heard of them but had never had reason to come into contact with the group.

They had excellent reputations, and not merely for mercenaries. Even in Imperial circles it was whispered that if they took a job, it got done. Clean, and no questions asked. The difficulty lay in getting them to accept a task, which was rather the polar opposite of most mercenary groups she knew.

Of course, The Gaian's had been around for a lot longer than most mercenary groups too, and their success had actually caused several other groups in the Free Stars to imitate their standards.

Not that there was every any shortage of the less discriminating type, she knew.

What are they doing here?

"Comm hail, Ship's Commander. From the Gaian vessel."

Kaela nearly snorted.

Of course it would be from them, who else?

Aloud, however, she merely nodded, "Put the signal through."

"Yes, Ship's Commander."

In an instant she was facing the visage of the Gaian Ship's Commander, or so she presumed. The woman had dark hair and was plastered with sweat, looking like she'd just finished a rather extreme workout.

Kaela had to reconsider that thought when the woman appeared to shift quickly, something about her motion looking fast and made with effort despite her not actually *moving* on the screen at all.

*Almost like she's working out **now**?* Kaela thought, confused. *In the middle of a fight? How bizarre.*

"I am ship's Commander Kaela Eurydice," She said. "Who am I addressing?"

"Captain Samuels, you can call me Cardsharp," The woman answered quickly, still in motion. "You appear to be having a bit of an issue here, Ship's Commander."

"Indeed… but how is it that you came to be here yourself?" Kaela asked tensely.

"We were following you," The *Captain* told her simply.

"Pardon me," Kaela demanded, uncertain if she'd heard that correctly.

"We were following you," The Captain repeated, smirking slightly. "Are your Comms intact?"

"I heard you fine, *Captain*," Kaela snapped. "I was merely giving you a chance to provide another reason that didn't involve *spying* on an Imperial vessel. I had heard that you Gaians don't take contracts against the Empire."

"We don't take *combat* contracts that involve the Empire," The woman answered, "Keeping an eye on Imperial activities is another matter, but for the moment I believe we have more pressing issues to deal with."

Kaela gritted her teeth, but couldn't disagree with that.

"Agreed," She bit out. "I suppose I should ask why you deign to help us?"

"Had some run ins with these beasts over the years," Cardsharp answered easily. "Never in these numbers, or in a monstrosity like this, but enough to know that they're not to be taken lightly. Can you withdraw?"

Kaela grimaced, "Yes, however we must know what they are doing here!"

"Not going to be able to find out anything if they eat that ship out from under you," the woman told her. "How many are on board?"

Kaela snarled, looking down at her panels, hating that she had to admit what she had to admit.

"I do not know. We have lost five decks... six now," She said. "We cannot track them."

"Rig your systems for thermal," Cardsharp advised. "These things, whatever the hell they are, run hot. Normal life scans won't show a damn thing, but thermal will."

Kaela tipped her head toward Sunnam, who was obviously listening while trying not to be obvious and failing miserably. The Chief nodded quickly and set to work.

"Have them," He said a short while later. "Multiple contacts, moving through the decks. Directing internal security to intercept."

Kaela blew out a breath, hating the fact that she was about to say the words coming to her lips.

"Thank you for the help," She ground out unwillingly.

"Not a problem, no one deserves these beasts," The woman told her, looking straight into her eyes across the screen. "*No one.*"

Kaela felt a chill, but couldn't identify what caused it. Something in the woman's voice, perhaps, but more likely the situation.

"Do you know what their goal is?" Carsharp asked her, almost casually, but the sharp look of intensity in her eyes told a different story.

"They are *beasts*," Kaela snarled. "They have no plan. They run on instinct."

"I've never seen them leave a ship intact as these have," Cardsharps said evenly. "They're myths of the spaceways to most, preying on ships in the outer reaches. Most don't even really think they exist, but my people have dealt with them… and the aftermath they leave. They're leaving your ship *intact*, Ship's Commander. They have a purpose."

"Then they will fail. The Empire will not fall to *beasts*."

The woman paused, her focus going elsewhere for a moment, and Kaela noted a series of beams slag through another group of the beasts before her attention returned, Cardsharp's expression seemingly resigned.

"As you say, Ship's Commander. Would you permit me to dispatch Marines to aid your people in repelling boarders?"

Kaela sucked in a breath, eyes fiercely blazing as she prepared to respond.

Cardsharp cut her off with a wave, "I understand your concerns, Ship's Commander. I would be hard pressed to accept such help myself. Consider it, the offer remains."

Kaela bit back her instinctive response, forcing herself to merely nod.

"Very well," Cardsharp said. "Then shall we finish

cleaning up this mess?"

"Yes. We shall."

The connection went black.

Kaela rose to her feet, eyes on the gleaming vessel beyond her own ship as it blazed fire through the abyss against their enemies.

"Coordinate fire," She ordered. "Clean this space of that *filth*!"

"Yes, Ship's Commander!"

Kaela stood straight, eyes fierce as she glared at the screens, but inside her mind was racing across what felt like a thousand topics all at once.

None of them made any sense or provided for any answers.

*****

The *Casino*

"Surprised you didn't press on sending the Marines, Boss."

Cardsharp twitched her head slightly, "She was going to tell me in no uncertain terms to take a flying leap. If I let her, then her pride would have kept her from asking later."

"Think she's going to need them?"

"Yeah." Cardsharp answered as she through full power into the warp drive, snapping the little ship around in a tight spin that brought their beams onto the next target batch. "The Drasin don't give up, and they are *seriously* intent on getting aboard that damn ship."

The whine and click of the beam capacitors discharging in near constant succession was rapidly becoming an irritant, but with other things on both their minds, the pair put it all out of their minds as far as possible to focus on the situation.

"Don't know about you, Boss," Roy said, "but I didn't read her as lying when she said she didn't know what they were after."

"Yeah. Me neither," Cardsharp admitted. "That worries me."

"More than the rest of this?"

"If the Empire had sent her out here with a purpose, such as *leashing* those fuckers again," Cardsharp said, "Then that might make some sense, but my read was that she was surprised by the whole situation."

"Concur, Boss," Roy agreed.

"In which case, the Drasin aren't after her ship in particular, maybe?" She murmured while flying the gunboat in a tight twist to avoid a swarm while letting their beams slag them to bubbling molten masses. "That worries me more than if they were striking at a specific target, but I don't… I don't know why."

"Don't worry about the bullet with your name on it, worry about the one addressed to 'whom it may concern'?" Roy jokingly asked.

Cardsharp fell silent for a moment.

"Yeah. Yeah, exactly that."

"Boss, I was joking."

"I know, but I think you might be right. Why target that ship? Because it's Imperial? Because it just showed up?" She asked as she flew the gunboat. "If it's a target of opportunity, why break with pattern? They have to be *after* something. We need to find out what."

"Just tell me how, Boss, and I'm right there with you."

"Never a doubt. You'll be the first to know if I work it out." She said, firming up her jaw. "However, in the meantime?"

"Task at hand, right boss?"

"Right you are. Slag these fuckers."

*****

CHAPTER 29

The *Casino*

Now out of stealth, the cool air from the conditioning systems was a balm on Cardsharp's sweat-soaked skin, but the activity and tension she was experiencing was certainly working to keep the sweat pouring out.

"Another swarm, Boss," Roy told her. "To your HUD."

"Got them. Still the small fry," Jenn grunted as she tagged the swarm and cleared beams to engage with a thought and a twitch of the muscles in her hands and fingers. "No sign of their Capitol class units yet."

"A bit odd, don't you think?" Roy asked, sounding concerned.

She didn't blame him. The starship sized versions of the drones were lethal beyond measure and more than capable of standing toe to toe with a Heroic Class Cruiser, or the Priminae and Imperial equivalents, and as such were the *last* damn thing they wanted to see in this situation.

That didn't mean she was *Happy* that they weren't there.

No, it just meant that she was worried about where they actually were and what they were doing.

"We've announced our presence thoroughly, Boss, what's say we go active on scans?" Roy suggested.

"Do it."

The Archangel Class gunboats were packing well over their weight class in many categories, particularly weapons and combat capacity, but part of fighting was being able to find your targets and so the designers hadn't skimped in scanners either.

Roy brought up the full sensor suite and through everything they had through the system, starting with a wideband FTL pulse that would illuminate everything within the sphere in short order.

Cardsharp twisted the *Casino* through space to avoid a group of the alien drones before they could get purchase on the smaller ship in the meantime, tagging them as they passed for the beams to take care of.

Being in a smaller vessel like the Archangel was a bit of a mixed blessing in this regard, she knew well. The size made them *much* harder to target, especially for low maneuverability drifting drones the likes of which the Drasin were currently deploying. The flipside of that, however, was that if any of them *did* get on board, the damage they'd cause would be well out of proportion to their size.

Archangels had *far* too much technology packed in as densely as possible, and even with redundancies there were limits to how much of a beating you could take when you were small.

"No hits of larger contacts within the sphere," Roy spoke up. "We look to be clear…"

"Don't believe it for a second," She countered. "If they're not in space, then they're parked inside parts of the construct, or hiding in the shadow of the shell somewhere. We're just not important enough for them to deploy… for some reason."

Roy nodded grimly, "I'm going to scan the Jupiter Brain, see what it's hiding, if I can."

"Roger that."

*****

IC *From the Flames*

"The Gaian vessel is performing high level combat scans," Sunnam said, a hint of surprise in his tone. "Impressive sophistication for a Free Stars *mercenary* group."

Kaela nodded, "So it is said. Imperial Intelligence believe them to be a defector squad from one of the higher tier polities, a group that fled with prototype vessels, most likely. Which one, we have not identified to my knowledge, but likely one that lost one of the many wars the Free Stars are known to fight."

"I am uncertain that I would like to be forced to engage whoever *won* that war, in that case," Sunnam said, jokingly but with feeling nonetheless.

Kaela hummed in partial agreement, but she knew that the upper levels of technology in a culture were not a particularly good measure of the *average* levels that existed.

If a polity invested fortunes into developing new technology, but were only able to deploy a handful of ships while the majority of their military wallowed in obsolete and ruined equipment from decades past... well, even a much lesser force on paper could likely take them in a serious fight.

"Do we have any indications of what they are scanning for?"

"Initial omnidirectional pulse, followed by a more directed beam that we're only catching the edges of," Sunnam said. "I believe that is directed at the anomalous object."

That didn't surprise her, either one actually.

"Cleared the area, looking for more opposition, and now they're investigating the likely source of the beasts then," She said. "Leave them to it so long as they continue to fight."

"Of course, Ship's Commander."

"Yseb, keep us clear of the swarms," She moved on.

"Working on it, Ship's Commander, but they just keep coming!" The beleaguered helmsman said plaintively. "And they're maneuvering. It is making it difficult to thread paths that avoid their approach."

"Just do as I say," She growled, again shifting. "Reports from security?"

"They're falling back again, Ship's Commander," Bekram Orram responded instantly. "The enemy are nearly impervious to our shipboard beams. It's taking massed fire to put one down, and by the time that works, the rest have cut our teams to shreds."

Kaela hissed, clenching a fist up tightly and slamming it down into a nearby console.

"Dispatch more teams. Put beams into every crewmember's hands if necessary, we *must* stop them. How far have they penetrated."

"The Dorsal decks are now theirs," Orram confirmed the worst, "They're now spreading through the central decks."

Kaela's face soured like she'd bitten into something truly unpalatable.

Left unsaid in that report was the fact that the Command Deck was centered within the Central Decks.

"Arm yourselves."

*****

The *Casino*

"There's a *lot* of power running through that thing," Roy said, somewhat unnecessarily to Cardsharp's mind.

"It's a Dyson Construct, Roy, that's precisely what they're built for."

"Realize that, boss, but I'm pretty sure I'm looking at a *massive* computer program, live processing."

"You think you can decode it?" She asked sharply, the intensity shedding off her in waves.

"Unknown. Not my specialty," Roy said. "I've got a couple people working on it, but we're not really built for intel work like this."

"Understood. Do what you can, record everything though," She ordered with a smirk, "I know someone back on Prometheus who'd give his left nut to have a shot at cracking that... and he'd probably do it to."

"Do what? Crack it, or give his left nut?"

"Yes."

Roy snorted, but left it at that as he continued to work.

Jenn, for her part, put that aspect out of her mind for the moment. She had more pressing matters to deal with at the moment.

*****

IC *From the Flames*

Kaela ordered the command deck locked down, but didn't know how long the security protocols would hold against the beasts that now prowled the corridors beyond the deck's secure doors. Her beam weapon was gripped in a sweaty hand, though she refused to acknowledge the fear coursing through her at the moment.

"Security reports contact just outside the Command Deck, Ship's Commander," Orram told her tensely.

She nodded, not trusting herself to speak.

Hand Beams were quiet weapons, so there was no sound of the fighting through the bulkheads that she could discern, but her imagination filled it in for her.

Alien shrieking, scrabbling of hard carapace against the deck, the subtle whine of the beams discharging... the screams as the men were cut down.

Keala hesitated only briefly before she returned to her station, "Give me a channel to the Gaian vessel."

"Yes, Ship's Commander."

*****

Cardsharp was surprised when she saw the hail, but automatically accepted and directed it to her HUD.

"Yes, Ship's Commander?" She asked professionally while the majority section of her mind was tagging another group of the never ending alien menaces for the Archangel's beams to deal with.

"Ship's Commander Samuels," The blond woman was speaking through gritted teeth, which told Cardsharp all she needed to know.

A flick of her fingers opened up a shared link to Colonel Keenan, who popped up on a separate channel, listening in but wisely remaining silent.

"Ship's Commander," Cardsharp said, "I would consider it a great favor if you allowed my Marines to help secure your decks. Your vessel is too powerful for us to lose in this fight if my people are to escape this alive."

The Imperial Commander paused, processing that, and slowly nodded.

"Yes, I… can see that. Very well, Ship's Commander. I will allow you to provide aid."

"Thank you, Ship's Commander. I will dispatch people as quickly as possible. Was there anything else?"

Unsurprisingly, the Imperial Commander shook her head.

"No, no I do not believe so."

"Then I will leave you to your duties, Ship's

Commander," Cardsharp said, letting the signal go quiet a moment later, after which she turned to Keenan. "You heard?"

"Yes Ma'am. Suited up and ready to go."

"Clean that ship, Colonel," Cardsharp ordered, "But try to find out what the *hell* the Drasin are after while you do."

"Understood. Keenan out."

*****

"Move it! Launch positions," The Sarge said, browbeating the squad into motion as Amanda listened, checking her own gear for the fifth time as she shuffled into place for her turn along with the rest.

The team was a well oiled group, thankfully, and needed little input from her as they got ready for the deployment.

My first combat deployment and we're going to go against the Drasin... This is insane.

Insane or not, however, it didn't appear to be a dream... or nightmare, more appropriately, as much as she wished for either.

The Marines swung themselves into the launch tubes, basic MMU systems strapped to their power armor. Being thrown out across the black with nothing more than a few gallons of reactant fuel and their initial vector between them and a *long* trip through the black had somehow become the *norm* to them.

Amanda wasn't quite there yet, and the shaking of her arms told that tale all too effectively.

"Relax, Lieutenant," The Sarge said quietly through his unsealed helmet as he took up the space at her side. "Be right with you the whole way."

She nodded gratefully, but remained silent.

"Vectors are usually good without alteration," He said,

"so don't use the MMU unless you absolutely have to. We usually dump them, still fully loaded, on the exterior hull."

"Got it, Sarge."

"Watch your gravity sensor, though, that ship has its warp fields up," The Sergeant went on. "Don't get sucked into either field, they'll pulp you in your armor like squeezed fruit juice."

"Thank you, Sarge." She said, somewhat more acerbically.

He just grinned at her.

"You've got this, Ma'am."

Glaring at him, she nodded and refocused.

I've got this.

"Next group!"

Amanda was the first in, sliding feet first into the tube, only pausing to look back at the rest, upsidedown from her perspective.

"Well, what are you lot waiting for? Those fucks ain't gonna kill themselves!"

With that she slid the rest of the way in and everything went dark.

*****

CHAPTER 30

The *Casino*

"Watch your eight low, boss, swarm inbound."

Cardsharp swore, hitting the warp field hard to pop the gunboat over the swarm, noting that they tried correcting to intercept but failed to maneuver as quickly as her ship was capable of.

"Looks like they've taken note of our presence, finally," She said as she dropped back down into the previous vector after the threat had passed. "How many swarms are we tracking now?"

"Too many," Roy snorted, but checked the numbers anyway, "At least fifteen so far, no individual count on the drones themselves... and that doesn't count the ones pulverized by the Imperial warp field, or slagged by either of our beams."

"Of course it doesn't," She said dryly. "Alright, good watching out. Stay on it. I'm going to get the Marines lined up."

"Aye Skipper."

Cardsharp had seen a lot of things in her time, she'd been recruited by the Confederation military right at the tail end of the last war on Earth worthy of the name, wanting nothing more than a slot with the *legends* themselves at a time when they were shutting down the Archangel program entirely in favor of more mundane fighter craft.

That wasn't to be her fate, however, and through work, preparation, and finally a lucky break... she got her ride.

And it all led me here, Jenn thought with grim amusement as she got the ship into place. *Somehow it feels like the universe doesn't just have a sense of the perverse, but positively wallows in it.*

She had work to do, however, and her eye flicked aside as she saw the vectors start to line up.

"Alright Marines, time to go out and play," She called over the comm. "Green Vector, say again, Green vector!"

"Roger Green Vector," Keenan called back. "Squad one, launching. Squad two, you're up next, get ready."

The fighter/gunboat shuddered as the magnetic launch system catapulted *people* out into space, leaving Cardsharp to again wonder at the universe's sense of the perverse and where it had brought her.

Ultimately, though, it really didn't matter that much.

After all, she knew all too well that her own sense of the perverse was *at least* as deep.

*****

The Cat launcher felt like a kick between the shoulder blades, but it was a sensation Amanda was well used to dealing with. Training had *sucked*, of course, but it had gotten her used to the beatings she'd have to deal with in the Marines.

Everything blurred around her briefly, and then it all went *shockingly* still as the confines of the launch tube were replaced by open space. She felt her guts rebel for a moment at the disconnect between what her eyes claimed was happening and what her body knew to be true.

She got a firm grip on the sensation, though, because puking in a breathing unit was *heavily* discouraged in training. If you couldn't control that reflex, you washed out. Period.

The startling immobility of the black around her took a toll though, making it hard to tell that she was still moving as it all felt too still around her to be real. That was merely an illusion of parallax, however, the distances to everything in her line of sight were so large that no matter how fast she was moving, she couldn't get any sense of motion.

Focus on the target.

The Imperial cruiser was hanging there ahead of them, barely visible at the current range, with only the light of the distant white dwarf and the Infrared illumination of the Super Jupiter sized beast out there reflected off it. It was growing larger, however, and she got a sense of movement again by focusing only on that for the moment.

The comms were silent, as was procedure she knew, but Amanda trusted that her squad was close as they flew in to the target, crossing the void with little more than faith in the crew of the *Casino*'s aim, and the small Manned Maneuvering Units limited reactant to keep them on target.

The insanity of it was like a drug, Amanda realized, as she started grinning at some point through the flight. She wondered if this was what the early airborne units felt like, jumping out of perfectly good aircraft all for a tactical advantage?

It felt good, realizing that link, that connection to legends of the past.

Her reveling in that sensation nearly cost Amanda, however, as she nearly missed the sudden increase in size of the target, and realized that the ride was almost over.

Approach vector... looks good, ok, don't need to maneuver. Hands off the control overrides, She thought, calming the spike of panic that had for an instant threatened to stage a coup against her mental state.

In the last hundred meters, her armor fired the MMU thrusters, spinning her sharply in space to put her feet down to the imperial ship, then a short burst slammed her down into the boots of her armor right before contact.

She flexed her legs on landing anyway, hearing the massive gong like clang conduct through her boots and up into her armor as she landed in a crouch before slowly rising back to her feet.

Imperial ships use magnetic hulls, unlike the Prim, She reminded herself as she stuck there. *All secure.*

A flash of light caught her eye and she turned to see another Marine jerked upright by his thrusters, then *hammer* down into the deck hard enough to make her wince. She was surprised when he easily rose back to his feet, though.

Did I hit that hard? It didn't feel like it, but...

Amanda didn't know, honestly, it was hard to tell sometimes when you were *inside* the suit exactly how hard, fast, and such you were actually doing things. From the outside it always just looked *painful*, though.

The Marine glanced in her direction and she held up a fist while looking around. He signaled back that he'd gotten the message and dropped to one knee, moving to cover the perimeter while she looked around to see several more Marines burn their thrusters hard just before hitting the hull.

Amanda got their attention one by one, circling her right hand in the vacuum with two fingers straight and visible. The Marines took the command quickly and circled her position, covering the perimeter as well as the sky, while the Sergeant stomped over to her in the peculiar way one did while using magnetic boots.

Once in close, she painted his armor with a low powered comm beam. Not quite a laser, but focused enough to remain coherent over a few meters to a few hundred if needed. She had hers tuned down as minimal as possible to ensure that it would be nothing but a weak flashlight to anything that might intercept it more than a dozen meters out.

"Ma'am," He said.

"Is everyone down?" She asked.

"Yes Ma'am."

"Good, let's get everyone moving. We'll use the enemy's access point for ingress," She said. "If I'm reading my charts right, we have a march to get there."

The Sergeant paused for a moment, presumably checking his

own charts, but a moment later his suit bobbed.

"Right you are, Ma'am. Should we perhaps wait for the Colonel, however?"

Amanda considered briefly, but twisted her torso visible in the negative, "No. The other teams will be here shortly, no doubt, but our job is to secure the LZ. Watch for Deltas as we move, make sure everyone knows to flatline those fucks on sight... but also to make *sure* of their targets. We have friendlies inbound, no one shoots the Colonel, right?"

The Sergeant's tone was amused, "That would be a bad thing, yes Ma'am."

"Let's move."

*****

IC *From the Flames*

The sound of fighting had faded from outside the sealed command deck, along with communications with anyone in the immediate area beyond the security doors, leaving Kaela little doubt as to the fate of her security teams.

She handled the weapon in her hand nervously, eyes flicking to the doors every few seconds but there was little to nothing that she could do about things which, of course, only made things worse.

"Do we have anything from the other side?" She asked Sunnam.

"No, Ship's Commander. The corridor scanners were disabled, either from the fighting or by the enemy," The chief responded, his tone even but with the same undercurrent of nerves that she knew she too had.

"Understood. Eyes on the void then," She ordered. "We don't need anymore invaders if it can be avoided.

"Yes, Ship's Commander."

*****

Amanda lowered her rifle, if you could call it that, to the ready position from her shoulder. She hadn't needed to fire, the rest of the squad had turned the inbound Deltas to shards with short bursts the moment they'd been spotted, and nothing more than a rain of molten material spattered down around them.

She held up a closed fist a moment later, then shifted to a flat palm that she swept forward.

The signal was repeated a few times from Marine to Marine before they got moving together, but that only took a couple seconds.

She spotted the ingress breach up ahead a moment later, holding up a flat palm for a moment before looping her finger in circles.

The Sergeant repeated the signal a second later and the Marines got moving, surrounding the hole and securing the position.

Once they were in position, she ensured that the team was in range and wide pulsed her beam comm, ensuring that everyone was included. Again, beyond a dozen more meters or so, it would only be a weak narrow frequency bit of noise to any would be listeners.

"We secure this point and wait for the Colonel and the others," She ordered. "Watch the skies. Confirm your targets, but don't hesitate to drop them."

"Hoorah."

The melding of voices that responded sounded both odd and comforting to her as Amanda took up a position near the hole, looking down into it briefly.

"Thoughts, Ma'am?"

Amanda hummed, "Give me two men to watch the hole. I doubt they'll be coming out but..."

The Sergeant bobbed his suit, "Better safe that sorry. Yes Ma'am."

He quickly painted two suits with beams and the chosen Marines moved over to take up position at the hole into the ship.

"Anything moves, frag it," the Sergeant ordered. "Ain't none of ours in there, and doubt any Imps will be bobbing around in the vacuum anyway... if there are, well, we got an excuse, right?"

"Yes Sergeant."

Amanda shot him an amused look that he couldn't *possibly* have seen, but the sergeant seemed to know it somehow as he painted her suit with a comm beam.

"No love lost between Marines and the Empire," He shrugged.

"None between any of us and the Empire," She said, not telling him to change his orders.

She highly doubted it would come down to it, since the odds of the Empire having men crawling out of a hole in their hull into hard vacuum were somewhat less than the chances of her sprouting wings and flying impossibly around the airless void. Still, it did bring to mind something important.

"Just remember, once we're on board, no one has any *accidents*," She told the Sergeant sternly. "We're not Terrans here, we're *Gaians*, and the Gaians have no quarrel with the Empire. Right?"

"Right you are, Ma'am," The Sergeant told her, her tone of voice *almost* sounding like someone praising a particularly cute puppy for doing something clever.

It chafed on her, but there wasn't much she could say about the man's tone, and his words had been entirely correct and respectful.

So she just nodded in response and settled in to wait.

*****

"LZ secured, Colonel."

Keenan looked up, noting the Marines at the entrance point to the big ship and nodded.

"New Lieutenant's squad?"

"Yes Ma'am."

The new butterbar seems to know her stuff, Keenan thought with satisfaction, *Or at least knows to listen to her non-com... which is the same thing at that rank, honestly.*

Either way she was pleased not to have a fuckup on site, such things always made her irritated after a mission, and none of her people enjoyed it when she was irritated in that way.

"Alright, get the portable airlock into place," She ordered, continuing her march to the target.

"Yes Ma'am."

They got there a few moments later, the perimeter security parting to let them through.

Keenan bobbed her suit to greet the young officer standing there, waving on the engineer team at the same time as they got an inflatable airlock into place and triggered it a moment later. The tough carbon fiber construct looked like nothing more than a pool toy as it inflated and was maneuvered into place, a fast curing liquid sealant being sprayed around its base.

"Alright, this won't hold off the enemy, but it'll make it easier as we access in deeper," She said or local beam comm, "Assuming we can keep it intact that is. Michaels, take your squad through, secure the other side. Stay in contact, use radio comms. The Imperials don't monitor those frequencies, but even if they do notice it's not an issue."

"Hoorah, Ma'am."

Keenan bobbed toward the lock.

"Be about it then."

*****

CHAPTER 31

Captured Destroyer

Eric Michaels was trying not to look jumpy as he stood watch, now back at Ops once more as the Chief took the shift at the Helm.

They'd been *screaming* through space since they'd decoded the flash traffic from the *Casino*, but it still felt like they'd been crawling the entire time. Free Star space was well behind them, the very edge of the Galactic arm was looming, but even at full military power there was only so much space that could be crossed in the time they'd had.

The Captain had the maintenance team running overtime, keeping the reactors from flying apart and that was at least one area that they had a solid and experienced team ready to handle if nothing else. Eric couldn't help but be more concerned about the command team, of which he considered himself to be the weakest link, but even discounting his presence at Ops, they were light on experience and *still* flying headlong into a likely fight with some of the most dangerous things ever encountered by humanity.

Despite that, no one... least of all himself... was questioning it.

"Target coordinates within a few lightyears now, Skipper," The Chief announced.

"Understood. Ops, Let's step up passive scans, I want the sensor mast right to the edge of the bubble," Reid ordered. "No surprises, clear?"

"Aye sir," Eric confirmed as he adjusted the system. "No surprises."

Running any sort of scans from within a warp ship was a difficult process at the best of times. The warp field bent spacetime in order to propel the vessel forward at effective FTL speeds, however those same fields *also* bent spacetime such that almost no particulates down to *photons* could effectively pierce through the warp to be picked up on sensors.

This was a great thing for keeping radiation from cooking the crew, micro-meteors from putting holes through everything until the ship looked like swiss cheese, and other safety issues... however it rather made *seeing* a difficult proposition at the best of times while at high warp when the twisting of spacetime was at its maximum.

The solution to that was to extend an incredibly durable mast *through* the warp, *almost* to the edge.

Almost being the key phrase.

If the mast penetrated the warp and extended out into the unwarped region of space, it would no longer be *technically* moving at FTL but rather it would *actually* be moving at FTL. This was a fundamentally bad situation, given that anything with mass that was moving at lightspeed would have all of the energy converted to mass instantly... essentially, for the tiniest fraction of a second, massing as much as the entire universe, at least theoretically.

Suffice to say that wasn't a tenable situation for the mast the sensor was mounted on, no matter how durable.

Horror stories abounded in the Free Stars of misaligned sensors that just vaporized ships when they were extended too far.

All apocryphal, of course, because there was no chance of anyone ever surviving such an event if it did occur. However, since no one had ever survived such an incident to his knowledge, and the math made it clear that this was a bad thing, Eric was generally willing to accept the stories as true until proven otherwise.

Most ships flew blind, trusting their charts and the warp itself to protect them from anything they might encounter. Military vessels had other options, but the majority of tactical operations were conducted at medium to high *sublight* velocities, and those warps could be fairly easily compensated for, so even most military ships he knew of just didn't run the risk.

However, they had the *option*, and on occasion... like now...

were called upon to exercise it.

So he *carefully* moved the mast forward, millimeter by millimetre, while observing the readings he was getting back through the Mast's hardline to ensure that he didn't overshoot. Once he was close to the very edge of the field and was seeing a reasonably clear image beyond, he stopped and relaxed marginally.

"Mast extended, telemetry to the board," He said.

"Thank you, Lieutenant, on the primary if you please," Reid ordered.

"Telemetry up."

There wasn't much to see, honestly. Interstellar space was like that with only about one atom of hydrogen per cubic centimeter and far less of anything else.

"Localize the target."

"Aye sir," Eric said, highlighting the coordinates on screen.

Noting appeared at all.

"Scan for thermal, adjust for blue shift."

"Aye," Eric said, fingers splaying out on a touch sensitive panel as he slowly twisted them, bringing the frequency down from where it was, way up past ultraviolent, compensating for the doppler effect as he slid it down through the visible spectrum, and finally to the infrared.

That was when it appeared.

Someone on the Command Deck swore, and Eric though it might have been the Captain, but wasn't sure. He wanted to himself, but really wasn't that comfortable in his own skin for the moment.

The massive ball out there, cut from the black sky, couldn't be missed if you had the right eyes... and they had them in spades at the moment.

"Well, ain't that a thing," Reid said after a moment. "Shame we'll have to bust it up."

*****

Gaia's Revenge

Steph fought back the urge to hurl with the experience of someone long used to dealing with the Transition drive.

Technically he probably shouldn't have used the Tachyon Transition Drive, given that they knew that the Empire had at *least* confirmed that Terran vessels had some form of near instantaneous travel between the stars before the fall of Earth, but at the moment he didn't care.

The Nest could censure him if they wanted, hell they could even take his command for all he cared. There was a nice patch of land on a Priminae world with his family's name on it anytime he cared to ask, and everyone knew it.

His daughter mattered more than any of that.

"Damn," Tyke gagged, wiping drool from his mouth. "I'd forgotten how much that *sucked*."

Steph snorted.

Being broken down into the Tachyon equivalent of your composite particles and instantly jumping across lightyears was a little hard on the constitution of many.

"Pussy," He said aloud, shooting his second a wry look.

"Get bent, poser brat," Tyke shot back.

Despite the tension in him, Steph chuckled easily as he checked their position.

"Right on," He said with satisfaction. "Switching to thermal… let's find us a target."

"You got it, Boss," Tyke said as he made some adjustments.

It didn't take long, the thermal bloom off the Dyson construct couldn't be missed if you tried, presuming you were on the right frequency.

"Yeah. Can't say I ever wanted to see something like that again," Steph breathed out.

He heard a sound from behind him and twisted, spotting Milla as she stared at the screen with a haunted expression that held a tinge of fear he'd never seen her show before, not even when they were honestly terrified… and both of them had been more times than he could recall.

"She'll be fine, love," He swore.

"You cannot promise that," Milla told him, though she offered up a weak smile to offset the rebuke.

"No, I suppose I can't, but I can promise I'll do everything I can to make it true," He said, nodding to one of the side stations. "If you would?"

"It would be… not a pleasure," She admitted, "not this time, I am afraid, but…"

She shook her head, but then just silently crossed the space and slipped into the cramped section of the gunship that controlled the direct access to their scanners and weapons.

"I get it," He told her. "I wish you were back on the Nest, you know… but I don't know anyone else I'd want at that station right now either. Complicated."

Milla nodded, "Yes. Complicated. A good word."

Steph smiled at her briefly, then turned back to the situation.

"Alright, we're moving on approach. Sound General Quarters, and rig for silent."

"Aye skipper," Tyke responded. "Sounding General. Rigging for silent running. Camplates shifting to black hole settings, all transmissions secured, IFF disabled. We're dark and quiet."

Steph stepped into the suspension field, lifting off the deck as he felt the ship's passive scanners feed in through his nerve endings. The heat from the big beast of a construct was like a warm summer sun on his skin as he leaned into it and sent the ship hurtling forward.

"They'll spot us the second we cross the boundary," He warned, "Our warp field and mass will give our position away once we're inside that thing, so watch for them to setup an ambush."

"Eyes peeled, boss man. Don't worry."

"My job to worry," Steph said with a grin, "your job is to put up with me."

"I believe that would be Milla's job, actually," Tyke countered with a laugh.

Milla glanced up, a hint of a smile wafting on her lips, "It is a difficult one too, very long hours."

"Be a ship's Captain they said," Steph rolled his eyes. "You'll be respected they said... liars, the bunch of them. Alright, let's do this."

*****

Bellerophon

"Transition drive disengaged, Captain."

Roberts nodded, not showing his discomfort. He'd always hated that system, no matter how useful it was. Warp travel was slower, of course, but by far preferable under most circumstances to his mind.

"Thermal bloom located, hoo man, yeah that's a big boy."

"On screen."

The Dyson construct filled up the screen an instant later, bringing Roberts back over *forty years* in a brief flash. He actually looked over to his right, expecting to see Eric Weston there in the command chair of the Odyssey for a split second before reality reasserted itself and he shook himself to clear the memory.

"Take us in," He ordered.

"Stealth settings, Sir?"

Roberts shook his head, "No point. They'll spot a warp as big as ours a long way out, if they haven't already, and once we're inside? You can track a mote of dust inside that thing by it's gravity signature. White Knight settings, sound the alarms. Bell, we're going to war."

"Yes, Captain," The entity known as Bellerophon responded as the ship filled with claxons. "We march."

They began to move, the massive construct growing larger on the screens, constantly threatening to grow past the screen's size, forcing them to back off the zoom level in a constant smooth action.

Blazing white armor announced their approach, as the Bellerophon marched upon the enemy, banners unfurled and all but actively taunting the enemy with their presence.

*****

Prometheus Facility

Aiden Pierce was having a rather... active day.

The Flashtraffic from the *Casino* had truly set the foxes amongst the chicks, as it were, and the moment the Drasin announcement had been made he'd been forced to deal with everything from fear among the populace, to volunteers wanting a ship, *any ship*, to go fight the bastards.

He, being ever the opportunist, seized on that second group and got them signed up fast and intro training.

Over the years, they'd run into a problem he believed could be called *ennui*. The feeling of wondering whether there was really any point to doing something.

They couldn't strike at the Empire, not really. They could burn the planets to cinders, of course. Promethus' gravity lens, coupled with the Transition technology, would allow that... but wholesale slaughter of innocents, even Imperial innocents, didn't sit well with anyone.

The Empire had been effectively decapitated by Prometheus' own action in the final hours of the invasion. Many had wondered why they didn't do it sooner, but he knew that they hadn't because it wouldn't have *done anything*.

The Empire, after the strike, was just as strong as it had been before the strike. Merely... under new leadership. Hitting their true power, the ships, as well as the men and women who commanded them, was a monumentally harder task than striking at worlds whose positions had been carefully pre-plotted.

And thus many people had been left to wallow in the grief that flooded them all in the aftermath, with little true outlet to focus it into. Grief turned to despondency, and that into depression.

They'd lost so many to suicide in the few years that followed the invasion that it didn't bear thinking on.

Now, though, Aiden could see the fire in the eyes of people who'd been moving day to day by rote up to this point.

The Drasin may be monsters, but a monster could save your soul... if he played this just right.

*****

Ranquil

"Admiral?"

The slight nature of the man in the room might have confused people when compared to his reputation amongst his people, but for him it had never been a deserved reputation anyway so he largely ignored it while he served and since.

"No longer," Rael said wearily as he rose to his feet and turned to face the speaker, a young pup who likely hadn't even been in the forces before he himself had left them.

"Priority message for you, Sir," The boy said simply. "From the Elders."

Rael Tanner snorted, "For me? They've not had much use for me in some time. Why now?"

"I was not informed. The message is encoded."

Rael scowled, but finally acquiesced and crossed the room to take the message. The encoding was to his genome, unsurprisingly, and unsealed shortly after he touched the device. Rael glanced pointedly at the young officer, who stepped back out a bit while he turned his focus to read the missive.

Halfway through he stopped and just stared for a long quiet moment.

Finally he shifted his thumb, shredding the message irrevocably, as he rose up to his full height which was quite a bit shorter than the young officer there.

"Bring the skimmer around," Admiral Tanner ordered. "I'll work on the way to Central."

EVAN CURRIE

*****

CHAPTER 32

IC *From the Flames*

Amanda controlled her descent through the hull of the ship with a hand on the line they'd tossed down ahead of them, the strength of the armor servos allowing her to deal with the rapidly increasing gravity curve as she breached the armor and dropped through the outer shielding and into the deck below.

Corporal Jan Smith was there ahead of her, along with the Sarge, securing the perimeter in as much as they could as she dropped to the deck and quickly cleared the route for the next one in.

"Report," She ordered simply, her rifle... if one could call it that, coming up to the low ready as she surveyed the deck around them.

It was a wide corridor, the lighting still intact despite the evacuated nature of the environment. There were no bodies to be seen, but her spectrometers detected iron and copper in the spattered stains that marked several sections of the deck and bulkheads.

Imps fought from the looks of it, but I bet they didn't last long against those things with explosive decompression sucking the air out of their lungs at the same time as the attack. Well, no one ever said the Imps were cowards. Bastards, yes, cowards? No.

"Area secure as it can be," The Sarge told her simply. "Can't promise anything beyond the curves of the corridor, though.

Amanda nodded curtly, bobbing her entire suit to convey the message. The Imperial cruiser was built to largely identical specifications as the Priminae cruisers as well as the Terran's own Heroic Class ships. Made sense, of course, since they all used the same effective blueprints, albeit with major alterations in the case of the Heroic Class and later generation Priminae cruisers.

After the first invasion of Earth, the Priminae and Confederation governments instituted a wide scale tech sharing, in which Earth got the plans and means to produce the Heroics, and the Priminae received Tachyon Transition technology among other bits of divergent technical innovations that Earth had managed to develop independently of the shared Imperial/Priminae tech tree.

So while Heroic class vessels did have major divergences from the Imperial design, few of those were in the general layout.

"Anyone on the squad spent time on a Heroic?" She asked.

"I did, Lieutenant," Corporal Danvers spoke up.

"Alright, Smith, Sergeant, you take point. Danvers, you call the ball. I'll follow your lead," She said, looking around. "The rest of you guys, take drag and cover the rear."

"Hoorah, Lieutenant."

"We need to find the path the Drasin took deeper into the ship," She said. "Orders from on high are to clear the vessel if possible, but our real priority is to determine what the hell the Drasin are up to. Colonel's brief says that they're acting counter to their normal SOP, and that makes the Captain nervous."

She looked around, "Let's calm the skipper's nerves, Hoorah?"

"Hoorah!"

She bobbed her suit once, then checked the access point they'd used, noting that the second squad was dropping down.

"We move out as soon as Second Squad has secured the ingress."

*****

Colonel Keenan observed the Lieutenant in action, using the suit sensors built into the young officer's own suit as well as those of her squad, but didn't make her presence known.

Micromanaging her Marines would only serve to piss them off, and likely get someone killed, and she knew it. Usually she didn't even really like to be looking in on them if she could avoid it, too many things could be taken out of context when viewed through the limited feed of a suit's scanner.

While incredibly detailed in many ways, there was a substantive difference between watching from a remote position and *being* on site. She'd seen people who directed fighting from on high in that way start to treat their own troops like game pieces rather than thinking, breathing, human beings... and the less said about how they treated non-combatants the better.

Decisions should be made on site, not over a computer feed.

With a cherry Lieutenant leading her first squad, however, she was making a bit of an exception. Thankfully, though, she was seeing no reason to step in even if the young officer was making a couple calls she probably wouldn't have made herself.

Despite the brief, it wasn't really the Lieutenant's job to worry about the overall mission objectives. That was Keenan's job, but the Colonel trusted Michaels' Sergeant to keep the little firebrand on target when it counted, and there wasn't anything really wrong with alerting the squad to the overall objectives so long as they didn't lose sight of what was in front of them.

Satisfied with how things were going, Keenan slipped out of the squad's feeds and looked over the situation on the surface of the ship's hull.

The next two squads were ready to move, and then her own team would take up the rear, closing the door behind them with anti-personnel weapons that should make a decent mess of any Drasin that tried to come in the back door behind them.

It wouldn't hold them out indefinitely, or really for very long at all, but it would take out a few of the bastards and give her teams a decent warning to watch their ass in the process.

Needs must, sometimes, she supposed as she waved the next team in.

*****

The *Casino*

"Target on vector to intercept the Cruiser, boss."

"Got them, Roy, good spot," Jenn said as she haloed the targets and passed them to the weapons control officers who were handling the majority of the *Casino's* beams at the moment.

She had a pair of linked ribbon emitters under her control, mostly for close to medium range interception, but preferred to leave the long shot potting of targets to people with less distractions to deal with.

"Special Weapons are hot and ready."

"Tell the powder monkeys to sit on them until I call for the fire," She ordered. "No opening that can of worms unless we have no choice."

"Aye, Ma'am."

Special Weapons was the code term for Antimatter Torpedoes, little balls of hellfire that had to be contained in precision magnetic fields lest they turn *her* ship into a volume of expanding gas and energy large enough to likely inflict some serious harm on the Imperial Cruiser at their current range. They were one of the few weapons that could reliably destroy *anything* they might encounter, but had the disadvantage of being both incredibly dangerous to maintain and practically a signature weapon of the Confederation forces before the second invasion.

If they opened fire with those, she would have to ensure that the Imperial ship went down with the Drasin in the ensuing conflagration.

Not something Jenn was entirely opposed to, frankly, but if she could avoid it she would choose the latter option for the moment.

If the Imperial saw those weapons launched from a 'Gaian' vessel and reported back to Imperial Command, there likely wouldn't be *anywhere* the Archangels could continue to operate in Free Star or Imperial adjacent space.

Losing access to that source of Intelligence was to be avoided if at all possible.

"Colonel reports that her teams are making ingress to the cruiser. They've secured both sides of the access, and are preparing to sweep the inner decks."

She nodded, "Excellent. Now we just have to keep the beasts of their backs."

Roy snorted, "Ask for something hard next time, right?"

"Don't jinx us, Roy."

*****

IC *From the Flames*

Kaela started as a scratching *shriek* could be heard from the other side of the armored bulkhead, and she wondered exactly what was out there trying to get in. Well, part of her did. The logical and rational part of her knew *exactly* what it was, it was just that part of her mind refused to fully process it and insisted that the situation she was in was patently impossible.

She kept a clammy grip on her hand weapon, eyes flicking to the door even as she continued to command the ship in their attempt to keep *more* of the beasts from being able to land.

What are they after? It makes no sense...

Everything she knew about the Drasin was from legend more than anything else, but they were the source of stories that people told to scare children.

Be good and loyal to the Empire or the Drasin will get you. That sort of thing.

They weren't supposed to be *real*!

Normally, she would have been eminently confident that the armored doors between her and the beasts would hold out indefinitely against any sort of assault... but they'd cut through her ship's *hull* in next to no time.

With that in mind, Kaela was honestly more surprised that they weren't already in the ship.

"Sunnam," She said, "Do we have scanners active in the corridors?"

He glanced back hesitantly, but nodded almost against his will.

"To my personal screens," She ordered.

"Yes, Ship's Commander."

Kaela pulled the screen to her as it lit up with the feeds she'd wanted, and in a heartbeat saw the source of tension in her scanner chief's demeanor.

They were swarming outside the Command Deck, dozens of them she though, though it was hard to tell as they moved over and under one another with ease and fluidity, making counting a chore. There were no signs of her security teams, however, other than some suspicious stains on the decks in various places.

*No bodies. Did... did they truly **eat** them?*

The legends described monstrous beasts that devoured *everything*, even entire worlds. That was impossible, of course, but eating her crew was... sadly, well within the realm of possibility. The shudder of disgust she had to suppress was in no way feigned, and Kaela regretted the fate of her people in that moment.

It wasn't time for mourning, however. That time was rarely upon an Imperial Officer to her experience, of course. One did their duty and moved on to do it again when the call from above came down. It was the way of things.

What are they doing? It's like they're... confused? Looking for something?

Kaela didn't know for sure, but there seemed to be an indecision among the beasts beyond the blast doors.

She snorted softly.

Unfortunate that they were not so inflicted earlier.

*****

"Delta down." The Sergeant said firmly as he lowered the smoking barrel of his weapon.

The shot had ablated slightly in the barrel, leaving a superheated residue that expanded rapidly in the vacuum as he'd dropped the target, leaving whisps of white smoke falling from the barrel to the deck below, there being no air for it to float up through.

Amanda moved forward, taking a moment to examine the body of the Drasin drone the Sergeant had dropped.

"Good shot," She said as she took a knee by the body and set her suit's analysis suite on it.

The molten interior of the Drasin fit the records they had on the creatures, however she could see variations that definitely diverged from what she had one file as well.

New variants? Evolution maybe? Amanda thought, shaking her head.

There was no way to tell, unfortunately, so she just logged everything with a priority tag and rose to her feet.

"Corporal, which way to the Command Deck?" She asked.

Danvers hummed, considering, "Straight line or through the decks proper?"

"Straight line."

"Pretty much straight down, Lieutenant," Danvers told her. "Assuming they use the same layout as the Heroics of course. We buried the command deck deep, but not in the center of the ship. That's where the singularity is housed. It'll probably be a few decks up from main engineering, where the reactor is, and several sections forward."

Amanda nodded slowly, "Roger that. Ok, pair up, scout out the deck. Find me where the Drasin cut through to the next level."

"Hoorah."

*****

The *Casino*

Jenn snarled as she triggered her ribbon emitters, lazing a group of the drones that had slipped through their outer perimeter and nearly got in close to the *Casino* without being spotted.

She felt a sensation like being hit with a hot rain as they flew through the molten slag that was left of them, but despite her skin crawling she didn't think any of them had made it to the hull intact.

"That was too damn close," She said aloud, taking a deep

breath.

"Not going to argue there, boss," Roy said. "Sorry. My bad."

"Not your fault, slippery bastards. I'm going to put a little more distance between us and the cruiser, no sense in making it too easy for the fuckers."

Roy nodded, "Makes sense… I think… wait, hold one."

Cardsharp looked over sharply, "What is it?"

"Contacts inbound."

"More swarms?" She asked grimly, her heart pounding.

"Negative. Farther out, and bigger. Shit…" Roy swore. "Enemy Capitol units inbound, hot and heavy, boss."

"Fuck," Cardsharp said succinctly as she reviewed the data, recognizing the profile the scanners were showing.

"Looks like the honeymoon's over," Roy said dryly.

*****

CHAPTER 33

IC *From the Flames*

"New contacts, Ship's Commander! Fast approach vectors, likely readying an attack," Sunnam called.

"Helm, standby to respond."

"Yes, Ship's Commander," Yseb responded.

Kaela was trying very hard not to think too much about what was beyond the blast doors securing the Command Deck as she had a great deal of other issues to deal with and more seemingly piling on, but the scrabbling that could be heard beyond it kept drawing her attention despite those efforts.

What are they doing out there? They should be through the doors by now, Kaela thought, hints of desperation filtering in to her private thoughts even if she did her very best not to show it to anyone around her.

This wasn't how the legends said the beasts acted, and it left her questioning everything about the situation. Was she right about what they were? They *looked* like Drasin, and certainly aspects of what she was seeing matched... but the differences in behavior from legend were *not* minor.

Something had changed, and she didn't know if the change was due to the legends being altered over time, or if it were something about the creatures *themselves* that had changed.

For the moment, however, she had to deal with the problems at hand... whether she was ready for them or not.

"Tracking inbound contacts," Sunnam said. "Vectors sent to weapons control. Mass and profile matches historical reference in our database. They are Drasin combat vessels."

Kaela blinked, "We have those profiles in our database?"

Sunnam nodded, "I was surprised as well, Ship's Commander. The database unlocked them when I ran the scans. They must have been sealed by Imperial Command at some point, but left a means of unsealing them automatically at need."

Kaela nodded slowly.

That makes some sense, She supposed, though she would have preferred a better brief than the computer noticing something was up and feeding her the data at the last *possible* moment.

At least we have proper confirmation now, and are not merely leaning on legends.

"Mark the inbound vessels as priority targets," She said absently as she accessed the system now, running a search to see just *what* had been unlocked.

"Yes, Ship's Commander."

There's more in here than I expected, Kaela's eyes opened in surprise as she found a massive list of entries that she could now see that simply had *not* been there before.

"Hail from the Gaian vessel, Ship's Commander."

Kaela looked up reluctantly from the data, grimacing slightly but nodding, "Put them through."

*****

The *Casino*

Cardsharp's eyes flicked to one side as the holographic screen popped up in the periphery of her vision, "Ship's Commander. I presume you have the new contacts on your scans?"

"Of course," Ship's Commander Eurydice said.

"I would like to suggest coordinating fire, and perhaps *withdrawing* from this region," Cardsharp said. "We are fighting within their territory, and no doubt they have us perfectly located due to the massive array of potential scanners surrounding us."

The Ship's Commander's eyes widened slightly, and Cardsharp could see her making the connection in the moment.

"Of... Of course," Eurydice said, with a hint of an almost rueful tone. "We will begin withdrawing."

"Excellent. I have Imperial codes from earlier operations we conducted on the behalf of the Empire," Cardsharp replied. "If the protocols remain the same, we should be able to interlink our systems to prevent targeting the same foes."

The Ship's Commander hesitated, but something over her shoulder that didn't register on the image or sound transmission caused her to start slightly. After she returned her focus forward, Eurydice nodded slowly.

"I agree," She said. "We will accept your codes and interlink our fire control system."

Cardsharp noticed the Ship's Commander's eyes flicker down several times during the conversation, like something was on her mind, drawing her attention off frame.

"Ship's Commander, are you alright? You appear... distracted?"

"It is nothing... no," Eurydice grimaced, taking a deep breath, "Our database unlocked considerable data on the enemy when we scanned the profile of the incoming vessels. We had previously not had any hard intelligence, now I fear we may have *too much* for the time we have available. I am... frustrated."

Cardsharp snorted, "I can only imagi... Wait."

Eurydice raised an eyebrow, "Pardon?"

Jenn held up a finger, "A moment please... something... something you just..."

She closed her eyes and in that moment the connection snapped into place, causing them to snap back open.

"You have a *database* on the enemy?" She leaned in, intently.

"Yes, however I cannot share it, I do apologize however the data is highly restr-"

Cardsharp waved her off, "We have encountered these beasts before, we know the legends... and we know the rumors. Some decades ago, when they first began to show up, the rumor was that the Empire had unleashed them on some of its enemies."

"Preposterous," Eurydice said instantly, "I assure you..."

"Ship's Commander, you were not even aware that the database existed," Cardsharp reminded her, "but more importantly, the rumor was that the Empire had restricted the generational cycle of the creatures as a safety precaution."

Eurydice shrugged reluctantly, "That would be a good means of ensuring that the damage they caused could be limited."

"Yes, it would," Cardsharp hissed out, "however... would any information on *that* be in your database?"

Eurydice frowned, shaking her head, but looked down involuntarily as her hands worked something out of frame.

Silently, Cardsharp watched as the Ship's Commander scrolled or searched or did whatever it was the Empire did to move through their intelligence database.

She knew that she hit paydirt, despite wishing she hadn't, when the Ship's Commander went pale and her hand snapped out to kill the connection instantly.

"Fuck a duck."

"Boss?"

"Oh we have real trouble," Cardsharp said. "Get me the Colonel. *NOW!*"

*****

IC *From the Flames*

How did she know?

Kaela couldn't answer that question, all she could do was stare at the sheer *nightmare* she was looking at, and try to will it into nonexistence.

The Empire did it. They actually unleashed those beasts on our enemies...

Who believed that to be a reasonable response to their foes,

Kaela wanted to know... if only so she could *shoot* them herself.

The Drasin were a nightmare, literally and figuratively. The database itself stated that in no uncertain terms.

Left unchecked, they would turn entire star systems into barren wastelands, stripped of all raw materials right down to the cometary shield in the very outer realms of the star's reach. They left nothing in their wake, save a star burning in the wastes with nothing left to warm. The records indicated that they were created by some ancient enemy, but there was no evidence supporting that she could find, though Kaela could admit that meant little at the moment.

Whatever their origins, they needed to be *destroyed,* not *leashed.*

Kaela had no sympathies for the enemies of the Empire, *none,* but this was not a weapon. It was a rabid *beast* that could only turn on its handler. Legends were passed down, generation to generation, for a reason.

This reason had been made clear long before.

Do not toy with these **things.** *Destroy them.*

"Ship's Commander, enemy combat vessels nearing maximum effective range."

"Share data with the Gaian vessel," She ordered absently, "fire as we can. No mercy."

"Yes, Ship's Commander. No mercy."

The Empire may have made this mistake... but I will not.

*****

"Hold the line!"

Amanda had a tightness in her chest as she sheltered behind a corner section of the bulkhead, the roar of the squad's weapons spitting supersonic rounds through the airless halls only reaching her as it was transmitted through armor to deck and then back to armor again.

It was a faint rumble, sounding like it was miles away even

though the guns were spitting rounds only meters away.

They'd made it down three decks and were looking for the next egress point when the swarm of Drasin erupted up out of a hole in one of the bulkheads that they'd not noticed in their initial pass. She didn't know if the damned things had camouflaged the hole somehow, or if her people had just overlooked it, but she'd be checking the recordings later to be sure.

At the moment, however, all they could do was *shoot*.

The bodies of the drones were startling to pile up, providing good cover for her squad and an excellent disruption for slowing the enemy advance, but the Drasin didn't seem to give damn.

"We're going to run out of ammo before they run out of drones, Lieutenant," The Sergeant warned between shots.

"Understood." She confirmed, breaking out her spare mags and tossing them to the Sergeant, "Pass those around, I'm going to call for backup."

"As you say, Ma'am," He told her, accepting the magazines while she eased back from the fight and opened up a comm signal.

*****

"Colonel, First squad is tangling with a swarm situation. Requesting ammo and backup, either or would be appreciated, both would be ideal."

Keenan nodded, "Get Two and Three moving, tell them to ruck whatever spares we have from the deployment delivery with them. I want First squad reinforced within two minutes, clear?"

"Hoorah, Colonel!"

So far the entry to the ship had gone smoothly, so she supposed that they were overdue for some problems.

Can't be too bad if they're calling for ammo, Keenan thought with grim amusement.

Calling for evac would be far worse, of course.

"We need a way into the pressurized sections of the ship," She said, "squad four, find me a sealed door that we can put an airlock over."

"Hoorah, Ma'am."

Colonel Keenan paused in her preparations and directions as she received the priority hail from the Casino, coming in on a high powered bandwidth that certainly wasn't going to be missed by anyone with ears.

Skipper is all het up about something, She thought as she cleared the signal.

"Keenan."

"Colonel, we have a problem," Cardsharp said, her voice deadly serious.

Keenan instantly stiffened, "Ma'am? Beyond the obvious?"

"Far beyond. The Empire ship maintains a Database about the Drasin."

Kennan nodded slowly along with that, it didn't seem like something that was surprising.

"Can't say that I'm shocked by that," She responded as much.

"Intel from after the Drasin war indicated that the Empire had imposed a generational limit on the Drasin, after so many replications, they start to break down, lose the ability to do the things that make them so damn lethal," Cardsharp explained.

"Again, makes sense. I wouldn't want to let any sort of bioweapon out into the environment without *some* measure to keep it from blowing back in my face." Keenan said cautiously.

"The ship has a database that has at *least* some intel about that limit. Colonel, I think that's why the Drasin are acting atypically. They're not there to eat the ship, they're there to *jailbreak* themselves." Cardsharp said firmly. "This whole damn thing... the Dyson construct, the signals everyone followed here, all of it... was a trap to bring in an Imperial Cruiser."

Keenan swallowed.

"Oh fuck me," She said.

"Now we're on the same page, Colonel... *do not* let them have that database," Cardsharp ordered. "I don't know if it has what they need, but we absolutely cannot risk it. *Clear* that ship…"

Keenan didn't need to be a genius to figure out what Cardsharp wasn't saying.

Clear the ship… or die trying, but make damn sure that everyone of the Drasin died too.

Even if it meant the lives of every Imperial sailor and officer… and the lives of every *marine* on board.

Keenan swallowed, but bobbed her head in the suit.

"Hoorah, Skipper."

*****

CHAPTER 34

IC *From the Flames*

Fighting in a vacuum was a strange beast indeed, Amanda thought as she fired a single round from her rapidly dwindling remaining magazine, putting the heavy tungsten round through the carapace of one of the drones and blowing molten silicates out the back of it's body in the process.

There was no boom, though she could hear the weapon discharge as the sound was conducted through her armor to her ears. It sounded more like a very dull thud, however, than anything else.

The smoke from the ablated round didn't waft around, filling the air around her, because there was no air to waft in and fill. Instead it dropped, almost like a stone, straight down to the deck and accumulated there in a bizarre fog that was composed of ash and tungsten dust and kicked up as they walked through it, only to settle again momentarily after they passed.

The enemy was screaming or hissing, she could *see* that much, but no sound was to be heard.

It was a distressingly peaceful firefight, one that lulled her into a near zen trance as she picked her shots and dropped targets with precision shooting rather than attempting to deliver high levels of firepower.

"Empty!"

"Fall back, Corporal," The Sergeant ordered, stepping forward to cover the Corporal's withdrawal.

The Marine did as he was bade, letting his rifle drop in its sling as he did, his sidearm filling his fist a moment later as he fired into the horde with a steady staccato beat even as he stepped back.

Amanda patted him on the shoulder as he reached her, nodding back over her shoulder, "Squads Two and Three have been dispatched to bring ammo. Head back, meet them and guide them here."

"Yes Ma'am!"

She moved forward, taking the Sergeant's previous position as she flipped her rifle to one side briefly to check the witness holes in her mag before putting the bead back down on the target.

Half empty.

"Clear breach!" The Sergeant bellowed over the comm, "Warp Out!"

Everyone, Amanda included, fell back a pace automatically as the Sergeant lobbed the Spacetime Grenade down range with a hefty heave.

The deceptively small device flew down the hall, bouncing off the ceiling once before caroming off a carapace and finally landing amid the scrambling group of alien monsters charging their way before the Sergeant send the detonation signal.

Once more, there was no noise to speak of, but Amanda had to scramble hard to keep from being pulled *toward* the enemy as the warp grenade suddenly compressed spacetime into what was very nearly, but not *quite*, a micro singularity.

The gravitational tug was significant, despite the sharp shear of spacetime caused by the small device, sucking the ash and dust from the floor around them right into the enemy's position, obscuring the lot from vision for a brief moment.

Then the effect was gone and she, along with several Marines, fell back from the pull that had suddenly stopped, landing hard on their ass in the process.

Amanda scrambled back along the deck, struggling to get her rifle back on target as she stared at the results of the warp grenade.

The Drasin that had been caught in the weapon's radius were broken, but not *dead* as best she could tell. They were still twitching and clawing at the deck at least, as though trying to pull themselves forward, but seemingly couldn't get enough traction to do so.

"Jesus fucking Christ, Sarge," Corporal Smith swore, "A little fucking warning next time?"

As much as Amanda agreed with the sentiment, however, she didn't think that was the time to hash it out. She rolled to her feet, moved back to her position, catching everyone's attention.

"Can that shit," She snapped. "Eyes forward and guns the same damn way. We're not done yet."

*****

Kaela Eurydice swore as she felt a slight tug pull at her even as warning screamed from their systems, causing her to bolt upright as she looked around.

"Report!"

"Gravitational anomaly, Ship's Commander," Sunnam said, sounding confused. "Too brief to localize precisely… but it was from *inside* the hull."

She paled, "The core…?"

"Negative," He said with a firm shake before jerking his head upward, "From above us."

Kaela looked up at the deck plates above her, confused, "How?"

Sunnam just shrugged helplessly, "I have no idea. There shouldn't be any materials in that area that even *could* cause such an event, and there are no scanners still intact thanks to the Drasin's progress. We're blind."

Kaela swore under her breath, rubbing her face, "Fine. Ignore it."

He half turned, eyes wide, "Ship's Comma-"

"Can you do anything about it?"

Sunnam swallowed, but reluctantly shook his head, "No, Ship's Commander."

"Then leave it. If we live, we'll find out what it was and ensure it *never* happens again." She said.

If we live.

"Yes, Ship's Commander."

"Focus on the enemy we *can* fight," She ordered, nodding to the screens.

He nodded slowly, turning back, "Yes, Ship's Commander."

Kaela firmly got everyone facing the right direction, fighting the enemy they could fight, but even as she managed that she couldn't help but look up and wonder just what in the *abyss* that had been?

*****

Colonel Keenan looked up as her armor practically screamed at her, then turned back to what she was doing.

"Someone popped off a warp egg," Her Gunny grunted. "I wanted to be one of the first to use those in a fight."

Keenan snorted, "Let others have some fun once in a while, Gunny. We have to worry about more than just popping some spider-crabs for shits and giggles. Best guess is that the ship will have it's primary database secured near engineering and the Command Deck, so we need to find the fastest way there from here."

"No reason to care about collateral, I'm guessing?"

"None at all."

The Gunny nodded as he considered that, looking over the same augmented imagery that she was using, most of it based on the layouts of Priminae cruisers pre-invasion.

"We can start cutting decks here," He pointed. "Blow through fast and hard, don't give anyone… not the Spideys, not the Imps, a chance to figure out what we're doing. Problem is, we can't be precise when all we have is a guess as to our destination."

"Agreed, but we'll have to take our chances," Keenan said simply. "Nothing else to do, not with the stakes this high."

The Gunny nodded slowly, "You've got it, Ma'am. I'll see to it."

"Thank you, Gunny. Be about it then."

"Hoorah."

Keenan let him be about his task as she examined the reports she was getting, checking the munitions deployment report specifically.

Sergeant Jessup tossed that egg. Huh, well good for him, I suppose.

The warp grenades were still technically experimental, only intended to be used in extreme circumstances... generally the brief was that they were for busting enforced bunkers, and Keenan was pretty *damned* sure that there were specific notes about being careful about using them on *ships* for obvious reasons... but those were written with Free Star Destroyers in mind more then Imperial Cruisers.

She was looking forward to seeing what the lethal little egg did to the deck of a cruiser, frankly, but that would hold for a while yet.

*****

"I'm out!"

"Same!"

"Fall back," Amanda ordered, dropping her own rifle in its sling just after the last round had been expelled from her weapon. She drew her own sidearm, the bulky pistol fitting her armor shod grip perfectly as she brought it up to her chest and pushed it out toward the targets just as she'd been trained.

The pistol bucked in her hand as she fired quickly downrange as she withdrew with her squad.

She was cursing silently with every step back, losing the ground that they'd fought to gain was galling, but there was little choice.

Where the fuck is the backup and resupply? She swore to herself, glancing toward her chronodisplay, *Its already been... fuck. It's only been a minute and change?* **How?**

It felt like *hours* had passed. She didn't even know how it was possible for so little time to have gone past, it felt so impossible that she briefly wondered if the warp grenade how somehow inflicted a relativistic effect on them somehow. It was patently absurd, of course, the weapon had been thoroughly tested, and anything like *that* would have been in the brief for sure.

That just left her with the idea that less than two minutes had *really* passed, though, and it just didn't seem possible.

"Lieutenant!"

She looked over her shoulder to see the Corporal legging it back in their direction, a pack over one shoulder, with two squads of Marines hot on his heels.

Oh thank God.

"Sergeant, get that ammo passed around."

"Yes Ma'am."

*****

The *Casino*

Jenn hissed to herself as she examined the telemetry feeding back to her from the now combined scanners of the *Casino* and the Imperial Cruiser.

That's a lot of Drasin ships.

Calling them ships was a bit of a misnomer, of course, at least as best she knew.

They Drasin were really multiple… variations on the same basic foundation, but some of the variations were wildly divergent. Possibly even massively extreme evolutionary shifts from the warrior drones to the capitol class ships, as humans identified them.

Research after the first invasion had made it clear that she wasn't really looking at ships. They were… organisms, of a sort. Not alive in every sense of the word, but close enough for military work. The ships represented a larger and more powerful foe, but one that had scaling weaknesses that could be exploited.

The smaller drones were incredibly durable, able to survive atmospheric entry temperatures and even *impact* at terminal velocity with a planet.

That was a level of toughness that was hard to imagine, given that *smaller* was something of a relative term and the drones in question were several times the mass of a human wearing *powered armor*. Nothing that had evolved on Earth could survive those sorts of stressors... but there was a limit to how well *anything* scaled.

As you added size, you geometrically increased mass... and *every* material had limits.

For the Drasin's ultra durable silicate/aluminum construction, those limits were visible as they reached the size of capitol ships.

Impacts that a smaller drone would easily shrug off would utterly destroy the larger ships, thankfully, otherwise she had no doubt that they'd just turn themselves into asteroid impactors and destroy everything for miles around their landing site before starting to eat the debris and replicate.

Unfortunately, there were a lot of things about them that researchers had been unable to completely understand... or understand even slightly.

Cardsharp despised fighting with incomplete intel, but such was life she supposed.

"Halo the lead elements, split the targets with the Imps," She ordered.

"Aye, lead elements haloed, boss," Roy said automatically. "Target data shared."

"Fire as they enter effective range," Cardsharp ordered. "Set beams to best average absorption based on our database of Drasin composition."

Roy nodded, entering a few more commands.

"Beams set. Firing in... three... two... one."

The augmented view of the space around them lit up with computer generated beams that lanced out from the *Casino* at the speed of light.

They would only take two minutes to reach their targets.

"Standby evasive maneuvers," She ordered. "Don't expect us to stay on any given vector longer than it takes for light to reach the enemy and return, anticipate new firing vectors."

"Aye."

Fighting at relativistic distances required a different mindset compared to dogfighting, she knew. The enemy, at the current range, would not see any move they made for approximately two minutes.

Of course, neither would they.

The trick now would be to guess where the enemy was when the *Casino's* beams arrived, while preventing the enemy from doing precisely the same thing.

How did the Skipper manage to make this look so damned easy?

*****

CHAPTER 35

IC *From the Flames*

The enemy vessels, assuming you could qualify those abominations as vessels, did not hesitate in their approach even as the combined beams of the *Flames* and the Gaian vessel *Casino* tore into their ranks.

Kaela supposed that she wasn't shocked by that fact. The Drasin had far superior numbers, and were clearly engaging on their own home turf with the disregard for their own survival that the monsters were known for in the legends.

Individual survival did not appear to be something that the species, assuming they were to be considered such, had coded for... or been coded for. She could see how some fools might believe them to be a perfect weapon, their suitability as devastating shock troops could not be denied. However, to what *end*?

They destroyed everything you might want to wage a war *for*. Nothing was left of value when they passed. The former system her ship was current fighting in was a perfect example of that.

The only objects that remained of a once valuable, albeit distant, resource system were the great shell that surrounded it all and the abomination of a world-construct that currently took up half of her viewer as she attempted to direct the fighting while withdrawing her vessel from the danger she had placed it in.

It was all so *infuriating*.

"Ship's Commander, reports from around this ship," Sirra said, distracting her from her thoughts for the moment. "The Gaian forces have entered the ship through the same path as the Drasin. They have been spotted moving their soldiers through portable atmospheric seals into the inner decks."

Kaela nodded curtly. She had honestly wondered how the Gaian had expected to deliver her forces onto the *flames*, but that made sense. It neatly avoided the fore and aft docking bays, which were heavily defended by the warp fields since they were considered natural weak points in the ship's design, and were never used while at high warp anyway.

"Understood. Instruct our teams to work with them as possible, and not to engage them. We have enough issues at the moment, we have no need of compounding them."

"Yes, Ship's Commander."

"Ship's Commander," Sunnam spoke. "We're crossing the warning point."

"Yseb, adjust course, random vector, place us clear of any beam vectors that may have been fired at our projected position."

"Yes, Ship's Commander."

The big ship smoothly responded to the change in the warp, no sensation of movement made it to anyone on board as everything on the ship, including the bodies of the crew, naturally moved in the same direction at the same moment thanks to the warping of spacetime.

If only everything were so smooth.

*****

The *Casino*

"They're bulling through, Ma'am. Not even sure that they've returned fire yet," Roy reported as Cardsharp slid the ship out of the path of any potential incoming fire.

"Yeah, they do that," She answered. "Confederate Intel was of the opinion that the Drasin are a hive species. Individual drones are irrelevant, and so long as one survives... they all do."

"Well... shit."

Jenn didn't blame him for that reaction, though she doubted he really had a concept of what it truly meant. Few people actually understood just how devastatingly effective a hive species could be.

One Earth, up until the second invasion at least, there had been *two* species that essentially shared dominion over the planet.

Humans... and *ants*.

Ants, despite having no technological base and requiring approximately two and half million drones just to equal one single human in mass, had managed to colonize every continent humans did.

Not evolve into those ecosystems, but actually had *colonies* of the *same* hive on *every single continent* save Antarctica.

In many metrics, they had outcompeted humans by a large margin.

The Drasin... were worse by any measure.

Ants that massed several times that of a single human, could self replicate nigh endlessly just from feeding on raw material, and were interstellar capable.

Frankly, Jenn was entirely uncertain how it was that the Drasin hadn't already managed to devour the galaxy.

Whatever the reason, they hadn't yet managed it, and that meant that it fell to her and hers to stop them here and now, Cardsharp supposed.

"Approaching one lightminute and still closing *fast*, Ma'am."

"Roger that. I'm going to stay glued to the Imperial cruiser, cover them as best I can..." She said before hesitating, then taking a breath, "Maintain a torpedo lock on the cruiser at all times, Roy."

Roy looked at her, shocked for a moment before he swallowed and nodded.

"Aye Ma'am."

Cardsharp set her focus forward, intent on making sure that she didn't *need* that weapons lock, but there was no way in *hell* she was going to let the Drasin get what they'd come for, not even on the slightest hint of a chance that she was right about it.

Not a single chance in hell.

*****

The Drasin formation was loose and messy, but that mattered little to the massive organisms of silicate and minerals that made it up. They had a task assigned to them, not by some other being, but embedded in their very construction itself. Instinctual service to the collective was the first order of every Drasin of any caste, with following tiers of instincts that mandated every decision that was to be made.

If a single Drasin made a decision, *every* Drasin would make the same decision.

There was no sense of concern over survival, under normal circumstances. If one survived, all survived... and *one* **always** *survived*.

However, in this moment, their normal hatred of *the red band* that signified the life infection was being overridden by something no Drasin could remember ever happening before.

An existential threat.

Their very selves had been coopted, crippled, turned into a *mockery* by the red band. It was an abomination, and it was *not* to be allowed to continue.

Before their proper response could be made, however, the mockery had to be undone.

No cost was too high, only failure was an unacceptable price.

So the Drasin endured the searing heat of the *Red Band's* beams, some falling to the destruction, but most passing through into the close range where the enemy would not be able to evade and waste the Hive's energy.

As they closed into the deadly close range after the brutal slashing of enemy beams cut down their fellows, the bulk of the surviving Drasin all made their decision as one.

They opened fire.

*****

IC *From the Flames*

"Forward warp field just registered heavy beam strikes, Ship's

Commander," Sunnam snapped upright. "Beams attenuated by the warp field, but they won't hold for long."

Kaela snarled, but understood the truth in that statement.

The warp field would bend incoming beams, to a point. Currently they were powering their warp to the maximum levels they could, specifically to protect the ship… from the Beams, yes, but also from the drones that were still attempting to gain purchase on the exterior of her ship.

It placed them in a vulnerable state, unfortunately, because to reconfigure their warp for efficient motion it would take a moment.

In that moment, they would be particularly vulnerable.

A shriek of metal from behind her served notice that she *still* had unwelcome visitors on her vessel to deal with, and ignoring them could easily prove fatally costly.

Just one moment to make a decision without the enemy being able to cut me down for doing so, that is all I ask!

However, she might as well ask for the deed to Kraike itself, and she knew it.

Honestly, She suspected that she would have a better chance with the deed.

"Return fire! Hold nothing back! Cut them down!"

"Yes ship's Commander!"

*****

The *Casino*

Cardsharp swore as the *Casino* registered beams cutting through space all around them. They easily slashed through the section of space that she would have been in if she had continued on her previous course, unsurprisingly, however they also did a fair job of bracketing likely divergences from that projection as well.

Only the relatively tiny size of her ship had kept the *Casino* from being carved up by the lethal beams, and while that great and all… their size also meant that they just didn't have the same warp field strength or sheer mass of armor that the Imperial vessel could boast.

As things stood, if the *Casino* took a strike, it would be all over.

Her hand swept over to the controls that would bring the active defense systems, the Archangel's Camplates, fully online but she paused.

If she activated those, the Gaian legend was burned the second the Imperial ship made it back to Empire space. She didn't actually think that the crew of this ship would recognize or know what that technology signified, but Imperial Command *would*.

They would hunt down the Nest, and burn the Archangels and everyone else out.

Cardsharp clenched her fist and withdrew it from the controls.

"Tell everyone to get strapped in," She ordered. "We're going for a ride."

Roy swallowed, but nodded in understanding.

"Aye Ma'am." He said simply as he reached over and flipped a toggle. "All hands, all hands, this is the Pit Boss. Secure for maneuvering. Say again, secure for maneuvering. If it's not tied down, get it strapped in *now*. Cardsharp is in the house."

She smiled thinly as she threw full power to the *Casino's* Counter-Mass Generators and opened up the conduits to the spacetime warp fields at the same time.

"She is indeed," Cardsharp said through that smile. "And you know what they say... the *house always wins*."

*****

IC *From the Flames*

"Put them down!"

Amanda had given up on precision shooting as she tapped a corporal on the shoulder, letting him fall back out of the line to reload while she stepped into place with her weapon roaring. They had enough ammo now to hold up a small war if they needed, and time was counting down.

The Colonel had pulsed a message ahead, throwing the priority for the mission up several notches, and basically telling them that there wouldn't be any retreating.

That sent a chill through her when she'd heard it, because that basically meant that the mission was well above the sorts of priority the Marines normally dealt with.

Generally, retreat was frowned on, but if the alternative was losing your men... it was better to regroup and plan another sortie. The Colonel had made it clear that there would be no regrouping here.

Finish the mission, no matter the cost, was the order of the day.

Amanda didn't know why the priority had jumped that high, certainly an Imperial cruiser wasn't nearly valuable enough for them to sacrifice marines to save... but from the Colonel's message, she didn't get the idea that *saving* the ship was the mission. She wasn't sure what it *was* yet, but Amanda figured that she'd find out if she needed to.

Probably.

She hoped.

The last of the Drasin swarm went down in a pool of bubbling molten silicates and other minerals as the distant sound of weapons firing slowed.

"Is... is that it?" Smith asked, uncertainly.

"Sergeant," Amanda stated dryly.

"Got it," The Sarge said, slapping Corporal Smith on the back of the helmet.

"Ow, what the f-..." Smith swore, looking around.

"Don't taunt Murphy, Corporal," Amanda said as she started moving forward. "First thing we learned in boot, so you should damn well know better."

"Ah... right you are, Lieutenant," The Marine sounded chagrined, but Amanda was already putting it out of her mind as she examined the carcasses.

They were already cooling, turning into congealed masses of silicates and various minerals. She supposed that they would be hell to clean off the decks.

Glad that isn't my job, She grunted as she stepped over one of the still searing hot globs of what was, essentially, stone now.

"Make sure they're dead," She ordered, "Then push forward. We have a job to do."

"Yes Ma'am," The Sergeant confirmed, waving to the squad. "You heard the LT. Get it done."

The men moved to comply, along with Gunmen from the other two squads as well. Amanda nodded to her fellow officers and their NCOs as they joined her.

"Well, Colonel's orders are clear," She said, "Any ideas? I'm open here."

"We're going to have to split up," Captain Jace McEnroe said as he looked up and down the split in the corridor, trying to judge the situation. "My team will move forward. We should find the Command deck there."

First Lieutenant Warren Bradford nodded, "I'm good with going aft a bit. Might get lucky, but at the very least we'll probably find Main Engineering and the singularity."

Amanda considered that, "Well guess I'm low man on the pole, so my team will flip a coin. Heads we go port, tails we go starboard, unless anyone here has a better idea?"

The assembled group looked around, but no one had anything constructive to say.

Amanda nodded, then reached automatically before stopping and sighing, "Ok. Anyone have a coin flipping app in their suit? I seem to have forgotten my purse on the *Casino.*"

*****

CHAPTER 36

The *Casino*

"Watch your one high," Roy called as Cardsharp flipped the ship under a sweep of the beams trying to track their position.

"Got them," She called, haloing the target with a flicker of her eyes before she unleashed the beams from the ribbon emitters under her control to slag three quarters of the way through the closest.

The fighting was getting close and personal now, well under thirty lightseconds and closing, and she was sinking deeper into the familiar zen-like state that took her when she delved deeply into the NICS controls and let them fully wash over her.

In a real way, Cardsharp *was* the Casino, and the deeper she delved the more that became true.

The armor that lined the hull was her skin, she could feel light and dust rub against her as they moved. The warp field were her limbs and shield, propelling her through the black at unimaginable speeds and deflected away the threats that came for her.

Her beams were her sword, great blades of photons that could deliver hellfire onto the target she chose.

The *Casino* responded to her will, and even to her *instinct*, faster than she could even fully think... if she allowed it to do so.

And right this moment?

She was not merely *allowing it*, Cardsharp was inviting it in like a favored guest.

Flipping the gunboat end for end as the enemy beams again attempted to sweep in their directions, Jenn ducked clean under the lethal weapons' fire, every beam on the little ship lashing out in response.

Her augmented display was running at full burn, taking every slight piece of data it could find in order to locate, identify, and track the enemy beams using the fluorescing track they left as they vaporized the few little bits of dust and gas that did remain inside the construct.

That more than emptiness was making things harder on the computer and on her, though, as there were relatively few particulates available to analyze the enemy beams from, and each was already incredibly hard to spot even under normal circumstances.

"I'm unlocking the adaptive beams," She stated.

"The Empire…" Roy said curiously.

"Minimal risk," She answered. "Doubt they'll be able to spot the variations in our beams, not if we're not actively aiming at them. So advise our gunners that we'll need an additional time to score the best strikes."

"Aye Ma'am."

Up close it wouldn't amount to much, of course. The scattering of photons could be analyzed by the computers in a fraction of a second, but the farther out the fighting was conducted, the more of a liability it would be to wait for their beams to adapt to the enemy armor composition perfectly enough to not waste any unnecessary energy in reflections.

Similar to the Camplates, the adaptive beam technology was very nearly a signature of Terran forces, though the Priminae had put them into full production after the tech share as well, of course. Being identified as part of either group would be death for the Archangels and the Nest, of course, but this was not a particularly large risk.

Any evidence of the adaptation would be lost in the noise of the battle, easily chalked up to scanner interference rather than anything nefarious.

"Paint the enemy, get a reading on them all." She ordered grimly. "No more wasted energy. We're going to need everything we can scrounge up."

"Aye, Skipper."

*****

IC *From the Flames*

"Gaian vessel is… engaging the enemy, Ship's Commander," Sunnam reported, sounding mild to moderately shocked.

Kaela didn't blame him, the Gaian ship was showing incredible acceleration potential far in excess of what the *Flames* could manage even at maximum warp, and combining it with maneuverability that she'd never even considered *possible* for a ship.

I always wondered how the Gaians managed to survive this long when their core fleet was composed of vessels far smaller than even a Destroyer. I suppose I have my answer.

The small vessel was also packing serious beam power according to their scans, cutting into the Drasin with nearly a match for the *Flames* weapons on full power no less.

Whatever polity designed those cannot still exist, She decided, thinking on the rumors attached to the Gaians. *If they did, they most assuredly would have come gunning for their missing ships by now.*

Initially, the Gaians had been believed to be a cat's paw for one of the major Free Stars polities, but that had never really materialized. Ultimately, Imperial Command decided that the ships had been a last ditch effort by a failing polity that proved to be too little, and far too late, with the crews fleeing the collapse of their world and setting up as independents.

The Empire had searched, in fact, for any evidence of which fallen government it might be… unfortunately, the Free Stars were chaos incarnate, with pocket empires rising and falling quite regularly across over a hundred inhabited stars in a loose shroud surrounding Imperial Space.

Determining which might have created such ships was ultimately decided to be a waste of time and resources.

Kaela was not so certain that was true, having now seen them in action, but she had more pressing concerns to deal with.

*****

Amanda didn't get to flip her coin, but she opted for the port side simply because they were already slightly to port as it stood so it was marginally less walking. Not a great reason, but given no other current factors to influence the decision, it was as good as any she supposed.

"Smith's reporting back," The Sergeant told her, "Thinks he found the entry point the Drasin burned through to the next deck, but it's sealed."

"This far over?" She asked, surprised. "And what does he mean sealed?"

She held up a hand even as she finished that, "never mind. Tell him to secure the location, get everyone else moving. We'll meet him."

"Yes Ma'am."

Smith had been scouting just down around one of the curving corridors, so it only took a minute to get everyone moving and less time again for Amanda to find herself standing over the glop that had once been the deck in that area.

"Shit," She swore. "They moved through and melted it behind them?"

"Yeah," Smith said, "No fucking clue why."

"Going to assume that they wanted to maintain atmo," She said with shrug, "though *why they'd want that,* I'm a lot less sure of."

"Can't be good," Sarge grunted.

Amanda silently agreed with them. To this point the Drasin had been content with slaughtering and *eating* anyone they came across, or so she assuming given that they'd not found a single body... just blood spatter boiled off the deck, leaving the dried remnants behind in the vacuum. If the crew complement was anything like a Heroic Class, dozens had to have died at least, possibly hundreds.

So why the fuck are they preserving atmo this deep in? She wondered cautiously.

"We ain't getting through here," The Sarge said firmly, the

boot of his armor kicking at the cooled slag. "We need another way."

Amanda nodded absently, "There should be inner locks on this deck. One every deck, for that matter, let's find one."

"Then what?" Smith asked, "It'll be locked down, sure as shit."

"Then we knock politely and ask to be invited in."

*****

The *Casino*

"Skipper, I think I've got a pattern here," Roy called from behind her as Cardsharp dove the fighter/gunboat relative to the current plane of combat to avoid another sweep of the alien beams.

They were getting closer, the range between targets now almost point blank for lightspeed weapons, and that was making her job a hell of a lot harder.

"All ears," She said, not looking back.

"They're avoiding firing on the Cruiser," He told her. "At least with serious intent. Looks like they're more aiming to keep the cruiser pinned down, so the Imps won't risk resetting their warp field for a full run."

"Shit. Yeah, ok, that makes sense." Cardsharp gritted out, thinking it through.

It presented both problems *and* an opportunity, however, she was certain.

Fuckers are keeping us from making a run for it, they want the ship intact... at least until they get what they're after, or determine it's not there, She decided. *But that also means...*

"Got it," She said, snapping the fighter over hard enough that everything keeled over as the maneuver somehow managed to exceed the capacity of *both* the CM and warp field's inertial nullification, putting them on a new course.

"What the hell," Roy snapped, hanging on to the console. "Goddamn it, Skipper, how the hell do you *do* that anyway? I thought warp field mechanics prevented *any* sort of acceleration on board!"

"Only if you *just* use the warp field to maneuver," She said with a smirk. "I've got the thrusters running at twenty percent over rated maximum, and the CM field maxxed out. Side note, we're going to need some time in a repair dock when this is over."

"Just fabulous," Roy grumbled.

"You know me, any excuse to spend some R&R on Ranquil," She quipped.

"You've *torched* the hull *that bad*?" Roy exclaimed. "We're *lightyears* from home!"

"My baby can take it," Cardsharp grinned.

"Maybe, but I doubt *I* can take it!"

"Suck it up, buttercup. We have a job to finish."

Roy swore some more, but ultimately just shook his head, "Where are we going?"

"Back to the cruiser. I need me a nice big chunk of *cover*."

*****

IC *From the Flames*

"Ship's Commander, reports from the deck crews are... becoming less frequent..."

Which means few of them are left alive, Kaela scowled, but merely nodded silently as she waited for Sirra to continue.

"More of the Gaians have made their way through the outer decks, finding ways into the still pressurized areas," the comms officer went on.

"Good. Direct them to any of the enemy we can find," Kaela ordered.

"Yes, Ship's Commander."

"Do we have any localized groups of the enemy located? Preferably on scanners?" She asked curiously.

"Some," Sunnam answered, cutting in.

"Where?"

"Near Main Engineering, just outside the Command Deck, a

few other places." He said uncertainly.

"What are they doing?"

"Nothing as far as we can tell, Ship's Commander," Sunnam answered. "Milling about, almost... lost? It is very strange."

Kaela grimaced, but didn't say anything more.

Strange is not an apt descriptor, She thought grimly. *They have a goal. What is it? What does it have to do with those locations?*

"Run a full analysis of every location they've been localized in," She ordered. "I want *all* commonalities cross referenced."

"All?" Sunnam looked shocked. "Ship's Commander, on a ship... that's going to be a *long* list."

"Do it anyway. I want the list, I want it *now*."

"Yes, Ship's Commander."

"Ship's Commander!"

She snapped around, eyes on Yseb, who was staring at the screen ahead as he looked like he wanted desperately to be *doing* something but seemingly didn't know what in the abyss he could do.

"What is i..." She trailed off in shock, eyes going wide as she watched the Gaian ship charging *right at them* at speeds she did *not* want to consider an impact at. "Sound collision alarms! Eva..."

Before she could complete the order, however, the ship flip itself *end for end* and narrowly skirted the *Flames'* warp field as it positioned itself *behind* the bigger ship.

*They're using us as a **shield**,* She seethed, bracing for the impact of the enemy beams... only for the impact to not come.

Heart slowing, Kaela crossed to Sunnam's station and reached over his shoulder to slide back through the data of the previous few seconds.

The Drasin pulled their beams.

Realization took only seconds.

They want us intact... for the moment. Kaela considered what she'd seen in the records that had been unlocked.

Nothing there would explain this, it was merely dry facts about previous operations, and she doubted that the Drasin cared about espionage in that sense.

But...

What if there were more in the computers? Data that hadn't unlocked, that she didn't *know* was there?

*What are they after that is this important? Surely there wouldn't be anything in my systems about the leash the Empire shackled them with? Imperial Command could not be **that** stupid...*

Even as she thought it, however, Kaela knew that she couldn't *count* on it to be true.

Abyss damn them all.

*****

CHAPTER 37

IC *From the Flames*

"I can't believe that worked."

"Can it, Corporal," The Sergeant hissed back at the whispering Marine. "Look professional for once in your sorry career."

Amanda heard both of them, but opted to ignore them as she used her suit's external feed.

"Thank you for allowing us access," She told the clearly frightened Imperial deck crewman who'd cycled the internal lock for them. "The Drasin melted their entrance points behind them beyond this deck."

The crewman look at her and the other marines nervously, but only nodded as he replied, "Orders from the Ship's Commander. We've been unable to put the beasts down effectively…"

He helplessly hefted the beam weapon in his grip, shaking his head, "Nothing I have seen was ever like this."

Amanda bobbed her suit, resisting the urge to pat him on the shoulder as she felt that he likely wouldn't take it as intended.

"The Drasin are resistant to beams," She said, hefting her own weapon. "Ours should prove more effective. Do you have any reports on their position?"

He shook slightly, "No. We've lost most contact with other security teams. The last positions confirmed were near Engineering and then the Command deck, but neither had been breached."

He hesitated, before going on. "Doesn't make sense."

"What doesn't?" She asked, looking in his direction as the last of her squad made it through the lock.

"Why did they not breach the Deck, or Engineering?" He said, almost sounding like he was complaining. "They came through our armor, through deck after deck... after they pass, there's nothing but blood on the decks. Why stop where they did? It makes no sense!"

Amanda didn't have anything to tell him about that.

"Man has a point," The Sarge told her quietly over a private frequency. "There's something at play we can't see."

She bobbed her armor, speaking on the same frequency. "I know it. Until we figure out what it is, though, we can only act on what we know."

"Yes, Ma'am."

She flipped back over to her external speaker, looking to the crewman, "Could you guide us to the closest contact you know of?"

The Imperial looked flat out terrified, but gestured his agreement.

"Ship's Commander's Orders," He said, sounding more resigned than enthusiastic, not that she blamed him.

"Good," Amanda said. "You're not in armor, so stay in the middle of our formation. We'll cover you if you have to run, but can't promise more than that."

To the others, she sent an attention ping, then lifted her hand with two fingers up, circling it around a few times to bring her squad in.

"Our friend here is going to guide us in," She said. "Standard escort formation. The Imp and I will take the center position. Sarge, you're on drag, Corporal Javins, you and Smith take point. The rest of you know your positions, so lets get moving."

"Hoorah," The group answered, in the clear and over speaker, startling the crewman briefly.

It took only seconds more to be ready to move, though, and the big armored Marines surrounding them seemed to calm the Imperial somewhat, Amanda noted.

"Where to?" She asked him intently.

"This way," He gestured.

She nodded, giving the hand signal to the others, "Let's move."

*****

The *Casino*

Cardsharp flinched as the enemy beams flashed past, close enough that the corona of the beam could be felt on her skin through the hull sensors and the NICS interface. The ship jerked slightly in space in response to her involuntary movement, moving away from the source of the heat, but the bulk of the beams had been solidly deflected already by the massive warp fields of the cruiser.

"Prepare to fire," She sent over the command channels, "popping over the warp field in three…"

She mentally counted down before executing the popup maneuver that cleared them from behind the Imperial cruiser, and the Archangel's beams lanced out in response to burn through the charging enemy formation.

While the gunners were handling that, Cardsharp focused on getting an overview of the battlespace, however, and found herself not liking what she was seeing.

The enemy were swarming, with more ships appearing from within the Jupiter Brain construct, making it clear that the object was more than they'd guessed, but she was hardly surprised. There were few places to hide an enemy fleet within the Dyson sphere, after all, so the enemy had to be coming from somewhere.

"We need to get the Imperial cruiser enough time to reset their warp," She growled, "otherwise those fuckers will drag us down with numbers!"

Roy shook his head, "We don't have the firepower, Skipper. There's too damn many!"

She seethed, but he wasn't wrong.

What the hell did I do, sending those men and women over there? I should have blown that bastard with torpedoes and ran like the devil himself was chasing me right from the start, She lambasted her decisions to that moment.

However, she hadn't, and now that meant that she was being inexorably forced into a corner with only one way out.

Once more, her hand twitched to the controls that would unlock the Pulse Torpedoes.

This close, a full salvo would punch through the Imp's warp field, no matter how deep and steep they had it tuned. The antimatter payload would turn the ship's own armor into a warhead capable of shattering everything on board.

The fight would be over in a flash, and the Casino could easily escape in the midst of the energy pulse that resulted.

All it would take would be sacrificing her Marines to do it.

Jenn clenched her fist again, cursing herself for a fool one more time before she refocused on the battle.

The Drasin were about to overtake, and when they did that the cover of the Imperial warp fields would lose a great deal of their value. Monsters to her back, front, and sides... well it made for a lousy way to run a battle if you wanted to survive, let alone win it.

"Beams free," She ordered. "Gunners target any Deltas of opportunity, don't wait for a Halo command."

"Roger that," Roy said. "Gunners free."

"Standby HVMs and Torpedos," She said. "Fire on my command *only*, but be ready."

Roy nodded, confirming. "Standby alternate weapons, Aye."

"Maintain target lock on the Cruiser, priority for torpedo guidance," She said dully, swallowing.

This time there was a long pause.

"Target lock, Imperial Cruiser, aye," Roy said reluctantly. "Torpedo guidance... Aye."

Cardsharp snarled silently, more at the situation and her own decisions than even at the enemy.

"Hold on tight, this fight ain't over yet."

The *Casino* ducked back behind the cruiser briefly before

suddenly darting to port, clearing the Imperial warp field in an instant. Cardsharp drove them out into the swarm at the full acceleration the ship could muster, and only the suspension field around her kept the strength of it from slamming her into the rear bulkhead.

With beams free, and targets easily available, the emitter ribbons placed in every arc of the gunboat's hull blazed with hot fire as they cut through the enemy with abandon.

*****

IC *From the Flames*

"Cover them!"

"Yes, Ship's Commander."

The powerful beams lancing out from the cruiser slagged through one enemy after another, but the Drasin seemed unmoved by the felling of their fellows, still pouring on their position with no change in pace.

Kaela gripped the side of her console, knuckles white with the strain as she looked it over.

There was little enough she could do, and that was worse than the looming specter of the abyss before her. The Drasin clearly wanted her ship intact, but she would *not* permit that to happen. In the worst case, she knew that she could blow the fields containing the singularity.

In minutes, after that, it would lose alignment and shift until it colliding with the wall of the containment unit. Once that happened, there was nothing that would save the *Flames*, or anything left aboard her.

If you've come here for data, She thought with wry humor, *you'll find nothing but death and whatever is to be learned from the afterlife.*

She didn't know what the Empire may have secured in the computers on board, but her duty was clear despite that lack. The enemies of the Empire would find no succor from her, not in any form.

*****

"Contact, Lieutenant."

"See em," Amanda said, watching the drones up ahead, curiosity trumping fear. "What are they *doing*?"

"Can't tell."

She hummed, shifting over to her external speaker but turning the sound *way* down as she turned to the Imperial crewman.

"What is in the bulkheads there?" She asked, gesturing around the corner.

The Imperial man hesitated, but glanced around quickly before paling and jerking back. He shook slightly, but didn't lose it.

"I don't know," He confessed. "I'd need an Engineering Crewmate to say for sure."

"No guess?" She asked.

"power conduits, communication filaments," He shrugged. "Might be a junction box, perhaps?"

Amanda frowned, "Communications filaments? What about Data transfer?"

"That too," He confirmed, "possibly anyway. Sorry, but I don't handle those repairs."

Amanda bobbed her suit, frustrated but holding her urge to express it.

"Understood. Step back please," She said, pushing him gently to the rear, not that he was resisting at all. She switched over to the squad frequency with a twitch, "How many Deltas?"

"Looks like a dozen, baker's maybe." Javins responded.

"Alright, Javins halo the Deltas and share the targets," Amanda ordered as she got her rifle ready. "Don't know what they're up to, but we'll worry about that when the threat is down."

"Hoorah, Ma'am."

The team setup carefully before emerging from cover, their

weapons leading the way. They had their primary and alternate targets already loaded into their HUDS, thanks to Javins' providing the data. Amanda had them check fire until her entire team was ready to fire, noting that several of the Drasin were focused on whatever they were doing, while the rest were operating as security... in a very rough definition of the word.

Initially they didn't seem to notice the Marines, leaving her a bit of hope that they'd manage a clean sweep, but that hope died stillborn when one turned in their direction and hiss/screamed at them.

The rest reacted instantly, causing a thrill of fear to run through her.

"Ma'am."

"Fire." She ordered automatically at the nudging from the Sergeant, her word almost swallowed by the roars of their GAR-22s splitting atmo.

This wasn't like firing in vacuum, the roar of the weapons could be *felt* through her armor, and the rounds ablated in the air around them almost looking like beam weapons as they left a burning trail of tungsten and depleted uranium composite in their paths.

The heavy shells hammered into the lead drones, spattering the deck with molten silicates and other minerals as the enemy's carapaces were shattered.

The others, however, responded with their own sweeping beams.

"Cover!" She ordered, dropping to her belly as the attack when overhead.

Javins suit went red in her HUD, but Amanda didn't have time to check as she kept on firing.

Her GAR-22 slammed repeatedly into her shoulder as she serviced targets, falling into the rote actions trained into her at the Academy, part of her mind gibbering in fear as she saw the searing heat of the beams cut the deck and bulkhead around them.

The air was rent by the roar of their weapons, both sides, burning away the oxygen and turning the air inside the ship to heavy metal poison in that corridor.

It felt like it went on for hours, but she knew it couldn't have been more than a few seconds because that was how long it would take to empty her mag and the weapon in her mitts had just locked open as the last of the enemy slumped in its own molten blood.

"Ma'am… ma'am," The Sergeant nudged her. "You ok?"

"Yeah," She answered shakily, climbing to her feet as she ejected the mag and let it clatter to the deck, retrieving a fresh one from her kit. "Javins?"

"Fuckin beam cut him in half."

"Shit."

She took a breath, shocked that she felt as numb as she did actually.

"Secure the body," She ordered. "I'm going to take a look at what they were up to."

The Sergeant hesitated, but nodded after a second, "Yes Ma'am."

She started forward, but noticed the Imperial starting forward again. Amanda gestured him back sharply.

"Hold back," She ordered in the open. "The air is toxic now, let the scrubbers suck up this smoke."

Fearfully he nodded and fell back.

Now, She thought grimly. *Let's see what you bastards are up to?*

*****

CHAPTER 38

IC *From the Flames*

Amanda cautiously approached the remains, intent more on what was beyond them than in the Drasin bodies themselves. Grimacing, she realized in short order that she had to cross the mess they'd made to see what the monsters had been up to, and began testing the cooling mass with her boot as she proceeded.

The thinner mass that had spilled out had cooled quickly in contact with the deck, enough that it took her weight with little to no deformation, but as she found deeper puddling of the molten silicates that made up the interior fluids of the alien creatures her boots compressed it more as she tentatively tested the cooling skin.

It was like walking on a water mattress, only with molten rock beneath her feet instead of water. Gritting her teeth, Amanda pressed on though, testing each step carefully as she could while she clambered over the mass to get to the bulkhead beyond.

Finally there, she leaned in and braced herself on the jagged edge of the hole cut into the bulkhead, leaning in to see what they'd been working at.

"Alright, I see conduits here," She called back. "Looks like a power system from the magnetic eddies I'm detecting, definitely a trunk line. Probably enough power running through here to light a small city."

"Weapons' lines, likely then Ma'am," Corporal Smith answered back. "Only thing on these ships that need those kind of Joules. Maybe they were going to disable the beams?"

Amanda shook her head, though she knew it wouldn't be seen.

"Don't think so," She said aloud. "No sign of damage to that…

hang on, there's another line here, smaller... barely any energy reading on it at all."

"If it's that efficient, it's likely a data line," Smith answered.

"Here," Amanda said, sharing the imagery back to the squad.

"Hmm..." Smith said after a moment, "Yeah. That's a data cable, but I don't think I've ever seen one that big."

"Whatever it is," Amanda said as she cleared the hole and stepped gingerly back, "That's what they were after. I can see what looks like a data tap bored into the side... weird."

"What's weird?" The Sergeant asked sharply.

"That it looks like a data tap," Amanda answered simply. "Shouldn't it look like some strange alien growth? I'm just surprised how similar it looks to our kit."

"Form follows function," Smith answers. "We built our gear in response to Imperial tech. Maybe the Drasin did too?"

"Maybe," Amanda said sourly as she made her way back. "I need a screen."

Smith nodded, easily retrieving a ruggedized screen from his kit and handing it off, "Here you go Ma'am."

"Thank you."

She snagged the screen as she walked past him, loading her captured imagery to it, and headed straight for the Imp.

The Imperial crewman was staring past her to the mass of former Drasin, mouth gaping slightly.

Not a great look, She thought wryly, but didn't care to make a joke as she lit up the screen and showed it to him. "Do you recognize this?"

"You killed them so easily..."

Amanda snorted bitterly, "Not so easy. We lost a man. I need you to focus, do you recognize what this conduit is for? The Drasin were *very* interested in it."

She waited as he collected himself and looked over the image with interest, but after a moment he just frowned.

"That's not... what?" He mumbled, looking confused. "No..."

"No you don't know what it is?"

"What? No, it's a data conduit, but it's too large by far," The crewman complained. "and it's *under* a power system? No one would run those lines together like that, interference would be a pain to compensate for... I mean, you can do it, but why?"

Amanda leaned back, letting him ramble.

I am not liking this. If he's right, it's an Intel pipe, She thought it through. *Classified to the highest, I'd expect. Which begs two questions... what Intel... and, more importantly, how in the ever loving hell did the Drasin even know it was there?*

Questions she didn't have the answer to, but thankfully that wasn't her job.

"Colonel," She called over the comm. "Have an update. File's coming your way."

*****

Keenan paused, noting the alert from Squad One. A quick check made her grimace.

Fuck, how'd they lose a man? She wondered, briefly checking the system without finding a log entry as of yet. She didn't have time to check the records, however, so she moved on to the alert from the Lieutenant.

Data pipe, hidden under a power conduit? Interesting, and the crewman didn't know it was there. Definitely an Intel Tap, Keenan thought, agreeing with the Lieutenant's evaluation.

That put things in a different light, a light that lined up too well with the Skipper's conclusions for her to easily refute. *The Drasin are after something the Empire both needs to hide, but also needs to have access to. Have to assume worst case until proven otherwise, and that means that they're here to jailbreak themselves, just as the Skipper predicted. Fuck.*

She checked the squad reports and noted that Squad three was heading for the general vicinity of Main Engineering.

"Bradford," She sent out over the squad channel.

"Ma'am."

"Take your team and secure Engineering," She ordered. "I want you to make certain that the Drasin don't take it."

"Yes Ma'am."

"Go scramble. Command Alpha Three.":

There was a pause before his voice returned, this time on the encrypted command channel, "Roger scramble, Colonel. Command Alpha Three Niner One Two."

"Roger Scramble." She replied, confirming the handshake. "Lieutenant, you have warp grenades on hand?"

"Full load still, yes Ma'am."

"Here's what I need your squad to really do…"

*****

The *Casino*

We are way to damn close for this shit!

Jenn was gritting her teeth as she maneuvered, ducking the sweeping beams or popping up over them… relative to her own position, of course. She'd trained for over the horizon fighting, originally, an age ago at ranges that, while much closer than she was currently dealing with also made use of weapons far slower than lightspeed beams.

With the Drasin so far inside her defensive circle that she could practically *smell* them through the ship's scanners, Jenn felt like she was knife fighting with terra-watt powered blades, and just focused as hard as she could on *not being* where the enemy beams were slicing while her gunners focused on potting the enemy ships where they were.

"Watch your six, skipper," Roy called out. "Got a pair of them coming around from there."

"I see them," She grunted. "Boxing us in. Hold on to

something."

Roy paled, hugging his console instinctively despite being strapped in. When Cardsharp said hold on to something, he'd long since learned that she *meant it.*

A second later the whole ship spun around him, or so it felt, as she did *something* to the CM field, thrusters, and the warp field that flung them helter skelter, limbs akimbo it felt. The urge to throw up came and went quickly as he forced his vision clear with panted breathing intended to keep blood where it was supposed to be.

"I can't believe I used to question why we had to wear compression suits," He bitched as he hung on for dear life, fighting against the urge to vomit and black out at the same time.

"Suck it, you big baby," Cardsharp said through clenched teeth, her eyes not looking away from the fight.

The Drasin were converging on her position, largely ignoring the more powerful beams as the Imperial cruiser lashed out at them relentlessly.

Never thought I'd see the day that an Imp was giving one of us covering fire, She thought with wry amusement despite the situation.

"More of them, boss," Roy called. "Vectoring in... Nine low. Eight Low. Six high..."

"I see them, I see them," She growled, feeling the noose tightening around her throat.

There was only so much maneuvering you could do, particularly in open space, before you... ironically... ran out of places to run.

She slagged two more with her paired emitter ribbons slashing out independently as the ship split the distance between two Drasin vessels with a lightning maneuver that caused them to maneuver wildly in their attempt to get her back in their sites.

Unfortunately, that pair was only a small part of the opposing force in this case.

Cardsharp screamed, more from shock and anger than pain,

as a beam made it through the warp field and scored across the *Casino's* hull. Her instinctual and autonomic response to move away from the pain jerked the ship sharply from the beam's path, but the faint burning sensation along her back told Jenn that they'd not gotten away clean.

"Report!"

"Moderate hull damage, Ma'am, no breach but we can't take another hit there," Roy said quickly. "Cam plates are roasted all in a line from forward dorsal line on the starboard side to the aft port. Don't get hit again."

"I wasn't *trying* to get hit *that* time," She snapped, her anger directed more at herself than him however.

She knew too well that only her autonomic reaction time, combined with the NICS interface, allowed them to survive *that* strike.

The fight was quickly going from unpalatable to untenable.

Reluctantly she gestured to again access the system locking down the Pulse Torpedoes, fingers tapping out the code.

"Pulse tubes unlocked," Roy said, his voice thick with concern.

"I know," She answered grimly. "They don't get whatever they're after, Roy. They just… *don't.*"

"Yes Ma'am."

Cardsharp rolled clear of another strafing run, letting the beams silently pass by into the deep black, the gunboat's beams firing back furiously. She ignored the fighting briefly to ensure that they had an active lock on the Imperial cruiser.

With all the scanner energy bouncing around, she knew that they wouldn't be able to tell that the *Casino* had a lock, but it still sent a shiver down her spine when it pinged clean.

"Cruiser locked in."

Cardsharp looked around carefully, noting that the Drasin were still swarming them. In a few more minutes, if that, she would have nowhere left to run.

Fuck.

"Standby to fire," She ordered, twisting away from an enemy sweep, returning the beam fire from her own emitter ribbons. "Not until *I* give the command."

"Aye, Ma'am. On your command only," Roy agreed, voice subdued.

She didn't blame him. They had Marines on board that ship, but...

Goddamnit, there has to be a way out of this!

"Drasin closing again, Ma'am. We're running out of room to maneuver."

I can see that, Cardsharp thought angrily as she ducked the ship behind the cruiser's shielding spacetime warp, letting beams warp off in random directions as they tried to transit through the fields.

"Check fire. Not until we have *no* choice," She ordered, returning fire *through* the warp, but angling her beams so that they would deflected into the enemy's path, like playing a lethal game of pool among the stars.

"Check fire, aye." Roy said quietly, "Six more, inbound. Another five coming around from the aft. Ma'am... we're out of time."

Fuck!

"Fine, open..."

She was interrupted by a crackle in the air as a signal came through, broadcast in the open.

"Sorry we're late. Tuck in, Jenn, you've got backup."

Cardsharp twisted, eyes wide as she spotted the beams in the augmented system a moment later, sweeping across space to cut down the closest Drasin with a single pass, slagging them to molten silicate.

"Who?" Roy looked up.

"It's The *Revenge*," She grinned. "And it's about *damn* time,

Crown!"

*****

Gaia's Revenge

Steph rolled his eyes, "Everyone's a critic. You don't want last second rescues, then don't go getting into trouble out in the middle of bumstead nowhere, Jenn!"

He glanced aside, cutting his comm, "Status of the *Bell*?"

"A few minutes behind," Milla answered nervously. "We are too fast for them to keep up."

"Looks like we got here just in time, so let's keep up the pressure," He returned focus to the fight. "All gunners, beams *free*. Cut them down."

"All gunners, beams free," Milla answered as she sent out the commands. "I believe that the enemy has noticed our presence, Steph."

"Well, let's greet them nice and proper then, shall we?"

"But of course."

*****

CHAPTER 39

The *Casino*

Cardsharp bit back a sardonic response as she heard the tone that signified Steph had cut her off.

"Arrogant old bastard," She grinned as she again leaned into the suspension field, hitting the thrusters to match, and felt the ship surge forward around her as she threaded the needle that Steph had just opened up for her. "Thank God for him."

"The *Revenge* is a welcome bit of backup, skipper," Roy said nervously, "but it won't be enough. We still have more contacts inbound."

"You might be right, but if the *Revenge* is here, I'll bet dollars to donuts we have more backup coming." Cardsharp said simply.

She put the *Casino* into a tight roll, bringing them under the plane of the enemy attack even as they started to react to the *Revenge* coming in from above. There was a brief moment of indecision among the Drasin, and in that second the two gunboats *tore* through their ranks.

Drasin vessels were slagged in a line of devastation long enough that you could measure with a flashlight and a *stopwatch*, buying the *Casino* some much needed breathing room in the void.

"Skipper, hail from the Imp Cruiser."

"Fuck. Alright, put em through."

*****

IC *From the Flames*

Kaela bolted upright as the new contact surged into existence on her screens.

How good are their stealth capabilities? She wondered in shock as the ship was identified as *Gaia's Revenge*, the lead ship that the Gaians fielded, one she knew had long been Captained by a man who called himself *Teach.*

Over the years, the Empire had managed to learn that was not his real name, but rather a reference to an ancient mariner from whatever world the Gaian's hailed from. Teach was supposedly a pirate of some renown which was ironic, she supposed, when considering the number of anti-pirate operations the Gaians seemed *eager* to take on.

The pair of vessels immediately fell into a *dance* as they moved across her screens, responding to one another without the *time* needed to properly communicate their actions. It was the sort of thing you only saw from warriors who knew one another *beyond* mere trust. They didn't trust each other, because they didn't *need to.* At that level it was more like one being.

Does your left hand trust your right?

For trust to exist, the *possibility* of betrayal also needed to exist. She saw none of that in the tableau before her.

These people are dangerous. Imperial Command has clearly not comprehended just what these people are.

"Ship's Commander, the surge of the newcomers assault has pushed back the enemy." Sunnam said. "Beam density is dropping quickly!"

"All decks, standby for acceleration!" She called, seizing the opportunity. "Balance the warp field, set for maximum acceleration!"

"Yes, Ship's Commander! Field ready to balance, maximum acceleration... on your command!"

"Do it!"

The background hum of the ship faded briefly as they all felt a shift in gravity, tugging invisibly at them as the system briefly went out of balance. In a moment it all came back, the humm surging as power ran fully through the systems.

"Contact the *Casino*." She ordered.

"Yes, Ship's Commander," Sirra answered automatically, connecting the systems to open the hail. "On display, Ship's Commander."

The face of the Gaian looked back briefly from the screen before her eyes flicked slightly to one side.

"Ship's Commander," Kaela said firmly. "We have succeeded in shifting stance and are applying full power to acceleration now."

"I see it, *go*," The Gaian said shortly, obviously running her ship while speaking. "We'll catch up."

"We can provide necessary cover to extract yourself and your..." Kaela started to offer.

"I said *GO*," The woman snapped fiercely. "They want your ship, not mine. Ship's Commander, be aware, I will not *allow* these beasts to have your ship. Get clear, before I am forced to destroy your vessel myself. Whatever these things want, no sane minded person will *ever* allow them to gain."

Kaela stood, stone faced for a moment, before she inclined her head slightly.

"Very well. Stars grace your fight, Ship's Commander." Kaela said simply before gesturing to have the channel cut.

She was not particularly happy with being *ordered* to do anything by a Non-imperial citizen, but frankly the Gaian was correct. Whatever the Drasin wanted, had to be denied them at all costs.

Still, one cannot speak like that to me in public without any response... however... for another time.

"Get us clear of here," She ordered, eyes on Yseb who was trying very hard not to look in her direction.

The Helmsman nodded, still not looking over.

"Yes, Ship's Commander," He said, trying not to sound too eager.

The big ship curved smoothly in space, accelerating smoothly away from the massive construct and the swarm of enemy it apparently housed.

*****

"Secure the corridor," Amanda ordered as the squad came to a stop. She looked back to the Imperial crewman who was still reluctantly tagging along with them. "What's up this way?"

"Stores," He answered nervously. "Nothing critical."

Amanda glanced up the walls, her thermal overlay running as she switched over to the squad channel.

"Sarge, are you seeing what I'm seeing?" She asked dryly.

The Sergeant snorted, "You mean the completely unmissable thermal trail left by a horde of those fuckers running through here? What do you think?"

"I think I'm wondering why the Drasin, who seem to have been able to locate a data pipe that the crewman back there didn't know about seem so interested in the ship's stores," She answered.

The Sergeant nodded slowly, "You think there's more there than he knows?"

"I think if were to strip that data pipe, we'd find it led back this way."

"I believe you may be right, Ma'am."

"Let's move."

*****

Gaia's Revenge

"Jesus there's a lot of them," Steph gritted as he rolled to the left as a beam from the *Casino* slagged a Drasin trying to take him on the right. "haven't seen anything like this since the first Invasion."

"Jenn has sent her analysis," Milla offered. "She has concluded that the Drasin are likely attempting to remove the generation limits emplaced on them by the Empire."

That made him jerk around, the ship twisting with him briefly before Steph righted it.

"Is she *sure*?" He demanded, focus back on the fight in less than a second.

"No, but her conclusion is logical and fits the available observations."

"Well... fuck. Ok, grab everything she has, get it packaged up and tight beam to the *Bell* the *instant* she's in range. Laser comm, secure and encrypted. No bleed, love." He ordered.

She sniffed at him, "I am hardly ignorant of such things. Deal with what is on your plate, husband, and leave me my task, yes?"

Women, Steph rolled his eyes, but wisely opted not to say anything.

He didn't have time for it, after all, as much fun as it might have been.

The Imperial ship was now withdrawing from the fight, which in light of Cardsharp's revelations, made a hell of a lot of sense. He'd wondered briefly about their sudden acceleration and vector, since one thing he'd never associated with the Empire was cowardice.

Venal corruption, genocide, all manner of other ugly attributes certainly, but not cowardice.

If they were right about the Drasin goal, however, getting that ship *out of here* had just become a priority.

Would be easier to just blow it to hell and gone, part of his mind whispered, but he discounted it immediately, barring no other options.

It wasn't a matter of wanting to save the Imperials' a ship or crew, but rather that if Cardsharp's guess was right, it would be better than an *Imperial* ship and crew delivered the news back to the Empire. They would *need* to be on guard, and if the news came from anyone else, Steph suspected that the Empire might a little... slow... to implement new protocols.

"Cardsharp," He called in the open, "Reform on me, let's plow the road for the cruiser. Get them out of here."

"Roger that, Crown, I'm with you."

Steph hid a grimace, he could hear the hint of amusement as Jenn used the English translation of his callsign.

Never should have told her that story.

He put that aside, however, and snapped his gunboat around with full thrusters in addition to the warp fields running well past their rated maximum. The *Casino* matched the move, and both started putting up a wall of beams that slagged anything that came in their range, as the enemy seemed to get it into their skulls, assuming they had such, that the cruiser was in fact starting to get away.

*****

Bellerophon

"That's one hell of a furball."

Roberts ignored the softly spoken comment from the conn, mostly because he was too busy analyzing the situation. At their current range they could scan the Imperial Cruiser easily enough, and the two IFF codes from the Archangels were lit off bright enough to see from a lot farther out than the Bell currently was.

The Drasin contacts were numerous and swarming, making it difficult to get a proper count on the beasts, but that wasn't unusual in his experience.

It's been a while since I've been here, Roberts thought grimly as he glanced aside to look at the scans of the Dyson swarm that surrounded them. *Well, they know we're here. Let's make sure they never forget the sight.*

"Priority target Drasin contacts," He ordered. "All weapons free."

"Priority targets locked. Weapons Free." The Ops officer responded. "The Imperial Cruiser, Sir?"

Roberts was tempted to simply ask 'what about them', but for some reason it looked like the Archangels were covering their withdrawal.

Might be just preserving their cover, but let's prioritize the Drasin until we can ask.

"Tag them as non-hostile for the moment," He ordered, noting the sharp looks that bounced around the deck. "I want to get a better feel for the situation before we hole their hull and leave them drifting for their *little weapons* to turn into a meal."

There was little love lost for the Empire among his people, and Roberts had absolutely *none* of what little did exist.

"Aye skipper. Targets locked."

"Fire as she bears."

*****

Gravity accelerated antimatter pulses exploded from the magnetic containment of the *Bellerophon's* tubes, launching across space at vastly superior speeds to the versions originally mounted on the Heroic Class cruisers during the war, hitting near lightspeed in an instant as the positron mass was flung from the ship.

They were passed only by the beams of the great ship as the *Bell* opened up with everything in her inventory.

*****

IC *From the Flames*

"By the abyss!"

Kaela snapped around, angrily scowling at the speaker, "Chief…"

"New contact, Ship's Commander," He cut her off, "I apologize for the outburst, but… look to the screens Ma'am."

She looked up, eyes widening as the numbers began scrolling.

Abyssal beasts. What in the…

She didn't even think that Imperial Battle Cruisers could match the numbers she was seeing, though the basic hull profile appeared to match a standard configuration cruiser.

They were able to get some scans of the beams as they slashed past, rending the enemy vessels from their composite atomic bonds due to the sheer power she was reading. The Drasin were *exploding*, not merely melting as she might normally have expected.

It was the secondary scans, however, that set her back.

She recognized that weapon as the scans registered the pulses that flashed past her vessel at nearly the speed of light.

Negative matter.

The pulses *hammered* into the Drasin line, annihilating anything they struck with explosive force that would depopulate a *planet* if fired into atmosphere.

Not as a total, mind… but *each.*

There was only one culture she knew of that used such a weapon, and a chill went down her spine as she realized it.

The flame bringers… Terrans.

They live.

*****

CHAPTER 40

IC *From the Flames*

Amanda held up a fist, echoing the motion of the Marine in front of her, and waited for the squad to come to a stop before she shifted forward to see what had caught the man's attention.

It wasn't hard to spot, the small swarming crowd of Drasin drones were riveting to say the least, occupying the corridor up ahead, milling about, either on watch or just lost, though she wasn't betting on the latter of the options.

Picket force, then, but what are the guarding?

She waved up the rest of the squad, taking a knee as she shouldered her rifle and looked down the optics with a critical eye, selecting targets and sending them to each of the men in the squad.

"Take your positions," She whispered, shifting enough to let them set up around her. "Fire on my mark, as one."

"Hoorah."

She checked her GAR-22 on instinct, making certain it was loaded and locked on a round, then settled it back into her shoulder, her finger curling easily around the trigger as she waited. The squad moved smoothly and, more importantly, quietly as they got into position and signaled that they were ready.

The Drasin were down the corridor, almost out of sight due to the very slight arc that was a signature quality of Cruiser class ships built to the specifications of the Empire and Priminae blueprints, the curves allowing the floors to feel straight and flat despite the relatively close source of gravity in the singularity core.

"All set, Ma'am."

"Fire," She all but whispered.

The sound of her command was lost in the *roar* of the rifles echoing through the bulkheads as the slugs from their weapons cut burning trails through the air before slamming into the Drasin drones. The front line went down in shattered husks, already cooling before their fellows reacted to the assault.

Amanda's rifle slammed into her shoulder twice more before she called for a check on the fire and rose to her feet.

"Forward," She ordered, gesturing with her left hand while her right controlled the rifle briefly.

The team started moving on command, pushing into the smoky mess they'd just made, their suit air protecting them from the ablated tungsten and uranium dust that had been burned from their rounds by friction and heat.

The Drasin picket group had been eliminated, but Amanda was quite certain that they were not the bulk of the enemy forces in the area, and so she kept her team moving slowly as they cleared each door and side wall before moving past.

She glanced back only once to ensure that the Imperial crewman wasn't following, thankfully he'd gotten the message earlier and didn't seem intent on walking into the poison smoke that had filled the air from their shots even as the ship's scrubbers started to pull it from the air.

"Negative contact, Ma'am."

"Keep moving, Sergeant. They're up here somewhere."

*****

Colonel Keenan scowled as she stepped over the cooling corpses of the Drasin they'd just put down. If her team was correct they were near the Command Deck, but this group hadn't seemed to be doing anything beyond *scratching* at the walls without any seeming intent to actually cause damage.

What the hell is going on? She thought, confused as she spotted the bulkhead and sealed doors up ahead.

They were clearly blast doors, intended to take explosive decompression and even some direct fire if needed, but certainly not sufficient to do more than briefly slow the Drasin.

Keenan nodded to the door and gestured to the Gunny, who nodded in return and waved on a Corporal to step forward. The Corporal walked cautiously up to the door and then banged on it, hard enough to send an echo through the air around them.

"Ship's Commander," She called, "The corridor has been secured!"

They waited, but nothing seemed to happen, so she nodded again and the Corporal banged out a pattern again.

Several more seconds passed, before the Gunny turned back.

"Breaching charge, Colonel?"

"Negative, if there's anyone on the other side we'd just as likely cut them in half as not," Keenan answered. "We'll have to…"

She paused, hearing a sound from the door.

Her Marines shifted quickly, the Corporal falling back as they got their weapons almost up to the ready before Keenan signaled them back. The doors cracked open, barely, and a single person peered out with one of the Imperial beam weapons in hand. He looked at them for a moment before falling back quickly, yelling something she couldn't make out.

The doors ground slightly as they opened up then.

Doubt they use those much, sounds like they need lubrication, She thought wryly as enough room to properly admit a person opened up.

"You are the Gaians?" The man asked as he reappeared.

"That's us," Keenan confirmed. "Colonel Keenan, Marine Corps. Are you people alright?"

Part of her rebelled at asking the Imps if they were alright, given everything that had happened, but she'd been doing this job for long enough to bury that impetus. The job mattered, and right now the job entailed keeping the Imps in the dark.

"We are fine. Ship's Commander Eurydice would like to speak."

Keenan nodded, gesturing to the Gunny, "Secure this area. I'll be out shortly."

"Don't like this Colonel," The Gunny growled. "Not one bit."

"What's to like?" Keenan snorted. "Just keep the Drasin off our backs."

"Hoorah, Colonel."

Keenan nodded easily and strode past the squad, through the gap in the blast doors as she stepped into he Command Deck of the Imperial cruiser beyond.

*****

Kaela barely looked up from the screens as the Gaian Colonel entered, stomping hard enough to send vibrations through the deck in the heavy armor the soldier wore.

She was too focused on the newcomer to the scene, the ship that appeared to be a standard cruiser configuration but was so much more than just that.

In just moments it had wreaked utter havoc beyond what her own ship and the Gaians *combined* had managed in the entire fight up to that point. Those weapons, things she'd only read about in briefings, were far beyond what she'd ever expected to see, and now that she had Kaela found herself wondering what she could do if the Terrans opted to engage her ship.

For the moment they're spending their ire on the Drasin, for which I suppose I should be grateful, but what happens if we survive through to the other side of this fight?

She had to assume that they would destroy her vessel if they had the chance.

I certainly would theirs, given the opportunity.

Unfortunately, she didn't think that she was going to get it.

"Ship's Commander."

Kaela glanced up again, nodding to the Colonel briefly, "Colonel, is it?"

"Keenan, Ma'am," The Colonel said. "Colonel Keenan, Gaian Marines."

"I have to thank you for clearing my ship," Kaela said honestly, albeit reluctantly. "We've begun receiving reports again as my crew are able to retake positions thanks to your forces."

"Just our job."

"Somehow, I doubt that," Kaela said, straightening and turning her full attention to the Colonel. "I am afraid that we are far from out of the current troubles, Colonel Keenan, however we are attempting to withdraw as quickly as possible. Your Ship's Commander believes that something on the *Flames* is the target of these beasts. It would be best, I believe, for both our people that they fail to acquire it."

Keenan couldn't disagree with that.

"That matches my orders, Ship's Commander," She confirmed. "We're to clear the ship and ensure that it not fall into Drasin control."

Kaela looked up sharply, something about that last part and the way the wording was delivered nagged at her, but she couldn't decide what it was that bothered her.

"Very well," She said finally, with a gesture to the screens. "As you can see, the situation outside the hull is not particularly good."

Keenan looked over the numbers, and found herself moderately surprised. She had expected them to be far worse.

"Pardon," She said, "but it seems that the enemy numbers have been much thinned from my last update."

"Indeed," Kaela confirmed, tapping a command and showing something else, "We have a new problem."

Keenan looked over the specifications and inside her helmet her eyes widened as she recognized the Bell's colors and the scans that matched the signature of antimatter weapons.

"An Imperial cruiser?" She said aloud, not letting any of her relief filter through to her voice.

"No. Not Imperial," Kaela said tersely. "An enemy. A hated foe, one from before my time, but one that cannot be trusted all the same."

It took all her control for Keenan not to snort at that statement.

Some gall there, She thought, *Saying that **we** can't be trusted. It was your people who started the war, bitch, who committed genocide… or gave it a damned good attempt, at least. Just because we gave as good as we got, you want to pretend that **we** can't be trusted?*

The hypocrisy of the Empire galled her to her core, but there was nothing she could do about it in the moment.

"They appear to be focusing on the Drasin," She said neutrally instead.

"For now," Kaela answered that, with cold hatred in her tone.

"Then, for now, I suggest allowing them to do so," Keenan said. "We have enough problems, inviting more would be… unwise."

The Imperial Ship's Commander glared at her, but Keenan could tell that the heat was aimed elsewhere.

Reluctantly, the ship's Commander backed down.

"I am forced to agree, as much as I would prefer not," She admitted. "However, there is every chance that we will be in a deadly fight with more than one foe before this is over."

"Then we will deal with what comes, as it comes."

"Indeed. Thank you, Colonel. If you could," Kaela gestured to the blast doors. "Please, clear my ship. I will deal with the threats beyond the hull, if you help my security crews deal with those within."

Keenan nodded once, bobbing her suit to make it visible.

Blowing this damned hull to the heavens and back is looking better and better, She thought as she turned and left.

Behind her, the crew on the command deck of the Imperial cruiser continued as they had through the entire conversation, running weapons and scanners, fending off the attacks from the Drasin pursuing them.

*****

"Cover! Cover!"

Amanda pressed herself into the curving deck, trying to be as small as she could possibly make herself as the beams cut the air overhead.

She imagined she could smell the ozone in the air from the energy ionizing the atmosphere, but knew that it was just her head playing tricks. Struggling to get her rifle out from under her, Amanda pushed the GAR-22 ahead of her as she heard her squad return fire.

The Drasin had dropped from the overhead deck, somehow having been hiding right up there in the steel and cabling. Their only warning had been when the lighting flickered and went out, likely damaged by the alien spider crab's movement.

She didn't manage to get a shot off before the Sarge and rest put the bastard down, though, and found herself slowly picking herself up off the deck.

"There's something up here, Sarge, Lieutenant," Smith said, casting them a mirror of his suit scanners. "Way too much power draw in this sector for cargo or logistics supplies."

Amanda checked the numbers quickly, finding herself in agreement.

"That's enough to power a small destroyer," The Sergeant commented.

"Or a big processing system," Amanda said. "Look at the patterns. That's not random."

Smith nodded, "Yes Ma'am. I'm guessing encrypted, but it *leaks* enough that I can scan the processing from here."

"Record it. All of it," She ordered as she gestured the team forward.

They moved slowly up to the end of the corridor, finding themselves confused by the fact that it dead ended in place, with no sign of any door or other way out.

Amanda looked right and left slowly, shaking her head, "Access on another deck?"

"Then why were the Drasin here?" The Sergeant asked,

uncertain.

She shook her head, confused, "I don't know. Followed the signal, same as we are?"

"Why didn't they cut through the wall then?" The Sergeant said. "We know they *can*."

"I… don't know," Amanda admitted.

Something wasn't right.

"Thermal scan, Ma'am. Check it," Smith offered.

Amanda clicked over her thermal overall and took an involuntary step back.

"Oh shit…"

CHAPTER 41

Bellerophon

"Tight beam from the *Revenge*, Skipper."

"Send it," Roberts ordered, looking down to his console as the *Bell* continued to fire as they approached the fight from range.

"To your ID, Sir."

Roberts got the notification and moved on through, grabbing the summary page first once he saw just how much data had been sent over. It only took a few seconds for him to get deadly serious.

Well isn't this a stone cold nightmare? He thought grimly as he read the speculations, hating that he couldn't poke any holes in the guesswork. *If this is right… it has implications.*

It was also going to make figuring out what to do from here considerably more difficult to decide on. Just glancing at the overview, his initial thought was to scrap the Imperial ship. A few direct hits with the torpedo launchers would pretty much guarantee that the Drasin got nothing of value from what little was left, afterall.

The Marines on board were a problem, though put back to a corner, he'd make that call if he had to.

He wasn't trained to just think about the outcome of the battle, however, but also to consider the effect it would have going forward. Wars could be lost because you stubbornly insisted on winning a battle, or even winning all of them.

The only battle that truly counted was the last one you fought. Every battle before that is negotiable, and if losing a battle put you in a better place to win the *last* one, then losing was the winning move.

And that training was currently *screaming* at him, though it took a few moments before he realized just what it was warning him about.

No one puts this much investment into a plan like this and hinges it entirely on the outcome of one battle. They will have backups, alternate plays. What are they?

*****

Gaia's Revenge

"Imperial Cruiser has adjusted its warp fields," Milla announced. "They are in motion, heading away from the fighting."

Steph risked a quick glance, noting the vectors with some irritation, "Would have made it easier if they didn't adjust course to flee the *Bell* while she's *actively providing cover fire*."

Milla shrugged, unruffled by the situation. They'd dealt with worse, on every level, in the past.

"Likely too much to hope that they would approach any ship they identify as potentially Terran or Priminae at this point," She said easily enough.

She had a point, Steph knew, he just wished that she didn't.

"Still makes our job more difficult," He griped, but without much real feeling. "Did the Bell get our message?"

"Confirmed. No response, as yet," She said quickly.

"It'll take time for Jason to dig through that big of an info dump," Steph said, unconcerned with the lack of immediate response, "Just so long as he has it."

"Receipt confirmed, yes."

"Good enough," Steph said. "Jason will recognize the significance."

Milla had no comment to add to that, she had little doubt that the Captain of the *Bellerophon* would indeed spot the obvious significance of the findings. The formidable man in command of the *Bell* was not one to miss a detail, it wasn't in his character, though she had never been all that comfortable around him for reasons she couldn't place.

It was as though space itself became brittle around him, though not through any action she could detect. Words crackled from his mouth like broken glass, though he said all the right words when he did speak.

Steph had told her that some men were like that, but it was not something she had ever known, growing up among the Priminae.

Terrans are strange, and no amount of time is enough to fully acclimate me to their strangeness.

Milla was honestly uncertain whether she should be glad of that or not.

"Coming back around," Steph said, through her thoughts.

"Aye, targets open. Beams free," She announced, just ahead of his own mouth of the words.

Just because she couldn't get used to them didn't mean that she didn't *know* them.

Steph just grinned briefly at her before throwing the ship into the fight with an abandon.

*****

Captured Destroyer

"Well, shit."

Marcus Reid was unhappy to be anywhere within twenty *parsecs* of where he was currently sitting, but that wasn't about change his orders.

They'd come in hot as they could, but it was clear they were late to the party by a not insignificant bit of time. The *Bell* of all ships was here, and not holding back, while both the *Casino* and the *Revenge* were mixing things up in a cloud of what his IFF was now calling enemy contacts ever since he'd grabbed the update being broadcast from the pair of Archangel Class Gunboats.

The Drasin were from after his time, mostly. He'd been a young officer during the invasion, and lucky enough to be one of the ships the Admiral withdrew from Sol Space with. The only fighting he'd seen had been in the tail end, when they returned to push the remaining Drasin out of the system.

Too young to have had any real responsibilities at the time, and not enough of a prodigy to get them anyway, but he remembered the nightmares all the same.

Tangling with those beasts, nothing but a half refitted Free Stars Destroyer under his ass? Well it wasn't really on his bucket list.

*If only because it's a damn good way to **kick** said bucket.*

"Beams hot, Captain."

Marcus glanced aside to where his least experienced man was standing Ops, looking excited to be there rather than scared like any *sane* person might.

Children.

"Roger that," He said aloud. "Weapons free. If it crawls or flies and it ain't one of ours, light the fucker up."

"Yes sir."

Michaels gestured and his command went out, the powerful forward beams of the Destroyer screaming as the system sucked power at atrocious levels, making him wince.

Alignment's off on those conduits, Marcus thought grimly. *We'll be lucky if we have more than a few minutes of beam power at this rate.*

He reached out, opening a comm channel within the ship.

"Main Engineering."

"Kate, please tell me…"

"Doing what we can," Kathryn McGill told him firmly, "but we can't do much about the alignment while we're firing, skipper."

"How long…"

"I give you maybe five minutes at full power."

Marcus nodded slowly, "Thank you, do as you can. Reid out."

It was often a mixed blessing to have a good engineer under his command, in his experience at least. McGill was damned good at what she did, and better again at improvising when it inevitably became necessary. It was one of the things that made her invaluable on the prize crews.

She was also curt, prone to interrupting, and almost always answered questions before he could finish asking them.

Efficient?

Yes.

Annoying?

*Fucking **hell**, it's so damned annoying.*

*****

Gaia's Revenge

"Backup on location," Milla said cooly.

Steph didn't look up from his flying, "Who this time?"

"Marcus Reid's vessel," She answered. "No title listed on the IFF still, so a new one it seems."

"Reid? Oh *fuck*." Steph swore.

"What is it?"

"That's Eric's ride," Steph grumbled.

Her eyes widened, "I thought he was being considered for a position on the *Bell*?"

"He was, but she went dark before the orders were cut," Steph told her, nodding to the imagery he was surrounded by, "Likely chasing down this crap."

"But... a Prize ship?"

No one got sent out to prize ships for their first assignment, so he understood her confusion.

"It was either that or wait until something else opened up," Steph sighed, "And you know Eric."

Milla grimaced, shaking her head slightly.

She did, indeed, know her son too well, and his reaction to that choice was not one that would surprise her.

"Well, ring the bells," Steph went on darkly. "The family's all here."

Now let's get everyone back out again in one piece.

*****

IC *From the Flames*

Another ship? Scans as a Free Stars Destroyer, but why would they be out here? Kaela wondered as she examined the scans from the newcomer.

It only took a moment to answer that, noting that the ship was broadcasting *Gaian* codes.

She had heard that the mercenary people often opted to capture and press captures into service on their side, rather than building up a force of their own. It had seemed an odd choice to her, given the distinct quality of their smaller vessels, but she supposed it lay more credence to the theory that they had lost the logistics support of their own world in one way or another.

In any event, any additional firepower was welcome, but she doubted that a single Destroyer was going to offer up much difference to the outcome of this fight.

"Adjust course," She ordered as she made some alterations to their vector and sent the new numbers along.

"Yes, Ship's Commander. Adjusting."

The new course would bring them closer to the Gaian Destroyer on their way out, providing her vessel with slightly more cover and… in the worst case… at least a chance that the Drasin might split their attention with them.

It galled her deeply, but the Gaian who called herself *Cardsharp* was right. The Drasin wanted her ship, and likely wanted it for intelligence that Kaela couldn't even be certain she *had*. Unfortunately, she couldn't be certain that she *didn't* either, and that was not a risk she could take.

She would have a great deal to think on, once she and hers were clear of this mess.

A lot to think on, and to report to Imperial Command.

And have a few words with same, She thought darkly about just how she wanted that particular conversation to go.

*****

The *Casino*

"Pulse traffic update, skipper!"

"Highlights, if you would," Cardsharp grunted out as she threaded the needle and split the space between two Drasin vessels, the ship's beams raking them vicious even as their counter attack narrowly avoided slagging their fellows.

In space it would take too much luck to trick the enemy into reliably slagging their allies, but it was too tempting to *not* attempt once in a while.

"Reid and his latest fling just arrived," Roy told her.

She snorted, amused by the description.

"Roger that. Any help is good for the moment," She said with feeling.

"The Imperial ship is accelerating smoothly now, two thirds of the Drasin forces are broken off to pursue."

"Like hell they will, plot me a course too…"

"The *Bell* has advised we *not* do anything that you might be thinking," Roy cut her off, amusement dripping from his tone. "They're planning on erasing a few grid cubes, best I can tell."

That would be a good reason not to go chasing down the badguys, Jenn thought to herself.

"Tell me that we're not in direct comms with the *bell*," She pled, though honestly she wasn't certain that she wanted the answer she was asking for.

If they *were* chatting directly with the *Bell*, then secrecy was up… at least for this encounter.

"Nothing quite so obvious, no. They broadcast that in the clear on Imperial frequencies."

"Ah, very well. Give me solutions for making the Drasin survivors wish the *Bell* had finished them off, then."

"Vectors to your HUD," Roy advised as he'd been waiting for that request. "Watch the clock. Timing *matters*."

Cardsharp didn't bother to respond to *that* comment.

She knew damn well how much timing mattered, especially when the artillery strike you were about to charge into the aftermath of had been accomplished with *antimatter*.

A positron was no one's friend, especially when you ran your ship into it and a few billion of its pals.

*****

CHAPTER 42

IC *From the Flames*

"I think we have a problem, Ma'am."

"No shit, Sergeant," Amanda snapped as she stared at the bulkhead ahead of them.

There was a hell of a lot of movement beyond the bulkhead, and not one bit of it looked remotely *human*.

"Ma'am," Smith spoke up, "I think it's worse."

"Worse than *that*?" She gestured toward the bulkhead while looking at the corporal.

"Yes Ma'am," He nodded, bobbing his suit carefully.

Amanda groaned, wanting to do nothing more than just *rub her damned face* but couldn't because of the armor.

"Alright, drop it on me, Corporal."

Smith pointed, "See that extreme heat blob there?"

She nodded slowly, looking to the white mass that was barely visible beyond the bulkhead, several smaller masses moving around it fluidly.

"I see it."

"I think that's a Quantum Computer Solution," He told her. "Sig is different than ours, but it's distinctive enough that it's hard to miss."

Shit.

Amanda felt like she was saying and thinking that a lot on this mission.

A Quantum Computing Solution wasn't a piece of kit that

Earth had casually installed on it's ships. She thought that *maybe* a couple of the Heroics had one, but was dead near *certain* that the *Odysseus* was one of them and she'd gone down in the second invasion.

She didn't think that the Bell had one, nor could she say with certainty of the location of any aside from knowing that both the Nest and Prometheus had one apiece. The Priminae had several, at least, she knew of in a general sort of way but she didn't know if they put them on their ships as a rule.

The power of such a computer system was both in its ability to make intuitive leaps from fragmented data, but also in the essentially unlimited data storage capacity that was part of the systems by the default nature of how they were built. You could store *everything* on one, all human knowledge and history, and whatever else you wanted because the system actually created more space in the quantum structure of the computer as it was needed.

Oh, she was sure that there was *some* sort of data cap involved, but Amanda had never heard of anyone actually *hitting* it. The people who designed the things might know what it was, and if so it was probably in the manuals somewhere, but she'd never had need to read them so she couldn't say for certain.

"Right," She said. "I'm calling the Colonel. Sarge, find us a way in. Smith, I want everything bleeding off that beast recorded. To be *that* hot, it's running a heavy piece of kit. Figure out what."

"Yes Ma'am."

"You've got it, Lieutenant."

"Everyone else," She looked to the rest of the squad, circling her hand slightly with two fingers pointed up. "Perimeter."

They moved quickly, not questioning the order or looking to the Sergeant, she noted with a small shot of pleasure. That shot didn't last long, however, as her duty settled in on her again, and Amanda put in the call over the encrypted command channel.

"Colonel, Lieutenant Michaels."

*****

Keenan paused in her examination of the hot spots her teams were currently dealing with, the encrypted channel getting her attention.

"Go for Keenan, Lieutenant," She responded curtly.

"Colonel, we have a... situation here." Michaels said, sounding calm but the nerves were clearly bubbling below the surface.

"I think we all have situations at the moment, Lieutenant," She chided easily, not letting herself sound too annoyed with the young officer, "Perhaps get to the point?"

"Yes, Ma'am, apologies. We've located what Corporal Smith has identified as a likely QCS."

QCS? What... oh, shit. The Empire has those on ships? That's not in the briefs!

"Understood," She said in fast clipped tones as she reflexively checked Smith's jacket, noting that he was Comm and Computer Tech certified for field work.

That means he can probably tell a QCS from a reactor, at least, She decided. "I'm dispatching reinforcements to your location as fast I can. What can you tell me about the situation as it stands?"

*****

Amanda risked a glance out and around the corridor to get another glance with her own eyes, but quickly ducked back and used the Corporal's feed instead.

"We're looking for a way to access the area the QCS is located in, but the Drasin are already in there," She said.

"What are they doing?" Keenan asked sharply.

"Uncertain, precisely," Amanda admitted. "we're recording the entire spectrum bleed, though. At a guess, I'd say that *someone*... Imperial or Drasin, I can't say which, but someone is running a very cycle heavy bit of software on it."

She tensed up as she heard the Colonel swear over the link, but kept herself from reaction.

"Understood," Keenan said a moment later. "Lieutenant, I

really would prefer to get more forces on site... and someone with a little more experience in the hot seat, no offense."

"Non taken," Amanda answered back.

In all honesty, as thrilling as it was to be making calls and leading her squad, she had long since decided that she was not only in over her head, but the water was only getting deeper by the second.

"Ma'am," She said, tensing, "I have been getting the feeling that I'm missing something really important here. What are the Drasin after? Have we figured anything out?"

There was a long pause from the other side before the Colonel came back.

"Lieutenant, we don't know for certain," Keenan said, causing Amanda's guts to clench up. She'd really hoped that wasn't the case. "What we do have is a guess, and it's bad. You know the history, I'll presume."

"Of the Drasin?" She asked, "Yes Ma'am. Academy covers it, in detail."

"I know, do you remember the intelligence reports acquired concerning the Drasin from the Empire after the first invasion? The ones about the Empire putting Generational Limits on them?"

Amanda nodded slowly as she thought back to those classes, "Yes Ma'am. Those limits were why we'd concluded that the Drasin had burned themselves out, which was why we'd never run into them again."

"Skipper has a different theory, one that seems to fit," Keenan said quickly.

Something clicked in her head.

"They'd went into hibernation, working slower than they normally would," She said, thinking it through, "Planned it out. Laid... a trap? They want the QCS, *that* is what this is all about."

*****

Sharp, that one, Keenan thought, surprised. "That is the

working theory. Now, I have people coming your way, but this is too potentially deadly, Lieutenant. So I need you to disrupt their actions, however you can. Buy time."

She could hear the hesitation in the next seconds before the Lieutenant came back.

"Buy time, Hoorah, Colonel. We'll get it done."

"God speed, Lieutenant."

The connection closed, returning to its dormant state as Keenan looked up to the proverbial heavens.

"Colonel? Are you alright?"

"I'm fine, Gunny," She said wearily as she looked back down.

"As the Colonel says," The gunny responded, sounding doubtful.

"Just hating the job sometimes," She said simply. "Let's get back to it."

"Hoorah, Ma'am."

Sending children to die wears on a soul after a while.

*****

Amanda let the closed link sit in silence for a moment as she considered options.

The Drasin weren't pushing back on their presence, something she wasn't foolish enough to believe was due to the aliens not being aware of her team's position. They'd had to make noise to get where they were, and the creatures were purportedly a hive mind.

Which told her that they weren't interested in taking the ship in the conventional sense of things.

They want something other than the ship, something more important... something they don't even need to escape the ship with in order to succeed.

Data.

"Sarge, circle back," She ordered softly, glancing to Smith next.

"You getting everything?"

"Hoorah, LT."

"Make sure it's backed up to the network and shot back to the *Casino* at every opportunity," She ordered. "Leave it recording when we move out."

Smith looked up sharply, "Leave it?"

"Put a grenade on it," She said, knowing that the encryption keys buried in the system were too high value to risk being taken, "but I want it recording *everything* for as long as it can. Hoorah?"

"Hoorah, Ma'am. I'll get it done."

"Good man," She said, looking up as the Sergeant arrived.

"Ma'am."

"Orders," She said simply. "Backup is coming, but we're going to have to start the party without them."

The Sergeant looked grim, but didn't object at all.

"Understood. ETA to backup?"

"Unknown," She shrugged, "Few minutes? More, maybe, depends on how much trouble they have finding the way I suppose."

Or whether they got into fights on the way, ran into obstructions, or had to explain their presence to the Imps, or any of a thousand other things… but she didn't say any of that aloud.

"Right you are, Ma'am."

"In the meantime, our job is to disrupt enemy operations," She said firmly. "The Drasin are pulling intel we don't want them to have."

The Sergeant nodded slowly, "Understood. Any idea what that intel might be?"

"With certainty? No," She said, "however we're assuming worst case outcome."

"And that would be?"

"They're trying to jailbreak the generational limit the Empire slapped on them back in the day."

The Sergeant stilled for a moment, his armor almost vibrating with the suddenness of his stopping. It only took a second for him to come out of it, however, and he nodded firmly.

"Understood, Ma'am." He said, "I will get the men ready."

"thank you."

*****

Kaela Eurydice glowered as she watched the ship engaging the charging enemy that was racing up along their aft wake, weapons now clearly aiming to disable her fleeing ship.

It would seem that the Gaian's guess was closer than I would like it to be, She thought dourly.

The Drasin had quickly changed tactics when the *Flames* had broken clear of their encirclement, moving from merely harassing shots to beams that were clearly aiming to cripple her vessel. Thus far they'd taken it with a minimal impact on their operating means, but that wouldn't last. One good strike through the warp field that just got lucky enough would be enough to badly impact their acceleration, and she didn't even want to consider what would happen if the *Flames'* FTL capability was crippled.

"Gaian destroyer is engaging the pursuing Drasin, Ship's Commander."

Kaela nodded curtly, but inwardly wondered at the actions of the *mercenaries.*

There is more to them than we know. Or, at least, She amended the thought, *More than Imperial Command is briefing us with.*

Mercenaries don't throw themselves into a fight like this with no payment agreement in place, for one... and *intelligent* mercenaries wouldn't take a job such as the one the three Gaian vessels were engaged in for *any* price.

Money was difficult to spend when one was dead, after all.

Yet here, the Gaians were *throwing* themselves into this fight completely of their own accord as best she could tell.

Unless someone did hire them for this? She thought, though that made no sense to her at all.

And then there was the presence of the *Terran* vessel.

Kaela had been trying not to think about that one, almost as much as she'd been trying to convince herself to fire upon them with everything her ship could bring to bear.

Neither option was a good idea, however, and so she found herself stewing over the situation in which she and the *Flames* now existed.

It was all so very wrong, but she couldn't find any other path than forward at the best speed her ship could manage.

"Ship's Commander!"

Sunnam's sharp tone jerked her back to the present, "What is it, Chief?"

"Contacts. More contacts." He said dully.

"How many?" She asked, her gut sinking.

"I don't know, the computer is unable to get an accurate count."

Kaela closed her eyes.

*Can **NOTHING** go right on this abyss be damned assignment?*

*****

CHAPTER 43

Bellerophon

"Contacts, Skipper!"

"Count and localize," Roberts ordered.

"Still working on a count, sir, but…" His scanner chief shook her head, "Look to the screens, Sir."

Roberts looked over, and it took a moment before he recognized what he was seeing. The contacts were *pouring* out of the Dyson construct in multiple locations, the computer clearly having trouble telling them apart there were so many, so closely packed.

Fuck.

"Plot us an escape path," He ordered. "Open a comm channel, no encryption, wide beam."

"Aye skipper!"

"Channel open!"

"This is Roberts, Captain of the *Bellerophon*," He said firmly as he rose to his feet. "We are plotting possible escape routes now. Strongly suggest we cover one another on our way out. If that swarm gets any of us alone, we're done. Alone we die, together we *may* have a chance."

"Cut it," He said with a slash of his hand.

"Signal cut, sir," The Comm's officer said, looking over his way. "You think they'll do it, Sir?"

"I don't care," Roberts said. "That was just to give the Archangels and Reid an excuse. The Imperials can go hang with their monsters for all the *fucks* I give."

He looked over the numbers, not liking what he was seeing at all, not that would be much of a difference from any other time he'd dealt with the monsters out there.

The Drasin numbers were clearly well into the *millions* at a minimum, but unless he and his people got extraordinarily stupid or just as unlucky they wouldn't be able to bring even a fraction of that to bear on the *Bell* and the others. It was just in the nature of space and the sheer size of a construct the size of the Dyson shell, you could only move to any given point with so much speed.

"Make for that cluster there," He ordered, pointing to one of the stronger positions the Drasin had seemingly enforced.

"Sir? We could vector for the hole in the formation..."

Roberts snorted, "If that's not a trap, these bastards are getting dumber and we have nothing to worry about. We have the firepower to punch through where I directed, and they don't have enough forces in range to reinforce it quickly enough. Now, if you check the holes in their formation... well, go ahead and do it... plot the response time for all the Drasin units around the hole."

The Helmsman frowned, then turned around and did what Roberts suggested. It only took a few seconds before he paled and flinched back from the console.

"I figure it for at least... three hundred or so response groups in range to close that noose," Roberts said. "Sound about right?"

"Almost," The Helmsman nodded, "You couldn't see the ones on the far side of the scans... call it almost four hundred groups. How did you run those numbers in your head so fast? The computer..."

"Computers are faster than humans for getting precise numbers," Roberts said firmly, "but not even Quantum rigs can beat a human's ability to make an estimate based on minimal data. I didn't run the numbers, I didn't have to. I've seen it before, I know what they can do. Set the course."

"Already set, Skipper," The Helmsman admitted. "I put it in before I turned around to ask."

"Good man."

*****

Captured Destroyer

"get ready to put us on course to join the *Bell*," Reid ordered. "Do *not* engage course change yet, however."

"Aye Sir," The Chief responded immediately.

"Ops, keep an eye on the tactical situation, I don't want to be surprised by these bastards."

"Aye," Eric said determinedly.

"Comms, get me a tight beam to the *Revenge*," He said. "Don't worry about bleed through, but make sure the encryption is up."

"Yes sir. A moment, it'll take a few seconds to get the link."

Reid nodded, but said nothing as he settled in to wait.

"Link established."

"Michaels, Reid."

"Go for Michaels," The voice came back a moment later, "I'm assuming you want to know the plan?"

"Just confirming that we're going with Roberts' option," Reid confirmed.

"Ultimately, yes," Michaels answered. "We're going to make it look like we're hesitating first, however, and let Jenn try and talk the Imp into it."

"Roger that. We'll form up on your vector then."

"Perfect, welcome to the party."

"You do tend to throw the most destructive ones," Reid said dryly. "Reid out."

He checked the numbers quickly again, then nodded, "Helm, put us on course to match the *Revenge's* vectors."

"Aye sir. Matching the vectors."

*****

The *Casino*

"Well, don't we always seem to get the fun assignments."

Roy snorted at the dry sarcasm in Jenn's voice, but he certainly wasn't about to disagree with her assessment.

Talking the Empire into working *with* Terrans, even in a situation like this, felt somewhat like convincing the proverbial scorpion not to sting the fox. The Empire had *known* that Terrans could torch their worlds from afar, and yet they'd still gone on to challenge Prometheus to do just that. There was a level of arrogance in those actions that spoke of deep-seated psychological *idiocy*.

Some of the most insane tyrants in history knew better than to challenge nuclear powers, even if they had nukes of their own. How fucked in the head do you have to be for the likes of Stalin, Kim, and others to be saner than you?

Roy didn't know the answer to that question, but he suspected the answer was '*very*'.

"Nothing to it, I suppose." Jenn crumbled, "no point delaying. Give me a channel to the Imp."

"Channel open."

*****

IC *From the Flames*

Kaela didn't know whether to rage at the very *suggestion* of joining forces with the Terran ship, even for a short time, or to rage at the situation that seemed to make it a necessity for the survival of her ship and crew.

The Terran who's made the offer had not shown any of the smugness she had mentally filled in for that people from reading the reports. Instead his voice had been curt, a bubbling anger or tension behind the words, yet precisely crisp in the way she recalled from some of her trainers when she had signed on with the Imperial Forces.

It struck her deeply just how she would never have been able to tell the difference between him and an Imperial officer, if she hadn't already known.

"Ship's Commander, contact from the Gaians."

"Put them through."

"Yes, Ship's Commander."

No doubt asking whether I intend to accept the offer, She thought darkly.

Part of her wanted to refuse out of hand, but her practicality wouldn't allow that. The military training in her was already looking for a way to turn the offer to her advantage, but the truth was that the only advantage she could see… at least until they got *clear* of the trap… was the mutual protection offered.

Which, granted, was not to be underestimated of course, but the truth was that she wasn't completely certain that she could sell that as sufficient to join forces upon returning to Imperial territory and reporting to Command.

If we're right about the Drasin's goals, however, that might well be sufficient reason.

"Ship's Commander," The woman on the screen said, bringing Kaela from her thoughts.

"Ship's Commander," Kaela gestured in greeting. "I can presume the reason for this contact."

"Indeed?"

"Yes," Kaela said unhappily. "and my response is… that I have not decided."

The Gaian nodded, "We are on a time limit, Ship's Commander."

"Of that I am aware," Kaela snapped before pulling herself back and taking a breath. "What do you and your fellows intend?"

"Barring another option?" The Gaian woman shrugged, "We'll accept the offer."

Kaela grimaced, but nodded in understanding.

That was a fair response, she knew, no matter how little she *liked it.*

"I will contact you shortly with my decision," Kaela said, cutting the signal before any response could be made.

The quiet that followed left her feeling suddenly isolated in a way she rarely recognized in her position. Her Command crew would do as she told them, of that she knew without question, but at the moment they were all waiting in that anticipatory silence for her to come to a decision that would likely decide their fates.

She rose from her station, examining the situation as was being reported through the scanners.

The enemy swarm had increased *massively* when it was clear that they were making for an escape path, with most of them moving quickly to cut off the path that led to freedom and safety. The Terran ship was on a somewhat parallel course to the *Flames*, she could see, but they were diverging slightly.

Idly she tapped out a set of calculations into the console by her side and looked down to see the results.

They're aiming for… interesting, they didn't pick the obvious hole in the enemy formation, She noted silently, tapping in more calculations. *Ah, a trap. Clever, on both sides.*

The Terran vessel was aiming for a hard fight, but one that would allow them to punch through… if everyone worked together. The obvious hole that was clearly intended to tempt her, or them she supposed, was a trap.

Kaela just wondered if it were the only one or not.

"Match course with the Terran vessel," She ordered.

Yseb slumped a little, clearly relieved, but had the sense of propriety to half turn even as he was activating the new course, "Are you certain, Ship's Commander?"

"My orders stand."

"Yes, Ship's Commander."

She would not talk to them, nor even *acknowledge* the offer… but she was neither foolish, nor desirous of death sufficiently to throw her ship to the Drasin in some attempt to spite the Terrans.

For now, we work together, She thought angrily. *I cannot change the situation… but when it **changes**…*

*****

CHAPTER 44

IC *From the Flames*

"Cover the Sergeant," The Lieutenant growled over the tac-net, "Sarge, get that breaching charge in place!"

There was a vague 'hoorah' in the background of all the noise, but it was well drowned out by the rumble of the gravity rifles supersonic rounds shattering the atmosphere within the ship while on their way to shatter their targets.

Smith hugged the corner he was using for cover, methodically firing the rifle in his hands on remote as he picked out targets over the camera built into the weapon, keeping his head and body as safe as they could be, behind the bulkhead.

The Corporal had seen some sketchy fighting in his time in the corps, there was no question about that. Rooting pirates out on their own ships or bases was rough and violent work, treacherous beyond belief by times in fact, but it was nothing quite like this.

The Drasin, monsters that were still being used to scare children in at least *three* separate space faring cultures, were *creepy* in a way he had a tough time properly quantifying. They didn't *move right*, for one. The closest he could get to describing it was that they seemed to move almost like puppets, or the stop motion beasts in old movies.

It wasn't *quite* that, but it was the closest he could find in his experience.

It was subtle, but there was something *unnatural* about their motion, something that was triggering that uneasy sensation he associated with the Uncanny Valley, though there was nothing human about these things in the slightest.

His rifle bucked again and again as he watched the Sarge

charge out into the middle of the fight, a breaching charge in hand as he ran for the bulkhead.

Crazy bastard, Smith through admiringly.

You didn't make it in the *Gaian* Marines without being a little crazy, of course. Each group assigned to the Archangels, or to the prize ships, were the guys at the tip of the spear these days. For the Casino's *Dealers* that was no less true, but running out into that *mess*, with a breaching charge in *both* hands?

That took guts.

The snot nosed Second Lieutenant following behind him, rifle in her mitts roaring ceaselessly, also took guts he thought a moment later.

Lot of stupidity too, probably, but gutsy.

*****

"Begging the Lieutenant's Pardon, Ma'am, but were you dropped on your head as a baby?" The Sergeant grunted as he slammed into the bulkhead shoulder first, pressing close to it in an effort to minimize his target silhouette.

"Probably," Amanda grunted between shots. "My dad is the kind of guy who'd likely do that."

The Sergeant snorted as he twisted around and got the breaching charge set against the wall, where its geckostick surface took up the weight. Beams cut through the air around them as he grabbed the charges and expected them out in a large 'X' across the bulkhead, trying very hard to ignore the fact that his primary cover was being provided by a fresh butterbar lieutenant on her first mission.

"Alright, it's set!" He called as the last charge was put in place.

"Fall back!" The Lieutenant called, pulling him away from the wall as she continued to fire, now from her hip with only one hand on her weapon while they scrambled back from the bulkhead.

Her accuracy had gone to hell, he noted, but a distant portion of his mind also took careful note that she'd still pass the range requirements at Basic despite that. He was impressed, since it took a decent amount of skill to control a GR-22 on rapid fire with *both* hands, let alone one handed, and to do it while aiming through the HUD was… a complex endeavor.

It took more than training, it took dedication. Both to the rifle and to the suit and interface she was relying on. It wasn't the sort of thing a fresh Lieutenant should have in their quiver.

"Who did you say your dad was again?" He grunted as they slid back into cover, roughly impacting the far bulkhead.

She looked over at him, her suit's armor inscrutable as it seemed to evaluate his question.

"Stephen Michaels," She answered a moment later.

"Fuck. The Captain of the *Revenge*?" The Sergeant blurted out, shocked.

"Told you it was likely that I could have been dropped on my head a time or two," She chuckled, bringing up the detonation control for the breaching charge. "My earliest memory is my Mom screaming at my dad for letting my brother crash the flitter we were in. He just laughed and said it was a good lesson… my brother and I were like five."

"Blackbeard's kid herself, God and Gaia both save us," He muttered while rolling his eyes, "Cause I doubt either alone will be able to."

"Cute," She said, looking his way again briefly before turning back to the fight. "Fire in the hole!"

The Breaching charge erupted a moment later with little more than a dull thump, but the smoke and fire rolling back over them made up for the lack of sound.

"On your feet, Sergeant," The Lieutenant called as she rose to her feet. "We have a job to do!"

He struggled up, unslinging his rifle as he followed after her, the rest of the squad falling into formation as they moved forward. The smoke and heat provided concealment as they moved, but no cover to speak of as the beams from the Drasin redoubled.

*****

Kaela flinched as she felt a shiver run through the decks, the fighting clearly still going on throughout her vessel.

"Explosive discharge detected in the aft storage decks," Sunnam said after a moment. "We're scanning increased thermal presence through that entire sector. There must be *dozens* there, Ma'am."

What in the abyssal beasts would attract them to the storage decks?

Certainly, if they wanted raw materials, she supposed that might be an easier location to gather it, but the Drasin had shown no particular issues with *eating* their way through her ship to this point, so she doubted that they needed their meals in more accessible pieces. That implied that there was something in the holds that had caught their interest.

What that might be was something she couldn't even begin to guess at, however.

*****

The Drasin had thrown everything they had at the Marines the moment they hit the breach, the volume of fire was almost *desperate*, Amanda noted as she hutted the jagged hole in the bulkhead to evade the beams.

"Warp grenade?" The Sergeant asked, shrugging.

"Not just yet," She said, risking a peek past the breach. "I want to get eyeballs on that QC if I can."

He stared at her for a long moment, uncertain if he'd heard her correctly.

"Hey Smith," She called out, ignoring his stare.

"What is it, LT?" Smith asked from where he was covering.

"And chance you could decrypt that thing?" She asked, nodding through the breach.

Smith held up a hand, slowly wobbling it, "A QCS? Slim to none, boss. Best I could do would be pull the data as is, maybe one of our QC's could crack it later."

Amanda nodded, "Figured. Ok, that's your job."

"What?" Smith blurted.

"We've never had access to anything even *remotely* like this before now," She said intently. "Our intel has been peacemeal, pulled from captured prisoners, off the shattered remains of main computer systems… we've had entire Imperial cruisers in our hands before, but never found one of these systems or even a *hint* of them. Corporal, pull that data, the rest of us will keep your ass in one piece. Hoorah?"

"Hoorah, LT," He mumbled, a little unenthusiastically, perhaps, but she just nodded curtly.

"Sergeant," Amanda said, "Pop smoke and put a mix of flash bangs and frags through the hole as soon as the squad is ready."

He snorted, "We were born ready, Ma'am."

"Hoorah!"

That time the enthusiasm was back, bringing a smile to Amanda's lips.

"Very well then. Let's kick the boogeyman's teeth in."

*****

Flash bangs and smoke did little to the Drasin, unsurprisingly, but the chaos of the moment still seemed to disrupt their ability to aim and coordinate as Amanda led her squad through the hole. The Sergeant didn't allow her to go first, instead taking two men with him on ahead. She followed with Smith in tow, right on their heels.

Moving from one side of the bulkhead to the other was like being transported through a portal to hell, Amanda decided in a heartbeat as she stepped from relatively clear atmo to the smoke and fire of the battlezone.

Her rifle was running IFF hot, just because she didn't full trust herself not to frag one of her own guys in the back in this mess, not that she was overly keen to *entirely* trust the dedicated AI running that part of her kit.

Computer intelligence software never *quite* matched up with the real world correctly, just due to the limitations put on it. Without a body to experience things, the sophisticated software that ran most Terran systems seemed incapable of properly interfacing with reality.

Still, it was better by far than her own reflexes were likely to be in the mess she was trodding through.

Perfection was the enemy of getting the damned job *done*.

With her Marines arrayed around in front of her, however, it meant that her rifle refused to fire more often than it barked.

Sighing, she gave it up for the moment, and let the others handle the fighting.

"Smith," She said, "Get to the QC."

The Corporal risked a glance in that direction, where most of the intense fighting was coming from, and stared back at her, his body language clearly radiating disbelief.

"Lieutenant?"

She snorted, "Do you need to get a physical connection?"

"Not strictly," He admitted. "It would be faster if I could though?"

"Don't worry about what could be better," She told him. "Worry about what you can do *now*."

"Ah... yes, Ma'am."

*****

The Lieutenant moved to cover Smith as he setup the antenna for intercepting the bleed from the QCS. On this side of the bulkhead the bleed was *far* clearer, he noted almost instantly.

"Must have shielding in the bulkheads," He mumbled.

"What's that?" The Lieutenant asked from where she was standing over him.

"The bleed is clearer here," He said as he worked, ignoring the fighting as best he could. "The signal through the bulkhead was barely recognizable."

"Makes sense," She said. "This would be a highly protected area."

"No doubts there," He agreed. "Ok, I have the system setup and we're getting data. I can't search and grab anything that's buried in the matrix from here, though. Just what's being processed."

"Right now that's what we want."

"Right."

*****

There's a lot of them here, but they're… hesitant?

Amanda noted the change in the Drasin's fighting methodology with interest. She guessed that they were attempting to avoid damaging their target, the Quantum Computing System.

There was little in the database about that that even *hinted* that they were the sort to even be able to show caution of any type, so she noted it on her log with a quick subvocal entry before returning to the state of the fighting.

Her Marines were holding their ground, but the advance had ground to a halt as they'd been forced to grab cover and concealment as best they could in the moments after the breach. The aliens weren't pushing the advantage, though, seemingly wary of what that might entail, but neither were they falling under the Marines' advance.

"Hurry it up," She growled to the Corporal. "We're going to have to warp the deck if the move on us."

"I'm running as fast as the system will allow," He growled. "unless you can get me close enough, and find me an Imperial data port, there's not a damn thing more that I can do!"

She just swore as she leveled her weapon, getting an all clear tone from the IFF.

"If that's the way you want it," She said. "Fine."

"Fine? What? Wait!"

The Lieutenant opened fire, stalking forward from her position as her weapon boomed through the rending of the air around them, walking toward the QCS.

*****

"What in the *hell* is she doing?"

The Sergeant didn't know the answer to that question, but there really was only one proper response to the situation.

No fucking way am I letting these alien bastards get into me for a butterbar, even if she is nuts, He thought grimly as he vaulted over his cover, landing on the other side with rifle aimed.

"Deal out the cards, Marines," He roared.

"Hoorah!"

The Dealers of the *Casino* roared as they went over the top of their cover, weapons roaring before they even landed on the other side.

*Fucking **Blackbeard's** daughter, all right. I don't know who I fucked over in a past life to deserve this, but if ever find them in the next life… I'll fuck em over again.*

*****

CHAPTER 45

Bellerophon

"Imperial ship has paralleled our course, Captain."

Roberts barely grunted his response, as he honestly didn't care what the Imps did beyond the fact that it would allow the *Revenge, Casino,* and Reid's Destroyer to maintain their cover in case the Imperial cruiser survived to get word back to the Empire. He wasn't surprised that they hadn't openly accepted his offer, or even acknowledged it, though if he were inclined to be fair about it... Jason doubted that he would have made any such acknowledgement himself.

Not that he really cared about being fair to Imps at the moment.

Still, they were the least of his concerns.

The mass of Drasin forces showing up on his scanners were... quite frankly, terrifying. It was a sight he'd never wanted to see again, and one that he had actually managed to convince himself that he *wouldn't* see again.

More the fool, me, I suppose, He thought derisively.

"Standby strategic weapons," He ordered. "Check fire until I give the command. Beams remain free."

"Aye, Skipper. Strategic weapons, check fire, aye. Beams free, aye."

The augmented view of the space beyond the ship was lit up with sweeping beams that crossed the vacuum, slicing and slagging targets with vicious effectiveness, but Jason was holding back the heavy weapons for the very last moment.

"*Casino* and *Revenge* have slipped into standard formation with *Reid's Destroyer*," His scanner chief confirmed. "They're roughly filling out the flanking positions between us and the Imp."

Jason nodded, pleased that *years* of training were paying off.

He'd had no communications with any of those ships since arriving on site, nor they with him, but they knew their tasks well and didn't need him micromanaging… nor even giving them orders at all.

The perimeter of the Dyson construct was now *visibly* approaching, which was a damn good indicator that they were close even if he wasn't looking at the falling numbers. In space, distances were generally so vast that you just couldn't get a sense of motion until you were practically on top of whatever it was you were using for a frame of reference.

"Enemy count still climbing, Skipper."

"I see it. Ignore it," Jason ordered.

"Sir?"

"At this point, it doesn't matter how many they have," Jason said serenely, a hint of a smile on his face. "Let them come… but increase the fire rate on our beams."

"Sir, that will put them over the red line. We'll be risking burnout."

"I am aware."

"Aye skipper. Increasing fire rate."

*****

IC *From the Flames*

Kaela was so tense as they approached the edge of the massive stellar construct that she felt like she might break in half at the slightest provocation, though she would *never* admit it to be certain. That sort of admission, or even the rumor of it, could easily be enough to cost an officer their promotion path… or delay it significantly.

Imperial Officers were expected, and trained to be, stalwart defenders of the Empire.

Weaknesses were not to be tolerated, particularly in the officer's corps.

To herself, though, she could easily admit that what she was enduring just in that moment was far closer to the breaking point that she had ever previous experienced. The Drasin were nightmares from the old tales, and were *on her ship!*

And that wasn't even the *worst* of the situation she found herself in.

Her command deck was sealed, she didn't dare breach that seal to allow anyone in, nor let anyone out… by some miracle, or plot of the enemy (something she felt far more likely at the moment), the seals had held thus far. Protocol didn't allow her to open those seals, risk the command deck and crew, so long as they were holding… which, she had been getting the feeling that *somehow* the Drasin *knew.*

That was just insane, however, and she put that thought as far from her mind as she could manage.

"Commander," Sunnam spoke up, drawing her attention.

"What is it?"

"The ship identified as *Bellerophon* has increased their beam rate."

Kaela pause at that, eyes briefly flicking to the numbers that were scrolling along her displays. She had been quite certain that they were already pushing the very limits of any beam system, just by the heat radiation they had been able to scan off the ship, and her glance to the displays confirmed just that.

*They'll burn out in **minutes** at this rate, what are they thinking?*

Part of her wondered if the intelligence they had on the terrans was truly *that* bad? Did they have superior materials science? That's the only thing she could think of that would allow them to so wildly exceed the limits of their beam systems.

With the edge of the stellar construct just ahead, some might believe that they only had a few seconds left of the fight. Once they'd punched through into open space, after all, the enemy and structure would be behind them and escape would immediately be at hand.

However, the stellar construct, despite it's massive size, really only covered a small fraction of the gravity well of the local star. It's outer perimeter was not much farther out from its primary than Kraike was from its own, in fact.

There would still be *hours* left to climb before reliable FTL could be engaged.

Hours that the Drasin would be dogging their every step.

It makes no sense. What are they doing?

*****

Bellerophon

"Weapons at redline, Skipper. We're going to need a rebuild after this."

Roberts chuckled, "I'll call ahead to the Priminae and arrange an appointment. Kill power to the forward port ribbon emitters."

Aye, Killing power. Port emitters offline."

"Increase power through the starboard emitters."

That got him a look, but no questions this time.

"Power increasing to starboard emitters."

Jason had seen a lot in his years in the service, both from the pre-spaceflight days and especially since then. He'd watched horrors and miracles, heroes and villains, all of them rise and fall with a steady beat that almost felt manufactured.

Hell, he couldn't honestly say that they weren't, if he were being completely honest.

He, like most of the remaining Earth humans that were known, had made his home in his ship. Over *decades*, he'd learned everything about the ship, it's crews, it's capabilities… and even the Soul that he had, admittedly reluctantly, permitted to be cultured within its core.

However, he'd learned about more than *just* his ship.

Studying their failures had become something of an

obsession for him, one that had eaten away at too much of his life over the past decades. In hindsight, of course, there were so many ways they could have acted differently... but, as painful an admission as it was to him, he wasn't certain that anything short of genocide would have stopped the Empire from the death spiral that had caught the Priminae and Earth alike in it's clutches.

Every bit of Intelligence from within the Empire, before *and* after the invasion and destruction of Earth had agreed on one thing...

The Empire had been driven by some form of Xenophobic obsession.

It made no sense, not to him or to anyone who'd survived the war. The level of phobic obsession involved to *knowingly* throw away your own life and the lives of those you led in the way that the previous Empress had done...

It beggared belief.

However, he'd studied more than just the Empire.

The Drasin were, thankfully, *far* more understandable.

Feral creatures, by most standards, they acted on instinct rather than working to a plan.

It wasn't that they were incapable of planning, he knew with certainty, but they didn't default to it. They were creatures of simple pleasures, so to speak, with limited ability to delay gratification. That simplicity gave him an opening.

"Drasin are shifting, skipper, converging on the port side."

"Understood. No change to current disposition."

"Aye."

Roberts watched the Drasin reinforcements as they shifted automatically, heading for the opening he'd created in the defensive envelope of his vessel. He reached forward, keying open the comm channels.

"Safeties off Strategic weapons," He ordered.

"Aye, Safeties cleared on strategic weapons."

"Standby helm, I want a full spread of pulse torpedoes on the center of their formation," He ordered. "On my mark."

"On your mark, Aye."

"Kill power to starboard beam emitters."

"killing power, starboard emitters, aye."

The faint click/whine of the beams faded entirely from the background as the ship's weapons ceased firing. Roberts ignored the sudden quiet, a shift in sound that felt somehow oppressive despite the fact that it was barely a change in the normal ambient sound.

His eyes were on the Drasin as they continued to group up into the bunched clusters he'd lured them into.

"All tubes, fire."

"Aye, all tubes firing!"

"T-Cannons, standby to pick off surviving clusters. Load with pulse charges."

*****

The full spread of torpedoes leapt from the tubes of the big cruiser, flung into space by the gravity shears that powered their launch, moving faster than the old magnetic launchers ever could have hoped to match.

Twenty *KILOS* of antimatter lanced across space, flashing briefly as stray bits of dust self annihilated with the exterior corona of the warheads. At nearly the speed of light, however, the travel time was measured only in *seconds*.

Slamming into the forefront of the Drasin formation, the annihilation simply *destroyed* any of the enemy unfortunate enough to be directly contacted… but the devastation caused by the *energy release* radiated outward like miniature supernovas erupting in their midst.

The chain reaction spread through the closely groups clusters, *tearing* the Drasin from their component atoms with sufficient power to initiate *fission* in many of the closer vessels. At the outer range of the blast radius, Drasin vessels were merely crippled…

The Bell, however, was far from finished.

*****

Bellerophon

"Fire!"

"All Transition Cannons, Fire, Aye!"

The Transition Cannons were the last great superweapon developed by Earth technology before the end, and as a cap on all weapons technology ever developed on that blue green world… Roberts supposed that they could have done a lot worse.

Sending a tachyon surge through the antimatter warheads held in the gravity isolation fields within the weapons breaches, the warheads simply vanished in a puff of impossibility only to reappear *instantly* several lightseconds away just as the enemy had begun to recover from their previous attack.

Antimatter explosions again turned the interior of the Dyson construct into a mini-super nova, light and radiation erupting in all directions as the Drasin vessel *burned.*

"Make for the hole. Full power back to the beams."

"Aye skipper, making for the hole!"

"Full power returned to emitters!"

"Weapons free. Burn them down."

*****

CHAPTER 46

IC *From the Flames*

Amanda hit the deck in a slide, armor on plating screeching in protest as she slid under the swipe of one of the Drasin's outstretched claws. Her rifle roared as the heavy slugs tore through its underside, spattering her with molten silicates before she kicked the body over and started using it for cover as she kept firing at the rest.

"Are you insane!?"

Smith scrambled along behind her, barely keeping low enough to avoid being clipped by the searing sweep of a Drasin beam. He crawled in behind the cooling corpse of the alien spider-crab, swearing the whole way.

"You're the one who said you needed to get closer!"

"I didn't mean we SHOULD get closer!"

Amanda grinned through the adrenaline and thrill of terror that was fueling her in the moment, "Next time be more specific. Now, seriously, how close?"

Smith turned to look at her, his armor practically *screaming* disbelief.

"I'm not telling you that! Not after the last time!"

"I'll take that to mean much closer then, get ready."

Smith held up his hands, "No! Wait…"

She didn't wait.

Amanda popped up, dropping the barrel of her weapon on the body of the Drasin, using it to stabilize the rifle as she pivoted the muzzle across a firing arc and loosed a fusillade of shots across the deck.

"We're going to get close and secure the QCS," She ordered, this time using the squad channel, "The Drasin need it intact, they'll have to check their fire if we're in close! Move it!"

Her squad responded with a matching fusillade as they moved in, the Sarge in the lead. She waited for her chance and, when she saw it, kicked the Drasin corpse over and planted her boots in the cooling body as she went over it with weapon still roaring. Smith, cursing the whole way, stayed on her six as they fought their way across the deck to the Quantum Computing System.

The Drasin that were doing *something* with it were easy enough to dispatch, the single minded beings hadn't even looked up from their work as she and Smith had potted them, splashing molten silicates over the QCS in the process.

Amanda hoped that didn't destroy the machines, as she was hoping that Smith would be able to get more out of it than he'd managed thus far, but she wasn't really concerned either way. If the QCS was destroyed, then they would have achieved their primary mission goal, just not in the way she'd have preferred.

Keeping the Drasin away from the system was, without question, the more important side of things.

The pair of them slid in to the computing core, hugging close to it as they turned their focus outward to guard against attack.

"I've got this," Amanda said as she started providing covering fire for the rest of the squad. "See what you can get off the system."

"Hoorah, Lieutenant," Smith said, slinging his weapon and grabbing his portable comp.

The Sarge and the others were just seconds behind them, Amanda covering them as they sprinting in.

"Get behind the system," She ordered, "use it for cover!"

She doubted that it would provide much in the way of real world cover, frankly, and it was too small to even be effective concealment if the Drasin were willing to punch through it to get to them... but she was betting that the single minded beasts would tunnel vision in on their assignment and be unwilling to destroy what they'd come for.

I hope.

*****

Ship's Commander Kaela Eurydice stare at the screens in a mix of horror and hope, uncertain which emotion was going to win out as she watched the utter *devastation* the Terran vessel was wreaking on the Drasin.

They lured the beasts into clusters before unleashing their negative matter weapons upon them, She realized at that point, understanding why they'd faked the burn out of the beam emitters.

That was going into the log as a warning to any other Ship's Commanders that might find themselves dealing with these people, assuming she got the chance of course.

"The Gaian's are moving to aid with clearing the path, Ship's Commander."

"Follow them," Kaela ordered.

"Yes Ship's Commander."

Until they were clear of this mess, she fully intended to play along with the general movement of things. What happened after, well she would make that decision when the time came. For now, she was going to head for the hole in the Drasin net with the full power her vessel could manage.

That, however, wasn't the only thing on her plate at the moment.

Kaela looked aside to the displays that showed activities within her vessel itself.

What is going on in the storage decks? She couldn't figure it out.

Why were the Drasin focusing their efforts *there* of all places? She had even called up the full inventory and they had *nothing* stored on board that might be worthy of such interest as best she could tell.

None of this mess makes any sense.

*****

"Holy crap… Lieutenant!"

Amanda ducked down under the edge of the large piece of equipment and half crawled over to where Smith was.

"What is it?" She asked up close, looking over what he was working on.

The download he was working on seemed to be straightforward. Smith wasn't even trying to decode any of the data, of course. His gear wasn't remotely equipped to tackle the encryption on a QCS, so she'd be surprised if he were trying it.

"Over here, LT," Smith told her, pointing to a section attached to the QCS that she assumed was part of the interface for it.

"What is it?" Amanda asked. "Interface system?"

"No, thought that myself at first, but it's been *precisely* disconnected from the system," Smith said.

"Disconnected? By you?"

"No Ma'am, by the Drasin."

Amanda shot him a look, "Pardon?"

"Yeah, threw me too. Look here, close."

Amanda leaned in, checking the place he pointed to. At first she didn't see anything, but then it caught her eye and she toggled on the Armor's image enhancement.

"What the hell…"

"You see it, Ma'am?"

"I see something. What is that? It looks like the results of a shaped charge, but I've never seen them that small and precise before."

"Best I can tell the Drasin injected a squirt of molten or possibly gaseous metals, no more than a hundred nanometers across. Cut a sensor line without touching anything else. I didn't even see it until I started backtracking a signal being sent."

She looked sharply to him, "What signal?"

"I'm *guessing*," He stressed, "but I think it's a self destruct command. It's going to this right here…"

He tapped a metal band that encircled the entire computational core.

"High grade chemical explosive, matches Imperial demo team kit," He said. "High order detonation, more than enough to slag the entire rig and… if I'm right about where we are, blow out this section of the hull and eject the whole thing into space."

Amanda gaped at him, just shocked.

"They rigged their *own* ship to explosively decompress?" She demanded, utterly unbelieving.

"That's what it looks like, but knowing the Imps? That's not what surprises me," Smith said, shaking his head.

"Then what surprises you?"

"That the Drasin knew about it, and were able to short the entire thing as efficiently as they did," Smith said, dead serious. "If they hadn't, boss, I would have set the trap off when I plugged in."

There wasn't a curse word *invented* strong enough for what Amanda was feeling in that moment, something she only realized after trying a few dozen on for size only to find them all lacking.

*****

The *Casino*

"Tag those beasts before they can regroup, burn them out."

"Aye, skipper."

Cardsharp leaned into the suspension field, bringing the ship around with her as she did, and lay the enemy positions right into the firing arc of her forward ribbon emitters.

Between them, the *Revenge*, Reid, and the *Bell* they were doing a good job of clearing the space that lay between the small motley group of ships and open space but she knew that it wouldn't be over when they crossed the threshold and made it back out. The Drasin were already sending reinforcements in at their best speeds, which were pretty damn good, and while they wouldn't arrive in time to close the door… they'd sure as hell make it in time to give pursuit.

"Signal from the Marines, Ma'am. Colonel is converging on one of her squads who found the Drasin fucking with a QCS hidden in the cruiser's holds."

"What?" She looked over sharply, "Is she sure?"

"That's what the squad reported," Roy shrugged.

"Who's squad?"

"Michaels."

Jenn swore, closing her eyes briefly. She, like most of the other surviving Archangels, had positively spoiled those two brats growing up. The pair of them were like family, and now she had *both* of them fighting monsters from the Black on their first damn mission out.

She'd call them chips off the old block, except that not even Steph was *this* crazy or unlucky as a kid.

Still, she knew them both and was inclined to trust their judgement… at least in the absence of anyone more experienced.

"Tell her to secure that system."

"That is what she determined to do, Ma'am."

Of course she did.

Keenan was no fool, even for a Marine. She'd understand the mess in potential that clearly existed in the situation. Probably more so than Jennifer herself did, since the Colonel would have better ideas of what the Drasin were doing on that ship.

"Understood," She said in clipped tones, thinking furiously for the moment before coming to a decision. "Open channel, in the clear."

"Aye skipper. You're on the air."

"*Casino* to all points," She said in Imperial, "We are falling back to provide support to the *From the Flames*. Out."

"Channel shut."

"All hands," She said over the shipwide. "Standby for

deceleration."

Jenn nodded, killing forward power and hitting the thrust reversers in addition to the gravity warp field, throwing them ship into a hard deceleration that everyone on board felt.

*****

CHAPTER 47

Bellerophon

"The Casino is dropping back, Sir."

Jason nodded curtly, "Jenn's Marines are on board that Imp ship. With the limits the Archangels operate under we're not losing much tactical capacity. Continue as planned."

"Aye Sir."

They were so close to the perimeter of the Dyson construct now that motion of the collector swarm could be seen as the *Bell* and others began to cross into open space. The few Drasin in close to their positions were sitting ducks for the combined beams of the impromptu squadron, and the scanners could already see open space beyond the perimeter.

They were far from in the clear, however, Roberts knew well. The gravity well of the Dydon construct would still extend out the same distance as it would have when the system was fully intact. There was no loss of mass, after all, merely a redistribution of it. Once they cleared the Perimeter, they were still a long way from being able to breach FTL.

"Step up scans as we cross the construct's perimeter line," He ordered. "They'll have reinforcements waiting in the shadow of the plates."

"Aye Skipper."

Space warfare was rarely about subterfuge, Jason knew well. In generally, while space was *immense*, and thus relatively easy to hide in, you also had to get incredibly close... again, relatively speaking, if you wanted to actually engage the enemy, which neatly negating the ability to hide unless you deployed in 'quiet' ship designs, similar to the Rogue Class Destroyers.

The Drasin didn't.

So he fully expected to see the enemy coming from a long damn way off.

The trouble, of course, was that it rarely mattered.

Fleet engagements generally boiled down to who could inflict the most real damage in the shortest amount of time.

The equations were more complicated than that, of course. Armor, maneuverability, and yes even strategy played their roles... but more often than not, near peer battles quickly rendered themselves down to a slugging match and the last man standing was determined purely by who could dish it out better than the other guy could take it.

Terran ships had held a strong advantage in any comparable fight, thanks to the Cam-Plate armor that could effectively no-sell specific beam frequencies at need... but they'd always fought at the wrong side of the numbers divide, and ultimately it had turned out that quantity had a quality all its own when it came to fighting the Empire.

The Drasin turned that issue up to eleven, making even the Empire's vast resources look tiny by comparison... but, thankfully, were far simpler in every other respect.

As Admiral Gracen's *Middle Finger* had proven, no one sane wanted to be on the wrong side of an exponential growth system designed with even a modicum of intelligence, after all.

"Passing the perimeter... scans out... Bingo, boss, you called it. The swarm is moving to intercept from behind the plates."

"Engage at will," Jason ordered firmly.

"Aye. All weapons engaging."

*****

Gaia's Revenge

Steph observed the *Casino* as it dropped back from the formation and adjusted the course of the *Revenge* to cover the gap the other ship had left. The Dyson swarm plates were passing on either side of his ship in the moment, and he was steeling himself for the first look at the scans from the other side.

"Standby for scanner pulse," Milla said softly, her voice filled with an undercurrent of tension that he didn't even have to hear to *feel*. "Pulse out."

Here we go.

"Contact responses... To your display."

Steph watched as the other side of the plates were populated by a sweeping path of the pulse, showing *thousands* of contacts moving in from all directions. Most of them were too far out to reach them in a timely manner, but more than enough were within the intercept range that they'd calculated.

"Damn. Cover our sectors," He ordered. "Beams free."

"Aye, Beams free."

Neither of them were happy to be fighting this battle with one hand proverbially tied behind their backs, but that was the current terms of engagement in any situation that might be leaked back to the Empire.

"Transmit scans back to the *Flames* and the *Casino*," He ordered. "Tell them we'll hold the door as long as we can, but they'd better pick up the pace. They do *not* want this one to hit them on the ass on their way out."

Milla shot him a look.

"I will... adjust the wording slightly," She told him.

"Well fine, if you don't like a little creative language."

"What you Terran's call language is less creative and more an example of entropic decay in action."

*****

IC *From the Flames*

"Enemy contact data, transmitted from the Gaian vessel, the *Revenge*, Ship's Commander. The Drasin are swarming along the outer side of the stellar construct."

She could see that much, Kaela thought sourly.

"Show me our energy reserves and drive curves," She ordered, turning to the Engineering station.

"Yes, Ship's Commander."

The data she wanted was up on the secondary display quickly, and Kaela took a moment to examine it and come to a conclusion.

"Very well, increase power to the drives by a full fourth," She ordered.

"Yes, Ship's Commander." Yseb responded, half turning to look at her, "I am required by Imperial Regulations to inform you that such a change will put our drive beyond the maximum rated limits."

"Your information is entered into the log," She told him formally, nodding, "Increase the power."

"Power increasing."

The space warp curves tilted significantly, sharply increasing as more power was sent to the drives and the big ship surged forward.

She watched the telemetry, noting that the Gaian vessel *Casino* had dropped back into an escort formation with the *Flames*, while the *Revenge* and the Destroyer she had no proper ID on continued clearing the path at the vanguard of the fighting.

The Drasin assault on her ship had cooled, but enough of the stray drones were still throwing themselves into the *Flame's* Defenses that she was happy to have any support in close... the more so because it was clear that her ship was the priority target and they still had the thickest part of the gauntlet yet to run.

*****

Bellerophon

"Jesus, will you look at that. The damn Dyson construct *crawls*."

Jason didn't bother reprimanding the speaker for the comment, mostly because he was busy enough thinking the same thing that it never occurred to him to do so.

The deep space side of the construct was where the Drasin had been assembling their forces, clearly, and now they were setting those forces into action.

"Replen Time on the Pulse weapons?"

"Another three minutes, Skipper."

Three minutes was going to be an eternity in this fight, Jason realized darkly.

"Weapons free, Beams and Kinetic guns open fire. Load fusion devices into the Transition Cannons and standby for orders."

"Weapons Free, Aye. Beams and Kinetics engaging. Fusion clearance granted, Aye."

Unfortunately, he was too aware that the Transition Cannons had a glaring weakness that reduced their potential effectiveness by devastating margins and would severely curtail how he could employ them with Fusion loadouts. The Tacyon Transition system essentially teleported their payload across space, instantly, leaving it to reform naturally at the destination when the power charge ran out.

This made for a very effective way of essentially delivering a payload *directly into* the target.

Or, it would, if the reintegration wasn't scrambled by intense gravity gradients... like those used by almost *every single starship* and starship equivalent such as the larger Drasin drones.

With antimatter warheads this didn't make any difference, antimatter didn't care how it reintegrated... it was still antimatter, no matter what shape it held after all.

Fusion devices, however, were somewhat more... rigid in their functionality. They didn't work well when reduced to a clump of their component molecules.

That made deploying them via the T-Cannons less than effective against enemy starships and starship equivalents... but didn't mean that they were entirely useless.

"Target just ahead of the swarm," He ordered. "Set proximity fuses."

"Aye skipper. Target positions locked in. Proximity detonation engaged."

"Go to rapid fire. Empty the magazines."

"Rapid fire, Aye."

The *Bellerophon's* cannons pivoted onto target and began to fire on automatic.

*****

The Drasin could *smell* their targets across the void, the red band of the *life disease* triggering a deep and irresistible hatred in each of them.

That smell drove them forward, rising up what any naturally born species might call a blood rage, or perhaps a feeding frenzy, as the drones threw themselves across open space at the gravity gradients that they could sense around the enemy.

A few of them noted the odd FTL *puffs* that were registering to their senses, but largely ignored them as irrelevant as the frenzy overtook them all. The leading edge of their force was in range to intercept the forward target, and that was the only thing that mattered.

One of their number spotted it first.

An object that just *appeared* in front of them, previously not being on any scan and then… it was just *there*.

The query/warning went out to the swarm, looking for any sort of match.

No response had time to be made.

*****

A *Dozen* small stars exploded into existence for a fraction of a second, englobing the Drasin front line in temperatures and radiation not even experienced in the heart of the *hottest* of stars. The nuclear fusion devices detonated, quickly reaching *millions* of degrees centigrade, and simply *vaporized* anything in their direct impact path.

The radiation *cooked* anything past that, overloading even the

Drasin's extreme tolerances in an instant, and went on to utterly devastate the swarm for hundreds of miles in all directions from each device's detonation point.

Unfortunately, the Drasin were closing from *millions* of miles in every direction, and for each on that was destroyed... ten thousand more were already surging in to take its place.

The *Bellerophon* kept firing.

*****

Captured Destroyer

"Radiation shielding holding, Captain."

"Thank you, Ops," Reid said, not taking his eyes off the situation.

The *Bell* going full auto with their fusion devices wasn't entirely unexpected, but he couldn't held but rate the pucker factor as pretty damn high all the same. The sheer level of firepower being displayed by *one* ship was enough to creep him out, and he was fully briefed on the potential of the *Heroic* class vessels.

For all that, though, it was immediately clear that it was a losing battle.

The Drasin were just soaking up the losses and surging forward without any hint of hesitation.

No human force, Reid didn't care *how* brave they were, would *ever* have been able to just take losses that like without suffering absolutely terminal blows to their morale. The Drasin, however? They didn't even seem to care.

Briefings on them don't do it justice, He thought grimly.

Describing the beasts as inhuman really just served to make them feel somehow more *comparable* to humans than what he was seeing. They weren't *inhuman*, they were... *unreal*. He wasn't watching living things, he was watching game sprites charging to their deaths.

Damn the design of these destroyers. Beams alone won't slow them nearly enough.

He wished for a *tenth* the firepower that the *Bell* was pouring on, even as he knew that even the *Bell* couldn't hope to keep that up for very long.

"Pick off anything that slips past those nukes," He ordered, "but check fire on the main body."

"Check fire, main body, Aye," Michaels said by rote from the Ops panel, sending the commands automatically. "Targeting any strays, Sir."

"Get ready," Reid said then. "The *Bell* will run their magazines dry soon at this rate of fire. When they do, we go full beams along the forward lines in our sector."

"Aye aye, Skipper."

"Chief, watch for any that get through," Reid said firmly. "I do *not* want those *things* on my ship."

"You've got it, boss."

I'm really starting to miss anti-pirate actions.

*****

CHAPTER 48

IC *From the Flames*

Amanda didn't know what was the worst thing about this situation. The fact that the Empire apparently thought it worth loading their ships with data that the crew and *captains* didn't know about, a data core that they'd rigged to *scuttle itself* if tampered with... or the fact that the Alien *nightmares* that the Empire had unleashed somehow not only *knew* about the damn cores, but how to disable the *fucking* scuttling charges.

Those things are smarter than we ever credited them for, She thought grimly.

The Drasin were generally considered to be beasts, little more than animals that happened to be at home in the environment of deep space. An incredible threat, yes, but mostly due to their reproductive capacity. A single Drasin, in just a few generations, became an Armada that could literally *eat* your world if left unchecked.

For all that, however, everything she had read about them said that they acted almost entirely on instinctual drives.

Amanda was uncertain if that were true, but if it were then their instincts were more fine tuned than anything she'd ever read about. *Instincts shouldn't include an understanding of technology to this level, if at all, even considering how long the Empire has likely been using their current tech in it's current form.*

Of course, she hadn't admit that she wasn't entirely certain how instinctual drives would work in a species that appeared to have been constructed, but even so... for something to this level...

*Were the Drasin **designed** to be Empire killers?*

Whatever it all meant, Amanda only knew that she had more

questions now that she'd gained more information, than she'd ever had before when she had been ignorant.

"What do we do, Lieutenant?"

She glanced up, shaken from the thoughts that had raced through her head by the question from the Corporal at her side. In a second it all recrystallized for her, and she threw out the new questions she had because they were all useless in the moment.

The simple practicality of the Corporal's question reset her mind into the moment, where it needed to be.

"We've secured the objective," She said simply, "Now we hold it until we're reinforced. We'll deal with the rest of this after it's over. Get your gear recording, Corporal, and then get your rifle up."

"Hoorah, Ma'am."

She ducked back, crawling over to the Sergeant.

"Ma'am."

"What's the sitrep, Sarge?"

"Those fuckers are not happy from the looks of it, but they're not willing to just slag the whole damn thing, and us with it," The Sergeant told her, "So it looks like your... *courageous*... decision might have worked."

She snorted, pressing her back against the Quantum Computing System and looking over at him, "You don't have to soften your words with me, Sarge. Shall we split the difference with what you actually meant and replace courageous with reckless?"

"I suppose that'll do, Ma'am," The Sergeant said agreeably.

She grinned under her armor, but didn't push that line any farther, "We need to secure the QCS until the Colonel gets here. Can do?"

"We have a choice?"

She glanced down and patted the ring of high explosives that encircled the device, "See this?"

The Sergeant looked down, "Uh... Yes Ma'am?"

"Imperial Demo kit. We hold the objective, or we blow the whole thing out into space so the bastards can't get it."

He stared at her for a long moment, filling in the details without them being spoken. Particularly the fact that they would almost certainly be sitting *on* the explosives when they detonated.

"Right you are, Ma'am," He said, "We hold the objective until the Colonel arrives with reinforcements."

"Thought you'd see it my way, Sarge," Amanda said cheerfully as she rolled off the computer and shifted around to take a peek beyond their cover. "Hmmm… are they holding back?"

"Yes Ma'am," The Sergeant confirmed. "Once we took the room, the enemy wavered briefly before withdrawing."

Amanda grumbled, ducking back down.

She didn't like that, if only because if they enemy were doing exactly what you wanted them to… it was probably a trap.

"They're calling in reinforcements, aren't they?" She asked mildly.

"I would be," The Sergeant confirmed cheerfully. "In fact…"

"We are, yes I know," Amanda sighed. "Who's backup gets here first?"

"Every Marine's favorite game, Lieutenant."

*****

"Internal alert, Ship's Commander."

Kaela turned sharply, "Report."

"Drasin have broken off from almost every position they'd occupied, reports show them moving toward the storage decks."

Kaela stared for a long moment.

That section again. Something is very odd here.

"Find me a security team," She ordered. "I want people on site, reporting back as quickly as possible."

"Yes, Ship's Commander. It will take some time, however. I expect that we may have to build a new team, the assigned teams took heavy losses."

"Make it happen faster."

"Yes, Ship's Commander."

*****

"Down!"

Keenan ducked as the order was snapped out by the Gunny, who was scouting out ahead. She made certain that she was as well under cover as possible before she started to question *why* she was hiding, but by that point it was clear that the Gunny had spotted a problem.

"Shit that's a lot of fucking spiders."

"Can it," Keenan snapped, "keep the channels clear."

There was no certain evidence that the Drasin could detect the transmissions between their suits, and it *should* be all but impossible, but she wasn't inclined to take a chance.

That said, the Marine wasn't wrong.

Their was a line of the beasts that didn't seem to have an end, just looping back through the curved corridor until they vanished from sight.

Keenan crawled forward, reaching the Gunny's position to get a better look and to connect their suits so that she could send the signal through a hardline connection.

"How many?" She asked.

"Fucked if I know, Colonel," The Gunny said simply.

Back on the ship, if he'd spoken to her like that, she'd have snapped his knuckles, but the field was a different situation.

"Figure it out, if you can, and see if you can tell where the fuckers are going."

"That's the easy part, boss. They're going the same way we are."

"Fuck."

*****

The single bark of the Marine's GR-22 Main Battle Rifle echoed in the enclosed space as Amanda slid over to check what happened.

"Report," She snapped.

"Probing maneuver, Ma'am," The Sarge grunted. "Couple Drasin just testing our response time, unless I'm very much mistaken."

"Don't be," She ordered the man, risking a glance around the bulk of the QCS to see for herself. "We can't afford mistakes now."

"As you say, Ma'am."

The Drasin were milling around, she could tell by the extreme heat differential visible through her thermal kit when she looked over the bulkheads. The transfer wasn't good enough to see the individual drones through the bulkheads, but the mass couldn't be hidden.

Briefly she debated opening up on them through the decks, chances were that the Drones were packed tight enough that they'd score plenty of kills without even bothering to aim. Unfortunately, she was fairly certain that doing so would set off the attack they were hoping to repulse. With the squad's current ammo state, Amanda was really just hoping to put off the encounter as long as possible.

I suppose we have the answer to who's reinforcements got here first, though, She thought sourly. *If this is a Marine's favorite game, I hope we win it more often than we lose. Fuck.*

"Get everyone ready," Amanda ordered, "They're coming in."

One of the Marines snorted, "Real life Zerg Rush, guys. Always wondered how effective that would really be."

"Terran Marines for the win, everytime."

Amanda glanced over at the Sarge, shifting to the private channel, "What the hell?"

"I'll explain it later, Ma'am," The Sergeant said with a shake of his head, "Just Marines being Marines."

That didn't explain much of anything and yet it

simultaneously explained all the mysteries of the universe at the same time.

Marines being Marines, Amanda thought, amused by how much that reminded her of asking *What's the worst that could happen?*

"Let's not taunt Murphy, Sergeant," She said dryly. "Or, possibly worse, invoke Chesty Puller. We only want to stop the Drasin, not unleash something worse on the Galaxy."

The Sergeant stared at her for a long moment before slowly starting to laugh, getting the attention of everyone in the squad.

"Right you are, Ma'am," He said firmly, turning to the rest. "Enough chitchat, Marines. Stand ready to repel us some bugs. Hoorah!"

"Hoorah!"

*****

The roar of supersonic rounds shattering the air was mostly insulated from the ears of the Marines as they opened fire on the mass that flooded through the gaps torn in the bulkheads. The shockwaves could rather be felt more than heard, a deep dull constant rumble that shook a person to their bones.

Amanda was calling orders from the rear, having handed out her ammo to the others in her squad, keeping only one mag in her rifle just in case and her sidearm for her own defense. The Gunmen on her squad were all better shots than she was, and she knew well that *someone* needed to be running overwatch lest the enemy find a hole to sneak an attack through.

That last bit was a little less likely in the current situation, of course, just because there were fundamentally fewer potential holes to sneak anything through in the current area of operation. The bulkheads were constricting, and tended to funnel the action into small, but intense, firefights.

That didn't stop her from keeping an eye on the rest of the area, however, mostly out of habit from training, and she was glad that she had when something caught her eye.

"Sergeant."

"Yes Ma'am."

"Thermal bloom, bulkhead right over this way. Get that arc covered."

"Right you are, Ma'am, on it."

Amanda watched, letting the Sarge redirect a couple Marines to get the sector covered just as the bulkhead started to slag away under heat from the Drasin assault on the other side.

The rocky spider-crab monsters were greeting with supersonic rounds to the face as they started through the new breach, which was good news as far as it went but it had also split their attention and thus the firepower her squad could deliver on target.

Amanda could see the ammo count dwindling, and was starting to sweat for reasons that had nothing to do with the heat that was surrounding them.

"I'm out!"

"Smith, pass your mags up to Drake," Amanda ordered. "I need you to do something for me."

The Corporal glanced at her, his body language clearly reading as *unhappy*, but the man just bobbed the armor he wore in the affirmative. "Yes Ma'am."

The Sarge was out of ammo for his rifle as well, she noted as she got Smith working. The big man was down to his sidearm, firing it dry into the breach without bothering to aim much. The mass of the enemy coming through rendered precision a rather moot point, she supposed as she stepped over Smith and leveled her rifle down the arc he had been covering.

The recoil of her own rifle into her shoulder was slow and steady as she fired with the rote pattern drilled into her during Boot.

Molten silicate spattered the decks and bulkheads around them, but the Drasin masses didn't seemed to care as they clambered over the bodies of their dead and dying with no regard for either their fallen or themselves.

Out of the corner of her eye, in the periphery of her armor's HUD, Amanda watched the Sergeant toss his handgun aside and pull his fighting blade. She rather thought that was being somewhat optimistic on his part, since she wasn't certain the blade could actually reach deep enough to seriously harm the Drasin and, if it could, she was fairly certain that it would survive more than a couple plunges into the molten silicate material without compromising the blade.

Still, she figured she would probably do the same in a few moments when she ran out.

Useless or not, she'd rather go down with a blade in her hand than an empty pistol.

Two more Marines' icons showed empty as their rifles came up dry, the system having stopped calling for replenishment and was now simply screaming for *any* sort of logistical support available. She ignored it, dropping her left hand to Smith's shoulder as she kept her rifle on point with her right.

"Get ready," She ordered grimly.

"Yes Ma'am."

Her mag was almost empty, and the volume of fire from the squad had dropped to a weak peppering of sonic booms as the last couple rifles with ammo continued the defense, but the enemy was now surging through.

Her guts roiled, but there wasn't much more left for her to do, Amanda supposed.

"Blow i-"

A rolling thunder interrupted her next order, and Amanda Michaels looked up in surprise and hope as a shockwave split the air around them, the deck shaking under their feet.

"First Squad, take cover," Colonel Keenan ordered, her voice crackling over the tactical network. "We're burning these bastards out."

*****

CHAPTER 49

IC *From the Flames*

Kaela stared as the Terran vessel just *laid waste* to everything in its range, with an array of firepower that she'd only *read about*. It was different in person, and suddenly the formidable power of the Imperial Cruiser she commanded... felt wanting.

Fusion devices are obvious, though there must be some kind of interference because some of them don't appear to have shown up on our scans prior to detonation. Strange.

For obvious reasons, identifying the position of fusion devices was rather important to the scanners of any advanced warship. Such weapons, while arguably crude, could still deliver energy on target in numbers that were almost entirely unknown in the natural world.

Temperatures that far exceeded the core of the *stars* themselves were nothing to scoff at.

They were generally considered poor weapons for a starship, however, due to the size and relative difficulty in handling, maintaining, and so forth... Beam weapons, while somewhat less potent overall, were more efficient and delivered a *much* higher portion of their energy onto the target rather that wasting it in an englobing explosion.

Against warships of the Empire, while somewhat effective, fusion devices would largely be a waste of space and effort in comparison to beam weapons.

The same didn't hold true, however, when faced with a swarming enemy like the Drasin.

While still somewhat wasteful in absolute terms, detonating a fusion weapon in the midst of a dozen or more enemies most certainly delivered a much greater economy of energy than wasting well over ninety percent of your weapons energy into open space.

Despite that, however, Kaela feared that even the Terran's formidable array of weapons would not be sufficient to clear the way effectively in this case. She could see *thousands* of enemy warship class drones converging on their position, and there was simply *no way possible* that the Terran ship could remotely hold enough fusion devices to handle even a small portion of them sufficient to fight their way clear.

The only thing she could be certain of was that she refused to allow her ship to be taken, and certainly it would not be even destroyed without the best efforts she could put forth to make the enemy pay dearly for the victory.

If only the Drasin were like to care about such costs.

*****

Bellerophon

"Drasin pushing forward through the blast zone, Captain," Bell informed Jason, well before the systems had confirmed such for the watch team.

"Understood," Jason said in clipped terms, not questioning the statement. As the soul of the ship, he was all too familiar with its systems.

"Take fire control," He ordered Bell, "hold them back."

"Fire control is mine," The Entity said softly, the guns of the big ship answering to him though he didn't move from his place, "however I must inform you that I will not be able to hold them off for long."

"How long before they close the distance?"

"Within three hours."

Jason let out a groaning breath, rubbing his face briefly before he checked the data for himself. He didn't have Bell's instinctual understanding of the raw data that flooded the entity from the ship's scanners, and the minds of every human on board, but he was practiced enough to do a fair job of it.

Bell's proclamation looked right, and he could immediately tell that they wouldn't be able to reach a safe distance to push past the FTL barrier within that time.

"Do we have any scans on Lagrange points that are closer?" He demanded, looking for solutions.

"No, the mass of the Dyson structure has obliterated any local points," Bell responded stiffly. "Any potential points would be cast *far* out of the system. There may be some created by the Jupiter Brain construct but those will have been thrown off by the shell as well, and while they may exist we have vastly insufficient data available to calculate any of them."

Of course, it couldn't be easy, Jason thought grimly, snorting with some amusement as he considered all the times that he'd been critical of Eric's actions before the War, and how he'd now gone and led his ship right into a trap that wasn't even meant for them.

"Stay on course, maintain full fire," He said firmly.

"Aye, Captain."

He would have to figure out something, he supposed darkly.

Maybe they'll stop chasing if we let them have the Imperial bastards. A couple well placed shots will cripple them, Jason considered. He certainly didn't have any sympathy for the Empire, even nif he normally wouldn't wish the Drasin on his worst enemy... *Unless said enemy were the dumb pricks who unleashed the Drasin in the first place...*

Unfortunately, he didn't know why the Drasin *wanted* the Imperial ship, and while he had no care at all for the Empire or those that served it... Jason was *loathe* to give the Drasin *anything* they wanted.

The Empire were human, if nothing else. Apathetic to anyone not of their worlds, at best, and flat out evil at worst... but human. The Drasin... they were a *plague*.

*****

Captured Destroyer

Marcus Reid wasn't liking the way the situation was forming

up but he was a man who rarely second guessed himself once he committed.

Afterwards, when he got falling down drunk to forget how much of an *idiot* he'd been to commit in the first place, well that was when he would second guess himself.

For now, he and his crew were working to clear the edges of the approaching swarm, doing what they could to keep the beasts at bay.

"Beams along the port side are overheating, sir." Michaels at Ops informed him.

"Overheat them then," He ordered. "We're not worrying about repair and maintenance now."

"Aye, skipper."

The kid is holding up well, Reid thought as he glanced over to the youngest member of his crew, at least among the officers', *Shame this is shaping up to be his last mission.*

That wasn't something he would say aloud, of course, but he could see the situation well enough to tell that any escape windows were slim, assuming they existed at all.

"Sir we have a push."

Reid stiffened, head and eyes swiveling back to look more piercingly at Ops. "Explain that, Ensign."

"Drasin are making a major push through the fire zone," Eric Michaels said without looking up. "They're soaking up the fire from the Bell and using their own as shields."

"God damn it," Reid swore, "Target?"

"The Imperial ship, Sir."

"Of course it is," Reid fumed.

It put him in a bad spot, he knew too well. The Imperials were *not* worth the lives of his crew, but without knowing *why* the Drasin were after them they only had the worst case scenario, as proposed by Cardsharp, to go on... and there was *no chance in hell* he was going to let the Drasin unchain their generational limits if, indeed, that was the goal.

The galactic arm would be at war in months, if that, and the Galaxy itself swarmed under by the evil spider crabs in just a few decades.

Damn the empire for putting us in this position.

"Roger that," He said aloud. "Standby to reorient. Ops, target the Drasin push."

"Aye skipper."

*****

IC *From the Flames*

"Enemy closing, Ship's Commander."

"I see them, target and fire as we can," Kaela ordered firmly.

The destruction from the devastating attacks of the Terran ship had torn the enemy to slivers, to be sure, but the resulting radiation and debris had made establishing positive target locks with them scanners all but impossible at range. It was all clearing, fast, however, and the enemy drones were again appearing on the screens.

"Yes, Ship's Commander. Beams engaging."

By the Empire there are a lot of them.

Kaela felt a wash of near despair flood over her and briefly wondered what was the point of all that firepower if the Drasin were *already* swarming through it as though it had not even been fielded in the first place.

Her professionalism pushed those emotions and thoughts aside, however. She was not going to surrender to her emotions. The enemy may kill her, but she would be *damned* if she did the job for them.

The *Flames* weapons scorched their targets with sufficient heat that the energy stripped the molecular oxygen trapped inside the silicates and set the drones *aflame* with their own oxygen. Despite that, the enemy just pushed through without pause, charging right into the beams with no concerns for their own survival.

She grit her teeth, realizing that at *least* half the energy being put out by the *Flames'* beams were likely being wasted on targets already long dead. The Drones behind just kept pushing their fellows ahead of them like brutal shields until they were completely burned away and the next would take its place.

Not how I expected to end my time as an Imperial Officer, She thought with a grim deliberation. *It would not have been such a hateful way to die if I could at least ensure that the Empire was forwarned.*

There in lay the true tragedy of it all, she knew.

With the death of her ship here… there would be no one left to warn the Empire of the existential threat that was marshalling against them. Kaela bowed her head briefly, until a flicker in the corner of her eye caught her attention and she remembered something.

"Open a channel to the Gaian vessel, *Casino*," She ordered.

"Yes, Ship's Commander."

*****

Casino

"Communication from the Imperial, Skipper," Roy called.

"Put her through," Cardsharp hissed through clenched teeth as she guided the *Casino* around to bring their weapons to bear on the enemy from an off angle, burning down some of those hiding behind the corpses of their fellows.

Her HUD flickered, and the image of the Imperial Captain appeared there just out of the way of any vital information she might need.

"Yes, Ship's Commander," Jenn said crisply. "What can I do for you?"

"Your ships are known to be faster than most," The Imperial woman said. "I will not ask how much so, but I need to know… can your vessel get beyond the reach of these beasts?"

Cardsharp frowned, "Why are you asking, Ship's Commander?"

"Someone must warn the Empire," the Imperial Officer said wearily. "If it cannot be myself, I will cover your escape if needs to be to ensure that *someone* does it."

Well, isn't this a new twist, Jenn thought with bitter irony as she thought of all the times others had done just that against the Empire during the War, only for it to end in a loss that nearly brought both sides low from the destruction.

"Someone amongst us *must* survive to warn the Empire," She said earnestly. "The Drasin have flooded local space with disruptions, and we cannon break through that to send even a single transmission pulse... so this is the only option left."

Jenn nodded in understanding. She could see the other woman's point of view on the matter, of course.

"If the worst should come to pass, we will run for deep space, Ship's Commander," Jenn said firmly. "We are not interested in a pointless death."

"Can you do it?"

That is the question.

"I don't know," She answered honestly.

The Ship's Commander nodded grimly. "When the time comes, I will give you the lead you require."

The signal dropped and the image vanished, leaving Jenn shaking her head as she flew.

Well, ain't that a thing?

*****

The Drasin swarm was coalescing from all sides as the small convoy of ships fled the stellar construct. Shielding themselves from the defensive fire with their own dead, they pushed into the defensive space of the defending starships.

Lasers slagged the Drasin Capital class drones, first killing them, then turning them to molten silcates... but still the swarm pushed them ahead, forcing the ships to *vaporize* each drone entirely before they could reach their next target, requiring the expenditure of a hundred times the energy and a thousand times the *time* needed to merely kill one of them before they could take down the next target in line.

It only got worse as more drones were killed, giving more and more room for the swarm to take cover behind. More and more drones were turned into molten mass, moving forward, pushed by the drones behind. More and more laser energy was forced to be expended just to vaporize the slag that had formed a boiling, bubbling shield that closed on the small convoy inexorably from all sides.

*****

Bellerophon

"They're inside the outer exclusion zone, Skipper."

"I see it," Roberts said grimly as the lighting changed.

With the Drasin that close they were now within the range at which no effective point defensive or dodging would be possible.

"Load the last shells," He ordered.

"Aye skipper. T-Cannons loaded."

"Check fire until I clear it."

"Check Fire, Aye."

He did *not* want to open up with fusion devices at this range, but there would shortly be little choice. If he wanted much longer, he would not longer be able to fire them at all for fear of slagging the *Bell* right alongside the enemies.

As it was, the shock front from the nuclear devices would certainly cause damage...

Wait...

"How thick is that mass?" He asked, looking across.

"Can't tell exactly, boss, but best estimate puts it under a hundred meters at the thickest point."

"T-Cannons up," Roberts ordered. "Spread fire, lob the shots. I want them just beyond the slab. Let their shield cover us."

"We'll be firing blind."

"Do it anyway."

"Roger that. Solution input."

"Fire as she bears."

"Firing."

*****

The Nuclear fusion devices launched by the Transition Cannons puffed out in a brief pulse of Tachyons, traveling instantly across the intervening space and tunneling *through* the slag on a quantum level before reforming… mostly… on the opposite side of the shield composed of enemy corpses.

Several didn't reform completely, most of those losing the ability to properly detonate in the process, but more *did*.

The *Tera-Ton* level explosions lit miniature stars within the Drasin positions, the heat and radiation trapped by their own shield, as *thousands* burned like matches in a furnace.

Tens of thousands more, however, simply flooded in to take their place.

The corpse shield wavered, crumbled in places, but was shortly filled with more bodies and reinforced as it continued to press in.

*****

Bellerophon

"We're dry, Skipper."

"Understood. Make for open space, all head flank. Signal the others that they need to keep up."

"Roger that."

*****

CHAPTER 50

Casino

"Well that cuts it," Roy said. "The Bell is calling for all speed for open space."

"What the hell does Roberts *think* we've been doing," Jenn asked snarkily, though she did grant that the *Casino* and the *Revenge* were not quite operating at flank. They both had more held back under their hoods than they'd fully let out to the Empire, and ideally wanted to keep it that way.

They were running about as fast as the slowest ship, which was the Imperial Cruiser at the moment due to them having incurred significant damage, could maintain. The idea that they were *covering* for the Empire against the very weapons the Empire had fielded against them back when the war started was an irony that was not lost on her... but while it was a tactically *idiotic* situation to be in, the strategic value of getting as much intelligence as they could far outweighed that.

Theoretically.

*If we survive to get the intelligence **out** it should outweigh it all*, Jenn thought darkly.

That was a fairly big if at the moment, she was fully aware of.

"Get me Comms to the Colonel."

"Roger that."

*****

Kennan ducked back as a particle beam scorched the deck where she had been, the responding massed fire from her Marines tearing the drone to shards and spattering molten silicates all across the deck almost instantly.

She had a signal from the *Casino*, she noted, and signaled the Gunny to continue moving forward before she opened it up.

"Bit busy here, Captain," She said firmly, quick checking around the corner before she shouldered her rifle and stepped out from cover to follow her squad into the mess.

"Understood. Keeping it short. We're up against it," Cardsharp said curtly. "Need you *off* that death trap, ASAP. Can you extract?"

"If we disengage now, we lose a squad *and* the intel we came for," Keenan countered. "I'm not losing *either*, Captain, not if I can help it."

Silence came from the other end.

"Understood. Do your best, get the hell out as soon as you can."

"Roger that," Keenan said, letting the channel close.

She briefly wondered just how bad 'up against it was', but that wasn't her concern at the moment. If things were bad enough, the Captain could have ordered her out despite the losses. She wouldn't have liked it, but she knew the fortunes of war, and how they turned on you sometimes.

"Problem, Colonel?"

"Not yours, Gunny." She said simply as she caught up. "Clear this deck."

"You've got it."

They were winning this fight. That much was clear. The Drasin were monsters in close quarters, to be sure, but they didn't have reinforcements any longer, and had no time either to reproduce. The end of this fight was already written.

"Where's First Squad?" She demanded.

"Bunkered down behind the QCS," The Gunny said firmly. "They're completely dry of ammo, if the enemy gets to them they'll be fighting with knives and fists. Teeth, maybe, if they drop their suit helmets."

"If one of those idiots tries to use his teeth on these things, I'll shoot him myself."

The Gunny just laughed at her, causing Keenan to sigh.

It was a joke, yes, but she knew Marines too well not to think that one of them might not do it anyway just for the bragging rights.

"Let's just get those guys out of there."

"Right you are, Colonel."

*****

Amanda kept her head down as the sizzling sound of the enemy beams filled the air, hugging the Imperial Quantum Computing System. Backup was there for them, at least, so now they just had to keep their heads down and do their best not to get killed before the rescue could be effected.

"Smith," She half turned.

"Yes, Lieutenant?"

The Corporal looked up from where he too was covering as best he could.

"Keep scanning this beast," She said, thumping the QCS. "I want everything you can get off of it. Got me? Just dump everything, don't worry about the encryption."

He nodded, "Hoorah, Ma'am."

She nodded curtly as he refocused his attention, thinking about the situation. Whatever was on this machine, two things were clear. First, the Empire wanted it protected with serious effort and, second, somehow the Drasin knew enough about it to *circumvent* those protections.

The first, on its own, didn't surprise her much. She knew well that Terran ships had protected cores with all kinds of heavily protected data. Often they were encoded to only unlock under very specific circumstances, sometimes that could be as simple as a time lock, and other times it could become quite complicated.

The second, in combination with the first, however, that was something that was setting off every alarm her mind could throw up.

How in the hell would the Drasin have that information? Is this the first time they've tried to access this data? If it is, the Empire's relationship with them is sure as hell a lot deeper than we ever thought.

Every bit of intelligence they'd gathered during and immediately after the end of the war had indicated that the Empire had *discovered* the Drasin and repurposed them. However, if that was the case, it didn't explain the familiarity of the Drasin with Imperial technology and safeguards.

*Maybe they just **ate** enough Imperial ships to recognize the system, but if they didn't...*

She didn't want to think about the alternatives, because it didn't lead to anywhere good. The Empire were the evil tyrants of the Galaxy, at least as far as any Terran human was concerned. Perpetrators of Genocide against Earth, unleashing weapons of mass destruction upon peaceful peoples, they were without question the enemy of any Terran still breathing, no matter where they might be found.

The Drasin, though, they were the boogyman. The Monsters that were use to scare children, aliens from the depths of the void... but with them it wasn't personal. They were considered to be little more than instinct predators by most theories. It wasn't personal, it was just their nature.

If the Empire was deeper entwined with the beasts, though, they may be far more sinister than that.

She didn't know for sure, but Amanda was certain of one thing. Her squad needed to get this intel out, and they needed to make damn sure that the Empire never found out that they had it.

*****

The Marines hammered the Drasin back, catching them from the rear as they were intent on the QCS that First Squad had been sheltering behind, quickly turning the drones in the area to cooling slag on the deck with a precise application of overwhelming force.

For all that, though, Keenan was sweating bullets by the time the last of the aliens fell.

Their ammo was running low, and she knew that they

wouldn't be able to handle another fight like this without resupply.

"Lieutenant Michaels," Keenan called as they approached. "Are you in need of medical support?"

"We're alright," The Lieutenant said, rising from behind the large computational system. "However I would like to advise that we exfil without pause, Colonel."

Keenan frowned under her armor, "Is there a problem?"

"The QCS is rigged to blow this whole deck out into the void, Ma'am," Michaels informed her. "The Drasin circumvented the detonation system, but I really don't want to trust that they got everything."

Well that puts a unique spin on things.

"Very well," She nodded back the way she'd come. "Let's move."

She saw Michaels make physical contact with one of her Marine's suits, and her eyes narrowed again as she knew that the only reason to do that was to use an induction channel for a completely secure communication.

Something was up, and Keenan didn't like the fact that she was so far out of the loop.

That said, she had to trust her officers when they had more information than she did on the situation, and so said nothing as First Squad got their shit together and headed for the door. She did, however, slow enough to let the Lieutenant come up near her and reached out to put a hand on the young officer's shoulder in a sign of apparent comfort.

"Do you have something to tell me, Lieutenant?" She asked over the induction channel.

"Yes ma'am. We pulled all the data we could from the QCS," Michaels said, causing Keenan to both be surprised and not by the statement. "We have it set to blow, using the Empire's own explosives. Can disable, if you order it, but would advise against it just in case we left traces."

Keenan nodded, considering that as she let her hand drop

to push the Lieutenant out through the hole in the deck ahead of her. She glanced around, wondering just how far the deck breaches ultimately went, but finally decided it didn't matter.

"Good work holding out, Lieutenant," She said over the normal channels. "We'll leave the mess here for the Empire to clean up."

"Yes Ma'am," Michaels responded automatically.

They were quite some distance off when a dull crump could be felt through the deck, and the air suddenly whistled out around them, leaving the squad in hard vacuum.

"What the hell was that?" The Gunny demanded, twisting around in surprise with the rest.

"I don't know," Keenan told them over the channel. "But it seems that we'll need to find one of the airlocks. Best be about it."

"Yes Ma'am."

Keenan looked over to the young Lieutenant as her Sergeant approached and listened in on the comm.

"Hell of a first mission, Lieutenant."

"That it was, Sergeant. You good?" Michaels asked.

"Yes Ma'am... Lieutenant, Michaels, Ma'am."

There was a heartbeat of a pause.

"Thank you, Sergeant Powell."

Keenan frowned slightly, wondering what that little exchange was about, but put it aside. She had other things to deal with, and it seemed that the squad was both efficient and getting along.

"Gunny, let's finish op. I understand that there's been trouble going on outside."

"Hoorah, Ma'am."

*****

"Explosion detected in the cargo decks, Ma'am. We've lost pressure on several decks."

Kaela grimaced, but nodded. "Understood."

It could have been worse, but thankfully they'd sealed those decks up solidly already due to the fighting that had become focused there for whatever reason.

For the moment, to be frank, she had far larger issues to deal with.

The fighting retreat from the system was proving to be a losing case. She knew without question that's she was within only minutes of making good on her word to the Captain of the Gaian vessel to cover their retreat in the hopes of getting word out to the Empire by any means necessary.

This close to a Terran warship, and they're not even the threat that will be my death, She thought sourly.

There was something frankly insulting about that.

"Drasin drones are within our defense limits, Commander of Ships! We cannot hold them any longer!"

"We will hold them as long as needs be," She snapped firmly, rising to her feet. "Prepare to provide cover for the Gaian…"

"Commander of Ships! Look ahead!"

*****

Bellerophon

They were up against it, no question. Roberts could *feel* the Drasin as they closed in and he was looking to find anyway that he could risk a Transition jump to get the *hell* out, but even if he could find a point that would work, Reid's Destroyer wouldn't be able to follow.

Worst case, if he had to leave them, he would… but it *would* be the last possible option he entertained.

"Drasin are within our second perimeter, Sir. We just can't burn through the slag fast enough to cut the bastards down."

"I know," He said grimly, glancing at the immobile figure of Bell where the entity was standing.

A simple shake was all it took for Bell to answer the unspoken question, so he didn't give voice to it. Not even the entities impressive command over space and time would be of much use in the current situation it seemed.

"Standby for final defensive…"

"Skipper! Tachyon surge!"

Roberts came to his feet, eyes wide as he checked the scopes.

Ahead of them dozens… *no… hundreds* of signals blinked into being as one.

"Comm Relay!"

"Put it through."

"All ships, this is Admiral Tanner of the Priminae Fleet. Advise you optimize defenses for radiation shielding."

"Fuck," Roberts said, a shiver running down his spine. "Do it!"

"Optimizing!"

The sensors went wild as they detected the massed weapons fire from the Priminae ships as they opened up on the Drasin from long range with their peculiar answer to nuclear devices. As the first of them went off, the *Bell*'s radiation detection systems went *haywire* as the scans spiked well past the range that the Terran devices had set and continued to climb.

For the Drasin, though, being so clumped together, it was a massacre.

Roberts had been in system with detonating Priminae devices once before, and never wanted to experience it again. The damn things somehow managed to create radioactive chain reactions in all matter they interacted with, defying the inverse square law as they could *cook* an entire system.

The Drasin had been spread out enough at the time to largely shrug it off, but this time they were not so luckily positioned.

The entire region around them and, he suspected, far beyond reached levels of radiation that simply didn't *exist* in nature as Tanner unleashed *hell* on the Drasin with his convoy right in the middle of it.

Right down to the wire. Now we just need to hope that our saviors don't make us glow in the dark.

*****

EPILOGUE

Admiral Rael Tanner looked impassively at the scanner as he oversaw the cleanup after the fight. The Drasin had scattered under the nuclear fire he'd unleashed, those that survived. Unfortunately there was no way to ensure some didn't escape, not with the stellar construct as large as it was. Already, though, the closer sections of it were crumbling apart, and the effect was spreading.

This threat will never be gone until we end the Drasin to the last. We cannot afford to allow them to reform like this again. Central must listen to me this time. I will not allow otherwise.

The *Bellerophon* had continued up the gravity well in the wake of his use of nuclear devices, before turning and taking it's place in formation with his own ships. The others, however, had kept a safe distance.

He recognized two of them, both the ships as well as the faces on the screens as they mad their negotiations. They were known to him, of course, though neither allowed recognition to show as they looked on through the joined channel now.

The commander of the destroyer he didn't know, but the uniform told him the ship's true allegiance.

Ironic, the Imperial Agent there likely thinks she has allies. If only she knew the truth.

The *From the Flames* was a classic Imperial Cruiser. Every bit the match of one of his own, or close enough before accounting for the improvements made by Terran influence over the years. He had no intention of showcasing any of that at the moment as he looked evenly at her.

"Ship's Commander," He said slowly. "You are an incredibly fortunate person, I hope that you are aware of that."

She had a look of frustrated rage, and he could see her eyes darting aside… likely to look at the image of Jason Roberts if he were to guess.

"The Empire does not rely on fortune," Was her simple reply. "The Drasin will be no threat to us."

Tanner smiled thinly, "I am not speaking of them. If it were my choice, I would destroy you now for what your people did to the Terrans… if it had been my choice at the time, your Empire would not have survived their response. My people, and the Terrans themselves, alone stayed my hand."

"What *we* did! They burned the Imperial Tower! They burned…!"

He laughed, cutting her off in her raging.

"Your fleet destroyed their world, their home… their people. If I had my way, I would have ordered the job they started with your Capitol finished," Tanner said tersely. "My people refused, we are not a violent culture. A weakness, perhaps, but it is our way…"

He had retired in protest when Central had denied his plan, in fact, and stayed away from the politics of the Priminae Fleet until this moment as a direct result.

The surviving Terrans, though, hadn't seemed concerned with his people's lack of action.

It had taken him a long time to understand why.

"No," He said, "Perhaps I was wrong. Fortune doesn't favor you after all… Tell me, Ship's Commander. Do you know what is coming?"

She seemed taken aback, surprised by his question.

"What do you mean by that?"

"You struck down their homeworld," He gestured, "but failed to finish the job. You awakened the Drasin, and lost the leash you thought you had on them. You cast the seeds to the stars. How long, do you suppose, before the Empire reaps what it has sown?'"

She glared at him in silence for a time before finally speaking.

"Do you intend to destroy my ship?"

Tanner shook his head, sighing sadly.

"So foolish," He said softly before he waved, "Go. Return to your Empire. Just remember what I have said here today, Ship's Commander."

He stood squarely looking at the screen, his small stature no mask for the anger and steel that lay within.

"Harvest is coming, Ship's Commander."

With that he killed the communication channel and gestured idly.

"Get us out of here."

*****

Printed in Dunstable, United Kingdom